SEPTEMBER
Somewhere

SUSAN LERNER & NANCY MEYER

For information about permission to reproduce selections from this book, or coordinating in-person author readings and events, or special discounts for bulk purchase and charity fundraising, please contact Susan Lerner & Nancy Meyer at lernermeyer2@gmail.com

Cover Images Licensed from Getty Images, iStock Photo & Shutterstock
Cover Image Design: George Ntentis giorgosntentis@gmail.com
Author Photograph: Don Romero Fine Portraiture

Social Sparkle & Shine is a legacy and storyteller's publisher, creating even more authority for accomplished individuals, with artisanal-quality book publishing and thought leadership in media channels (strategic publicity), plus her signature "Fairy Godmother" consulting services to create your book results, impact, and contribution as you imagine. For a free assessment of your own publishing and bestseller potential, email Debbie Horovitch at debbie.horovitch@gmail.com
Visit our website at www.theSparkleAgency.com

Library and Archive Canada Cataloging-in-Publications Data:
ISBN-13: 978-1-77316-008-5
ISBN-13: 978-1-77316-009-2 (ebk.)

Published in Canada, Printed in United States of America
FIRST EDITION

Dedication

This book is dedicated to our parents
Leon and Geraldine, who showed us by
example the values of Education,
Humility, and Respect For Our
Fellow Human Beings.

A portion of the proceeds from this book
will be directed toward the Robert
Packard Center for ALS Research
at Johns Hopkins in memory
of our father.

For more information on the Packard
Center, please visit www.alscenter.org.

Acknowledgements

We would like to thank the following
people who encouraged us and guided
us on our journey to write our
first novel:

Martha Levin

Juman Malouf

Our Fairy Godmother Consultant

Debbie Horovitch

and

Our Wonderful Supportive Families

Prologue
San Francisco, 2012

Charlotte should be reviewing budget projections, not trying to justify buying an $850 purple velvet Alexander McQueen blazer she's eyeing on Net-a-Porter but that's exactly what she's doing (old habits), when her email pings. Obviously nothing good comes from an email with the subject line: SAD NEWS. With the day she's having (thus the retail binge), the last thing Charlotte needs is "sad news" but since it's from the Harvard Law Alumni Association she's hoping it's at least distantly sad, like a former classmate she barely knows has an entirely curable form of cancer and she can just write a check. Still, Charlotte clicks open the email with a sense of dread, quickly followed by shock as she reads that her beloved Professor Thomas Wallace, who taught at Harvard Law since 1959, has died at the age of ninety-one.

The first thing Charlotte thinks is, impossible. Though of course, it's anything but impossible, this eventuality was inevitable, and he was, after all, in his nineties. But Professor Wallace, his faint Irish brogue, his ubiquitous Red Sox pullover, his ability to recall the most esoteric case law, like his mind was made of wires and Pentium processors, not flesh and blood, seemed immortal, like he would walk the halls of Langdell Hall forever.

The second thing Charlotte thinks is, fuck, followed by an

acute wave of anxiety. She collapses back in her chair, closes her eyes, takes deep breaths. This is what her therapist tells her to do, let her emotions wash over her and wash away. Not for the first time she thinks she should be getting better advice for $300 an hour.

They will surely be at the memorial service, which she sees from the obituary is scheduled for this Saturday. If she wouldn't miss it for the world, then neither would Mari, or Ryan, who could bring Emily, if they were even still together. And this means she will have to face them.

Ever since what Charlotte refers to as the "Bermuda Blow Up"—the name intended, albeit unsuccessfully, to create a distancing effect between her and the actual events—she's done her best to put Mari and Ryan, their friendship, its dramatic end, out of her mind. She does this through a combination of disciplined denial—stuffing thoughts of them and memories in a locked suitcase in the back of her mind—and when that doesn't work, by reassuring herself with cringe-worthy platitudes. All good things come to an end...nothing lasts forever...it is what it is. And for the most part it's worked, because Charlotte is, if nothing else, an expert at compartmentalizing, but in this moment, as she sinks deeper into the buttery Italian leather of her executive chair, not so much.

As much as she wills it not to, her mind takes her right back to the beginning, to law school, to Professor Wallace who brought the three of them together in a way—hand-picking them as promising First Years in his intimidating but fascinating Jurisprudence seminar.

Even now Charlotte finds she can still conjure the smell of Professor Wallace's house after all these years, a distinctive blend of wood smoke and the inside of a tackle box, like it was a lake house and not a colonial smack in the middle of Cambridge. The three of them—Ryan, Mari, and Charlotte—spent so many Sunday evenings there. At The Prof's, as they affectionately called him, where they drank "good" wine, ate exotic cheeses that they, in their early twenties, had never heard of, and discussed what he called, the poetry of the law. He reminded them frequently, wistfully, of their bright futures, ones he commanded them to embrace. No, to seize. And, like puppies, they figuratively climbed all over each other, clamoring for his attention throughout their three years at Harvard, eager to prove that they were worthy of his unwavering confidence. How eager they were also to outdo each other, and support each other and be there for each other, united in a bond of lifelong friendship that was supposed to serve them just as much (if not more) than their fancy degrees and finely shaped minds.

Until everything fell apart. Until she made the biggest mistake of her life.

It was dizzying to think back to that weekend and try to make sense of everything, which is why Charlotte avoids it at all costs. But now, like suddenly being splashed with a bucket of cold water, more memories come back in intense flashes: The feel of cold sand on her back.

Mari shaking her head in outrage. Ryan unable to look her in the eye. Charlotte's own biting words, a childish and defensive reaction of last resort: "fuck you." The vodka-soaked six-hour flight home. The guilt. God, the guilt.

For a brief period after that dreadful weekend, Charlotte nursed a tiny flicker of hope, that maybe, just maybe, they could work through all this. She was prepared to take responsibility, throw herself at the mercy of her friends, repent, change, confront her demons, do what she needed to do to right the universe. She had even started therapy. A full on Charlotte Overhaul. But the weeks turned into months, which turned into years, and no one was in touch. At least not with her. Her therapist had recommended that she get off Facebook since Charlotte had developed a rather unhealthy obsession with comparing other people's lives with hers, and either feeling wildly superior or miserable, so she has no idea what Ryan or Mari (or, sometimes, it feels the rest of the world) are up to or if they're in touch. This is all for the best, she reminds herself. But god, god she misses them. Romantic break ups were one thing and she has had her fair share of those, but more than ten years of friendship exploded into unrecognizable pieces was another thing altogether.

Charlotte sits up, fights the sense of vertigo brought on by this unwelcomed trip down memory lane. Her eyes dart around her expansive office, filled with supple furnishings and accessories, all in various shades of grey and blue. The interior designer who redid the office when Charlotte took the reins of Mayfield Construction from her father had called the coloring "a calming palette." Charlotte wondered why the designer thought she needed calming. Why not a "bold palette"? The office also features floor-to-ceiling windows, which Charlotte turns toward now, the glass covering the entire east-facing wall, framing million-dollar views of the bay and the Golden Gate Bridge, which feel close enough to touch.

All of this was supposed to make her happy. The money, lording over her family's lucrative construction company, the 3,000-square-foot loft in Nob Hill, the corner office.

Everything she was groomed to covet. Her birthright. And yet...

Mari's voice comes into her head as loud as it was that day, that last conversation, the Blow Up. "You do have everything, Charlotte—you just don't ever appreciate it. You always want more! It's always poor, poor, Charlotte. And you want us to feel bad for you for the drama YOU create. That's all you do! Create drama." The unexpected truth of this statement may have hit Charlotte like the proverbial Mack truck, but it didn't mitigate the outrage she felt.

How dare she? Goody two shoes Mari and her sanctimonious judgments. And yet, what leg did Charlotte have to stand on after what she did?

A toxic mix of regret, longing, and nostalgia churns now in her stomach and she wonders if she's going to be sick. And then another thought, a whisper really: what if? What if it didn't have to be this way? What if there was a way back? What if, after all these years, they could get together and...talk? Forgive? Fix? What if, once again, Professor Wallace brings them together?

She's not so naïve or Pollyanna to believe that they could undo everything that's happened, obviously not, but maybe... She can't finish the thought, can't envision how they could come back together and what being a part of each other's lives again would look like.

Partly because it's genuinely inconceivable and partly because, even if she could imagine it, it risks being too painful to hope for such a thing. Giving up, moving on, not giving a shit is always, always the safer bet.

But still she feels a surge of energy as she closes her email and opens Expedia, beginning to look for first class flights to Boston. When she pulls up her calendar to see about cancelling her schedule, it hits her and she laughs out loud. The irony is too much. It's fucking September. Of course, it is. And that fact, that in a silly twist of fate poor Professor Wallace happened to die on September 9th, buoys her even more. Every year since they graduated law school, no matter where they lived, or what was going in their lives, they got together every single September and now they would again. Charlotte, who normally scoffs at the notion that things happen for a reason (the Mayfield mantra is that you make your own luck) chooses to believe that this has to mean something.

One thing's for certain—she's getting the McQueen blazer. If she's going to pay her respects and confront her past, she's damn well going to need armor.

Chapter One
Martha's Vineyard, 2002

She's been counting down to this weekend, literally marking X's on the calendar on her desk, and it's finally—finally—here. She takes a deep breath of salty sea air as to confirm to herself, yes, vacation has begun. Maybe it's the fact that she grew up in Florida or maybe it's that her ancestors are from Cuba, but nowhere is Mari happier than being surrounded by water. Though she prefers the white sand beaches of her native Hallendale Beach, Florida, the Nantucket Sound, which stretches around her like a nubby navy blanket, is beautiful and peaceful it its own way. Mari has the upper deck of the Seascape Ferry all to herself and so splays out on the wooden pew-like bench and lets her body sway with the waves.

Only a handful of other people are on the ferry, a sure sign that the summer rush has come to an end. Which is just as well as Mari didn't want to spend a weekend packed on an island with snobby financiers and old money types anyway. Perhaps it's unfair of her to stereotype "the Vineyard," as those financiers and old money types call it, in such a way but she can't help it and she damn sure doesn't want to be mistaken for a nanny this weekend. So all in all it will be nice for Ryan, Charlotte and her to have the island more or less to themselves.

The air is crisp and the wind whips her long dark hair around her face. She's been away for less than three months, but had already forgotten how fast summer flees in New England. In Montgomery, Alabama, her new hometown, it's still sticky and balmy.

When she landed in Boston and took a deep breath she remembered how you could almost tell the exact date by the smell and feel of the air alone. First weekend in September. Her favorite time of year. The twilight between summer and fall, which calls to mind for her the smell of fresh cut grass and of sharpened pencils and crisp textbook pages. The smell of promise.

She feels the tension lifting from her shoulders, her frayed nerves calming down after a stressful day of travel. Getting here was not easy, to say the least—a 7:00 a.m. flight out of Montgomery, which she almost missed having overslept after staying up way too late fretting over every sentence of a brief she was determined to finish before she left. Then a connection in Atlanta, which was more than an hour late, then a shuttle from Logan International Airport to the ferry terminal, and, finally a mad dash to make this 4:45 departure. All told she's been travelling now for almost ten hours. So, as excited as she was to see her friends, until this moment Mari had been cursing Charlotte, who had insisted they come to the Vineyard, all the way.

Charlotte's parents' friends had a "cottage" that Charlotte explained they could stay in for free, which was an enticement for Mari for sure, given her limited budget.

But surely convenience was a factor, too, in Charlotte's insistence that they come here, since both she, who was still in Boston, and Ryan, who's in New York City, arrived here last night in less than half the time it had taken Mari to complete just the first leg of her trip.

When they were deciding destinations Mari made a half-hearted suggestion that they come down south to Gulf Shores, Alabama, where her colleague said there were pretty beaches. Ryan actually guffawed. "You're crazy for moving to the deep South, Mar, and you're crazy if you think we're vacationing in Al-a-bam-a." He pronounced all the syllables with a thick Southern accent.

So there was that, and also had they gone to Gulf Shores or anywhere else, their accommodations would likely not have been nearly as nice, because, Mari, wise to the ways of the New England elite after three years at Harvard, knew very well that this "cottage"—owned by friends of the Mayfields no less—was likely to be a four-bedroom waterfront mansion. Which beats her Hampton Inn budget any day.

Mari shakes her head and firmly reminds herself of her promise that she won't think about her budget or paltry checking account this weekend, or just how she's going to pay next month's student loan bill, or just why in the hell, as a Harvard Law grad (cum laude, at that) she is as broke as she is. Well, she knows exactly why. While all of her classmates opted for well-paying clerkships or associate jobs at prestigious firms or consulting companies, Mari took a job at the Equal Justice Project, in which she earns exactly $32,000 a year, which is, she notes with some frequency, considerably less than a year of her law school tuition.

However, painful salary notwithstanding, Mari loves her job, the one she knew, with an uncharacteristic sense of certainty, that she wanted almost from day one at Harvard when EJP's founder, Ted Robinson, came to speak on campus about his work with death row inmates, trying appeals for people wrongly or unjustly sent to death row.

Mari was mesmerized listening to him talk about his cases, including one in particular about a boy in Mississippi who had killed his mother's abusive boyfriend, while the monster was in the process of lighting her on fire, and himself got sentenced to death row—at thirteen. Mari was not naïve; unlike a lot of her classmates she didn't grow up in a rarefied world shielded from (or willfully ignorant of) those sorts of injustices. But still, the story and Ted's passion and commitment struck her at her core, it lit a spark and gave her a sense of purpose. And with it came a sense of relief, to have the future, or at least the stretch of years she could see right before her, mapped out.

She had arrived at Harvard Law largely undecided about

exactly what she was going to do with her (expensive) law school degree—she had actually been somewhat ambivalent about law school all together. But after excelling at the University of Florida, Jacksonville, taking the LSAT and applying to law school had seemed like a good thing to do next, if for no other reason than to delay the "real world" everyone talked about so much. She applied to Harvard on a lark, but once she got in and got a decent-ish financial aid package, she decided to go. Granted she had wavered a bit thinking about the debt she would have, even with the financial aid, but her father put an end to it.

"You don't turn down Harvard, Mija. Period."

So she didn't and she's glad for that because she found her passion and she made lifelong friends and, most importantly, if she were honest, she discovered something about herself—she was special. Or if not special herself, at least she could run in circles with the "special" ones, the brilliant, the wealthy, the connected, and hold her own.

Harvard saved her from an insecurity she wasn't fully aware she had and prepared her to confidently be a part of the world of the haves.

Though in her new 600-square-foot apartment—the second floor of a house owned by an elderly widow—twenty minutes from downtown Montgomery, and her office, which is three metal desks in a strip mall storefront, she feels very far from those "special" circles. She feels very far from any circles at all actually. She had spent most of the first few months in Alabama clocking seventy-to-eighty-hour weeks reviewing and organizing case files and researching the status of appeals, and then grabbing Subway on the way home, scarfing down a Spicy Italian sub and falling asleep watching CNN.

Mari is excited by her work (a direct hand in justice!), but she is also, she realizes now that she has her first moment to take stock, very, very lonely. Yes, she talks to her friends, they email, keep tabs on Friendster, and she's met one girl who works in the dental practice next door to EJP's office who she hopes (more desperately than she'd like to admit) will be a candidate for friendship, but it's not the same. Hence her excitement for this weekend. But she also feels guilty about taking two days off, not even three months into the job. She doesn't want Ted, her boss, to question her loyalty or work ethic. And given how short-handed they are, she doesn't want to fall behind on any of their cases, to which she has almost immediately become fiercely dedicated.

But when she sheepishly asked for the days, Ted reminded her that it's a marathon not a sprint. "Go see your friends," he'd commanded. "No one's getting zapped this weekend." One of the other things she loved about the job—the gallows humor.

Mari looks up from the choppy water and sees the Ferry Terminal ahead, a growing speck in the distance. The sun is setting, a bright orange globe dropping fast and Mari feels a sharp twinge. Eagerness and anticipation. And also, unexpectedly, weirdly, nerves? She loves Ryan and Charlotte. They are her closest friends. But sometimes their trio just seemed...how would she describe it? Improbable.

Charlotte's family is so wealthy, capital W. And Ryan looks like (and more often than Mari would sometimes prefer, acts like) the quintessential plaid-shirted frat boy.

She realizes that she, working class, slightly chubby, first in her family to go to college, and the third leg of this tripod, is something of an oddity. Her (secret) theory about the origins of their friendship, and she's given this some thought, is that Charlotte and Ryan had an attraction to each other when they all met in Professor Wallace's notoriously tough Jurisprudence seminar first year—but they both were both seriously dating other people. Having Mari as a buffer whenever they hung out kept everything on the up and up. But then, quickly, the three of them had truly clicked with an ease and alchemy strengthened over dozens of all nighters, lots of alcohol (Pinot Grigio for Charlotte and Mari and Pabst Blue Ribbon for Ryan), many meltdowns, and a willingness to confess and accept each other's confessions of their darkest vulnerabilities, which seemed to flow unbidden (Mari blames the stress and Pinot). By the end of first semester, their threesome, however unlikely, was a thing, especially after they began to get the heady invite to spend Sunday evenings at Professor Wallace's. Including one particularly odd and memorable night where instead of debating law, politics, or current events as usual, they made a pie. Blackberry, she recalls.

So Mari knows it's silly to think that she's the odd one out when she's, in some ways, the glue that keeps them together. In fact, these weekends were her idea. She proposed it graduation night—that now that they would be scattering to the wind they would promise to get together every September. Fueled by expensive champagne (a gift from Charlotte's parents), and the anticipatory nostalgia that comes with graduation, they'd made a pact, that no matter what, they would meet up somewhere for a weekend every September to reconnect. And here they were. In fact, Mari, previously lost in her revelry and mesmerized by the sun tracing across the sky and being pulled closer and closer to the ocean as if it's a shimmering grey magnet, notices that she is literally here, the ferry is mere feet from the dock.

As Mari makes her way to the first floor deck, she, who has trouble parallel parking her tiny Civic, marvels that this huge vessel pulls so closely and seamlessly up to the floating wooden planks.

"SHEEEE'SSSSS HERE!!!" Mari hears the instantly recognizable chorus of Ryan and Charlotte's voices floating over from the parking lot on the other side of the terminal gate. Charlotte is waving frantically. Not for the first time Mari is struck by Charlotte, her perfection. She is always so gorgeous, so put together. She's clearly been out in the sun this summer giving her a deep glow, and she's let her blonde hair grow into long waves since Mari saw her last. The result is a seemingly effortless beauty that screams California girl, which, of course, Charlotte is.

Mari fights the urge to look down and assess her own crumpled outfit, black leggings, canvas slip ons and a hoodie with GO GATORS across the chest. She can't dare say this ensemble was fashionable when she put it on this morning, and after ten-plus hours of travelling it's that much worse for the wear, including a coffee stain on the sweatshirt. One day she hopes to be the type of woman who travels in crisp white button-ups, belted designer jeans, high heels. Women like Charlotte's mom, model turned socialite, Evelyn Mayfield. Charlotte once told Mari that her mom has never left the house without mascara on, not once, in her life. An astonishing fact that Mari has never forgotten and wishes now that she had taken to heart. She curses herself for not at least applying a little lip gloss on the hour-long ferry ride. But she doesn't have time now because Ryan and Charlotte are already hugging her, taking her bag, talking to her at once.

"How was your flight?" "Wait till you see the house!" "We got two cases of Pinot." "I have to pee." They talk at once and their chatter cocoons her. God, she missed them.

They pile into a sleek Range Rover, the wheels that apparently come with the house.

"I can't believe it. We're all here," Charlotte turns to the back seat and beams at her.

"Thank god, you're here, Mari. Charlotte asked me three times which dress she should wear to dinner last night. They all had flowers."

"Florals are the new black!" Charlotte exclaims.

Mari has never really had a close guy friend before Ryan and it surprises her how much patience he has with their so-called girl talk, which, frankly, when Charlotte goes on about clothes and shoes for too long is beyond even Mari's patience. But that's Charlotte, a clothes hound and don't dare call it frivolous as Mari made the mistake of doing once. (She got a twenty minute diatribe about how fashion is serious, it's art and believe it or not, you can be smart and love clothes...look at Sarah Jessica Parker.)

"So, how's the new gig?" Mari asks Ryan.

"He hates it. I knew he would," Charlotte says confidently before Ryan can answer.

"I don't hate it." He glares at Charlotte before turning towards Mari. "It's just not what I expected is all."

Actually Ryan does hate his job, but he won't give Charlotte the satisfaction of saying so, since she tried to talk him out of his move to New York and into taking the associate job that the

Boston-based McCladden and Associates offered him a month before graduation. He had interned there for the last two summers but—and he would never say this aloud even to Charlotte and Mari—he felt he was better than McCladden, a local firm. He belonged in New York and had his sights set on working at the Skadden Arps and the White & Cases of the world. So, with eyes on the prize, he'd turned down McCladden (much to their, and everyone else's, surprise) and moved to New York City the day after graduation. He had a place to stay—with a buddy from undergrad—in what he now realizes is the far reaches of Brooklyn, despite his roommates assurances that it would be about "twenty minutes to Manhattan."

That's not the only thing that took him by surprise. He'd arrived primed to secure the job of his dreams, but also ready to party, ready to take on the world, ready to enjoy the debauchery and delights of the city that never sleeps, but what he found was a New York that was more somber than he thought it would be, still jittery a year after 9/11. People seemed anxious; the drive and energy was there, but it seemed aimless somehow. It's like the entire city was waiting for the other shoe to drop, and people didn't know what to do with themselves in the meantime.

Ryan had sweated it out the first few weeks of unemployment—literally, NYC in June is frigging hot—but finally his relentless, some may say aggressive, networking paid off and he got a job as a junior associate at the blue chip, Barker, Jones and Simon. So take that McCladden.

And yet, another surprise. The promising job, the illustrious midtown address, the crisp business cards, were supposed to make him feel more important than he actually does. He shows up every day in a rumpled suit—he alternates between three $2,000 suits he got, thanks to Mastercard, at Paul Smith when he arrived in New York, because hey, you have to look the part—after the hour-long commute on a packed, sweltering subway train. He gets settled in his cube with his deli coffee and sad donut and feels like a schoolboy, an imposter, not a titan of industry. But it's still early yet, as Mari reminds him.

"You've only been there, what, three weeks! I know you're ambitious and all, but it's a bit soon to be running the place. All in good time."

"Well, in the middle of a meeting last week, my boss, his name is Tripper if you can believe that. I mean you have to be an asshole if your name is Tripper, right?

Anyway he asked me to run and make a copy. A photocopy. Like I am a fucking paralegal. I didn't go to Harvard to make copies." But still, Ryan wonders, thinking long term, it's better to make copies at a top tier, international firm in New York, than a small firm in Boston. Isn't it? Tripper is a dick to be sure, and obviously intent on hazing him in some weird way, but he also just settled a multi-million dollar suit against Pfizer last year, so...

"I happen to do all my own copying and filing if it makes you feel any better," Mari says.

"Well, that's because you're saving the world." Ryan turns around to grin at her.

"Not to worry, Ryan. Pretty soon, you're going to have your very own assistant that you can treat like shit. I know that's always been your dream," Charlotte teases.

"Besides, you can't complain," she continues. "You could have been in Boston with me, but noooo..."

"Well, the question is what the hell are you still doing in Boston? Your parents are practically begging you to take the keys to the kingdom and you stay on at some second tier firm?" Ryan realizes he's projecting with that second tier bit and hopes the others don't notice.

Charlotte opts to let Ryan's snark pass. He's right after all, the firm isn't her ideal job by any means, but she's not going to explain for the umpteenth time why she doesn't want to go home and run Mayfield Construction.

"I think the better question might be WHO am I still doing in Boston!" Charlotte laughs gleefully.

"Not the hockey player! Still?" Mari reaches up from the back seat and slaps her arm. "That was supposed to be a summer fling!" She catches Ryan's profile from the backseat and he doesn't look amused.

"You're still seeing him? I thought that was a one-night stand?" Ryan says and Mari detects something in his voice, a trace of derision.

"Well, it was. It was supposed to be. But I don't know...we've connected."

Charlotte's annoyed. This is not the reaction she was expecting when she envisioned this conversation. Her friends are supposed to be impressed, entertained...envious even.

"You've connected over what exactly? His criminal record? Your love of hockey?" Ryan scoffs. He (barely) manages to refrain from saying this out loud, and yes it's superficial, but bearded, burly James looks like a guy on a documentary about wrestling alligators, or someone who hasn't left an oil rig for ten years. He didn't even go to community college. But Ryan also knows Charlotte well enough to know that all of this is probably part of the appeal.

"Don't be so judgmental. He had a minor brush with the law. And we got him community service."

"Okay Charlotte, if you call a DUI in which he drove his car straight through the window of a Kentucky Fried Chicken a minor scrape. He could have killed someone!

The only reason he got community service is because he's a god in Boston. If he was just some kid from Southie, you know he'd be in jail, right?"

"I thought you'd think it was cool that I'm dating a professional hockey player?"

Charlotte says, with too much pout in her voice for her liking.

"Does your boss know, Char?" Mari interrupts.

Of course, Charlotte thinks, Mari wants to make sure everything is on the up and up. The truth is her boss doesn't know, no one at the firm does—even she realizes that lawyers who sleep with clients could get a...reputation. If there's one thing Charlotte understands it's appearances. And besides, the sneaking around has been part of the fun, but there's no point in telling everyone that.

"There's no official rule against it at the firm and I only work on his stuff peripherally. I'm working with a lot of other cases too—the benefits of a small 'second tier'..." She lets go of the steering to make air quotes. "...firm. You get to do it all."

"Well, so long as you don't do all your clients," Ryan says, hoping his attempt at humor disguises the fact that he thinks this romance, if you could call it that, is ludicrous and going nowhere fast. Jonathan Mayfield is never going to accept some roughneck from Alberta (he's not even American!) as a son-in-law.

"Ha. Ha. Very funny. Look, we're here, Mari."

Mari looks out the window as they turn into a long gravel driveway, with hedges that tower over the SUV on both sides. After about a hundred yards the driveway spills into a giant portico and a grey-shingled classic Cape Cod rises. Mari had pictured four or five bedrooms, but this looks much, much bigger and there is a full on guesthouse to the right that is twice as big as her parent's house.

"Holy shit, Char."

"I know, nice right? Wait till you see the pool. It's actually going up for sale next summer. Maybe we can combine our savings and come up with six mil." She gets out of the car, makes a sweeping gesture. "At ten acres, it's a bargain!"

"Why are they selling it?" Ryan asks, grabbing Mari's bag out of the back seat.

Inside he's thinking that, though he may not have $600 to his name right now, he very well will have a house exactly like this one day. Specifically by thirty-five. Forty with a grace period.

"Divorce," Charlotte explains. "Right after graduation, Devin, that's my mom's best friend, you guys met her at graduation. Well, she came out to the house for a long weekend thinking it would be empty. Grant, her husband, was supposed to be in New York for work. Turns out he was here with his mistress! The upstairs window in the back of the master bedroom still has a board on it from where Devin threw a vase through it when she found them!"

They're all standing on the porch now, which is lined with

six pristine white rocking chairs Mari is willing to bet have never been used.

"The divorce is getting ugly and there's all kinds of drama with the property and secret bank accounts and stocks and what not. I'm telling you, we all should have been divorce lawyers. We'd be raking it in!"

"Hey, I already lived through my parents' divorce. That was enough for me,"

Ryan says, taking in the predictably grand foyer they are walking into.

"It's just sad because the house has been in their family for generations. Devin's grandmother and my great grandmother became friends here. I told my parents they should buy it, that it would be a way of keeping it in the family so to speak. But mom says that Devin would find that awkward. Go figure. And also, well, the Mayfields really aren't all that welcome on the Vineyard anymore."

"What? Why?" Ryan tries to imagine his parents being infamous enough to be banned from anywhere, let alone their hometown, Lawrence, Kansas. Briefly he wonders if his parents have even heard of Martha's Vineyard.

"Oh, back in the 50s, my great uncle supposedly raped a waitress at the Navigator—it's a landmark place, we'll eat there this weekend—and then he tried to pay her off. The whole thing got really ugly and we Mayfields high-tailed out of the East Coast and now it's Palm Springs all the way. Which is way more fun anyway. Hey, we should obviously do one of our weekends there. I'm going to make cocktails." Charlotte breezes away leaving Ryan and Mari standing in the foyer. Mari almost forgot Charlotte's manic energy, how fast she talks, moves.

"Well, Char takes the ole Mayfield skeletons in stride, huh?" Ryan says, raising an eyebrow.

"Always has, always will. I need to shower. And not just because of that story,"

Mari laughs.

"Come on, I'll show you to your room. The blue room.

There's one for every color."

Mari laughs. "I would expect nothing less."

"Ry—I need you. Limes need juicing!" Charlotte calls from the kitchen as Mari takes in the blue room, where everything from the carpet to the ceiling is in varying shades of blue.

"You can tell me more about that skanky hipster you're fucking," Charlotte yells.

"Um? Skanky hipster? Should I hear this story before my shower?" It's Mari's turn to raise an eyebrow.

"Ha, ha. She's doesn't have it exactly right—she's not a hipster." He winks. "See you at dinner!"

Mari hears Ryan's laughter trailing down the hall. She missed this, missed them, missed being together. How good it feels to be here, she thinks, almost as good as this shower is going to feel.

* * *

"So she still hasn't found a job! And get this, I heard that security had to escort her out at her last interview!"

Mari walks into the massive kitchen and right into the latest gossip.

"Are you talking about Olivia? I heard that, too." Mari had always felt sorry for Olivia, who was one of those people who always seemed to be trying too hard.

"She was always a loon, but... what a nightmare. Harvard Law and you can't get a job. What the fuck?" Charlotte adds some fresh lime slices to the pitcher of margaritas and brings it over to the table. "But I mean, look at her. She wears gauzy skirts and Birkenstocks. She looks like a hippy."

Both Ryan and Mari roll their eyes. "I don't think she's not getting a job because of her skirts."

"You gotta look the part is all I am saying. And her look says Joan Baez, not, Ally McBeal."

"Ha, well done." Ryan reaches for the pitcher, fills all their glasses to the brim, takes a big swig thinking how precariously close he himself came to being one of those Harvard Law alums without a job.

"Ryan, can you check on the meat? Mari—we're doing burgers. I hope that works." Charlotte is up again, bustling about the kitchen. She digs in the curio cabinet.

"Let's eat outside, and I figured we might as well use the Wedgwood," she says, holding up a stack of plates that Mari suspects cost more than her rent for the month. "And the silver. It's a celebration after all."

"Here, let me help you," Mari holds onto each plate for dear life as they head for the deck.

"So sorry we're not having shrimp and grits. I bet that's what you eat now. At least you don't have an accent yet. I still don't know how you stand the South," Charlotte says in one breath as they set three places at the impossibly long farmhouse table.

"You forget I'm from the South."

"Florida is different from Alabama. Good lord. Or should I say, Good lawd a mighty!" She fakes fanning herself, exaggerates the accent.

"Okay, so Alabama might not be the first place I'd choose to live, but that's where the work is. I do miss Boston though. I would kill for a lobster roll from Charlie's Kitchen."

"James and I just went there last week! It was delicious, not to rub it in."

"Hmmm, I'm noticing that James keeps coming up in conversation." Mari bumps her hip to Charlotte's much bonier one.

Charlotte quickly reflects, feeling self-conscious. Has she been talking about James a lot? Shit. That wasn't her intention. She doesn't want to be that girl. After all, she's already decided that she's positioning this romance in such a way that she stars as the indifferent seductress to the completely whipped bad boy, especially after their reaction earlier. "Whatever. Don't worry, I'm going to be grilling you over dinner on what's going on in your love life."

"You'll be shocked that nothing has changed since you

grilled me last week about what's going on in my love life, which is still nothing. I know it's shocking I haven't found a hot eligible guy in Montgomery, Alabama, in the ten minutes I've been there." Mari's rather lackluster love life is a constant project of Charlotte's, which is endearing and also annoying.

"Burgers up!" Ryan appears from the other side of the patio in an apron that says, PRICK WITH A FORK. "I found it hanging by the grill. Too funny, huh?"

"And so fitting. Give those here, prick," Charlotte says placing the platter in the middle of the table.

"I bet Devin bought that for Grant and had no idea how true it was," Mari says.

"Or maybe she did and just didn't care," Charlotte shrugs. "Let's dig in."

An hour later, they are stuffed from the burgers, grilled vegetables and corn from the farmer's market, each thrilled to have a break from the carryout they all eat almost exclusively. And after catching up on all of their classmates, agreeing that Leah Marshall is doing the best, having secured a coveted clerkship with Justice Roberts on the actual Supreme Court and thus setting the competitive benchmark for their entire class, they end up on sitting on lounge chairs around a marble fire pit, even though they are all too lazy and drunk to actually start a fire. Charlotte has gathered a bunch of blankets and they huddle under them, warding off the nighttime chill. The Malbec also helps.

"I told you red wine warms you up!" Charlotte says.

"Then you should be on fire, because that's your fifth glass," teases Ryan.

"It also makes you so sleepy," Maris says, unsuccessfully trying to stifle a yawn.

She looks at her watch. "Jesus it's after midnight."

"Mari," Ryan says sternly. "Three months ago we would have just been getting started."

"True, I'm old. You'll recall I'm going to be twenty-five in two weeks. It's time to get eight hours of sleep a night."

"She's right," Charlotte slurs. "Otherwise, we're gonna get

wrinkles. It starts now. Seriously." She starts pulling at her cheeks. Ryan observes her closely with drunken concentration. Charlotte's skin is flawless, dotted with freckles that seem to have exploded since the last time he saw her, since even hours ago. He loves her freckles, especially the ones that dot her shoulders...the ones he traced with his fingers like they were constellations. Ryan shakes his head as if to erase the images from his brain, commands himself to stop this line of thinking immediately, blames the alcohol.

"Well, I'm going to bed and not because I'm going to get wrinkles, but because I'm exhausted. Those baby blue sheets are calling my name."

"That's what Ryan's skank says...those baby blue eyes are calling my name," a very drunk Charlotte imitates a high-pitched (skank-like?) voice, and then nearly falls off her chair laughing. "At least you don't have blue ballllls."

"Okay you're cut off. Time for bed." Ryan grabs the bottle of wine, which is empty anyway. He goes over to pour the last dregs in Charlotte's glass, and then joins her on her poolside lounger, which is big enough for two, just barely. She puts her head on his chest. She smells like expensive shampoo and oddly, but not unpleasantly, olive oil. The last time he was this close to her, where all parts of him were touching all parts of her, she smelled, pleasantly, like garlic from the pasta they'd eaten at Carmichael's.

Again, he implores his brain to shut down, focuses on trying to fall asleep, because even in his inebriated state he knows, that way danger lies.

* * *

A hangover never stopped her before and besides the ocean air is brisk and invigorating, a sure cure for one anyway. Charlotte runs barefoot on the beach, just as the sun comes up, three miles to town, she'll pick up bagels, three miles back. The sand is cold on her feet, bracing. When she gets to Raven Cove, a spot she swears she remembers playing near when she was little, she decides to stop, take in the ocean while she has the entire mile-long stretch of beach to herself. It's hard for Charlotte to quiet her mind, to silence her thoughts, the chatter, but it's so quiet here, so peaceful, she feels a sense of calm without even trying. Reward without effort is her most favorite kind.

She squints out over the ocean, takes off her shoes and socks and lets the white foam of the waves dance over her toes. The water itself is not as cold as she thought it would be. She holds her hand over her eyes to shield them from the rising sun gleaming off the water and this is when she sees it. At first she thinks it's her imagination, a trick of her eyes, it must be, what are the chances? But it's not. A giant humpback whale surfaces and dips and then surfaces again. Charlotte is not easily impressed, and can't say she's truly been awed, until right now. Holy shit, is what she thinks even if the moment calls for something more poetic. She wishes her friends were with her, that they could see this. But as the whale surfaces again and she's certain she can actually hear the slice through the water, she decides she's glad they're not. This is hers, all hers.

She moves closer to the water, so she's ankle, then calf deep and the whale appears to move closer to her, too. He (or she, she has no idea) seems to be swimming in a wide circle. He's not communicating with her, that would be silly, he's not even aware of her presence, she realizes this, of course, but for a moment, Charlotte feels she and the whale are kindred spirits. They are, if not communicating, then communing in some meaningful way. Charlotte decides this is a Moment. If only she had been looking for a sign for something, an answer to a "big" question. Should she stop seeing James? Should she move back home after all? This would have been the sign she needed, would have told her something. But Charlotte isn't in the market for signs right now. She's not making decisions; she's just letting her life unfold, come what may. It's liberating, exhilarating even. Charlotte considers that maybe this is actually a sign after all, that this approach is exactly right.

Suddenly she realizes that she wants to leave before the whale does—she can't bear to see it swim off. She takes one last look, says goodbye, even if it makes her feel foolish, and wades out of the water. She's lost the will for her run. Missing one day won't kill her, it's vacation after all. So she grabs her socks and shoes, and heads home, promises herself she'll run an extra three miles tomorrow.

By the time she gets back to the house, Ryan and Mari have cleaned the dinner dishes that they'd been too drunk to worry about the night before. Though they put $200 plates in the dishwasher and she'd have to fish them out later. They also packed sandwiches and their bags for the beach.

"It's chilly, but we figured we'd still spend the day at the ocean. I like a beach day where I can wear a sweatshirt over my bathing suit without looking ridiculous," Mari says.

"Perfect plan. Let me just go grab a shower and change." Charlotte bounds up the stairs, still thinking about the whale. A day that starts with a whale sighting is bound to be a good day. That has to be a law of the universe.

Hours later the trio is spread out on the beach, finishing up their third game of Scrabble on a very worn out board Mari found in the pool house.

"Z-e-p-h-y-r. Triple word. Boo ya!" Ryan slams the letters down so hard some of the tiles side off onto the blanket. He can't help himself. He's always been competitive.

Whatever the sport, activity, or challenge, he wants to be the best. Sometimes living in New York, he'll even find that he's racing the guy walking next to him to the corner.

A memory comes back to him now, his mom pulling him aside at a rec soccer game. He must have been seven or so, and though he doesn't remember exactly what he said or did to warrant his mother's lecture, he does remember her angry words.

"You're not going to have any friends, Ryan, being such a damn spoil sport." But Ryan isn't a spoil sport, he's a winner. He recalls also that his mother then reminded him,

"It's just a game." But that's the thing, nothing is just a game.

Or rather, it's not about the game itself, it's what you bring to the table, your drive, cunning, commitment. To Ryan, that's unwavering. You don't get to be the best, otherwise.

Ryan thinks about an interview he recently heard on the radio about a woman who is writing a memoir about being transgender. She explained how she was born a man and felt like she had spent her entire life in the wrong body, and so in her thirties decided to fully transition to living as woman. As hard as it was to wrap one's head around that, Ryan could relate. Sometimes he felt he was born into the wrong life, as the only son of Barbara and Roger Hart, who he wouldn't exactly describe as overachievers. Their highest aspirations seemed to be having the best dish at monthly bridge group and catching the biggest fish in Lake Buckeye, respectively. He loved his parents, of course he did, but he wished he admired them. He wished they were the sort who went to Europe, could name their favorite work by Philip Roth, didn't think blue cheese was exotic. In other words, come to think of it, he wished they were Mayfields. But as Jonathan Mayfield would himself say, as he had actually said to Ryan somewhat presumptuously at graduation, "it doesn't matter where you start son, it's where you end up." And Ryan was damn well going to end up with the life he was born to live.

"Earth to Ryan," Charlotte says, waving her hand in front of his face. "You win. Again. Happy?" She lies back on the blanket, looking out over the water, wondering if the whale will come back or how far away he's swum. She was going to tell Ryan and Mari about her morning, the whale, the "Moment," but the afternoon passes, and for some reason, she doesn't.

"Guys, I gotta eat. We finished the snacks hours ago. I need more sustenance," Mari says.

"Pick up pizza or go to the Navigator?" Charlotte asks.

"I vote pizza. It looks like it's going to rain." They all appraise the sky and the dark purple clouds forming.

"My treat! Whatever toppings you want," Ryan says, as they pack up their stuff and head to the car.

"Big spender!" The girls joke, but truthfully Mari is happy to let Ryan pay for dinner considering he makes more than double what she does. Although she always bristles when Charlotte opts to pay for things. Go figure.

The pizza is delicious, rivaling the best Ryan's tried so far in New York. The power naps are even better and by the time they wake up and reconvene in the massive sunken living room, it's pitch black out. Ryan begins a campaign to rally the group to hit up a bar.

"Ryan, it's 10:30 on Martha's Vineyard, not the East Village. And we have plenty of wine right here." Charlotte gestures toward the still robust but fast dwindling stock.

"Lame, lame, lame. We're in our twenties for godsake's! We should be living it up."

"True! Okay, how about shots?" Charlotte walks over to the bar and gamely holds up a bottle of scotch.

"I'm pretty sure you don't do shots with scotch, Charlotte. And especially hundred dollar bottles of scotch, which I am sure that is." Mari can spot a bad idea when she sees one.

"Okay, we'll do swigs, then!" Charlotte laughs and takes a huge gulp from the bottle and then coughs uncontrollably for several seconds. "Wow, that burns." But she is determined to be the sort of girl who drinks scotch, swirls a highball glass, sips gracefully, and without coughing. One day.

"Give it to me." Ryan tips the bottle back, a hefty pour flows straight into his mouth. "Very smooth." He is sure he has heard someone describe scotch in such a way before. "As...um, quaint as this is, I'm serious, next year, we're going someplace with more scene. And we're going out!"

"How about Miami!" Charlotte suggests. "Mari can habla the espanol and show us all the sights. Oh wait—Mari—we have to do a shot for your birthday! Shit, Ryan, why didn't we get cupcakes or something? Hold on!" Charlotte stumbles into the kitchen and returns a minute later with a Twix bar in one hand and a candle Mari recognizes from the dining room candelabras in the other.

"Happy early birthday, Mar. Make a wish."

It's childish, perhaps, but Mari takes birthday wishes seriously. More seriously than she should at almost twenty-five. She takes a deep breath, thinks.

"Any time now," Charlotte chides.

But Mari won't be rushed. One wish a year, it's important. Usually it's a matter of wanting so much it's hard to narrow it down, but this year Mari feels at a loss to pinpoint anything she wants and that's even more daunting. But then it comes to her, a viable option, a decent enough desire, given the fact that Charlotte is now dramatically sighing. She takes a deep breath. Wishes. Blows out the candles.

"Wow that must have been a good one. Don't worry we won't make you tell.

But I hope it was to get laid!" Charlotte cackles and bites into the candy bar.

Ryan passes Mari the bottle. "And now a birthday swig."

She takes one, a big one. It burns going down, but weirdly feels good at the same time. Like she's being cleansed.

"I know, I know, let's play the game!" Charlotte shouts.

The game started first year during intense study sessions. One day, after a marathon of reviewing for the first torts exam until their eyes were bleary they started talking about the best and worst things about law school, and then everything else— childhood, Britney Spears, road trips—and this diversion became their go-to break. Someone would say, it's time for the game, and they would go round and round asking best/worst, no category off limits, until one of them (usually Mari) got them focused again.

Charlotte recalls how she tried to play last week with James and all he said was, "I don't play games," which in Charlotte's experience thus far was not expressly true, but she wasn't dwelling on James right now and she sure as hell wasn't bringing him up.

"I'll go first. Mari, best/worst, your job."

Mari thinks for a minute. "Um, best: I feel like I'm making a difference, or will at least one day. Worst: that I make as much as I would if I worked at Starbucks."

"Charlotte's turn," Ryan says, pleased that the game has

given him this perfect opening. "James. Best/worst. Go."

Charlotte lies back on the leather sofa, she's very drunk, but determined to get drunker still. She takes a sip of wine, prolonging the moment. "Hmmmm, best. The sex. Sorry, Ryan." She gives him a pointed look. "Worst is..."

"Wait, wait a minute. Why are you apologizing to Ryan?" Mari interrupts, confused.

"Why should I care?" Ryan says, hoping it's convincing that he doesn't. Of course, Charlotte would bring this up, he fumes. Even though they'd agreed that it would remain the night about which they never speak. Fucking alcohol.

"Will someone please tell me what's going on?" The wine and the scotch, the unwise mixture of both, are making her thoughts muddy but Mari has the distinct feeling she's missing something.

"Ryan and I...we sorted of hooked up this summer after you left. It was nothing though, right Ryan?"

"Wait, WHAT?" Mari sits up so fast her head spins. This is her worst nightmare, that Ryan and Charlotte would become a couple and then she really would be the third wheel. But after their initial flirtation, they'd seemed to truly settle into just being friends.

Mari had even asked Charlotte point blank one day and she'd insisted as much, that Ryan was officially off limits. And now not three months after graduation, this? What the hell? Mari is confused and inexplicably, perhaps, hurt.

Ryan glares at Charlotte. "I thought we agreed we weren't going to tell her."

This cuts Mari to her core. They were going to keep this, whatever this is, a secret from her. They did keep it a secret from her. They weren't supposed to keep things from each other.

Ryan sighs, goes on: "So yeah, we did. But it was honestly no big deal... We had too much to drink one night and well..."

"He basically jumped me, Mari," Charlotte says, laughing.

"Don't flatter yourself, Charlotte. As I recall you were the one who was too tired to go home."

The banter is light, but there's an unmistakable edge and yet no one is sober enough to sort out the subtext, which may be a blessing.

"Whatever, it was a one-time thing. We're not right for each other. We know that. And we're not ruining the friendship. Etc. Etc." Charlotte says.

Ryan tosses a throw pillow at her, which he intends to be a playful gesture, but literally falls flat.

"Okay, time for a new subject. Mari ask a best/worst." Charlotte wanted Mari to know about her and Ryan, somehow knew it would "slip" when she was drinking this weekend, and she could use alcohol as an excuse, claim drunken regret. But she hasn't even sobered up and already she wishes she had just kept her mouth shut.

Ryan jumps in. "Hold up. You never told us the worst thing about James." He's taunting her, a little, but she deserves it. They had a pact. And besides, he wants to know.

"He's too smothering. He's just too into me." Charlotte laughs.

The game has lost some of its fun, but Mari plays her turn. She'll put the idea of Ryan and Charlotte out of her mind until later...or actually, better, until never if she can help it.

"Ryan. NYC. Best/worst?"

"Best, the skanks. Worst...the skanks." They all laugh and if there was any tension left in the room it breaks. The bottle of scotch makes another round.

"This went too fast," Mari says, suddenly pensive.

"It's not over yet! We don't leave until like 3 p.m. tomorrow," Ryan says.

"And we'll see each other at Cecily's wedding, right? I still think it's selfish to have a wedding on New Year's Eve, but at least I'll get to ring it in with you guys," Charlotte says.

Mari knows that Charlotte will offer to pay, so she should probably just lie and say she can't go because of work, but they'll realize even death row lawyers have holidays, so she's honest. "I'm not sure I can go. I looked at prices to LA last week and they were steep."

"Noooo, you have to go, I'll pay. Don't worry about it."
Charlotte is aware that Mari hates it when she offers to pay for
things. Their one big fight first year involved Mari screaming,
"I'm not your charity case." But it's only money. Charlotte also is
well aware that it's easy for her to say, only rich people say "it's
only money," but it doesn't make it any less true. She has money,
plenty of it, so why didn't Mari just let her pay. Ryan was always
happy to let her. Maybe a little too happy, come to think of it.

Mari knows if she declines that Charlotte will keep insisting
or worse, be hurt, so she says she'll think about. And who knows
maybe she will let her because the idea of sitting alone in her
apartment watching Dick Clark is depressing the hell out of her.

"I'll be back, you guys." Mari gets up and leaves Charlotte
and Ryan discussing the logistics for tomorrow. Bloody Marys, a
bike ride, then back to pack and head their separate ways.

There's something Mari wants to do, has been dying to do
since she arrived. She makes her way to the porch, appraises each
of the rocking chairs and sits on the one all the way to the left. She
could try all six like Goldilocks, but this one is perfect, situated at
the corner of the porch where she can see both the front yard and
the marshes to the side that lead down to the beach. She rocks
gently in the chair, then stops because the porch already feels like
it's spinning, thanks to the ill-advised combination and amount of
scotch and wine she's consumed and will surely regret tomorrow.

She feels a drop of rain ricochet from the deck railing onto
her cheek and then another. Soon a steady stream is falling,
making a pleasant pattering sound as it hits the roof above her and
the bushes around her.

She lies back, closes her eyes and an image of Charlotte and
Ryan kissing pops into her head. Ugh, it's like imagining her
sister, Carmen and her husband. The idea of them, together, throws
off her entire equilibrium, or maybe it's the rocking. She knows
both of them too well, knows just how terribly this could end up.
And with her right in the middle, choosing sides. She decides to
take them at face value, it was just a drunken slipup, it was a one-

time thing. These things happen. Well, not to Mari, who had never had a one-night stand in her life, but she knows she's not the norm. Damn Catholic school.

On the other hand, what if...she pictures being both the maid of honor and best man at Charlotte and Ryan's wedding, the touching speech she will make. She begins to compose it, feels a lump in her throat. Dammit. She's getting overwrought. This is what happens when she drinks too much. Ryan and Charlotte joke about this alter ego of hers; Maudlin Mari they call her. But she can't help it, being with her friends this weekend, moving away and starting her "adult" life, her upcoming birthday, it's all made her feel sentimental.

She thinks of her grandmother's ninety-first birthday party last year. After a long day of revelry, Cuban music blasting, and a battalion of kids running around her older sister's back yard, they wheeled Abuelita up to blow out the candles on the giant tres leches cake her mother had spent all day making. As the flames from the candles flickered in front of her, Abuelita leaned over and grabbed Mari's arm with her liver spotted hand, pulled her down to her and whispered, "But it went so fast, Maricella?"

She looked mystified, stunned, confused. At first Mari thought she meant the party, or the holidays—which to Mari were passing interminably slow, as eager as she was to get back to Boston. And then it dawned on her that what her grandmother really meant was her life. Ninety-one years had passed so quickly. And that concept is starting to sink in for Mari. That everything, a weekend with friends, life itself, could pass in a blur if she's not careful, and maybe even if she is. It could all, one day, feel as sweet and fleeting as a late summer rainstorm.

Chapter Two
Miami, 2003

Acknowledging that she is sometimes prone to dramatics, this has still been one of the most intense weeks in Charlotte's life and things show no sign of letting up as she frantically tries to make it to the airport for a flight that she is not, given that I-76 is a parking lot, optimistic that she'll make.

She tries to take deep, calming breaths but every ounce of air in the cab she's in is filled with the pungent combination of curry and body odor even with the windows rolled down. She fights the urge to cover her mouth with the scarf around her neck, swallows deeply to combat a wave of nausea, a sensation she's become all too familiar with in the past few weeks.

Glancing at her watch yet again does not have the desired effect of making time slow down. She leans forward in the seat, toward the cab driver who is chewing on a toothpick and nodding along to the radio as if he doesn't have a care in the world, which irritates Charlotte to no end. She needs him to feel her sense of urgency, for them to be in this together.

"Hey, I have a 7:50 flight that I really have to make." She looks at her watch for dramatic effect. "It's the last flight to Miami tonight. Is there an alternate route we can take or something? This is ridiculous." She sounds more entitled and impatient than she intends, she knows that this traffic is not his fault and yet she also needs someone to blame and someone to solve this.

"Nothing I can do," he says. "Probably accident up ahead. We just have to wait."

He offers a what-can-you-do shrug that further infuriates Charlotte.

Now, on top of the nausea, she swallows against the lump in her throat that rises when she pictures American Airlines Flight #25 taking off without her, when she imagines calling Ryan and Mari and telling them to have fun without her tonight.

No, that's simply not acceptable, she's been looking forward to this weekend, their annual weekend together, for months now. She'll just have to use her parents' credit card to book a charter or a last-minute one-way ticket on an airline that has a later option. What would that cost? A grand? Two? That seems a fair price to pay considering this is entirely their fault anyway. She feels a sense of satisfaction as she finds the proper scapegoat for her predicament and channels her frustration accordingly.

This week of all weeks, her father had to insist, with typical last-minute notice, that she come down to Philadelphia for a stupid reception where he was getting some sort of award from the Wharton Alumni Association. Even after sitting through the mind-numbingly stiff ceremony last night she still doesn't know what exactly it was...Distinguished Contribution in the Field of Amassing Money? Actually, it was probably more like Distinguished Contribution to the Alumni Endowment. When you give multi-millions they name buildings after you, but when you give hundreds of thousands of dollars, as Jonathan Mayfield does, they give you bogus ingratiating awards. That her father strong-armed her into attending this farce because, "it's important that my loving family is there, Charlotte...for the pictures," even though she had explained it meant her taking another day off work, on top of the one she already took this week ("You're a first year attorney, what is so important that you can't get away for a few days for something this important?"), and rearranging it so she could fly to her long planned weekend with Mari and Ryan from Philly— caused her no small measure of irritation.

That it also meant spending twenty-four hours with her family as her dad strutted around his alma mater like a dignitary from a foreign country and her mom and brother alternatively basked and cowered deferentially in his refracted glory, just made her tired. On a good day it's hard to manage her family, and after this past, utterly exhausting week, she just didn't have the stamina.

She sits back against the cracked leather seats of the cab and tries to pinpoint the moment when she started to dread her family. Certainly the Mayfields were never what you could call close; there was no pretense of Cosby-like shenanigans where "life lessons" were learned, no homemade pizza nights—unless you count Magda making flatbread—and no family road trips in the paneled station wagon, but Charlotte recalls having a perfectly pleasant childhood. She felt proud even, to be a Mayfield. In fact, one of her earliest memories is overhearing the headmaster at The Branson School talking about her parents to her third grade teacher as they arrived at back-to-school night. "Well, there go Evelyn and Jonathan Mayfield, charmed as ever."

For an eight-year-old who loved The Little Mermaid more than just about anything, Charlotte was taken with this description: "charmed," which conjured magic and destiny and good fortune. But now that she looks back she can detect the sneer in Headmaster Frankel's tone, the smug subtext that was lost on her then is pretty clear in hindsight, along with the realization that people don't really like her parents. Or more specifically, people don't like Jonathan Mayfield, and Evelyn is a casualty. They respect him, perhaps; are intimidated by him for sure, but like him? Not so much. Charlotte, who once upon a time might have considered herself a "daddy's girl" has come to understand that her father is, well, kind of an asshole, and this has been one of the most shocking and disappointing in a series of revelations adulthood has brought her. Now that she's come to this clarity, now that she sees their flaws and cracks, she can't un-see them; she's only able to observe her family with a sharp-eyed objectivity that her father would actually appreciate. ("Sentimentalism is for fools, Charlotte.") So when the four of them are together, which is really just the odd holiday and special event at this point, she is hyper aware of things she wasn't before: her dad's relentlessly condescending comments towards her mom, her mom's vacant stares and plastered smile, her brother's passive aggressive resentment. She wants to scream at them, why are we such fucking wasp clichés! But if she did, her mother would probably tell her how unbecoming it was to raise her voice and continue cutting flowers or whatever else she did to fill up her days.

She knew this evening's "talk" was coming, but it didn't make her dread it any less. The last thing she needed at this particular point in her life was to think about what she was "doing with herself," a variation of the conversation her father has been initiating ever since she told him she wasn't coming back West after law school to work at Mayfield. Because her Dad demanded it, he'd assumed it would happen and he found it increasingly maddening that Charlotte was not bending to his will.

Oliver missed this little tête-á-tête because he had naturally hightailed it out of there as fast as he could last night. Within an hour of the reception ending, her brother was on the Acela back to D.C., explaining that he had a very early meeting on the Hill with Congressman so and so. Partly this was offered as an excuse, but it was also Charlotte knew, a thinly veiled attempt for Oliver to impress their father with his career as a lobbyist and his access to powerbrokers, which Charlotte also knew would prove futile. Sure enough Jonathan just nodded and offered a cursory, "well thanks for coming, son," when Oliver took his leave.

Which was just as well because she hated to see the look of heartbreak and anger on Oliver's face whenever their father brought up the so-called "family business," the one that Oliver, once beloved heir apparent, was not so subtly pushed out of after he came out his senior year at Michigan and began dating Brice, who he was still with. It was unclear what was more outside of Jonathan's grand design, that Oliver went to a state school or that he liked to sleep with men. But neither sat well with their father and so despite outward assurances that he was "supportive," all too swiftly Jonathan began aggressively grooming Charlotte to be his Number Two—ostensibly because Charlotte majored in business in undergrad but everyone knew the truth: Jonathan took away the prize because he was punishing Oliver, or because he was ashamed to have him helm the company. She didn't know which was worse.

Charlotte wants to be close to Oliver, for them to be allies, if not friends, but if she takes over Mayfield that will never happen. If Oliver is a spurned protégée, then she is a reluctant one but she's been unfairly cast as the usurper, an unforgivable transgression. So rather than bonding with each other and bitching about their parents behind their backs, a favorite sport of siblings everywhere, they engage in polite catch-up conversation as if they are former colleagues and not flesh and blood. It breaks Charlotte's heart.

So it was a saving grace that Oliver wasn't there for Jonathan's latest interrogation about his strategic vision for the next five million years, and Charlotte's "timeline and goals," and what exactly she's doing with her life?

Oh god, how close she was to unleashing on him. Yes, Dad, good fucking question. Let's talk about what I am doing with my life. My boss is essentially sexually harassing me, but I get plum cases out of it so... I'm in love with a man—you remember James, the one who ordered a bottle of the most expensive scotch on the menu and then slid the bill over to you when you and Mom met him in May...and who didn't even bother to pretend we had options when I was told him I was pregnant. Oh yeah, that's right Dad, not seventy-two hours ago I was with child! Don't worry, now I am not, so one thing that's not in my immediate future is a baby at least. Happy?

It would have been priceless to see the look on his face. Girls like Charlotte Mayfield don't get knocked up and don't get abortions. But actually, it is exactly girls like her, Charlotte thinks ruefully, rich white girls with bright futures that can't be compromised and have $600 to burn, who have abortions.

Instead of unleashing, however, like a grown up, she calmly told her dad she was still evaluating all of her options. That she had a great case at work (true) that she was committed to seeing through to the end (a stretch) and by that point she will have been at the firm at least three years, which seemed like a smart time to make a move. In other words, she treated her dad like an eager recruiter, which seemed the best way to manage him at the moment. After all it was her father himself that taught her this trick:

"Always keep all your options open, Charlotte."

But another of his favorite maxims is, "Know what you want."

After bulldozing through the last twenty-something years on a course of success, accomplishments, privilege and prestige, she's been just one year in the so-called "real world," and she suddenly has no clue where that was all supposed to lead, no idea what she wants anymore. She only knows what she doesn't want: to be alone, to practice law forever, to move back to SF. Oh yeah, and to have a baby. The nausea crests again at the same time traffic opens up, and the fact that they are finally moving, and the influx of fresh air to the stagnant backseat, which feel like such gifts— she could cry. Actually, she does cry. Her emotions have been such a see saw she might as well still be pregnant, at least she could blame the hormones.

It's still so surreal, Charlotte muses, discreetly dabbing her tears with her scarf, lest the cab driver realize he has an emotional basket case in the backseat. Monday morning she woke up pregnant, and now she's not, the simplicity of that equation belies the complicated emotions she feels.

The nurse at the clinic, a lovely woman with an enormous bosom and a scrub shirt with penguins on it, which Charlotte normally would have found ridiculous but for some reason found comforting, kept reassuring her she was okay as she came up from the anesthesia. "You're okay, baby, you're okay baby," she said over and over as she rubbed Charlotte's forearm. And then in the most sympathetic voice possible when Charlotte was more fully awake, "How you doing, hon?"

Is she okay? How is she doing? The nurse probably did not mean for these to be existential exchanges, but Charlotte took them as such and truthfully, she had and still has no idea. She hasn't been able to clearly isolate a single feeling as they tumble through her like clothes in dryer. At first, looking at the stick, she felt total shock, though perhaps she shouldn't have given her carelessness with the Pill the last few months. Then she felt conviction to get rid of it as fast as possible, which James all too readily agreed was, "really the only thing that makes sense." Then she felt a little badass to be honest; she was a feminist and a grown up who was prepared to make controversial choices and exercise her rights. Then she felt...numb. Then it circled around all over again to shock.

The nurse explained to her this was normal, that she would feel a range of emotions—sadness, anger, guilt, regret. Check, check, and check. But the only thing she regrets, truthfully, is not calling Mari. She knew better than to call Ryan who would be so full of shock and give her a lecture about why she was still with James and can't she see he doesn't give a shit about her (she can't) and why wasn't she more careful (good question), and blah, blah, blah. She just didn't want to deal with him.

Granted Mari would have thought all of these things too, she's the most righteous of them all, but at least would have been generous enough not to say them aloud. And yet, she didn't call Mari. She was just too far away, what good would it have done? Mari couldn't hold her hand, bring her meds, stay up late watching Law and Order with her. And besides Charlotte had decided almost immediately that this was something she should navigate alone, mostly to steel herself against James' indifference. He seemed to equate an abortion with having a cavity filled and so she, too, convinced herself that was the case. No muss, no fuss, and certainly no tears; Charlotte was a beacon of practicality and cool.

Only when the clinic insisted that she had to have someone pick her up did she call Jill, a friend from undergrad who had also moved to Boston. She wasn't going to give James the satisfaction of asking him to come if he wasn't going to offer—and he didn't. In the moment she didn't have the emotional bandwidth to feel appropriately outraged about that. She just let it go, as she let so many things with James go and which he took to mean, as he always did, that everything was fine. In a twisted way, this made Charlotte feel powerful. She wanted things to be fine, too, and by sheer will, she made them so. So when James kissed her goodbye when she left for Philly with a, "have fun with the folks, kiddo. It's all good, okay?" she made the decision to agree. It's all good. She let herself feel reassured, hopeful even that they were going to turn over a new leaf, move forward in their relationship. Aren't babies supposed to bring people together? Maybe even babies you don't end up actually having?

She reaches in her handbag and takes out the Valium she swiped from her mom's purse earlier in the day. She was waiting to take it on the plane and chase it with a vodka tonic, but with thoughts of James becoming a jumble in her mind—the sooner she blots them out the better, and she needs some chemical help.

With sweet relief, she sees they are finally turning off on the airport exit, and even though she will have to ungracefully run through the airport O.J. Simpson style, it looks like she'll make it after all. And with this, this one small break, a mercy she may not deserve, Charlotte feels an overwhelming gratitude to the universe, the one that has lately seemed so bent on fucking her over.

* * *

Charlotte doesn't look so good. This is what Mari is thinking as Ryan pours another round of pre-game shots into the tumbler glasses in their hotel room. Since Mari herself arrived an hour ago, Ryan has been insisting that they aggressively pre-game before they go out in South Beach and Charlotte had barely dropped her bag in their room before he upped the urgency.

Charlotte is gamely chasing vodka, but Mari knows Ryan must also see the dark circles under her eyes and that she's very thin. Not the thin that Mari, in weaker moments, is jealous of, but the emaciated kind. She also, inexplicably, smells faintly of curry, even though Charlotte hates curry.

"Are you okay?" Mari asks, plopping down next to her on the double bed they'll share for the weekend.

There's that question again, along with the lump in her throat, which Charlotte attacks with a big swallow of vodka. "I'm fine." And the thing is, it's true—the relief of seeing her friends, the fun weekend ahead of them, the vodka giving her a warm flush, she's better than she has been in weeks. She rests her head on Mari's shoulder, squeezes her arm. "I'm really happy to be here, to see you guys."

Ryan sits on the double bed opposite them. "This weekend is going to be amazing. This room is sick, right?"

Ryan is very proud of himself for finding it. The Saxon is one of the trendiest hotels in South Beach, brand new and in the heart of everything. He'd overheard Tripper mention the hotel and that one of his clients was an early investor, so Ryan decided they had to stay here and then made a point of casually mentioning it to his boss. Yeah, that's right, Tripper, I have taste. Ryan knew Mari would balk at the price (and he didn't even get the ocean view suite he really wanted) so he lied about how much the room cost so she would pay less and then he and Charlotte covered her share. Well, Charlotte didn't exactly know they covered her share, but she was always opening her wallet and saying that's what friends are for, so Ryan reasoned that she wouldn't mind.

Ryan reaches out and lightly slaps Charlotte's thigh. "So what's going on, you've been MIA? I called you like a thousand times last week."

"I know, sorry. Like I said, it's been nutty," Charlotte says. "Work stuff," she adds quickly so they don't immediately start grilling her about James.

"Are you making progress with the Headly case?" Ryan had been keeping an eye on the case because his firm is involved in a similar proceeding, an ousted CEO suing shareholders. Charlotte was lucky to get such a plum assignment. For a split second, he sort of wishes he had a boss who wanted to sexually harass him. Men can never sleep their way to the top.

"Ugh. I don't want to talk about work." Charlotte doesn't want to talk about anything—work, James, life. She just wants to have fun. When was the last time she truly had fun? She's twenty-six for god sakes, all she was supposed to be having was fun. The vodka was already working its magic. "Can we just drink and dance?"

"Amen! That's my Charlotte!" Ryan yells, swigging from the Absolut bottle.

Though there's a small part of him that does want to talk about work since he's kicking ass and wants them to know it. But all in good time—they have the whole weekend to catch up.

"Why don't you shower and get changed and we'll hit the Delano, right down the street. Good DJ, strong drinks. Done and done. How do I look?" He stands up and walks over to the full-length mirror in the room, admiring his plaid shirt and dark jeans.

Charlotte is very over plaid button-ups and thinks the jeans are trying a little too hard, but Ryan still looks good. "You look great. Heartbreaker." She winks.

"I'm not even going to ask you how I look," Mari says. "Because this is what I'm wearing so don't try to convince me to change or to squeeze into anything of yours."

She'd made a last-minute trip yesterday to the Banana Republic in Eastdale Mall to grab two tops to bring for the trip—one the skin tight blank tank she wore now, which made her feel heavier but at least accentuated her boobs, and a flowy tank top with sequins for tomorrow night that she hoped looked "South Beach." It's funny, despite the fact the she grew up an hour from here, she never really came down to South Beach with friends. It wasn't, and Mari suspects, still isn't her scene, all bass and club kids and four- inch heels. But it's also not Montgomery, so she'll take it.

"You look fabulous," Charlotte says genuinely. Mari has that effortless appeal that comes from not trying hard at all, but still managing to be pretty, with her thick dark hair and impossibly long lashes. "But you know I'm going to do your make-up."

She nudges her friend in the elbow. The fact that Mari only

ever wears mascara and lip gloss is a running joke.

Ryan turns on the small radio in the hotel room and Beyoncé's hit, "Baby Boy," comes booming into the room while Charlotte heads to the bathroom to get ready as quickly as she can.

Ironically the exact same song is playing when they arrive at the Delano an hour later. Mari is almost breathless at how gorgeous it is. They go through the lobby of the hotel to the back terrace, which features a long pool, lined with cabanas draped in white linen and surrounded by colored lights and lush landscaping. Just past the pool is an outdoor bar, DJ booth, and a throng of glamorous people sipping on cocktails and gyrating to the music. Mari would normally feel out of place but she's too taken with the scene. Near the far end of the pool, right smack dab in the middle of the shallow water are two ornate white metal chairs and a small table. You'd have to tread through knee deep water to reach them, and then everyone would stare at you sitting smack dab in the middle of the pool, but it's all Mari can think about, sitting in one of those ridiculous chairs.

Ryan brings them a round of cocktails. Mari has no idea what's in hers, but it tastes fruity and exotic at the same time. Charlotte downs her in seconds.

"Daaaamn girl, slow down that's a $15 cocktail, not a forty." It's a sure sign that Ryan is drunk when he starts talking like an Eminem wanna be.

"Oh please, here." Charlotte opens her tiny snakeskin clutch and digs out her credit card, hands it to Ryan.

"Nah, I got you." Ryan makes a show of flashing his corporate card.

"Well, thank you Mr. Expense account. When did you get one of those?"

"Oh you know...I'm big time now." He flashes them a wide grin.

"Well, that's great but you realize we aren't clients right?" Mari says.

"Whatever, last week Tripper expensed a masseuse to come to the office and give him a full body massage at 10 a.m. so I'm not worried. Be back!"

He disappears into the crowd of sweaty people as Charlotte and Mari huddle around a high table and sway to the music.

"So how was your dad's award last night? Good times?" Mari screams across the table to be heard above Nelly—"it's gettin hot in here"—booming from the nearby speaker.

"Oh, the usual. Everyone kissed Jonathan's ass and we ate overcooked steak. Blah blah blah."

Mari was well aware that Ma and Pa Mayfield could be a sensitive subject so she didn't press. "I'm psyched to see my parents tomorrow. I haven't seen them since last Christmas! It's crazy."

Charlotte totally forgot they had planned to drive up to Hallandale Beach to visit Mari's parents. She should probably slow down so she's not completely wrecked and hung over tomorrow when they hang out with the Castillos, but Ryan arrives with another strong cocktail and a tequila shot and she downs them both with relish.

"Holy shit, Charlotte is gangsta." Ryan starts dancing behind her. "I'll be back y'all. There's a fine lady waiting for me at the bar."

Both Mari and Charlotte roll their eyes. Knowing Ryan as well as they do his idea of "game"—especially when he's drunk—cracks them up, but he's good-looking and friendly and generous with the drinks, which is a simple but highly effective combination when it comes to the opposite sex.

They keep eyes on him as he makes his way back to the bar so they can check out his potential conquest. There are three girls, almost identical, each with long blonde hair, sheer tank tops showing a few inches of flat tanned stomachs, all teetering in high heels.

"I wonder which one he's eyeing?"

"Um, any of them... All of them." Charlotte laughs.

They're quiet for a minute, people watching and nodding along to the music.

"Oh shit, Mari!" Charlotte says suddenly. "I'm the worst

friend! I totally forgot to ask you about the execution."

A few weeks ago, Mari attended an execution in Alabama. Some guy, Charlotte can't remember his name, but she does remember his crime—murdering his girlfriend—was put to death, and Mari's boss Ted got her a press pass through his connections so she could attend. He said anyone working on death row cases should see "what it's all about." Charlotte feels like such a self-absorbed jerk. She knew how nervous Mari was about it but with everything going on she forgot to ask.

"I'm so sorry, I totally forgot," she slurs again, hugging Mari.

"It's okay. But um, can we not talk about it now," Mari smiles and nods her head toward the couple next to them, a man who's at least seventy-five pounds overweight and a girl young enough to be his daughter, who begin feverishly making out not one foot away from them. "This just doesn't seem to be the place to talk lethal injection." Mari laughs.

"Uh, I think this girl is about to get a lethal injection," Charlotte says and they crack up. "Come on, let's dance!" Charlotte grabs Mari's hand and they make their way closer to the DJ booth where they find Ryan grinding enthusiastically with one of the blondes.

As if on cue, 50 Cent's "In da Club" comes on. Ryan sees them and dances his way over.

"Go Mari, it's your birthday," he sings along and pumps his arm with the music, which would look ridiculous if he wasn't so thoroughly committed.

"Happy early birthday, Mariiii!!!" Charlotte screams into the music.

"God, when was the last time we danced like this?" Mari asks rhetorically, or rather when was the time I danced like this, she thinks. For a girl who sometimes has a hard time "letting loose"— as Ryan and Charlotte are always urging her—tonight, fueled by the vodka, the music, and the desire to get her mind off the last grueling few weeks, she has absolutely no trouble.

The beat consumes them and they are exhilarated, energized, ready to dance all night. Or at least until 2 a.m., which is when the lights come up.

"What the fuck?" Ryan slurs. "It can't be closing. Clubs in New York don't close until the sun comes up." He steps up his dancing as if his energy will keep the club open a few more hours. Then he whispers a bit with the Bunnies, which is what Mari and Charlotte have taken to calling his three blonde friends.

"We should head back," Charlotte goes to grab Ryan's arm.

"You guys do that. I'm gonna head back to the W with the O'Neill sisters here."

He gestures over to the trio of girls in deep conversation a few feet away who are undoubtedly trying to negotiate the sleeping arrangements considering a stranger is coming home with them.

"Hold up. Those girls are sisters?"

Ryan grins. "Jackpot!"

Both Mari and Charlotte groan and hit him. "You're so gross."

"I'm only hooking up with one of them, don't worry. Well...two tops," he laughs.

"I'll be back by 9 a.m. so we can do our bike rides and then head to Mari's parents."

Mari and Charlotte bid Ryan farewell and lean into each other as they stumble the few blocks back to their hotel. Even though Ryan's bed is empty, they fall into their double bed together, fully clothed, and curl up like puppies, clutching each other as if that's going to stop the room spinning around them. Charlotte wills herself not to throw up.

Or maybe she should, that would be a relief. She's too tired to decide so she just closes her eyes instead and nuzzles against Mari's shoulder.

For a second Mari has a flashback to law school, when on the rare Saturday they could totally relax, they would lie in Charlotte's bed all day and watch Lifetime—a their "women-in-peril movie marathons" they called them.

"Hey Mar?" Charlotte slurs. "I miss you."

Mari turns, sloppily kisses the top of Charlotte's head. "I

miss you, too."

* * *

"Rise and shine, sleepyheads!" Ryan throws open the black out drapes covering the hotel room's large windows.

"Are you kidding me? Close those! What time is it?" Charlotte groans and buries her head underneath her pillow, willing the bright sun away.

"You're pretty chipper?" Mari says, also burrowing down in the sheets, which feel so incredibly soft, yet crisp. There's nothing better than hotel sheets.

"Oh getting laid will do that for you, you should try it sometime." Ryan flops down on the bed and collides with the pillow Mari throws at him. "Ha. Ha."

"So how was it?" Charlotte asks from under the pillow, her voice muffled.

"A gentleman doesn't kiss and tell."

"Um, then how come we know that Kimmie Reardon has a third nipple or that that the redhead you hooked up with after the Maroon 5 concert used baby oil as lube?"

Mari dies of laughter. "Omigod, I totally forgot about her. She must just have a constant yeast infection."

"Okay, stop. Talk of yeast infections is ruining my post hook up high. Let's just say a good time was had by all." Ryan rummages through his suitcase to find something to wear.

"Um, please tell me you're going to shower," Charlotte says, mock-horrified.

"Only if you'll join me," he jokes.

"Nah, you have to focus on washing off the cutie cooties."

"Never miss a chance for corny alliteration, do you Charlotte? Seriously you guys gotta get up."

Charlotte and Mari make no moves to leave the bed. "I can't. I love these sheets.

Do hotels buy their sheets in special places?"

Ryan looks at Mari like she has two heads. "I have no idea.

We're supposed to pick up the bikes at 10 so we can have them back by 2 p.m. Then we can shower and head to the Castillos. God, I hope your mom made banana bread." Mari's mom sent a loaf of homemade banana bread in a care package their first year and Ryan has not stopped talking about it since.

"Where are we biking? I can't be on the street, I haven't been on a bike in...forever. Mari didn't that guy Brent want to take you to rent bikes and ride around the Common our first year. I remember thinking that was so cute and romantic."

"Yep. But instead I convinced him we should go to lunch at Legal Seafood on the waterfront, which was the classiest thing I could imagine. Until he insisted we split the check and then itemized our bill down to the valet parking. Not so cute and romantic."

"I told you that guy was a douche. You guys need to listen to me. That's what guy friends are for: insider knowledge." Ryan looks pointedly at Charlotte. "Anyway, there's a nice bike path along the beach. Goes up to Bel Harbour and back. It's like five miles or so."

"We need to leave for my parents around 4 p.m. if that's cool. Should take like an hour to drive up." Mari suddenly feels apprehensive about going to her parents' house. She wonders what Charlotte and Ryan will think of it. She hasn't seen where either of them grew up, though she can certainly imagine—has actually spent an embarrassing amount of time imagining Charlotte's lavish estate in Marin. She smiles to think how her mom will no doubt put out fresh flowers today, which she does whenever company comes. "So we'll seem like the type of people who always have fresh flowers in the house," her mom explained.

"But we aren't," Mari had teased. "You only ever get them when someone comes to visit."

"But they don't know that," her mom had said and then swatted her with a dishtowel.

"I got us on the list for Shore Club tonight," Ryan says. There's nothing Ryan loves more than being on a list. He's now been in New York City long enough to know which club promoters to cultivate. He and his buddies get bottle service for $300, $400 a pop Friday or Saturday at Lotus, Spy Club, Marquee, nightclubs frequented by models and ballers—literally, Ryan spotted Latrell Spreewell at Lotus just last weekend. Now that certain promoters know he's ready to spend (thank you expense account), they put him on the VIP list so he goes right up to and quickly past the velvet rope no matter how many people are waiting to get in. Suckers wait in line is Ryan's guiding philosophy. "I can't imagine drinking again tonight," Charlotte says, blinking against the light. "Come on, all you need is a Bloody Mary and you'll be good to good," Ryan assures her, pulling her from the bed. "Hit the showers."

* * *

The Bloody Mary, or rather Marys, plural, did the trick. Charlotte actually feels fantastic as they ride up the wooden plank beach path. The Atlantic on their right is a sparkling blaze of blue waves and they could not have ordered a more perfect, cloud-free sky.

Charlotte tries to pinpoint the last time she was on a bike. She remembers getting a shiny green Schwinn for her tenth birthday. She recalls how she coveted the bike for weeks and months before her birthday, but funny, she can't remember actually riding it.

Fortunately, it's true what they say, though she's a little wobbly, getting back on two wheels really is "like riding a bike." Though for a split second she wonders if she's even supposed to be on a bike so soon after her...procedure, but fuck it, too late now.

Charlotte pedals faster to try to catch up to Ryan who is predictably riding as if he is in the Tour de France.

"This is amazing, isn't it?" he calls back, his voice carried by the wind. Mari is having the exact same thought a few paces back. She took it for granted how breathtaking the ocean can be when she grew up so near it. But this, white sand, brightly painted lifeguard chairs dotting the beach, the thick marsh grasses, it's all so perfectly picturesque, she appreciates it anew. As she follows Charlotte, whose hair is blowing in the breeze, and Ryan who is somehow already perfectly tan after just twenty- four hours in Miami, she feels like she's in a commercial for Bud Light or sunscreen or tampons. Tag line: Have the time of your life. Which she is.

She hears Charlotte call out something to Ryan though Mari can't make out what she says and this is when it happens, as if in slow motion. One moment Charlotte is coasting along, not even really pedaling and then a kid comes from her left merging onto the beach path. She swerves to miss colliding with him and then swerves the other way to recover and her front wheel slides in the sandy planks and then shoots right off of the elevated boardwalk. She lands heavily in the marshy weeds with the bike on top of her.

Charlotte sits stunned for a moment, long enough to see the kid disappearing down the path like an innocent bystander. She could kill that kid for almost killing her!

But that thought quickly fades as a more pressing sensation occurs to her, an incredibly intense burning, as if a sharp knife has sliced through her flesh. Or in this case, a sharp pedal. By the time she realizes what's happened blood has pooled in the sand under her, creating a dull pink sludge.

"Oh shit, Charlotte!" Ryan has circled back and jumps off his bike beside her. He blames the hangover and the lack of sleep for the serious case of dry heaves he has as he takes in the layers of exposed flesh of Charlotte's leg and the blood dripping out of the deep gash, which goes from her just above her ankle almost to her knee.

"Thank god, you weren't pre-med," Mari says as she nudges him out of the way and kneels down next to Charlotte.

Ryan recovers and slips off his T-shirt. It's his favorite Harvard T-shirt, but he has a lot and this is an emergency so he only hesitates slightly as he hands it to Mari to wrap around Charlotte's leg to stop the bleeding.

The pain is incredible but all Charlotte wants to do at this point is laugh.

Seriously, universe? Seriously.

A group of passerby gather and the locals point them to a hospital ten blocks north. An older woman with a Pomeranian that oddly looks exactly like her dashes off to the street ahead of them to hail them a cab, her terrier barking in excitement the whole way. Ryan and Mari help Charlotte to her feet, she drapes an arm over each of them.

"Well, that's going to leave a mark, huh?" Charlotte says, wincing in pain.

"Well, bright side. At least it's not your face?" Ryan grins and Charlotte gives him a murderous look.

As they walk he calls the bike place from his cell and explains the situation and the owner says to leave the bikes where they are and he can drive up to come get them.

Apparently this isn't the first time this has happened.

An hour later they are sitting in blue vinyl chairs in the Miami Dade Memorial Hospital Emergency Room. Charlotte's leg has stopped bleeding for the most part, but it's clear she'll need stitches, a lot of them, Ryan thinks. He can't understand why there is always a wait in the ER. Isn't the very nature of an emergency that you need to be seen right away and yet they've been waiting forty-five minutes and there's at least five other people in the waiting room also experiencing "emergencies." One guy has an arm that's clearly popped out of the socket. Ryan saw the same thing happen to someone on his high school baseball team once and recognizes the telltale dangling limb. And there's a woman sitting next to them holding a toddler who looks incredibly listless. At this rate they'll be here all night. He tries not to think about the Shore Club.

"Do you want to call James, let him know you're hurt?" Mari asks. Charlotte's leg is propped in her lap and Mari's been flipping through a People magazine. A picture of mom Laci Peterson before she went missing is on the cover, and Mari and Charlotte wholeheartedly agree that Scott Peterson killed her. It's always the husband/boyfriend.

"I'm not dying. It's just a scratch." Charlotte instinctively adopts a cavalier attitude though it would be nice if James were worried. Maybe she should call him, embellish her accident a bit, milk some sympathy points.

But then a nurse comes out and calls her name and she hobbles to the back, Ryan and Mari trailing behind her, and gets settled on a bed surrounded on three sides by a thin blue curtain. On the other side of the curtain a doctor is pretty vigorously interrogating a woman about her bowels and the three friends don't dare make eye contact lest they burst into laughter.

Thankfully a doctor walks in then and in ten minutes has given Charlotte eleven stitches and pronounced her good as new. He says a nurse will be in with pain medicine and bandages shortly.

As he walks out, Mari swears she hears a familiar voice down the hall, near the nurses' station. She pokes her head around the curtain and sure enough there is her mother, carrying two giant shopping bags.

"Mom! What are you doing here?" Mari exclaims, shocked.

"Well, you said you weren't going to be able to come up because of Charlotte's accident, so your father and I just decided to hop in the car and come down to you. El esta viniendo. Donde esta Charlotte? Esta bien?"

Her mother always slips in and out of Spanish when she's agitated or excited.

"She's okay, Mom, come in." Mari parts the curtain as if revealing a magic act.

And in some ways it is; she can't believe her mother has appeared. "Look who it is, guys!"

Emelda goes right over to Charlotte and embraces her. "Oh, honey I was so worried when Mari called and said you fell off your bike. Though I'm surprised it wasn't this one. She never was very good at riding a bike."

"I was too," Mari protests, half-heartedly because her mom is right. It is a surprise that she wasn't the one who fell today.

"Oh you know it's true. You had a lot of other talents. Did you know that Mari won the fourth, fifth, and sixth grade spelling bees? The only kid in Hallandale to ever do that."

"Yes, Mom, you told them at graduation," Mari says, rolling her eyes affectionately.

"Well, anyway, how are you Charlotte? Let me see." Emelda leans down to inspect the wound as if she's a battlefield nurse. "That will heal up very nice, no scar.

Okay little scar," she regretfully concedes, gently patting Charlotte's leg right above the scar. "Oh here, I got you something." She reaches into one of the shopping bags and pulls out a pink teddy bear wearing a T-shirt that says, BIENVENIDOS A MIAMI. "I know it's silly but I wanted to get you something, and we were in such a hurry to get here, we just stopped by one of those tourist centers. He's cute though, right? Cheer you right up." Emelda leans over and gives Charlotte a squeeze.

This is far from silly, Charlotte thinks. This may be the nicest thing anyone's ever done for her since...well, she can't even remember. The kindness threatens to undo her. She bites her lip so as not to burst into tears. A memory comes back to her: She's five or six, lying in her pink and purple striped room, coughing dramatically so her mother would come up and check on her. She waits and waits in anticipation, making sure to stay buried under her thick duvet, even though she's boiling hot, so her temperature will stay high. She imagines her mom reading her books and feeling her forehead and bringing her vanilla pudding, her favorite. But only Magda came with French onion soup (she hated the slimy onions) and two children's aspirin. Charlotte is surprised by herself and tilts her head as if to drop the sadly cliché memory out of it.

"Thank you, Mrs. Castillo," she says, meaning it. "He's adorable. I feel better already."

"Ahh, I bet that's the Vicodin," she says and everyone laughs.

"What else is in the bag, mom?" Heaven only knows. Mari was notorious in both law school and undergrad for getting the most random and inexplicably curated care packages from her mother. One of the more memorable ones consisted of a deck of cards, a giant bag of Twizzlers, and a glass figurine of a dolphin in a giant box. But it truly was the thought that counted.

"Oh I knew you wouldn't be able to come to dinner, but I made all your favorites so I brought them to you. You guys can snack." She pulls out banana bread, and Ryan dives right in, pulling a chunk from the loaf pan and pronouncing it delicious mid-bite.

Meanwhile, Emelda lifts plastic container after plastic container from the bags and Mari squeals with delight at each one.

Charlotte can remember the handful of times she felt envy in her life—when Rebecca Miller got homecoming queen, when her Stanford roommate's boyfriend decorated their room with one hundred red roses for Valentine's Day and now, when she sees Mari and her mom together.

"I'll leave you kids for a minute. I got to go find your Papi. He dropped me off and then was circling trying to find the closest parking space. You know how he is." She disappears around the curtain.

"Sorry, guys I hope that wasn't too weird."

"Are you kidding—it was the best," Charlotte says. She's clutching her teddy bear.

"Agreed." Ryan holds up a piece of banana bread as if toasting.

"They are the best, huh?" Mari is grateful to have this reminder of how special her parents are—she knows she often takes them for granted. Just last week her mom was fired up on her weekly rant about the nurses at the assisted living center where her grandmother moved in the spring and Mari tried to get off the phone for at least twenty minutes, finally all but hanging up on her in exasperation. She feels a sharp stab of guilt.

Would it have killed her to be more patient and listen to the woman who drove here with shopping bags full of thoughtful gifts for her and her friends? It's not like she hasn't herself been annoying. God, she cringes now to remember how obnoxious she was during her first visit home from Harvard, how much she wanted to impress her parents with her newfound knowledge and her fancy friends. She told one pretentious story after another, about her new friend Charlotte's dad, who might be governor of California one day, about how esteemed Professor Wallace, who was on the legal team (the good side) who argued Brown vs. Board of Ed, had taken her under his wing, about how she might go with a friend (it was Charlotte, but she was trying to give the impression that her circle was more expansive) to her family's house in Aspen for Christmas break. Finally, her mom turned to her and said, "Sounds like you've met some wonderful people, but, recuerda quien eres. Remember who you are. You're the impressive one."

As Mari reaches in the shopping bag to get another homemade cookie, she resolves, not for the first time, to be a better daughter, and to feel grateful that her parents love her friends and vice versa. No one likes Charlotte's dad. Not even Charlotte.

The nurse comes in with discharge papers and a medicine bottle. "Here are six Percocet. That should get you through the next couple of days. Don't mix these with alcohol." The three of them look at each other, preemptively guilty.

The nurse is no fool. "Just be very careful, okay," she says with a world-weary sigh she probably gives to all invincible twenty-somethings.

They reunite with Mari's parents in the lobby, who offer to drive them back to their hotel. It's only a forty-minute trip down to South Beach but Charlotte, fuzzy from the painkillers, nods off on Ryan's shoulder in the back seat with a car full of animated voices dancing around her. She dreams that she's in a panel station wagon, the only car driving across an endless desert highway, her parents are laughing in the front seats, she and Oliver have set up a game of Uno on the bench seat in the back, and she is happily letting him win.

* * *

Charlotte wakes up in a mood. She has no idea how long she's slept, but sees it's now dark outside, so at least a few hours. Ryan and Mari are on his bed talking in hushed voices so as not to wake her.

"So he's just lying there, Ryan. But strapped down so he can't move at all. And I thought it would be quick, but it takes him like, I don't know, twenty minutes to die. He can barely move with the restraints but you can still tell he's fighting and gasping and we're all just sitting there, looking on. It was barbaric."

Watching the life literally go out of someone is not something that Mari had ever imagined she would witness. It made sense why Ted wanted her to go to the execution, but it's affected her in ways that she can't fully articulate and doesn't really want to discuss with anyone but Ted who understands more than anyone since he's been to seven executions himself. Ted had warned her, "watching someone die, watching someone be killed. It stays with a person. It's something you can't un-see." But the thing is, Mari doesn't wish to un-see it. She's glad she went, grateful even. It was one of the most profound and affecting experiences of her life. And it reinforced her convictions and her commitment to her work, which was not just a matter of justice and fairness, but life and death. There was no greater injustice than an innocent person being put to death and she could think of nothing else worth dedicating herself to, worth fighting so hard and working such long hours to prevent. Though she would love to be able to get just a little more sleep.

"That sounds tough to watch. But you know he killed someone, too, so I am sure the victim's family didn't think it was so awful. Didn't you say they were happy about it? I bet they celebrated after. They got justice."

An eye for an eye. That doesn't make it right, is what Mari wants to say, along with all the statistics she has at the ready about how many innocent people are put to death, but then again the last thing she wants is to get into a debate about the death penalty with Ryan, on vacation no less. They'd already gone round and round about the war in Iraq this morning so Mari was thrilled to see that Charlotte was waking up at the perfect time.

"You're up!"

"I am...what time is it?"

"9:30. You down to go out?" Ryan is already dressed in a nearly identical plaid shirt to the one he wore last night. No, is clearly not an option. But she is ready, ready to go out, to get out of her mind yet again.

"For sure, let me just shower and get dressed." She still has the plastic bracelet from the hospital around her wrist, and looks down at the unsightly gauze covering her leg. "The hospital chic look is not exactly what I was going for when I packed my DVF wrap dress for tonight. I wish I brought pants."

"Are you kidding me? Guys'll love it. The whole damsel in distress thing. You can get some drinks out of it for sure."

And sure enough, Ryan's right. Charlotte's injury gives guys just the opening they need to approach her. From the time she hobbles through the front door, with the incredibly hot doorman offering a personal escort to a seat, to the bartender insisting her first drink is on the house, her mishap is proving to have some upside.

The Shore Club is perfect—it's set up like a lush tropical garden that might be straight out of Colonial India, with vibrant prints, tall leafy flowers, large bronze lanterns, and scattered groups of seating. If Charlotte pretends she is in someone's impeccably landscaped backyard, rather than one of the most popular hot spots in Miami, then she doesn't feel quite so silly that she has her injured leg propped on a table.

Per nurse's orders, she's trying to take it easy on the drinks that Mari and Ryan take turns ferrying to get her from the packed bar, but the painkillers and the vodka are giving her such a pleasant euphoric feeling, she just wants more, more, more. Charlotte better understands why some of her more rebellious friends at prep school dabbled in heroin. Who wouldn't want to feel like this?

Mari goes to the bar with the stern pronouncement that this is the very last drink Charlotte can have for the evening. Charlotte puts her leg down to go through her purse, ostensibly to find and re-apply her lipstick, but really to check her phone and see if James has called.

He hasn't.

"You should really keep that elevated." Charlotte looks up to see a tall, lanky, guy hovering over her. He looks like a slightly nerdier version of Ben Affleck, a comparison he's no doubt been flattered to get from time to time.

"Oh come on, is that the best you got?" Charlotte offers him a neutral smile, not sure yet how far she wants to take this.

"Well, I am a doctor," he says sitting down next to her. He's cuter up close, and he smells really good, which Charlotte has always been a sucker for.

"Yeah, right. And I'm a Victoria's Secret model." Charlotte sets him up for the easy compliment because hey why not.

"Well, you absolutely could be and really, I am a doctor. An Ortho resident in Phoenix. I'm here for my buddy's bachelor party." He points to a short Middle Eastern-looking guy across the bar who is gyrating against a tall blonde woman who from this distance could be one of the Bunnies. "He's getting married next month. Sucker."

Charlotte can read the subtext of this comment; he's trying to make clear before moving any further..not looking for anything serious, just want to have fun. Which is fine by her. That's what this weekend is all about. That's the thing that's most missing from her life, between her eighty-hour work weeks at a job she increasingly hates and the eighty hours a week she spends on James, venting, stressing, analyzing, strategizing, beating herself up. Jesus, her relationship takes more energy than law school.

Fueled by her buzz, she decides without realizing that she's made the decision that she's going home with him. She hasn't slept with anyone since she started dating James, hasn't even kissed someone unless you count the weird make out session she had with Ryan last summer. Maybe this is what she needs, exactly what she needs.

"Hey—let's go back to your place," she says abruptly. "Assuming you have a place?"

He raises his eyebrows, looks surprised, but pleasantly so. "Yeah, for sure. I have a room at the Loews, right near here. I may have to carry you, huh?" He grins.

"You may, I am very delicate," Charlotte flirts right back.

"And then I'll have to give you a thorough exam..." He leans over and kisses the side of her neck.

"Okay, you're going to have to quit with the lame doctor jokes right about now before I change my mind," she teases.

He laughs. "Okay, let me just go pay my check and we'll get out here."

He slides out of the couch and Ryan pounces as if he's been hiding behind a shrub watching them. Has he been hiding behind a shrub watching them?

"What's going on? Who was that?" He sounds more accusatory than curious.

"I don't know—I didn't catch his name over the music. Greg. Or maybe Craig. We're going to head to his place."

"You're drunk."

They're all drunk, Charlotte would like to point out. Instead she says, "So?" "So, it's not a good idea for you to go home with this dude."

"Why not?"

"Um, let's start with the fact that, again, you're drunk, and you're hurt and you don't know this stranger...and don't you have a boyfriend?"

"Ryan, you hate James. That's no secret. And you had some fun last night. It's my turn."

What is his problem? Charlotte wonders. She resents this slut shaming, this double standard. Ryan can do whatever he wants but she can't? Fuck that. And worse, he's ruining her peaceful high.

"I'm just looking out for you Charlotte."

That's true, she knows it's true, but she's already too drunk and frustrated and irrational to back down now.

"Yeah, right. You just want me to be some perfect, wholesome girl on a little pedestal."

The truth is, Charlotte loves that Ryan puts her on a pedestal, loves the version of herself she sees through his eyes. She realizes something then: that's why she didn't call him when she was pregnant by some guy Ryan can't stand, not because he would judge her, but because he would be disappointed in her somehow and that would be more than she could bear.

"Where did that come from? You're being ridiculous." Though, Ryan silently concedes that she's not altogether wrong.

"Leave me alone, Ryan. It's none of your fucking business." Lame and lazy as far as responses go, but it's all she's got. She realizes that she's out of line, that she is being unreasonable and petulant and Ryan doesn't necessarily deserve it, but she can't help herself. All of her emotions and thoughts are back in the dryer and the narcotics and alcohol have sped up the cycle to a mind-numbing spin. She wants Ryan to protect her, she wants James to protect her, she wants Ryan to like James more, she wants James to like her more. She wants everything to be different. She wants to be in love. She wants to be loved. She wants the room to stop spinning. And also, her leg fucking hurts. So she takes it out on Ryan because she can. Because he'll forgive her. And that's not fair, but she'll deal with that tomorrow. Tonight, she's leaving with Ben Affleck, who's walking up with a big smile.

"Ready?" he says.

She looks pointedly at Ryan when she responds. "Ready."

"Oh hey there, I'm Greg." He reaches his hand out to Ryan, who just scoffs.

Charlotte's not the only one taking out their feelings on the wrong party.

"Yeah, keep her safe okay." Ryan walks away without another word. He goe straight to the bar. He'll order a final shot for the road and then he'll find Mari. It's time to go.

* * *

He should have brought a blanket or a towel or something, he thinks as he sits down in the sand. Ryan hasn't slept at all, tossed and turned all night once they got home from the bar, so he decided to come out and watch the sunrise. Hokey yes, but he hasn't seen a sunrise since he was a kid and went on a fishing trip with his dad to the Gulf Shore. It was the first time Ryan, stuck in landlocked Kansas, ever saw the ocean, which was the most amazing thing he'd ever seen. He remembers asking his father a million questions: How big is it? What's on the other side? How far can we see? How deep is it? Will we see a shark? Until his dad just put a hand on his shoulder and said, "How about we just be quiet and enjoy this okay?"

Ryan feels someone coming up behind him on the otherwise completely empty beach.

"Hey, I woke up and saw you were gone. What are you doing out here? It's 6 a.m." Mari sits down next to him in the sand.

"I don't know. Couldn't sleep."

"Worried about Charlotte? She'll be okay."

"Yeah, I know. It's not that. I guess I just wanted some quiet, too. New York is so go, go, go. I didn't even realize that it's never quiet. I love it, but..."

"You want me to go so you can be alone?"

"No, no. Stay." He reaches over and puts his arm around her.

Both lost in thoughts, they sit in comfortable silence as the sun rises higher and higher in the sky. They look over at some point to see a figure walking toward them on the beach. Charlotte is still wearing her paisley wrap dress. She limps slightly and the bandage on her leg is a bit yellowed and frayed around the edges, and yet still she somehow manages to make the walk of shame this glamorous.

"Look what the cat dragged in," Mari reaches up for Charlotte's hand and pulls her down next to her.

"I went to the room and saw you guys out here from the window."

Charlotte feels sheepish and stupid. As soon as she got back to Greg's she had sobered up enough to realize that she shouldn't be there, not least because she had had an abortion not even a week ago and so anything below the belt was strictly off limits.

And she didn't want to be there, with this random stranger from Arizona who smelled good and that was about all. Yet, there she was drunk and alone in a hotel room with a stranger, who despite sending clear signals otherwise, she did not actually want to have sex with. Even if you hadn't been a volunteer with a rape safety organization as Charlotte had at Stanford, anyone with common sense would know this ranks high on dumb ideas. Luckily Greg didn't seem to mind when she crawled in bed with all her clothes on and pulled the cover up. All they did was spoon, which was weirdly kind of nice. Charlotte snuck out right at dawn leaving Greg drooling on his pillow. And here she is.

After a long minute, Mari turns to her. "What's going on with you, Char?"

There's something about the directness of Mari's gaze, her genuine concern, the fact that Charlotte can't hide anything from her and doesn't want to, that pierces her.

"I had an abortion. Tuesday." She just blurts it out.

"Oh, honey. Oh my god." Mari scoots over in the sand and hugs Charlotte, exchanging a look with Ryan over her head. He mouths, "fuck."

"I thought I was dealing. I guess I'm not. I didn't want my stupid drama to hijack the weekend. And then I end up in the ER? I'm so sorry, guys." Charlotte is now full on sobbing.

"You didn't hijack the weekend. I just wish you had told us weeks ago so we could have been there for you."

Ryan gets up and goes to sit on the other side of Charlotte, flanking her from the opposite side. "Do I need to kill James?" he asks.

"No, no. I mean, he's not winning any awards for boyfriend of the year but I'll figure it out."

Not boyfriend of the year? If that's not an understatement Ryan doesn't know what is. In all of the stories Charlotte has told Ryan about James over the last year, Ryan has struggled to find an ounce of appeal. Maybe that James is rich and somewhat famous, but even that's not enough to redeem him. All Ryan wants to do is grab Charlotte by both arms, look her dead in the eyes and say, "You are better than this, Charlotte Mayfield." Maybe one day he will, but now is clearly not the time. Right now, it's time to just let Charlotte cry, which they do.

"What can we do, Charlotte?" Mari asks after a moment,

rubbing her back.

"I don't know...get me an entirely different life?"

"I'm not sure we can do that." Mari leans over and wipes Charlotte's tears and snot with her T-shirt.

"Well then how about get me a bacon, egg, and cheese sandwich? I need grease."

"Now that we can do. Bacon fixes everything." Ryan is pleased to have a solution, however inadequate.

"I can't believe I have to get on a plane in three hours. Ugh. Ugh. " Charlotte collapses back in the sand. The other two follow suit, so they are all lying side by side in the sand, looking straight up at the lavender sky. Mari turns her head to face Charlotte, who still has a tear running down toward her ear. "We're going to talk about this much more when you're ready, Char. But you're going to be okay, I promise."

On some level Charlotte knows this is true, she will be okay. But she can also see that it's going to require some tough decisions to make it so. She's had her grace period and now it's time, time to fight the inertia and suffocation she feels, time to start figuring shit out. How she's going to leave James, her job, and possibly Boston, or in other words, leave her life as she knows it. She can do this, though, she knows she can.

She was top of her class at Stanford, she was All-American in track, she's a Mayfield, "tough stock," her Nana always said. She can do hard things.

"God, my leg fucking hurts," she says. "Safe to say my bone-deep gash was the worst part of the weekend."

"But what was the best? Mari asks.

"Easy," Charlotte says turning to look at Ryan and then Mari lying on either side of her. "Right now." She reaches for both their hands and squeezes.

Chapter Three
Crested Butte 2004

Ryan has spent the last fifteen minutes lying in bed watching particles of dust float in the ray of morning sunlight beaming through the large window, mulling over his inexplicable behavior. His plan had been to announce his big news to Charlotte and Mari as soon as they all arrived last night...and yet he didn't. Even though he's been waiting weeks—until they were all together—to tell them and is practically bursting with the news.

Charlotte picked him and Mari up at the microscopic airport last night, then they drove straight to dinner at a little bistro in the center of the town, which as far as Ryan could tell consisted entirely of a grid of eight streets, surrounded by ski lodges high in the mountains around them. And that would have been an ideal time, but Ryan hadn't wanted to steal the spotlight given they were celebrating Mari's big victory. It's not every day you win a major death row appeal, which EJP had done the previous week, thanks in large part to Mari's tenacious commitment to the case over the last two years.

That commitment earned her second chair when their client, a seventeen-year-old accused of murder, was granted a second trial by the court of appeals and then a full acquittal, thanks to conclusive DNA evidence, after five years on death row.

Ryan marveled at this, the idea of spending five years in a

dangerous, depressing prison for a crime you had no part of and then suddenly, improbably, getting a second chance, being spared. It's almost, Ryan would imagine, like having a near death experience.

Charlotte had called ahead to the restaurant and arranged to have two bottles of very expensive champagne—Ryan recognized the label from a recent client dinner with Tripper—chilled and waiting for them at the table. Then Charlotte herself was overflowing with updates and stories since she had just gotten back from Italy.

It felt like there was never the right moment for Ryan to interject. But now, if he tells them today, will it be weird that he waited? Maybe he'll tell them at dinner tonight, explain, honestly, that he didn't want to take the spotlight away from Mari last night, but he has a big update of his own.

I'm going to ask Emily to marry me! He rehearses the announcement in his mind.

Should he bring the ring to dinner, he wonders. That might be weird. But he brought it all the way to Colorado to show them, so they would give it their stamp of approval, affirm how much Emily will love it, though there's no question in his mind that any girl would fall all over herself for the 3.5 carat platinum ring. Cut: emerald; clarity rating: flawless; color rating: F, the second highest. He now knows more about the four Cs than he ever thought possible, but his fiancée's ring is first and foremost a reflection on him...and of his love for her, of course. He wanted the very best and he had spent days in the diamond district, not to mention a full third of his salary, to get the perfect ring, which he picked up last week and at this moment rests in the pocket of his suitcase. He was dumb to bring it, it's not even insured yet. But it was important for him to show Mari and Charlotte before it ended up on Em's finger at the end of next month, when he takes her to Bermuda and proposes almost exactly a year to the date that they met at last fall's New York City marathon.

Emily thinks they have the most adorable meet story ever and she loves telling everyone. Ryan would obviously not contradict this out loud, but to his mind it's actually pretty run of the mill. According to her version, which he's heard dozens of times now, they had spotted each other and made eyes a few times on their training runs with the Central Park Running Club in the months leading up to the marathon. In truth he doesn't exactly remember her, but to be fair there were always dozens of runners, and more than half of them were fit, pretty girls with high ponytails and tight tanks tops advertising previous races.

Emily will then recount how they never actually spoke until they crossed the finish line at literally—here she emphasizes the word—"literally, the exact same time!"

She marvels that it was her fastest time yet (5:10) and jokes about how keeping pace with Ryan motivated her. Here she usually makes a corny quip about how you can't outrun love.

Apparently, at the finish line, surrounded by throngs of racers and spectators Ryan spontaneously grabbed her into a hug, which he doesn't remember but allows is possible given the delirium that set in at mile twelve and the euphoria he felt in finally finishing his very first marathon. The story then goes that Ryan followed the hug with a high-five and said, "We did it! Let me take you to dinner tonight to celebrate."

Ryan actually remembers Emily saying, "That was amazing, I feel like eating a giant steak. You should join me." It stuck out because he thought it was very cool that she asked him out and that she wanted a steak, and not just any steak but a giant one.

But whatever the case, they did end up splitting a porterhouse later that night (after Ryan took a long ice bath) at Strip House in the East Village, Ryan's favorite restaurant.

Of course, Emily had been sweaty, hair in a bun, no makeup on for the race. So Ryan was pleasantly surprised when she showed up at the restaurant all dressed up and looking like a slightly, and only slightly, plainer version of Keri Russell. Mari and Charlotte once made him watch a Felicity marathon and Keri Russell was the only thing that made it tolerable.

Over the typical ritual of the first date information swap (hometown, siblings, college, job, etc.), they discovered that they were both in Boston at the same time.

Emily, whose parents emigrated from Ireland grew up in Charlestown and she was finishing at Boston College when Ryan was a first year at Harvard. She moved to New York two years before him to work at an art gallery and, as she put it that night, "to figure out how to be a grown up," an explanation he found adorable and a goal he found admirable since he was still trying to do it himself.

Emily tells people it was love at first sight, right there at the finish line in Central Park. Ryan agrees, naturally, because he loves her and understands that all relationships take on a revisionist romantic mythology. Obviously, he doesn't see the point in clarifying that it's not exactly true, that it wasn't until maybe their sixth or seventh date that he thought there might be something there. He wasn't even so sure when he spontaneously invited her to go home to Kansas with him for Christmas last year—after she not so subtly reminded him a few times over that her parents would be going on an extended visit to see her ailing grandmother in Dublin for the holidays, so it would be her first holiday all alone since she couldn't make the long trip with her work schedule.

It seemed mean not to invite her for his quick (Ryan declared a forty-eight-hour maximum for any visit home) trip. Though it would have been just as mean to invite her to meet his parents, with all that implied, and then break up with her two weeks later, but he decided he would deal with the consequences either way.

Turns out the trip home was great, the best he'd had in years. Ryan was used to feeling suffocated on these visits, as the only child, driving back and forth between his two parents, having polite quiet meals in front of the TV at his Dad's apartment and at an oversized dining room at his mom's that seemed like it was suited for a different family, one larger than two.

Ryan had long stopped wishing his parents never got divorced, if he ever even did, but he did find he was resentful that they didn't, at least, give him a sibling to commiserate with before they did so. Or he would even take some uncles or cousins to give their estranged family of three a little breathing room, to be a buffer and a distraction. But as it happened Emily was perfect for that. She handled going to both houses like a pro and brought thoughtful gifts, a scented candle for his mom, that he knows she'll display but never actually light so as not to "waste" it, and a personalized tackle box for his dad, that Ryan knew he would use that very weekend. Barbara and Roger were utterly charmed by Emily. And Ryan, who usually felt like his parents' approval was irrelevant given the vast gulf between his life and theirs, was surprised to discover how much that meant to him.

So when they came back to New York, Ryan looked at Emily and their relationship with new eyes. For him, she went from fling to girlfriend, a subtle but concrete mental transition that Emily was not entirely aware of given that she was already a few steps ahead of him and taking this as fact already. But now Ryan, too, was all in and they began to see each other regularly. Emily fit seamlessly into his life; she was pretty, his parents liked her, she knew about art, read decent books, and dressed well. She was, in short, marriage material and Ryan realized he was ready, more than ready, to get off the merry-go-round of random hook ups. Not that he was one of those guys who kept track, like his buddy Colin, but he was pretty sure if he did, he'd have a respectable number, high enough to feel confident that he wouldn't regret missing out, but not so high as to be completely sleazy.

The hazards of dating had definitely started to outweigh the thrills. Right before he started dating Emily, a one-night stand called him to say she might be pregnant and then strung him along for a very intense month before she would even take the test in a truly manipulative mind fuck. Ryan wasn't convinced she even actually ever thought she was pregnant, so felt more angry than relieved when she told him, in an overwrought telephone call, that "there was no baby." Then there was the girl who showed up crying at his door one night a few weeks into their hooking up because he hadn't texted her back. He just didn't have the wherewithal to deal with it anymore. And, moreover, he had more important things to focus on, namely convincing Tripper to put him on partner track before the other third years. Ryan was determined to be the youngest ever partner at Barker, Jones and Simon, and he understood it would be a by-any-means-necessary operation. Every advantage helps. So while some of the other associates his age are still coming to work hungover, hanging together in testosterone-infused clumps at firm events and hitting strip clubs under the pretext of "client engagement," Ryan plans to set himself apart. And Emily will help him do that.

He imagines, for the one-millionth time, sitting down to dinner with Tripper and his Barbie doll wife, Clare, he and Emily delighting them with charming stories about their wedding registry and apartment shopping, reminding Tripper and Clare of themselves in their younger days. Having a pretty wife, setting up a house, being a grown up, these are the accouterments to the partner track, along with aggressively bringing in big business, which was also a prong of Ryan's strategy.

So yes, even though he's maybe a little young to propose at twenty-six (at least in NYC standards), and even though Emily would probably wait, as long as it took, Ryan had made up his mind: the time was now. There is just one nagging sticking point, but he puts that out of his mind for now, as Mari walks through the Jack and Jill bathroom that adjoins their two rooms.

"My head hurts," she whined plopping down with a thud on his bed.

"Well, it could be the altitude, but most likely the fact that you drank almost an entire bottle of champagne last night?"

"I can't believe Charlotte's out running right now. That girl is nuts."

As if on cue they hear Charlotte come in downstairs. "Rise and shine! I have coffee and bagels!" she calls up.

"I hate her. She has way too much energy." Mari puts a pillow over her head.

"Guys? Are you up? The first band goes on at 11 a.m.! Let's get a move on."

They hear her humming and opening and closing cabinet doors in the kitchen of their rental, a very homey duplex Charlotte found online.

"We'll be right down!" Ryan yells, causing Mari to wince. She can't imagine spending the next twelve hours in the bright sun, listening to rock bands, but this is exactly what they came to Crested Butte to do. She convinces herself that with a bagel and a shower she'll be a new person.

"I'm going to go shower. That's going to help right?"

"You act like this is your first hangover. Come on girl. Don't get soft on me."

"I feel like I've been celebrating for a week straight though."

"Well you deserve it. Seriously, you rock Mari. I've said it before, but I'm seriously so proud of you." Ryan reaches over and squeezes her arm.

Hearing this, Mari gets a warm feeling in her stomach, like when she gets a laugh out of her baby niece, the feeling of hard-won approval from a source not to be taken for granted.

"Thank you, that means a lot," she says sincerely, pushing herself off the bed with exaggerated drama. "Let's just hope this gets me a damn raise." She smiles widely from the doorway. "I'll see you down there."

Ryan gets up, starts rifling through his bag for a T-shirt and khaki pants. He pulls out the black velvet box from the inside flap of his suitcase. It makes a satisfying sound as it snaps open. The ring sparkles in the sunlight, shines as if it's illuminated. Seeing it gives him an unexpected sense of vertigo, which he chalks up to the altitude.

* * *

The band that's playing when they arrive, Rocket Sprocket, is just about as terrible as its name, but the crowd doesn't seem to mind, contented as they are by the perfect weather, and the picturesque surroundings. Charlotte has loved Aspen since she started going there every winter with her family when she was a toddler, but this little town of Crested Butte, nestled in a tiny flat valley surrounded by several tall ridges of the Rocky Mountains, is arguably even more gorgeous and serene. Her friend, Rick, whose parents have a second home down from the Mayfields in Aspen told her about this music festival, Rock the Rockies. Rick is one of the investors and promoters. It's only the festival's second year, but it's packed. At least a thousand people dot the vast grassy knoll in front of the main stage, lounging on colorful blankets and lawn chairs.

The lead singer of Rocket Sprocket sports requisite skinny jeans and skullcap, and is singing at the top of his lungs. Actually it might more accurately be classified as screaming rather than singing, about someone, presumably his ex girlfriend, who stomped his heart like grapes in a barrel.

"Dude, this song is terrible," Ryan laughs.

"Luckily every band only gets a twenty-minute set," Charlotte responds, yelling over the song, which has taken a visceral turn; said broken heart is now oozing a river of blood the color of merlot.

"Well, he's really committed to his blood/wine metaphor. I'll give him that."

Mari laughs and tips back her own plastic cup of wine, pleased that she has rallied to the point of drinking again, a feat that seemed impossible two hours ago.

The applause is generous as Rocket Sprocket leaves the stage, probably more from relief than anything else. The next act comes on and it's a gorgeous girl with long, wavy red hair. She comes out on stage with just a guitar and a stool and from the first note you can tell she's going to be good. Her voice rings out in the air, high and pure, as if it's echoing against all the surrounding mountains and bouncing back to them.

I'm tired of waiting for a love that just won't come
I'm tired of playing at a game that can't be won
But then I'll look at the clouds, at the great big beautiful sky
And wait for the rains to come down, and wash these blues
goodbye

It's the wine, it's the sunshine, it's being with her friends, but Charlotte is touched by the music. So much so that she feels tears threaten, which she, feeling silly, swallows down with a swig of wine. She was never a music aficionado, she has no clue if this song is objectively good or in key or the right pitch or whatever. She has no idea what Simon Cowell and Randy Jackson would say, but she knows she fucking loves it. It speaks to her. For a moment, as she listens, Charlotte wishes she were an artist, that she could affect people with a note or word like this wild-haired girl, and not a lawyer.

Then it occurs to her she's actually not a lawyer anymore. She's not anything, officially, except for maybe unemployed, but she's not sure she would even fall under that category since it's willful. All she's done is wander around, in every sense, for the last few months. This is probably why the song speaks to her:

I need a map to find my way to me
I need an outlet for these dreams as big as the sea

When Charlotte gave notice, to her very shocked boss that was precisely her goal: to find my way to me. Though she would never have been able to articulate it that way. In fact, she articulated it pretty terribly on that freezing December night when she called her dad and told him her plan. Charlotte had never done anything truly impulsive or reckless in her life, unless you count the time James convinced her to have sex with him in the locker room after one of his games, when supposedly everyone had cleared out for the evening. Turns out "everyone" didn't include the overnight maintenance crew who got quite the surprise. Then again, Charlotte wasn't a fool, hockey players having sex in the locker room was probably not so infrequent an occurrence to scandalize anyone that came upon them.

But that night last year, as she walked home from drinks with colleagues at a Back Bay wine bar where they had discussed people and cases and any array of subjects she could not have cared less about, a feeling welled up inside her, or more precisely, it was like a voice starting speaking to her, becoming louder and more insistent as she got closer to her house. You can't do this anymore, it said over and over. "This" was vague but Charlotte took it to mean a lot of things: date someone who you can't pretend is something other than exactly what he is (an asshole) anymore; pretend that you love working at a place you hate, and where everyone hates you because of your boss's blatant favoritism; ignore the fact that you've grossly miscalculated the first quarter of your life and even though you did everything "right" you are still lonely and unhappy.

This is what Charlotte explained when she called her dad as soon as she got home. In a rare moment of empathy, Jonathan listened, sympathized as Charlotte cried, even though neither could remember a time when she'd shed tears in front of him.

Then he said two words: "Come home." That this invitation served Jonathan's grand plan did not make it any less sincere or appreciated. Charlotte realized that this was the out, the parachute she was looking for and that she was lucky to have such a formidable Plan B. Right then and there she acquiesced, she would go home and work at Mayfield, under one condition. Normally Charlotte wouldn't dare voice "conditions," but she saw a chance to capitalize on the moment since Jonathan seemed to be feeling indulgent.

So she made her one demand: she would throw herself into the company business but only if she didn't have to start for one full year.

Many people, including a few of Charlotte's prep school friends, took a gap year after high school, but since sixth grade Charlotte had been on a relentless pace of perfection; the best grades, the best test scores, the best extracurriculars, the best Ivy's, the best internships every summer, the best—okay a solid—law firm. And where did all those "bests" leave Charlotte? Exhausted. She was turning twenty-seven in a few months and burnt out. She just needed a year, to travel and breathe, to reset.

To find my way to me.

Charlotte realized this was perhaps immature and certainly indulgent in a world where seven-year-olds work eighteen-hour shifts in factories, but it didn't make it any less true. And really was it too much to ask, to have a minute to take stock, to regroup, to not have a goal or a milestone or an expectation on the immediate horizon?

Charlotte didn't think so. In fact she thought it was vital, so she made the case to her dad. It's not like she needed her parents blessing, she had the means thanks to her trust fund, she could do this with or without their support, but who was she kidding, she spent the last twenty-six years working at all those bests precisely, if not always consciously, to earn their approval, and she wasn't in a place to stop now. She needed someone, namely her dad, to say that it was okay to drop out of her life. And much to her surprise, shock really, Jonathan said, perhaps more curtly than Charlotte would have liked: "Take the year. You'll start January 2nd." And that was that. She gave two weeks notice the very next day and told her landlord she was moving out at the end of the month.

For someone who has always had a plan and focus, this last year was incredibly liberating. First spring in Brazil and Argentina, and then back to New York for a week, then to Aspen for the summer, staying at her parent's place and hanging out with all the off-season ski bums. And the last three weeks in Greece and Italy. Somewhere in all of those travels, much to her pleasant surprise, she got over James, who she broke up with over a text, a cowardly move that still shames her a bit, but no more than their whole relationship shames her.

It helped her to get over James that she got under someone else; a torrid affair with a university student in Florence who drove a moped, chain-smoked, and wrote bad poetry did the trick. It was like she was in the world's most cliché, embarrassing, and saccharine romantic comedy. In other words, it was perfect.

But now she just has eleven weeks and three days—not that she's counting—left of her proverbial gap year and the thought of starting the rest of her life, opting back in, fills her with a panic that she keeps at bay with a constant stream of distractions, some healthier (reading) than others (vodka).

Charlotte zones back in just as the singer finishes her last song and is met with loud, genuine applause. Charlotte is inspired to jump to her feet.

"Now that girl was good," Mari says. She, along with much of the crowd, has joined Charlotte, standing now. The singer looks sincerely shocked and touched as she waves, thanks the audience over and over, which makes them cheer even louder. A hush of soft murmuring falls over the crowd as everyone settles back down and waits for Turnkey, the next and last act, the headliners, one of the only bands where people will likely know at least some of the songs by heart.

"I'll be back you guys. I'm going to brave the porta-potties," Mari says, fortifying herself to deal with the lines and the smelly bathrooms. Music festivals were all fun and games till you had to go.

"Good luck. Here." Charlotte hands her hand sanitizer from her bag.

Ryan lies down in Charlotte's lap, closes his eyes. "I'm going to power nap until Turnkey comes on."

She stares down at him, sips warm white wine from her Solo cup. She knows people looking at them, lying together like this, would think they were a couple. Were a good-looking couple at that. They belong together, people would think. And then she realizes something: they've been together for twenty-four hours and Ryan has hardly mentioned Emily. When she was in New York last spring visiting it was all, "Emily this and Emily that." Which Charlotte chalked up to new infatuation, as tedious as it was.

When Ryan first mentioned that he was digging her, Charlotte had asked him point blank why, why specifically, he liked her. "She's uncomplicated," was one of the attributes he offered. Charlotte, now having met Emily, would go as far as to say, "simple." Charlotte immediately sized her up as one of those girls who wouldn't voice an opinion unless she was sure everyone would affirm it. Emily wasn't the type to rock the boat, in fact, she wouldn't even get in the boat. Charlotte suspected that she had a tattoo of a flower on her ankle and it made her feel badass. Not that Charlotte had a tattoo at all, though if she did get one, she likes to think it would be truly badass. Maybe she should, come to think of it.

But lukewarm first impressions aside, Charlotte sees Emily's sweet, easy appeal, especially for a guy like Ryan, who thinks he likes a challenge but really doesn't. And yet, Charlotte suspected that it was only a matter of time before he was bored to tears with Emily. At their one dinner, Charlotte had found her pretty boring. Some might argue there are worse traits. Not Charlotte. In fact, maybe Ryan already realized it and that's why Emily's name hasn't come up. Ryan has moved on, and just as well that it dawned on him that Emily wasn't right for him without Charlotte having to eventually, gently, point it out. She's making herself a promise that she'll resist the urge to say, "I knew it," whenever Ryan announces they've split, when Mari stumbles back over.

"You've been gone forever. What the hell?"

Mari looks a little glassy-eyed.

"Are you okay?" Charlotte asks, as Ryan blinks awake, sits up.

Mari holds out a fist, which she unfurls to reveal two skinny joints.

"These guys by the bathroom asked me if I wanted to smoke up and then gave me these." She giggles and reaches for the bag of Cheetos.

"Maribella Castillo. Are you high?" Charlotte mocks shock, but she actually is shocked, she's never known Mari to smoke before.

"What? It's not big deal. I'm living a little." She licks orange Cheetos powder off her fingers.

Charlotte and Ryan exchange a look and then burst out laughing.

"Well, when in Rome?" Ryan shrugs and grabs one of the joints. He knows so many people who do coke on a regular basis in New York, his guiding philosophy is always, what's a little weed?

"We're not in Rome or even Amsterdam, kids." Which was the last place Charlotte smoked, in a coffee shop, with a bunch of very rowdy Australians. But what the hell, this year is all about full throttle adventure so she leans over and asks the guy next to them for a light and the three of them take turns passing the joint.

"Are we going to get arrested?" Mari giggles, picturing the three of them, three Harvard lawyers, sitting in the local lock up.

"Are you kidding? This town probably has one cop. I think we're okay."

The weed hits fast. Charlotte feels like she's floating on air, like her senses have heightened and everyone is staring at her. She conveniently has forgotten that weed makes her anxious and paranoid.

"Ted is working with state legislature to legalize marijuana. It's like his pet project, besides, you know, getting people off death row. He insists that weed will be legal in the next few years. Can you imagine?"

"Mari, are you in love with Ted?" Ryan asks abruptly.

"What?" She nearly drops the joint. "Are you serious? He's fifty and bald. Nooo. Why would you ask that?" She's outraged.

"I don't know, you're always talking about him. And you haven't dated anyone else. Since..."

"Forever," Charlotte interjects helpfully, taking a long drag of the other joint.

"Ted is my mentor and I know you guys think I'm some sort of prude but I'm not. I just...have a lot going on. I don't have time to date at the moment."

"We don't think you're a prude," Charlotte leans over and hugs Mari as if to reaffirm the point.

But Ryan and Charlotte do believe Mari is a prude and have devoted countless hours over the years to discussing her love life, which, as far as they know, has thus far consisted of a one-year relationship in undergrad (her first...everything) and two months-long flings in law school.

Ryan does not find three a number high enough to make the "no regrets" threshold, though he allows that men think different about this. Still, it offends his straight man tendencies that Mari is so "completely fuckable and yet doesn't realize it," as he told Charlotte just a few months ago. Ryan and Charlotte have both tried to hook her up with guys over the years, but to no avail. Every time they bring up the issue they are met with an array of excuses: I'm too busy, I'm not looking, he doesn't seem like my type, I'm tired or today's, I have a lot going on.

This litany of excuses and her voluntary celibacy has convinced Charlotte and Ryan that Mari is cynical and scared, with a dash of insecurity mixed in. In fact, the opposite is true, and it's her best-held secret. Mari is a hopeless, incurable romantic.

She wasn't scared to date, she wasn't avoiding intimacy, she just wasn't interested in wasting her time. Thirty years ago, her parents met (and fell in love) when they both showed up to look at a room for rent in a house in Miami. Mari's dad deferentially ceded the room to her mother, finding another place across town and the two began dating. And her sister, Carmen, married her high school sweetheart with whom she fell in love as they passed notes in homeroom freshman year. Similarly, for Mari, it is not a numbers game, it is simply a matter of waiting for lightning to strike. And from the time she was a little girl, she believed, with 100 percent certainty, that it would and that when it did she would just know. Obviously, Mari knew you can't say these things out loud, even to your best friends, because you'll sound like a seven-year-old who watched

Cinderella one too many times. It's better to be thought a prude, than ridiculous.

"Are you in love with Emily?" Mari asks. When in doubt shift the focus, lawyering 101.

"Yeah, for sure." It's Ryan's turn to be outraged. Wasn't it obvious? So maybe it's because he's feeling defensive (and so very high) that it's now that he blurts out his news.

"In fact, I'm going to ask her to marry me!"

For a split merciful second, Charlotte takes this to be a distant, nebulous goal...as in, one day I'm going to Paris.

Then Ryan adds, "Next month. I got a ring."

Charlotte experiences a sudden and strange disorientation like someone has pushed her into a pool with all of her clothes on. She feels muffled and confused as she tries to process her thoughts. Ryan is getting married? To Emily? Boring Emily? She hears Mari screaming with excitement but it seems far away.

"Ryan!!!! That's so great. I know I only got to meet her for two seconds, but she seems great and Charlotte thinks she's great too, right Charlotte?"

Charlotte tries to respond but her lips won't move. She just smiles and nods.

"This is so fabulous," Mari continues, gleeful. "When? When is the wedding???"

"I don't know Mari, I haven't even asked yet. Maybe next fall?" Ryan, having said the words out loud—I'm getting married—for the first time to another living soul, his best friends, is struck by how real it all is now.

"We'll be in the wedding, though, right? Best wo-men. We can wear tuxes instead of dresses. Or is that cheesy? What do you think Charlotte?"

It's clear that if drinking makes Mari maudlin, smoking weed makes her positively manic. Ryan wishes he could enjoy her, be amused as he would normally be, but he's distracted waiting for a response from Charlotte who hasn't said a word.

"Charlotte?" he asks tentatively. Her reaction, his nagging concern. He shouldn't care as much as he does, but...

She leans over and hugs him, whispers in his ear. "I'm so happy for you, Ryan."

As far as Charlotte can remember that's the first time she's lied to his face.

"You know Emily really likes you." It was true, but Ryan made sure it wasn't an option not to. He understood that Emily would feel intimidated by Charlotte, most women were, and their friendship. And sure enough when they were first dating, Emily would see pictures of Charlotte on Facebook and comment about how pretty she was, willing him to disagree. He was proud of his sensitivity around this matter, constantly reassuring Emily and Charlotte both that they would love each other, in advance of their meeting. And that turned out to be true enough from what he could tell.

"What about the ring?" Mari asks.

"I actually brought it," Ryan offers, feeling sheepish.

Mari actually squeals. "I can't wait to see it!! I bet it's beautiful."

Everyone turns to look at the stage as Turnkey takes their places and the lead singer steps to the front of the stage and screams out, "How are you dooooinnnnnng tonight Colorado?"

Good question, Charlotte muses. Good question. She has no idea and decides she'll have to wait till the pot clears her system to have any chance of sorting it out.

The crowd screams as the opening notes of Turnkey's hit song ring out. The lead singer invites everyone to get to their feet and sing along. Ryan doesn't know the song, but he gets up anyway. He wants to give Charlotte a minute to collect herself, and maybe himself, too.

"I love this song," he lies as badly as he dances, but does both with conviction and with enough contagious enthusiasm that Mari and Charlotte rise to join him and the rest of the crowd. The sun sets, the music blares, the crowd sings and sways.

The song is called "The One You Love" but Mari, Charlotte, and Ryan aren't in the right state of mind to appreciate the irony.

* * *

When they get back to the rental they are like children who have been at the playground all day—tired, anxious, out of sorts. They are also newly, but not entirely sober, after eating the rest of the contents of their picnic and walking almost a mile back up the mountain back to their rental. But there is something about sobering up at the hour in which one might typically start drinking that is disconcerting.

The first thing they do when they arrive back at the house, at Mari's demand, is have a look at the ring. Ryan runs up and gets it out of his suitcase and brings it down to the kitchen where they sit on barstools at the butcher block island.

Charlotte has three thoughts when Ryan snaps open the black

box, which occur in rapid succession. Holy shit. It's gorgeous. And then: it should be me. Not in the sense that Ryan should be proposing to her, per se, but that she should be wearing a ring this perfect. Charlotte is no stranger to diamonds, and this one is flawless.

Mari has one thought: Jesus, that must have cost a fortune!

"Oh my God, Ryan it's beautiful. It must have set you back," Mari says turning the ring over and over in her hand.

"Well, you know..." He smiles proudly as if his infant daughter is on display and not a gemstone.

"Emily is going to love it." Mari holds the ring away from her and then brings it close. She's seen any number of girls, usually tall, skinny, and blonde, wearing rings like this, dotting the campus of Harvard and at some of the fundraisers EJP has held for the so called "country club set" in Alabama. The rich in the South may be a whole different beast than the rich of the Northeast, but look at the ring finger of both sets and the baubles line up.

Mari would prefer her engagement ring (one day!) to have more character, be more interesting and unique, and maybe even diamond free since she'd read enough about the industry to be queasy at sporting one, but a large solitaire like this certainly makes a statement, even if it's just, we are people that can afford this.

"Do you have a plan to propose?" Mari realizes she's been hogging the ring and hands it to Charlotte, who fights the urge to try it on.

"I haven't thought it about it too much yet," Ryan says. "I figured nice dinner on the beach, sunset, get down on one knee, etc."

"That sounds perfect. Doesn't it, Charlotte?"

"It does. I think we should celebrate!" Charlotte is almost entirely sober and not altogether pleased about it. She grabs a bottle of red from the counter and looks around for the corkscrew.

"No way, none for me. I seriously can't drink any more tonight. Especially if you're dragging me for that hike at the crack of dawn."

"Come on, Mar." Charlotte is eager, desperate to keep the party going despite the flagging energy all around.

"You two have at it. I'm going to bed. I'll be back in action tomorrow." She gets up and kisses both Charlotte and Ryan goodnight.

"Ryan?" Charlotte holds up the bottle by way of invitation.

"Sure," he smiles gamely, but Charlotte can tell he would just as soon go to bed then stay up drinking with her, and this make Charlotte feel incredibly lonely, albeit irrationally so.

They move over to the living room and Ryan flips on the gas fireplace. There's a chill in the mountain air and they wrap themselves up in a heavy quilt on the plaid chintz sofa and pass the bottle of wine between them, not bothering with glasses. Charlotte is close enough to feel Ryan's heart beat, which she listens to for a full quiet minute.

"You're happy for me right, Charlotte?" Ryan asks, tentatively, breaking the silence.

"Yes. I am. It's just all happening so fast. Everything is changing. I hate change."

"Says the girl who upended everything so she could change her life?"

"I guess." She raises the bottle in a half-hearted toast to her so-called adventures and takes a big swallow. She suddenly wonders just how much she really changed. It's like that expression, wherever you go there you are. Here she is.

"What's next for you? Any more trips?"

"I have no idea, actually." One of the points of the year had been to not plan too far ahead. She had thought about going back to New York, but she's reconsidering it if that means being a third wheel with the newly and happily engaged couple. She wanted to visit Mari in Montgomery. She was also going to see her friend Jill, who moved to Austin. Then she'd have to go apartment hunting in San Francisco. Arrange to move her stuff from storage. The idea of having a place to live again, that's all hers, putting pictures on the wall, sleeping in her own bed, is appealing. The downside of all of this travelling is being unmoored. Charlotte all of the sudden wants moors.

"Will you guys come to SF next year for our weekend?" she asks.

"Yeah. That sounds great to me if Mari's down. Em's never been."

Shit. So now, Emily is coming on their trips? That should have occurred to her, that one day they'd bring their spouses on these weekends, maybe kids even. She just thought it would be in some way distant future. Like when they were thirty-five.

She takes another big sip of her drink, realizes she's had three drinks for Ryan's one. He's just drinking to humor her, but that's okay. Except now she's drunk...again, and that may not be okay. Essentially she's been drinking for thirty-six hours straight.

When you're gainfully employed and having a bender it's one thing. But in the situation Charlotte finds herself, it may be another all together. How fine the line is between aimless adventurer and wandering drunk.

Charlotte takes just one last swig and puts the bottle down. She snuggles deeper into Ryan's shoulder, tucks her head under his chin and has a seductive, subversive thought: what if Emily walked in right now? Would she feel jealous? Threatened? Not that she wants her to feel these things necessarily, but she does want her to understand that in some ways Ryan will always be hers.

That said, she instantly regrets what she does next. She doesn't even know why she does it. It's like when she was a girl and went through a phase of inexplicable tantrums long after it was appropriate. Magda would look at her standing there, crying and stomping her feet, usually because she couldn't find the right flips flops or because Oliver had once again hid her favorite American Girl Doll, and say, "What's gotten into you, Charlotte?" She didn't know then, like she doesn't know now. It's as if her body is not under control when she tilts her head up and, when Ryan looks down at her, kisses him.

He settles in for a split second and then pulls back as far as he can, which is only a few inches given how entwined they are on the sofa. She still feels his breath in her face, which smells and tastes, oddly, like coconut.

"What are you doing, Charlotte?" He asks it calmly, as if she's about to jump off a bridge and a sudden movement could be disastrous.

"I don't know," she answers honestly. Is she imagining it, or is he less shocked and displeased then she would have thought?

"Well, we can't do that. This. Anything. I'm with Em now." Again, it's as if he's explaining things to a slightly deranged person, which she supposes, in this moment, might qualify.

"I know." She just doesn't like it.

Ryan is flattered and confused. After all, it was Charlotte who put on the brakes when they hooked up a few summers back. She said it wasn't worth ruining their friendship, which, fair point. So what's the deal now? Granted, it's not like he never imagined that one day he and Charlotte would realize they were more than friends, confess their love and ride off into the sunset, like a bad Anne Hathaway movie, but he had always felt silly for doing so. And now he has Emily, loves Emily. He can't let Charlotte and whatever this silly flirtation, this push/pull between them that used to be fun and exciting, but now is just old—come between them. Any of them, he and Emily, or he and Charlotte.

"I'm just scared, Ry," she says after a moment. "I blew up everything to create a new life. But what if I hate that life, too?" Charlotte decides to use her current instability as a cop-out for her impulsive behavior though she's not entirely sure if and how they are related.

"Then you'll create another," Ryan says confidently.

"How many lives do you think we get exactly?"

"As many as we need," he says seriously, philosophically. "Look, for the girl who has it all, I just don't know why you worry so much about the future, Charlotte. If I've said it once, I've said it a thousand times, you're going to be fine. Better than that, you're going to be amazing. You're going to be the best deputy CEO Mayfield has ever seen. You're going meet a great guy. One who's far better than he I shall not mention.

And he's going to appreciate you and want you to have like ten kids with him." He pulls her chin up so he's looking directly into her eyes. "You're going to have everything you want."

"How do you know?" Charlotte is impressed he addressed all of her doubts in one fell swoop.

"Because you're the magical Charlotte Mayfield, kicker of ass, breaker of hearts.

You and I are special. Exceptional. Destined for greatness." It's times like this when Ryan is his most charming. He looks a little bit like a dirty blond version of Rob Lowe in every heartthrob role he ever played. Charlotte can't believe Emily snagged him.

"You know you're too young to get married, right?

"I know. It does feel very adult. But I'm ready." He realizes he is, and somehow this conversation is affirming it for him. He knows that Charlotte will be okay, but it's also hard not to know what the future looks like. He knows exactly what his future holds and he's grateful for that.

They sit in silence, watch the flames dance in the fireplace.

"Um, so, sorry I kissed you a second ago. Let's pretend that never happened okay?" Charlotte smiles sheepishly.

"What never happened?" He grins down at her then grazes the top of her head with his lips.

He should get up, brush his teeth, go to bed, it's getting late. He should also call Emily and say good night. But he doesn't do any of this. He just sits in front of the fire and nods off holding Charlotte. His last thought before falling asleep is how good Charlotte's hair smells, like lemons and sugar.

Chapter Four
San Francisco, 2005

Mari slams her cell phone down on the pretty mosaic table. The loud clang it makes startles the couple sitting next to her. For a split second she wonders if she can make it to the bathroom in time. She's in a lovely little coffee shop in Hayes Valley, surrounded by freelance writers hunched over their Macs, tourists with maps of San Francisco sprawled open and, next to her, a teenage girl with a disturbing number of tattoos, furiously writing in a journal. She doesn't want to ruin the vibe, she doesn't want to be that girl, but she can't stop herself, the floodgates open and Mari bursts into tears.

The teenager looks up curiously and then looks back down to her journal as quickly as possible when she realizes what's happened. The man and woman at the next table also look over, smile sympathetically and then pointedly avert their gaze as if a force field has come between them even though they are only four feet away. Mari is grateful for this attempt at privacy, but it also makes her feel worse. Crying in public is somehow so much lonelier than crying in private, not to mention much more mortifying.

She wills herself to pull it together, dabs at her eyes with a napkin, grateful that she didn't bother even with her usual mascara this morning. God, it had been such a good morning, too, until now. Still on Eastern time after arriving in San Fran late last night, she woke up bright and early in Charlotte's king size bed, in her gorgeous king size waterfront loft. Charlotte had to go into work today, but she left her a note saying that she could sneak away for an afternoon coffee, along with a map of the city marking all of her favorite spots.

Mari had started her day at the Ferry Building, where she discovered Elaine's, a charming bookstore, where Elaine herself, the impossibly energetic proprietor, offered her book recommendations. Bookstores being one of Mari's favorite places, she spent an hour browsing the shelves, then another fifteen minutes debating whether she should buy a new bestselling novel about a girl who goes to prep school and feels like an outsider, or a memoir about a woman's unorthodox childhood in West Virginia. Finally, she decided to treat herself to both, because she's on vacation, and needs some good, escapist reads more than ever.

Then she sat at the nearby wharf and read the first two chapters of both books, stopping periodically to people watch and observe the sways of fog slowly dissipating over the Bay Bridge. She marveled over the engineering feat that allowed these bridges—she could also see the Golden Gate behind her to her left—to stand for so many decades; sixty-eight years for both she recalled from the city guide book she had flipped through at Elaine's. These architectural feats made her ponder permanence and fleetingness, and life, and then for obvious reasons, death. Before she could go down the rabbit hole too much further she decided to walk, walk as fast as she could up Market Street and away from those thoughts, which were always fast on her heels these days.

She was just settled here at this little coffee shop where she's to meet Charlotte when her sister called.

"Hey Carmen," she had innocently, cheerfully, answered.

"Oh, Bell," she said, using her childhood nickname for Mari who could tell instantly that Carmen had been crying. "It's awful. She's awful. I don't know what to do."

"Slow down, what are you talking about?"

"Mom, duh. I was just over there. The chemo is so much worse than the doctor said. She was fine yesterday, right after the treatment, but now she can't keep anything down. She's pure white and just listless, Mari. I can't see her like this."

Mari felt like she was sinking. Actually she was sinking, slouching lower and lower into her chair as if to physically get away from the phone and what Carmen was saying. Chemo? Now? Why didn't she tell me? She must have talked to her mom fifteen times in the last week. Mari had called her twice daily since her diagnosis, which her mother complains about ("I don't need you fussing over me, Mija") but Mari knows she loves it, needs it. But at no point did she mention she was starting chemo yesterday.

Mari realized exactly what happened: her mother didn't want Mari worrying about her during her weekend with Ryan and Charlotte so she conveniently neglected to mention that she was having her very first treatment. For a brief flash she was furious at her mother. And at Carmen for that matter. Why didn't her sister tell her?

"She didn't tell me she was starting chemo, Carmen. When I asked her last week she said she didn't know exactly when her first treatment was. Why didn't you tell me?"

"I assumed you knew!" Carmen seemed taken aback. "Where are you anyway, work?"

Mari paused. "No, I'm...I'm in San Fran. It's my annual weekend with Ryan and Charlotte, remember?" The guilt that Mari felt threatened to overwhelm her and she had to remind herself: I didn't know. I would have been there. I didn't know...

"So, let me get this straight. You're on vacation?" Carmen didn't bother to keep the outrage out of her voice.

"Carmen! I didn't know! Mom didn't tell me. Or I—"

"Or you, what? You would have come home?"

"Maybe...I don't know."

Mari had flown home as soon as her mom was diagnosed last month, when the doctor noticed some "troubling findings" after a routine colonoscopy. She was on a flight two days later so she could be there for the next round of doctors' appointments and second opinions—the exorbitant cost of the ticket was wince-worthy but of course Mari didn't even consider not clicking the buy button.

Her parents had picked her up at the airport and maintained pleasant chitchat all the way home, asking her about work, talking about the weather, telling stories about Carmen and the kids, as if this was just a normal visit. Mari, too, tried to keep up the cheerful charade. If they were going to pretend that this wasn't happening she would too, however surreal and ridiculous that endeavor. But the next morning, as they sat in the oncologist's office where he spewed—that's how Mari saw it, all of the words coming from his mouth like vomit—horrible, horrible words like, "malignant," "stage three," "terribly aggressive," she could no longer maintain her composure or the hope that this was all just a big mistake. When she started sobbing, right there on Dr. Rosen's green leather chairs, her mother, fully composed, leaned over and started rubbing her back. Mari was horrified, at herself, at the situation, at the fact that her mother was comforting her rather than the other way around.

Mari thinks of that moment now, of her mother in her favorite floral Ann Taylor Loft blouse ("I just thought I'd wear something cheery today, you know?") leaning over and wiping Mari's tears and telling her that everything was going to be fine. "I'm not going to die anytime soon, honey, if that's what you're thinking," she'd said. And that was exactly what Mari was thinking at that moment, and throughout her whole conversation with Carmen. Actually, it's what Mari has thought just about every moment of every day since she left the doctor's office: What if my mom dies? What if *my mom dies? What if my mom dies?*

"Okay, well I don't want to keep you. I'll let you get back to your friends. Just wanted to give you an update," Carmen said, clearly unable, still, to keep the note of sarcasm out of her voice.

"Please don't be like this, Carmen," Mari pleaded. This was the dynamic between them as of late: poor stressed-out and put-upon Carmen who carried the weight of the world on her shoulders and the carefree baby sister who flitted around having adventures because she had no responsibilities, like a husband and kids and aging parents two miles away. No question, Carmen often, too often, liked to play the martyr, even though, as far as Mari can tell, having a husband and two children is not akin to forced labor in a prison camp, but that's the way her chronically beleaguered sister carried herself. But hell, just because Mari doesn't have a husband and kids doesn't mean she doesn't have responsibilities, obligations, stress of her own. And Carmen didn't have to live two miles away from the house they grew up in for that matter. That was her choice. Mari had felt herself getting worked up, but she knew better than to point all this out. She just wanted to be allies again, for her sister to forgive her, even if for a crime she didn't commit.

"I want to be there. I do. When is the next treatment? I'll be there." And she will. When she told Ted about her mother's diagnosis he promised her she could take as much time as she needed. He had also blurted out that his own mother had died of cancer and then seemed to immediately regret it. "It was a long time ago though, they have much better treatments now," he'd assured her.

"I'm sorry, I know you want to be here," Carmen said. "I know she wanted to protect you. I'm just frazzled. Jasmine was up all night, too. And I'm already late picking Marco up from soccer. Just dealing with a lot. I got it handled though. Don't say anything to her. She'll be upset that I told you how bad it is—especially if she doesn't even think you know she's having treatment. This is probably the only time Mom has kept a secret in her life." Carmen managed a laugh.

It's true their mom was a truly terrible secret keeper. When they were little girls, their mom would be so excited for their Christmas presents she would "secretly" tell Mari everything she got Carmen and then secretly tell Carmen everything she got Mari, leaving them the burden of keeping their presents a surprise. At some point, they decided to reveal just one present to each other every year.

Mari again dabs at her eyes, smiling at this memory.

"Shit, Mar. Are you okay?"

Mari looks up to see that Charlotte has materialized in front her with a latte already in hand, which she places on the table and then leans over and hugs her. "What's wrong?"

"Oh, I'm okay. Sorry. I just got off the phone with Carmen. Apparently my mom started chemo yesterday. She didn't tell me. And apparently it's bad. She's not doing well."

"Oh God, Mari. I'm so sorry." She collapses into the chair opposite Mari. Charlotte still has a big soft spot for Mrs. Castillo. The teddy bear she'd given her in Miami a couple years back was one of the first things she unpacked when she settled into her loft.

"There's nothing I can do, I know. But that's the worst part, feeling helpless."

"You do help, a lot. Your mom is lucky to have you, and Carmen. And she's going to be okay."

Charlotte has been repeating this to Mari like a mantra since her mom was diagnosed. Mari knows she means well, she knows everyone means well, but is at the same time sort of fed up with the pointless words and empty platitudes people offer at times like this. That they know "she'll beat it," and that "she's in their thoughts," that she should, "stay strong," and that's not even to mention the unsolicited advice that's often grotesquely absurd like the co-worker who was emphatic that walnuts cured her cousin's cancer. Walnuts! It's enough to make Mari want to scream. Some days she does scream, into her pillow, hoping her poor landlady doesn't hear. But then again, what are people supposed to say? "Sorry to hear about your mom. Hope she doesn't die?" Actually, maybe Mari would appreciate that refreshing change of pace. But what she would prefer most of all these days is everybody keeping their mouth shut all together, even if they mean well because more than anything, she hated talking about her mother's cancer—hated even the phrase, "her mother's cancer," as if it's something that belongs to her, a possession. It makes her feel lonely and exhausted like she's shouting across a chasm and the person on the other side can't understand a word she's saying. "Thanks, I know she will be," Mari says, even though she doesn't know and that cruel reality is precisely the problem. But pure optimism is the only thing that makes people comfortable, and the quickest way out of "cancer talk." Yep, it's all going to be fine. Next.

She takes a final dab at her eyes, convinced the flow of tears has stopped for good. "Okay, subject change. Stat. Is Carlos going to be there tonight?"

She can tell by Charlotte's smile that she doesn't mind this particular subject change at all.

As soon as she hears his name, Charlotte pictures Carlos' olive-skinned shoulders, which though she's normally not a shoulder's girl (is anyone?) is for some reason her favorite feature. Though Carlos has a lot of features to recommend, not to mention an accent that makes Charlotte swoon. Carlos' family's Madrid-based firm won the bid to design Mayfield's new commercial and residential development in Mission Bay, an up-and-coming area near SBC Park, and Carlos is serving as lead architect, which is how they met a few months ago.

The multi-million dollar project is Charlotte's first major undertaking as Senior Project Manager at Mayfield. She is determined that it be a success and go smoothly so as to counteract the unavoidable taint of nepotism that still follows her nine months into the job. That she is so much younger than everyone she supervises also doesn't help.

In that light, having a liaison with the project's lead architect is probably not the best idea. But their business meetings and drinks became increasingly flirtatious despite all efforts to restrain themselves—until last week and the week before, and well, the one before that, too, when Carlos had ended up coming back to Charlotte's place after work drinks and late nights at the office.

Each time they've agreed it's best they don't tell anyone (which somehow makes it hotter) and that they should stop things before they go too far, (which also somehow makes it hotter). But Charlotte, though perfectly aware of how messy this could be, is realizing she is very much ready to let things go too far if too far means amazing sex. And if the hot and heavy make out sessions they've have had so far are any indication, it will indeed be amazing.

"Earth to Charlotte. You're blushing. You got it bad, girl."

"I know, I know. I can't wait for you to be meet him. He'll be there tonight for sure. He knows how important this is to Jonathan."

Charlotte's father was hosting a party at the Mayfield suite at SBS Park and had invited everyone from the mayor to Harrison Ford, a family friend, and many others whose palms he had greased or whom he had wined and dined to get the green light for the Mission Bay build, one of the biggest commercial development projects in San Francisco in decades. Tonight was both celebration and kickoff for supporters, and a lavish "F-you" for the few naysayers Jonathan had invited to prove a point, namely that Jonathan doesn't stop until he gets what he wants.

Charlotte normally finds these events a lethal mix of pretension and tedium, but the fact that Mari will be there, and Ryan and Emily, too, who are coming straight from the airport to the game, will make it bearable. And that they will get to meet her new love interest, that she even has a new love interest attending, might even elevate the event to fun.

"Well, I can't wait to meet him. I haven't seen you crushing this hard in a while."

"I know. I haven't. I mean I had that fling with Jackson last year and dated that guy Steven when I first got back, but Carlos is the first guy in a while that I feel a real connection with. We just have a lot in common. He's also going to be taking over his family's company, which he wants to expand into the U.S. This project was a major coup for him."

In fact, they had celebrated this very achievement, in bed, the last time he was over last week, an evening she's been replaying in her mind since.

"This is a big opportunity for me, Charlotte, and I need to keep your father happy so you tell me what I need to do and I do it," Carlos had said with that seductive accent.

"Well, right now, I think we should focus on what you need to do to keep me happy. I'll give you a hint." And she had leaned over and kissed him, empowered by the sexy, bold side he brings out in her.

Still, she's determined to take things slow, have reasonable expectations, not to get too invested and all of the other things advised by the stupid women magazines she reads when she gets manicures and pretends to hate.

Charlotte glances down at her watch. "Ugh sorry. I have to dash back for a meeting." She looks at Mari and can see that she is still worried and distracted as much as she's trying to hide it. "Are you going to be okay?"

"Yes, for sure. I'll walk out with you. I'm going to walk around a bit. Clear my head." Mari is determined to figure out how to be a person who gets up, works, laughs, reads, eats, etc. at the same time her mother battles cancer. It doesn't seem possible that those two things would happen, but she knows they must.

Charlotte hops in a cab after giving her a longer than usual hug and Mari begins to walk. She misses walking, something she did all the time back at Harvard, but never in Montgomery. The day is cloudy and getting chillier, but she doesn't mind—it matches her mood. She doesn't know where she's going until she does, until it looms before her, above her—Grace Cathedral. She remembers seeing it the guidebook she flipped through this morning, but it's even more beautiful and imposing in person, perched high atop a hill in the middle of the city.

She slowly climbs the long, wide staircase to the entrance and then steps into the soaring main sanctuary, which is hushed and dark, and timeless. She feels a familiar sensation, the one she experiences whenever she walks into church: serenity. She loves this feeling, even if it's fleeting, that someone, some high power, is taking care of her.

Sister Nunez used to tell her and the other elementary school kids in Sunday school to imagine that God is holding them in the palm of his hand and nothing can happen to them. It was comforting then and is so now, too. Yet, she hasn't been in church since her grandmother's funeral last spring, and before that, not on a regular basis since she left for college, much to her mother's horror. Mari resolves to start going again as she lights a candle. She stands for a moment watching the flame and then she prays; silently, fervently, and with an utterly un-self-conscious abandon she hasn't felt since she was a little girl in Sunday school.

* * *

Charlotte can't decide what's worse, that this local Assemblyman is a close talker who has yellow teeth and horrible halitosis, or that he's grabbed her waist twice and called her "little lady." Either way, she can't get out of this conversation fast enough. She's been eyeing the door, anticipating Carlos' arrival, but is just as happy to see Ryan and Emily walk in giving her an escape.

"Excuse me, Mr. Jenkins. Friends of mine have arrived," Charlotte says as politely as she can, and then silently adds, *and see a freaking dentist, you jerk.*

They arrive holding hands. Emily is pretty, more striking than Charlotte remembers, and she's cut her blonde hair into a sleek straight bob, and wears perfectly fitted dark jeans. Charlotte takes this all in as she makes her way over to them. And Ryan, as always, looks good, tan, happy. Perhaps they both still have the newlywed glow since it's just been weeks since their wedding and Mediterranean honeymoon.

Mari had been disappointed when Ryan and Emily decided to get married in a small, immediate family-only ceremony in Ireland so that Emily's ailing grandmother could be there. But Charlotte was sort of relieved that the wedding wasn't the big to-do she'd anticipated, mainly because she didn't have any good prospects for a date and also, maybe a little because she was worried about how she would feel actually seeing Ryan standing in front of a priest, making vows, pledging his undying love to Emily, till death do them part. Not that she's completely off the hook. They're having a big celebration in New York in December and Charlotte is determined to have a date by then, a role she's grooming Carlos for, even if he doesn't know it just yet.

"You made it!" Charlotte takes turns hugging them both.

"We did! Thanks so much for having us," Emily beams. Her face-framing haircut and new highlights—Charlotte sees them now that she's closer—has somehow made her eyes pop and appear even bluer.

"How was your flight?"

"This one snored the whole way," Emily nudges Ryan. "But it was fine. Thanks for arranging the car, that was really nice of you."

"Company perk! No problem. The driver will take your suitcases to my place."

Mari races over from where she had been trapped on the other side of the skybox talking with Charlotte's mom who had been ranting about how Tahoe just isn't what it used to be, a topic Mari, having never been to the old or the new Tahoe had zero feelings about, so she was equally gleeful to escape.

"Hi guys!" Mari hugs them both quickly.

Ryan, who's been worried about Mari since her mom's diagnosis, is happy to see she looks to be in pretty good spirits. He'd gotten a text from Charlotte when he landed that Mari's mom had started chemo yesterday. They were determined to cheer her up this weekend, or at least distract her.

"Well, let me see!" Mari grabs for Emily's left hand, which sports the engagement ring, along with the addition of a slim, tasteful matching diamond band. Charlotte has a flashback to last year: sitting on the toilet in the bathroom of their rental in Colorado, secretly trying on the engagement ring, while Mari and Ryan made breakfast. She feels strange now, it's like she's worn Emily's underwear or used her toothbrush and put it back.

"So pretty. I can't wait to celebrate with you guys in December," Mari says.

"Um, speaking of celebrating. This suite is sick." Ryan coos, looking around. A bartender serves top-shelf drinks, there's a table in the corner overflowing with food—grilled shrimp, prime rib, a tower of different breads and cheeses. And then the view: they can see out over the entire stadium and even the Bay just beyond it.

And the giant scoreboard feels close enough to touch. He's also pleased to see that his Royals, who happen to be playing the Giants today, are beating them 2-1. But people seem to be paying less attention to the game at this point, than they are to enjoying the open bar and looking around to scout out who's who in a room full of "who's who." Ryan recognizes San Fran's popular young mayor chewing on a lobster slider a few feet away.

This is totally his scene, he thinks as he grabs a glass of champagne for himself and one for Emily off a tray held by a white-gloved hand. He sips the sweet bubbly and thinks about all the useful connections to be made tonight.

"Is Carlos here yet?" Emily asks, smiling conspiratorially. This catches Charlotte off guard. But, of course, Ryan would have filled Emily in on Charlotte's love life, and it's not as if her three dates with Carlos have been a secret, from her friends at least, but she feels oddly betrayed. Would she be able to tell Ryan anything in confidence anymore?

"Not yet, but he should be soon. I'll bring him by for sure." Charlotte returns the conspiratorial smile. After the initial shock of Ryan's engagement last year, Charlotte has been determined to bring Emily into the fold, and she has made an effort, asking about the wedding plans, reaching out on Facebook and giving her a lavish day spa package at one of the most expensive spas in the New York City for her bridal shower, even though she, understandably since they barely knew each other, was not invited.

At the last minute Charlotte had added Mari's name to the card for the shower gift, unbeknownst to her, worried that it was too ostentatious coming from just Charlotte, like she was overcompensating, which let's face it, she was. But this weekend, their first weekend all hanging out together, will be the true test.

"First, unfortunately though, I have to schmooze for a bit. Groan." Charlotte takes a gulp of her vodka soda for dramatic effect, and also because she needs it to fortify herself for said schmoozing, which is by far the worst part of her job. "I'll find you guys a in a bit. Enjoy! Eat!"

She goes off to track down her dad who wanted her to make

a point of charming Susan Millet, a local assemblywoman who was making a big (and to Jonathan's mind quite unwelcome) stink about building more affordable housing units at the project.

Charlotte was supposed to somehow find a way to appease her, or as Jonathan put it bluntly: "Get that bleeding heart hag to back off. I'm not in the business of operating shelters."

The box, though quite spacious, is crowded now with about thirty or so people, but she still sees Carlos as soon as he walks in fifteen minutes later. It's as if his path is illuminated as he makes his way over to the corner where she and Jonathan have been listening to Susan recite facts and figures as if she's at a City Council meeting, not a cocktail party. ("San Francisco has the highest rates of homelessness in the U.S. A quarter of the homeless are families with children.")

Close on Carlos' heels is a tall, impeccably dressed woman who could be a dead ringer for Selma Hayek. Before Charlotte can fully process the scene, Carlos is upon them, leaning in to kiss her cheek hello and then shaking hands with Jonathan and Susan, who looks star struck.

"I'm Carlos...and this is my fiancée, Christiane," he says directly, cheerfully. Very fucking cheerfully.

It's like a scene in a movie where everything and everyone suddenly stops, only no one and nothing does. Just Charlotte's heart. Everyone else continues smiling and chatting as if Carlos hasn't come up to her and slapped her in the face, which is exactly what this feels like.

Fiancée. Fiancée. Fiancée. Charlotte says the word over and over in her mind as if to process and she wills herself not to run, not to throw her drink in his face, not to scream, ARE YOU KIDDING ME RIGHT NOW? Instead, she plasters a smile on her face, shakes Christiane's delicate, bird-like hand and begins slowly counting down from ten in her head as she nods along with the conversation, which at present is Susan commenting on how beautiful Christiane's ring is. Charlotte can't look down at it, can't look at Carlos, can't find anywhere for her eyes to be, until they focus on a large, unsightly mole on Susan's wrists, which holds

Christiane's hand so as to further examine the ring, while Carlos explains that it's a family heirloom.

"Will you excuse me for a second? Ladies' room calls," Charlotte says as gracefully as she can, though it takes heroic amounts of strength to get her voice above a whisper. If Carlos has taken pause at the scene unfolding, her reaction, he doesn't show it and the sheer audacity of this, of his being so entirely unflappable, fills her with such a rage it's all she can do not to throw her glass tumbler across the room.

Instead she puts her glass down calmly on the nearest table, and fights to walk at a normal pace out the door of the suite, before she all but breaks into a run to the bathrooms down the hall. She hears someone behind her and looks up to find Mari rushing to catch up.

"Is that Carlos? I saw him come him and recognized his picture from Facebook."

The way she says it, hesitantly, tells Charlotte that Mari has put two and two together.

"Yep. And that model with him? His fiancée."

"Fuck," Mari says, pulling Charlotte into the mercifully empty bathroom. She locks the door behind them.

"This is so humiliating. What a liar! How do you forget to mention that you've asked someone to marry you? I guess his tongue was too far down my throat." She looks in the mirror, immediately starts comparing herself to Christiane—Jesus even her name is glamorous—and rummages in her bag for lipstick as if that's going to magically transform her into someone who this isn't, wouldn't be, happening to. This is an instinct from her teenage years. Whenever she would get in a petty fight with one of her girlfriends, or have her heart broken by the boy of the day and not want to leave her bedroom, let alone the house, her mother would say, "Well, put on some lipstick, honey, you'll feel better." As if lipstick, even if it is Chanel and glides on like butter, has ever solved anything. Still she reapplies, puckers.

"This is all on him, Charlotte," Mari says firmly looking at her in the mirror. "You didn't know." Mari is relieved to realize

Charlotte didn't, in fact, know. Her first impulse was to worry that Charlotte had just forgot to mention she was dating a married man, then she immediately felt bad for not giving her friend enough credit.

"Yeah, but I still feel dumb. And cursed. I seriously have the worst track record with men. It's...stunning."

It's hard for Mari to argue with that. As much as Charlotte has going for her, which to Mari's mind is everything, she really doesn't have the best of luck with men.

It's one of life's big mysteries. Up there with how a healthy fifty-six-year-old woman gets life-threatening cancer, Mari thinks before she can help herself.

"Nope. Do NOT feel bad," Mari says firmly. "He's the asshole. And you're going to walk back in there like he doesn't matter, because guess what, he doesn't matter. You two kissed a couple of times. It's not the end of the world."

"I want to get him fired." A girl can dream, Charlotte thinks.

"Well, we can plot revenge later. We can always borrow from the Jennifer Jackson playbook?"

They both break out into laughter thinking back to their friend at Harvard, who pretended to be from the Health Department and tracked down everyone her cheating ex had ever been with, including his new girlfriend, and reported to the women (falsely, at least at the time) that he had herpes.

Laughing feels good. Charlotte tousles her hair, takes a deep breath, smiles in the mirror. "You're right. Fuck him. Let's get out of here. I know the perfect bar." The fact that Carlos was the one to introduce her to said bar, where they recently snuggled up in one of the dark booths, is either masochistic or a nice bit of irony, depending on how you look at it. Charlotte chooses the latter.

Mari goes to round up Emily and Ryan while Charlotte squares her shoulders and makes her way back over to where Carlos and Christiane are still talking to her dad, like the best of friends.

"It was lovely to see you, and lovely to meet you, Christiane. My best friends are in town for the weekend, so we're cutting out early. Going to head over to Bourbon and Branch. You've been there, right?" She looks pointedly at Carlos and feels satisfied as a quick cloud passes over his face. She's not going to say anything, but he can't be a hundred percent sure of that and she needs to see him sweat.

"I have something to discuss with you first thing Monday, Dad." She can't resist twisting the knife a little further.

Her dad looks perplexed, but that's okay, she'll find some bogus reason for meeting on Monday, but the point is to leave Carlos wondering.

By the time they get out of the stadium and into a cab, Carlos has sent her a nauseatingly predictable text—I CAN EXPLAIN— which everyone implores her to ignore.

And by the time they make their way across town to Bourbon and Branch, Charlotte has almost convinced herself that she feels fine. With her friends egging her on, she had nearly completed the full about face—where Carlos went from suave prospect to dirty leech who is not worth her time—that would make it possible to get over this. Anger is better than self-pity any day. It helped when Emily explained that the same thing had happened to her.

"Before I met Ryan I dated this guy, an i-banker, for like three months and only found out he had a wife when she called me to confront me about sleeping with her husband! She had seen my number on his phone. The worst part was that she didn't believe I didn't know. I don't know, I was so insulted by that. That she thought I would knowingly sleep with a married man."

"Wait—you never told me this story before," Ryan says.

Emily just shrugs. "Not one of my finest hours."

"Well, just like Charlotte. It's not your fault. I mean how would you know?" Mari says and then thinks, see this is why I am holding out; or not bothering, there's such a thin line between the two.

"I guess, it just makes me nervous that I would miss the little things," Emily says.

"There must have been signs. I just like to believe in the good in people—I guess that's naïve."

They sit quietly thinking about this as the cab pulls up.

"This is the place?" The group looks around tentatively. All they see is a dark street and a plain black door.

"Best kept secret in San Francisco," Charlotte says gleefully. "It's a speakeasy!"

Sure enough, she buzzes a hidden doorbell and a man opens a small window in the door.

"Hawk flies," Charlotte says and the door opens.

"You have to call and get a password! It's so hokey, right? But I love it."

The non-descript door opens into a large bar with a bordello-like feel, blood red luscious wallpaper lines one wall and opposite it is a wall made entirely of exposed brick. It seems to only be lit by candlelight and low wall sconces, giving it an intimate, cave-like feel. Since moving to New York three years ago, Ryan has admittedly become one of those people who thinks everything is better there, but this place is one of the coolest places he's ever been to.

"Love this place Charlotte," he says as they settle in a leather booth. "The vibe here reminds me of Strip House, my favorite restaurant in NYC."

"Where we went on our first date!" Emily says, placing her head on his shoulder.

They trade bits of gossip about the party as they look over the menu filled with artisanal cocktails featuring liquors they've never heard of.

"So, your dad asked me to play golf with him tomorrow." Ryan can't lie that this took him by complete surprise and made his day.

Charlotte is also is a bit surprised and annoyed—even she hasn't been invited to play golf with her dad since she's been back home. Not that she's in a hurry to hang out at his stuffy country club. But still.

"Let me guess, girls aren't invited?" Emily says.

"Not to worry, I've booked us for brunch and then manis and pedis tomorrow," Charlotte says. "And then we have a Napa wine tour on Sunday." Charlotte remembers that she was going to subtlety invite Carlos on the tour and her outrage momentarily returns, like a forgotten bug bite that starts itching again.

"I gotta up my golf game since I've been playing regularly with Vince and crew.

And they take that shit seriously."

"Are these the potential clients you were telling me about?" Charlotte says. Ryan has been at full-court press to woo them to his firm and is convinced this will be a career-making move.

"Yeah, I met them at a Nets game. Vince is a big import/export guy who's having some trouble with tariffs. He's not happy with Aiken and Watson, wants a bigger firm with more...influence. If I can bring in their business, I'll be golden."

"Well, cheers to that," Charlotte raises a glass, though from what she's heard, these guys sound pretty shady.

"Speaking of Vince...did Ryan tell you guys we found an amazing apartment to buy? Vince gave him the lead on it."

Charlotte gives Ryan a quizzical look across the table as Emily continues.

"It's a new building going up on Park. They start construction in January, but there's a great pre-sale deal happening now if you get in on the ground floor. So if we can get in—and Vince says he can make it happen—it's practically a steal. $975,000 for a two bedroom south of 96 is practically unheard of, especially with the amenities."

Mari almost spits out her drink. Almost a million dollars for a two-bedroom apartment? I mean she knew her friends have done well, but this well?

"The place sounds amazing, Emily," Charlotte says, but she's looking at Ryan who is staring into his drink.

"Hey—did you guys hear about Brad?" Ryan asks abruptly. Charlotte doesn't know if the others catch how eager he is to change the topic, but she does.

"Yeah, crazy," says Mari.

Brad was a classmate of theirs who secured a plum job clerking for a federal court judge. Turns out he then started a blog

(Don't Judge Me) in which he dished about the judge and added his personal "take" on her rulings, which were often contrary, if not downright snarky. When the judge got wind of it he promptly got fired.

"It's no surprise. He was always so pompous and had no common sense, a bad combo. Clearly."

"I talked to Professor Wallace a couple weeks ago. He called me when he heard about my mom—so nice. And he told me that Brad called him to see if he would put in a good word with the judge. Try to help him get his job back."

"Is he going to?"

"No. I believe his exact words were: "You are where you are because..."

"...that's where you want to be!" Ryan and Charlotte join in to complete Professor Wallace's oft-used quote, which essentially implied that good or bad, your actions and decisions have landed you in whatever predicament you find yourself. Mari used to buy into this, found the logic of it fair and comforting—but now that her mother has cancer, she's not so sure. Life is capricious and sometimes you find yourself somewhere you do NOT want to be, with no say in the matter.

"How is your mom, Mari?" Emily asks, as if reading Mari's mind. She reaches across the table and holds Mari's hand, which is a strangely intimate gesture that with anyone else would be too affected, but somehow with Emily, direct, earnest Emily, it manages to exude sincerity.

"She's okay. I had a little bit of a breakdown earlier. She started chemo today and didn't tell me. And apparently it's been awful."

"That's brutal," Emily says, squeezing Mari's hand. "But she'll be fine. That's what we have to believe." Another familiar platitude, but somehow Emily says it with such conviction and frankness, that Mari almost, if just for a precious second, fully believes it. And the surge of hope makes her feel powerful. Or maybe it's the absinthe.

"Well, I propose a toast," Ryan raises his glass. "To Mari's mom getting better and to being where we want to be."

* * *

Since she was a little girl Charlotte has always been a terrible sleeper. In her mother's histrionic re-telling Charlotte didn't sleep more than ten hours total between the ages of one and three, although Magda would be a more credible source on the subject.

When Charlotte can't sleep these days, which is often, she heads to her balcony that overlooks the Bay and the long row of Victorian houses on the sloping street below and she watches the city sleep and she waits, to get sleepy or for the sunrise, whichever comes first. She's more than a little surprised to find Ryan out here at 3 a.m.

"You too, huh?"

"Yeah, can't sleep. Jetlag I guess." He scoots over so she can join him on the patio loveseat.

They sit listening to the night for a while.

"So I gather you didn't tell her?" Charlotte says quietly.

Ryan doesn't seem shocked by the question; obviously he knew it was coming.

"No," he says simply. Then, "Not yet."

Charlotte is quiet for a minute trying to decide how to proceed. It was already awkward enough when Ryan came to her shortly before the wedding and asked if he could borrow $100,000 to for a down payment on an apartment. Not necessarily a staggering figure for Charlotte, but an audacious amount to ask of a friend. He at least had the decency to be sheepish about it, but still, that he put Charlotte in the position was uncomfortable for them both. Her father's words, "never lend money to friends, period," echoed in her ear. But it was Ryan, and she had the money, how could she say no? So she agreed to $50,000, telling him that was all that she could access from her trust fund at any one time, a small white lie. Not on par with, say, not telling your wife that you borrowed $50K.

Finally Charlotte speaks. "It's just...well it's big secret to keep from her, don't you think.? And really it's no big deal. You should tell her."

"Look, I want to be able to give Emily a life she deserves, we both deserve, and this is a once in a lifetime real estate deal. When I sign these clients, my bonus next spring is going to be big enough to pay you back, with interest, in one fell swoop."

"Ryan, it's not the money I'm worried about. Come on, you know that." Though, if she's honest, it is a bit about the money, because it's a lot and it sort of hangs there between them in ways they probably both didn't foresee. "It's that, I don't know...if I were Emily, I would just want to know, is all."

"I know, I know. Em is just weird about money. And she wouldn't have wanted me to borrow the money from you."

Charlotte resists the urge to ask, then why did you?

"Is everything okay? You've seemed a little stressed lately and Emily mentioned that you weren't sleeping and now here you are."

"She told you that?" He sounds rather hurt.

"Well, Mari and I were talking about Law and Order and Emily mentioned you were watching it a lot because it comes on local TV in the middle of the night. She wasn't trying to have an intervention or anything. Well, maybe she was on Mari and me. When we started listing our favorite detective pairings, she decided we watch way too much Law and Order." Charlotte attempts humor and is relieved when Ryan smiles.

"You do watch way too much Law and Order." A pause. "I'm fine. Just a lot of pressure. I have a wife now—one who is already talking about babies. And I have the five-year plan..." Charlotte is well aware of Ryan's five-year, which was taped to the inside drawer of his desk for all three years they were at Harvard.

GRADUATE
BLUE CHIP FIRM
MAKE PARTNER
MARRIED
KID AFTER PARTNER

EARN 250K/YR BY 30

OWN PROPERTY/INVEST

BIG TRIP (Patagonia? South Africa? New Zealand)

"I have this weird feeling, Charlotte, like I'm running out of time."

"I'm going to give you the same speech you gave me not so long ago—it's all going to be okay. Better than okay. It's going to be...stupendous. Because you're the

Amazing Ryan, kicker of asses."

He looks at her and smiles, but there's an anxiety that she can still see behind his eyes.

"I'm serious, Ryan. It's all going to be good. Okay?"

"The sun's going to be up soon," he says by way of response. They both look off to the distance where a barely there yellow glows hovers around the horizon.

"Shit." The idea of sunrise isn't exactly welcome right now. "Em and I are going running in less than two hours. What time are you meeting my dad?"

"Seven, sharp."

"He doesn't ask everyone to play, you know. You're like the son he never had.

Don't tell Oliver I said that!"

"Speaking of, how is he?"

"Oliver? Oh, the same. He and my dad aren't speaking— again. Oliver is furious because he found out one of our major investors is this guy Randy who runs Campaign for California Families, which apparently is trying to get some sort of anti-gay marriage bill passed here. But he should know Jonathan better than this, he's not political, he's equal opportunity. I'm sure he has some pro-marriage people on the payroll, too. But Oliver took it personally, as a slap in the face. More evidence that 'you hate that I'm gay' and all that. Then he calls me in an absolute fit, as if I have anything to do with anything, and tells me that he's not speaking to me either unless I resign from Mayfield."

"Dramatic much, Oliver? Jesus," Ryan says.

"Tell me about it. He makes these extreme lines in the sand

and backs himself into a ridiculous corner. I'm going to give him a couple months to cool off and then call and act like everything's fine. Thanksgiving should be a blast."

Ryan takes a minute to appreciate not having siblings.

"Okay, I'm going in." Charlotte sighs and picks herself off the sofa. She doubts she'll sleep but at least she can stretch out in her bed for a bit. She turns back when she gets to the doorway.

"Tell her, Ryan okay?"

He offers the subtlest of nods.

* * *

It's still dark and the air is crisp and cold, so much so that Emily and Charlotte can see their breath coming at regular intervals as they run. No one, least of all Mari and Ryan, understands Charlotte's desire to get up at the crack of dawn and run every day, no matter the weather, or her hangover or how much sleep she's had, but to Charlotte it's an exquisite torture, like jumping in an ice cold pool. And also, no matter how chaotic or unsettled Charlotte's life feels at any given moment, she knows that between 5 and 6 a.m., she'll be doing the same thing and the ritual of it—not to mention the endorphins—always make her feel calmer. Though this is usually her precious alone time, it was Emily's idea to join her this morning and it would have been impossible to say no.

"I can't believe this. This is truly amazing," Emily says.

They are running along a path on the north coast of the city, which will take them straight up to and across the Golden Gate Bridge. Usually Charlotte stays in her neighborhood and runs a six-mile loop on her streets, but when out-of-town visitors come, she always brings them here to walk or run because the view is breathtaking.

It's early, even for some of the morning people, and they all but have the path to themselves. Charlotte's relieved that Emily is not a chatty running partner—the worst.

As they approach the stairs that lead to the bridge they see flashing lights and that a small crowd has gathered, some fifty feet ahead of them, towards the middle of the bridge. A guy an in bright orange vest comes over with traffic cones, blocking their path.

"Sorry, guys, closing down. We have a potential jumper," he says.

They can make out a figure on the other side of the giant orange metal stanchions, staring down into the choppy waters.

"Oh god," they both say, almost in unison.

"Don't worry ladies, we're prepared for this. We have an official talking to him now. Hopefully we'll get this all sorted out."

Growing up just outside of San Francisco, Charlotte is well aware of the statistics, that the Golden Gate Bridge is one of the most popular places to commit suicide in the world. Some 1700 people have leapt off this bridge, including Lizzie MacComber, a girl from her prep school, freshman year. Rumors were that it was because John Mackie didn't ask her to Homecoming, which in the midst of teenage melodrama actually seemed a viable reason. But to Charlotte now, remembering this, it's the most heartbreaking thing in the world.

She tugs Emily's shirt. "Come on, I know another path."

Emily follows her back down the path from where they came. It's clear that they're both shaken up by the jumper on the bridge, by the life that literally hangs in the balance. Charlotte realizes if they keep standing where they are, they will have a perfect view if the person does jump, which is not something she wants at all, so she again urges Emily to start running and takes off at a faster pace in another direction.

A few minutes later, Emily stops, breathing heavy. "Can we take a quick break"?

Charlotte didn't realize how fast she was running.

"Sure, let's sit." There were benches dotting the walkway that looked south out over the water, away from the bridge. They perch on one, catch their breath, drink water.

"When I was little, about six, I almost died," Emily says out of nowhere, with the same matter-of-fact tone as she if she just shared she was once a girl scout.

"I had a really severe infection that turned to sepsis. I was in the hospital for more than a week and just kept getting worse. And I remember overhearing the doctor talking to my mother when things seemed really grim and he said she and my dad were much more scared than I was. That, at six, it was a blessing that I didn't fully comprehend what was happening so they shouldn't worry, that they could let me go. I know that brought my mom comfort. I could tell. But it was a lie. I knew what was coming and was terrified. Completely and utterly terrified. And I knew, more than anything, that I didn't want to die. That it was an oblivion—even if I didn't have the word for it—that threatened to swallow me. I knew I had to fight. And I did. I remember giving myself these peps talks inside my mind. I would constantly tell death to "go away," the same way my dad had yelled at the monsters under my bed. And I got better and then everything after that was simple. My priority in life was simple: all I have to do is live. Everything else is icing."

Charlotte thinks of poor young Emily lying in a hospital bed too big for her, of the jumper, of Lizzie whose yearbook photo she now can't get out of her mind. All she had to do was live. But she didn't. They had all grown up but Lizzie was fifteen and still dead. She hasn't thought about her in ten years, and still this fact, it's brutal simplicity, bowls her over. Charlotte realizes she hasn't said anything and before she does Emily speaks again.

"I want you to like me, Charlotte," Emily says apropos of nothing, or maybe of everything.

Again, she's caught off guard by Emily's directness, her earnestness, which Charlotte initially took as simplicity and a superficial desire to please and to fit in but now she understands that Emily has a complexity and a grit to her that belies her straightforward exterior. Her total lack of self-indulgence is novel, and a little scary, Charlotte realizes, because Emily, she's learning, is the type of girl who isn't afraid to invite you in, who isn't afraid to go there, who sees you.

"I do like you," Charlotte says firmly. And she realizes she does. Not just out of obligation because she's Ryan's wife, and not just by default because there is nothing obvious not to like, but because there is something captivating about Emily, about her vulnerability, her openness. She hopes Ryan doesn't fuck this up, because she feels, in this moment, clear as anything, that she's made a friend for life.

"Good. Back to it then?" Emily says tucking her water bottle back in her pocket.

They get up to resume their run and Charlotte can't help but to wonder about the jumper. Did he? Didn't he? Is he still suspended up there, trying to find a will to live? How did it get so bad? Who will miss him?

Charlotte doesn't know, will never know, but that's okay because on some level she understands that sometimes not knowing is for the best.

Chapter Five
New York City, 2006

Emily would never harm the baby. Of course, she wouldn't. After all, the last few weeks since Owen arrived have been the most miraculous of her life and she loves him with a ferocity she can barely comprehend. True to every cheesy platitude she had ever heard about motherhood, it is a profound and mind-blowing experience. It's also the hardest fucking thing she's ever done, second only to almost dying as a child. She feels a bone deep fatigue and a certain level of overall disorientation at trying to navigate her new life—and this is how she thinks of it, since her old life, her pre-Owen life, is all but unrecognizable to her at this point.

So there are times, not often, but maybe once or twice a week that she finds that she's gripped by fantasies that Owen has disappeared. He's not hurt in any way, he's just gone, tucked away someplace safe for four hours or six, just enough time for Emily to regroup, sleep, feel like a human again. To take a shower, a sweet, long, hot shower, as she does now with Owen under the watchful, fawning really, eyes of Mari and Charlotte down the hall.

Emily feels ashamed though as she stands under the hot stream of water—has as a shower ever felt so good?—that she all but threw the baby at Mari and Charlotte when they had barely just wheeled their suitcases past the front door. But there had been so much that she was trying to get done before they arrived since Ryan had been a maniac that everything be perfect for this visit, the first to their new apartment. Fresh Direct had delivered groceries at the crack of dawn, then the house cleaners came, she had run to Whole Foods to get fresh flowers, and in between breast fed Owen several times. And she hadn't had a chance to shower today, or yesterday she now realizes.

When Charlotte and Mari arrived from the airport Emily was wearing sweatpants—she had lost track of how many consecutive days she'd worn them—and one of Ryan's t-shirts that said ROCK THE ROCKIES across the front, covered in spit up.

Fortunately, Mari and Charlotte were so distracted by the apartment, which Emily admits, thanks to six months of work by a zealous interior decorator, is gorgeous, as well as the baby, who is also pretty gorgeous, that they didn't seem to notice how disheveled she was.

Fifteen minutes in, before they even put their bags in the guest room, she asked if they would mind if she just took a quick shower. When Mari grabbed the baby and said, "yes, go," Emily could have cried with happiness.

And here she is, sitting on the Carrara marble shower seat, enveloped in water and steam. She even lit one of the as yet unused $70 soy candles she'd bought a few months back, because when is the next time she's going to have time to do that.

As she massages a deep conditioner into her hair she feels yet another wave of guilt.

Mari and Charlotte shouldn't be spending their annual weekend visit here in Babyville, with a frazzled new mom. They should be out living it up and dancing till dawn, having fun.

Emily tries to recall the last time she drank and danced with total abandon—it certainly wasn't over the last nine months of a pregnancy that left her completely wiped out. A flash comes back, last New Year's Eve, her in only a bikini top pressed close against Ryan's sweaty body at a dive bar in the Bahamas their cab driver had told them about. There was a live band and lots of rum and a bathroom filled with graffiti. And after the festive countdown to 2006, they'd stumbled back to their room and right into bed. In their drunken stupor they couldn't find the box of condoms, but Ryan had slurred, "What are the chances? It's fine," as he eased inside of her and Emily, reckless with rum and pleasure didn't make a single move to stop him, and then probabilities and biology both conspired to mock them. "A surprise," they had told everyone. "A happy surprise," which is more or less the truth.

Emily finds it laughable that last month, right before Owen was born (three weeks early), she had actually told Ryan that he should still plan to go away with Mari and Charlotte as usual. Just because they would have a brand new baby, didn't mean he should miss this tradition that's so important to him. He should go, she'd insisted, ever the loving and generous wife, she would be fine, she could handle a newborn solo for a couple of days. Little did she know! Thank god, he had the good sense to refuse a getaway and suggest that they invite Mari and Charlotte to see them for the weekend instead. She tells herself that Mari and Charlotte won't mind, don't mind. It is New York City after all. They'll still have fun—a different kind of fun. Emily's whole life is now a different sort of fun.

There's no clock in the bathroom and she's lost any sense of time. She could have been in here for two minutes or two hours but she feels like she needs to get back; all good things, even showers, must come to an end. Besides she feels the heavy weight and warm tingling of her breasts filling up. She'll have to feed Owen soon.

After she's toweled off, dressed in clean clothes and brushed her hair, she feels utterly transformed. Gone is the sour smell of old spit up and unwashed hair. Fortified, she heads to the living room where she finds Charlotte and Mari cooing over the baby.

"Em, he's so adorable and tiny. I can't even take it." Mari looks down at the tiny finger gripping hers. She could sit here holding this warm bundle all night. She's certainly been hogging him since she arrived an hour ago, but Charlotte, who's been scrolling on her phone seems unconcerned.

"He is, right?" Emily face lights up with a smile but Mari can tell she's exhausted.

She looks—and smells— better than she did when they showed up at the door an hour ago, but she still has dark circles under her eyes and a slightly unhinged look in her eyes.

Mari remembers this exact look on Carmen's face when both her niece and nephew were born. A heady mix of exhilaration mixed exhaustion.

"I'm taking a turn soon," Charlotte says. Though he is so small Charlotte is afraid she'll break him, or worse, look and feel inept as she handles a newborn, whereas Mari looks the picture of maternal confidence.

Emily barely settles on the massive sectional couch that anchors the living room, before she anxiously jumps up again and heads over to the adjacent kitchen. "I'm such a bad host! Did you guys get something to eat? Drink?" She begins pulling bowls of fruit and bottles of sparkling water out of the fridge. "We have everything..."

"We're fine. Sit down. Relax," Charlotte and Mari both assure her.

Just then Emily's phone vibrates on the counter and she flips it open to check the message. From Ryan: All okay? Client meeting going to run late.

Home 10ish. Sorry babe.

So he's just going to leave her here entertaining his friends, she fumes and then feels bad because they are her friends, too now, but still! Ryan hasn't been home before 10 p.m. for the last three weeks and he promised an early night, knew how much it meant to her. And all she gets is a lame, "sorry, babe"? She places both her hands on the cool stone countertops and takes a deep breath.

"Everything okay?" Mari asks. Both she and Charlotte are staring at her hesitantly.

"Yes, yes, sorry." Emily comes back to the living room and sinks down on the sectional. "Ryan just texted that he's going to be late—again."

Ever since he made junior partner in the spring, it's been like this, longer and longer hours. Most days, she gets it, she does, she knows what she signed up for and she knows how much pressure Ryan is under—how could she not since he is constantly reminding her—as the youngest person to make partner (even junior) in the firm's history. There are higher expectations and "haters" who would love to see him fail. But he has a son now who would love to see him at all. So, it's just frustrating...not to mention lonely as hell.

"That's the life of a corporate lawyer," Charlotte says, and then thinks, looking around, and the one that pays for all of this. She is still stunned by how lavish Ryan and Emily's place is. Taking in the spacious apartment with its impeccable finishes and décor—there must be four hundred silk throw pillows on this couch—and thinking about how much this all must have cost gives Charlotte a slightly nauseous feeling. She tells herself, it's none of my business.

"Yeah, I know. What I signed up for, right?" Emily smiles half-heartedly. "I had thought we could all go to dinner when he got home, but honestly, I'm exhausted. Do you guys care if we just do delivery?"

"Sounds good to me!" Mari says cheerfully, raising Owen from her lap to over her shoulder. "I'm exhausted, too. This week has been brutal. I haven't been back to Montgomery at all. I flew straight from Florida to Kansas City for a conference and then here."

"Oh yeah, your mom's party last week! Six months in remission. Such great news." Emily was so proud of herself for managing to get it together enough to remember to send flowers to Mrs. Castillo.

"The flowers you guys sent were really nice. My mom loved them. Naturally, she'd endlessly complained about the party and how there was no need for a fuss, but I'm so glad we did it. Every positive milestone is important to celebrate and after all she went through with chemo, radiation, and surgery, it was nice to get together for a good reason. And not have to go to a damn hospital or doctor's office."

"So she's feeling good?" Emily asks.

"Yeah, she has to go for scans every six months from here on, but otherwise, she should be okay. The docs say she was very lucky."

Though luck seemed like an understatement to Mari. Luck is a winning lotto ticket or stumbling upon a forgotten umbrella just as it's about to rain. This was something so much more, that her mother survived, that she is cured when that's not the outcome for so many people with her exact diagnosis. Is it providence? Grace? A miracle? Mari hasn't been able to find any words to fully capture what it means that they get even just one more day, let alone months and quite possibly years to be together, that her mother can still yet one day meet her future husband and future children. All she knows is that she feels profoundly grateful. But even that feels like a gross understatement.

"Well, speaking of celebrations, you know what? I'm going to have a beer." Emily abruptly gets up again and goes to the fridge trying to remember when was the last time she'd had a beer. A year ago? "Is that crazy?"

"Not at all. I'll have one too," Charlotte calls. She was hoping for wine, but doesn't want to put Emily, who is clearly a little on edge, out. So a beer will do, anything really.

"Me too!" Mari calls, startling Owen who jerks slightly in his sleep.

Emily returns to the living room with delivery menus and three IPAs. Ryan has long since graduated from Pabst.

"It's surreal. I can't believe you actually have a baby," Charlotte says, quickly opening her bottle to catch up with Emily who's chugging with so much speed and gusto it might as well a Gatorade.

"I'm his mother and it's still surreal, believe me. Especially here in NYC. I'm twenty-eight, but in New York standards, it's like I'm sixteen. My friends at the gallery acted like I had a rare and contagious disease when I told them I was pregnant. The very first thing my friend Molly said when I told her the news was, 'are you going to keep it?'

Can you believe that?"

What Emily would never admit was, in fact, that that was her very first, instantaneous, reflexive thought, looking down with utter shock at the plus sign on the pregnancy test. Am I going to keep it? Now that she sees Owen, holds him, smells him, she's horrified that she even let the thought cross her mind in that panic-inducing moment, alone in the bathroom, her pants still around her ankles, but all she could think was that she and Ryan weren't ready. Yes, they wanted to have kids, and both being only children themselves, they were determined to have multiple kids, but they were so young, not even thirty yet, there were childless adventures to be had. But then Ryan lit up like the Empire State Building when she told him when he got home that night. He picked her up and swung her around the living room, screaming, "we're having a baby!" and just like that they were.

"It's not like we planned it," she continues. "And it would have been nice to have more time with just Ryan and I, but...you are where you are because that's where you want to be, right?" She smiles. "Anyway what do you guys want for dinner? Thai okay?"

Both Mari and Charlotte agree that Thai is perfect even though neither cares for it that much.

"I ordered a whole bunch of chick flicks from Netflix thinking I would have all this time to watch movies when the baby came. Yeah right. But we could watch tonight."

Emily goes over to the media console and flips through the stack of DVDs on top of the giant plasma TV. "Love, Actually, anyone?"

"Love it," Charlotte says. And she does love rom coms but why exactly, she doesn't know since they are all total and complete bullshit and make women, herself included, long for things, grand romantic gestures and perfect happy endings that they'll likely never get. Then another alarming thought: shit when did I get so jaded?

"This is so fun—an old fashioned sleepover." Mari raises her beer bottle. She and Carmen were never allowed to go to sleepovers when they were young and having been denied this adolescent ritual she holds it in that much higher regard. Though she's thankful to have outgrown spiked Slurpees and truth or dare and gone straight to wine and movie night.

Emily goes over and takes Owen from Mari, realizing how much she's missed his nearness, his weight, all eight pounds of it, in her arms. "I'm already in my PJs. You guys should go get changed while I call for the food."

They all scatter to change, make calls, wash faces, brush teeth. Emily feeds Owen, changes him into pajamas, pays the delivery guy, sets out the food and then they're all, finally, an hour later settled in comfortable repose around the living room, watching the opening scene of Love Actually, which even without hormones pumping through her veins never fails to make Emily tear up.

It is only then, settled on the couch with Owen asleep on her chest, twenty or so minutes into the movie with the hectic-ness of the evening behind her, that she realizes something: Mari and Charlotte have barely said two words to each other.

* * *

Charlotte is awakened by angry, hushed whispers coming from the master bedroom.

She looks at the clock on the cable box: 5:50 a.m. She'll run in twenty minutes, even though she feels groggy and stiff. Sleeping on the living room couch was not a good idea, but she fell asleep here before the movie ended and didn't bother relocating to join Mari in the guest room when she woke up at 1 a.m. and again at 3:30. She wonders what time Ryan ended up getting home, it was after they had all fallen asleep.

She tunes back into the voices, listens intently, but can't make out what they're saying, though the unhappy tone is clear. She has flashbacks to sleepovers at her friend Denise's whose parents, it seemed, were always, always fighting. There is nothing more awkward than being in close quarters with a couple who's fighting, or worse even, aggressively giving each other the silent treatment. Charlotte worries it's going to be a long and uncomfortable day.

Abruptly, the voices stop and it's quiet for a few minutes. She sits up, rubs her eyes and then to her surprise, Ryan appears in the living room dressed head to toe in running clothes. "Hey there. You're up. Thought I would join you this morning?"

Charlotte doesn't bother to hide her questioning look. As far as she knows Ryan hasn't been on a run since the '03 NYC Marathon after which vowed to "never run again."

"What?" he says, shrugging. "I just feel like a run, okay. Come on."

"Sure, give me two minutes to get dressed."

"Cool," he says, but he's already typing away on his Blackberry.

Charlotte sneaks as quietly as possible into the room where Mari is asleep and rummages through her suitcase to grab her running clothes and shoes, then quickly throws them on. They make their way through the lobby, where a drowsy doorman sits at a sleek black marble desk. He perks up when he sees Ryan, attempts to look busy shuffling the stack of New York Times on the desk. "Morning Mr. Hart."

It's early yet and the traffic on Park mostly consists of trucks making morning deliveries. Charlotte puts her leg on a fire hydrant and begins stretching.

"Um, is it cool if we don't actually run?" Ryan says.

"Wait, what?" She looks him up and down to reinforce the fact that he's dressed from head to toe in premium Nike running gear. "You don't actually want to run?"

"I just had to get out of there," he says, and starts walking fast south on Park Avenue. "Come on, let's get a drink."

"Ryan! It's not even 7 a.m." She quick steps to catch up with him.

"I know—that's why we're getting mimosas." He flashes her a grin but Charlotte feels uneasy. Ryan seems on edge, tightly wound and she's not exactly cool with sneaking around. Also, she sort of does want to run. But she keeps following him and soon they're settled in a small upscale diner a few blocks away.

"Are you going to tell me what's going on?" Charlotte asks before the waiter even fills their water glasses.

Ryan runs his hand through his hair, nervously taps his fork on the table.

"You're not going to ask me for money right?" Charlotte jokes. Well, half jokes, because part of her thinks of the silk throw pillows and the Bose stereo system and wonders if this is exactly what's about to happen. Thankfully Ryan had recently sent her a check for the full amount he'd borrowed, with ten percent interest, and a note—I think we're both glad you didn't have to break my kneecaps. ☺—but she's not eager to have this be a revolving line of credit. To this day, she wonders if he ever told Emily.

She's never asked again, but her guess is, no.

"Relax, no, I'm not going to ask your for money..." They pause while the waiter drops off menus, rattles off the specials.

"So what is it?" Charlotte asks as soon as he walks away.

"I don't know, Charlotte..." Ryan pauses, looks out the window. "It's just...been crazy lately." Another pause. "I never told you this, but you know what my very first thought was when I came home from work and Emily told me she was pregnant? It was, fuck. What kind of dude thinks that when his wife tells him she's having a baby?"

A lot Charlotte would imagine, but she doesn't say it.

"I mean obviously I didn't say it out loud. Emily was so excited, so I pretended to be happy about it, until I was actually happy about it. It was sooner than we would have liked, but whatever. And god, I love that kid, Charlotte. But with work and the baby and Emily... It's like she's never happy these days. She doesn't get it, I'm stressed, too. I'm trying to deliver at work, make her happy, help with Owen and I swear all she does is nag at me when I get home. It's just tough." He stops, refills his glass from the pitcher of mimosas the waiter has delivered.

Charlotte isn't sure what to say, but she knows the last thing she wants to do, is qualified to do, is weigh in on anyone's marital troubles, least of all not Emily and Ryan's. So she just waits, hopeful that he just needs a sounding board, and sure enough he continues.

"But I know Em and I will get it figured it out. She's anxious, I'm anxious and we have no idea what the hell we're doing. It is what it is. Shit, that's not even what I wanted to talk about. I need some work advice actually...and a favor."

Charlotte is pleased to be on firmer ground and to possibly be able to provide a solution. "Shoot."

"I worked my ass off to convince Vince to bring his business to the firm and it worked. As soon as I did, my billing was through the roof and Tripper had no choice but to make me partner. But I have may have..." Here he stops talking as if trying to figure out what to say. "I may have implied that we had more...shall we say, influence in D.C. than we do, or at least I do. Vince has been happy with our work so far, but now he's having some issues with Customs and he has a shipment stuck in San Paolo.

"This shipment is...legal right?" Charlotte continues to feel that there is something shady about Vince. Working in the international construction business, Charlotte is all too familiar with the Vinces of the world.

Ryan feigns shock. "Actually, yes, totally legit. It's emeralds, if you must know.

But there are a lot of regulations and loopholes. He's losing hundreds of thousands a dollars a day and he expects me to fix this."

"What does Tripper say?"

"Well, that's the thing. Let's just say, I didn't fully disclose the extent of Vince's...expectations. And besides I want to handle this myself."

"It sounds like you're getting into some really tricky territory here." Charlotte sips her drink, tries to think, though the champagne is not helping matters.

"I know, I know..."

"So how I can help?"

"Well, I'm hoping that maybe Jonathan has some

connections in D.C.? Or Oliver? Isn't he still working at Capital Lobby? He got friendly with Senator Sandler on Commerce, didn't he? I just need to start making these connections. I need some political capital. Maybe Oliver could make an introduction? I could easily go down to D.C....next week?" Ryan is trying to keep the eagerness out his voice.

"I mean, I'm happy to ask him, but you know I'm not my brother's favorite person. He's not going to bend over backwards for me, you know?

Ryan starts anxiously tapping the fork again.

"But I'll ask him," she quickly adds, reassuringly. "And I'll ask Jonathan, too. God knows he'll have a connection. And he likes you. He'll want to help."

"Okay, cool, thanks. I appreciate it. And I'm working a few other angles, too, so it'll be good. Could you keep this discreet though?"

She drinks and nods, worried that this is yet another secret from Emily. Although then again, Emily clearly has her hands full, she may not want to know the ins and outs of Ryan's work issues. Maybe she's taken a page from Evelyn Mayfield's book: as long as he brings home the bucks...

"So while we're here...having a heart to heart..."

Charlotte knows exactly where this conversation is headed. She readies her defense.

"Emily told me it was pretty chilly between you and Mari last night?"

"It's not chilly, it's just...weird," Charlotte says.

"Okay, weird then," Ryan concedes. "But that's not good. What do we do to...un-weird this?"

"I don't know, I guess, honestly, I'm still a little mad." Charlotte leans back in the booth, sighs. "She's just so judgmental sometimes, Ryan, you know she is, and I can't take it."

"Charlotte, you were sleeping with a married man."

"Engaged," she says more forcefully than she should given it is such a weak defense and Ryan just raises an eyebrow. But it's not as if Charlotte needs any reminders of her ill-advised, to put it mildly, ten-month-long affair with Carlos. She'd had every intention of breaking it off as soon as she learned about the fiancée—Charlotte can't bear to say, or even think, her name. But then Carlos had told her all about his doubts, about how his fiancée was someone his parents were pushing on him, a business alliance more than anything, how he just needed some time to sort things out, that Charlotte was who he really wanted to be with blah, blah, blah. Now, with the cruel clarity of hindsight, she can see all of it for the calculating, manipulative bullshit it was, but at the time... She's so ashamed, of the affair yes, but mainly of her own stupidity.

It's all the oldest cliché in the book and Charlotte is better than clichés. Or so she thought.

Ryan is staring at her, pointedly. "She just cares about you. She hated to see you get hurt like that. That was a train wreck, Charlotte."

"I know, I know. I get it." She does, she really does. "I'm a train wreck."

"I didn't say you were a train wreck, Char. But the situation was."

Ryan is kind to say this, but the truth that Charlotte is coming to realize is that she is a train wreck, a fact proven by the countless mistakes she's made with men pretty much since she lost her virginity to her crush Elliot Mason, junior year on the Branson School spring break ski trip, only to find out he only slept with her because Bradley bet him twenty bucks he wouldn't be able to get her to do it. At this point she has a pretty clear picture of her countless missteps and stupidities, if not the why and the how to change it. It feels like every time she tries to turn over a new leaf, it blows away in the wind. But her love life is punishing enough, she doesn't need her friends piling it on, too.

"I get that. But sometimes I just feel like Mari can be so sanctimonious. And when I called that weekend, I was devastated, Ryan. I really thought he might change his mind. Instead he walked down the aisle with...her. And while I'm sobbing, what does Mari say? 'Pull it together, Charlotte. You knew this was going to happen.' Which was basically the same as saying, I told you so. And isn't the number one rule of friendship that you don't never say, I told you so! And worse? Her tone, Ryan!"

Charlotte is getting all worked up again thinking about their conversation. "She was dismissing and patronizing. Like she didn't have time to deal with my petty drama.

That just wasn't what I needed in the moment. I needed a friend, not a lecture."

Charlotte's eyes threaten to well with tears as if they'd had this conversation yesterday, not two months ago.

Ryan nods sympathetically. "That was harsh for sure."

"I just feel like you're there for your friend even if she's making a mistake. And you don't judge. Right?"

"Well for the record, I know she feels bad about how she reacted. You have to cut her some slack, too, though. She was dealing with everything with her mom. You both had a moment. Can't you just move on?"

He thinks back to how Emily had drama for weeks with her friend over some slight at her baby shower. Why is it so hard for chicks to move on? He can't remember a time when things were ever "weird" with him and his buddies. Even when Colin had sex with Emily's cousin at their New York wedding celebration, after he specifically said to him per Emily's orders: "Hands off Emily's cousin, okay?" Ryan still all but forgot about it a week later.

"We have moved on. We're here, right?"

"Yeah, but apparently not really talking? It's time to truly clear the air, make nice."

Ryan's Blackberry buzzes on the table. It's Emily: Coming home soon? He can't tell if there's a note of sarcasm in the text, but he chooses to give Emily the benefit of the doubt.

"Come on, let's get back." He downs the last dregs of mimosa in his glass. "I have some making nice to do myself."

* * *

A thin stream of clouds moves swiftly across the steel grey

sky. Fall announces its arrival with an unseasonably chilly afternoon for September; "sweater weather" as Emily's mother would say. Emily is all too pleased by this because fall in New York is her favorite and all too fleeting time of year, and because she is all too happy to hide her still puffy "baby body" under many layers. She's snuggled Owen into a crochet sweater Ryan's mom made for him, which is too big since he wasn't meant to wear it for another month or two but adorable nonetheless.

It seems to take her forever to leave the house these days, but at last after packing the diaper bag, one last change of clothes—Owen's and hers—double-checking she has the pacifier, an extra blanket, an extra pair of clothes, an extra...everything, she, Ryan, and Charlotte are finally making their way to Central Park. Of all of the amenities of their apartment, that it's only ten blocks to the south end of Central Park is her favorite. She and Owen have whiled away many afternoons there, which even when crowded still manages to feel like her own private oasis.

There are so many nooks and crannies and wonderful parts of the 800-plus acre park to explore and yet most days, she sits on a bench right near the southeast entrance, at the water's edge of the aptly named, "The Pond." She rarely talks to anyone, well anyone but Owen. But every Wednesday at 1 p.m., like clockwork, an elderly woman appears and sits on the bench next to the one Emily considers "hers."

The woman is always alone, and has no book, no music, not even any bread for the ducks. She just comes and sits on the bench for exactly an hour and then leaves.

Emily has watched her for a few weeks entertaining a fantasy that one day she'll work up the nerve to go talk to the mysterious stranger who will be warm and wise and impart all sorts of unforgettable and life-changing wisdom to Emily over a series of weekly chats. Or the woman could just be crazy and start speaking in gibberish. In New York City that was the chance you took with just about every encounter with a stranger.

But Emily has a sense that it's the former, that the woman is charming and sage and maybe a little lonely. This is because Emily generally believes in giving people the benefit of the doubt, while Ryan believes that everyone is out to "get theirs." She wonders what point of view will prevail upon Owen and which is better? Taken to the extreme, is it better to go through life being naïve or cynical?

As she ponders this—and lately she spends enormous chunks of time pondering, what will Owen be like?—Ryan grabs her hand, and it's such an unexpected delight she feels giddy, the tension lifted. Her mother once told her, "It's not how much you fight, it's how well you make up," and Emily is proud that she and Ryan do at least tend to make up well. So far.

"So Mari's meeting us here later?" Charlotte asks, determined not to feel like the creepy third wheel in the wholesome tableau of Mom, Dad, and Baby. Do they have to hold hands?

"Yeah, when she left she said her meeting would be a couple of hours. I told her we'd be in the park and to call us," Emily says.

Before she and Ryan got back from their "run" Mari had left for some sort informational interview with a friend of Ted's. That was really all that Charlotte knew since she and Mari hadn't spoken beyond swapping a few perfunctory, logistical emails in the weeks leading up to this weekend. Ryan's words ring in her head, make nice.

"Speaking of work. When do you go back, Em?" Charlotte asks as they settle on a bench.

"Oh...I'm...I'm not." Emily should not have been caught off guard because this is a perfectly reasonable question and yet she is. She didn't have time to calibrate her tone of voice to say this more confidently, proudly.

"Oh...really?" Charlotte is very surprised. As far as she knew, Emily loved her job at the gallery and was doing well.

"Ryan and I just thought that it would be better...me staying home with the baby..." Emily admonishes herself again for her hesitance, for the uncertainty that creeps into her voice when she explains that she's going to be a stay-at-home mom.

She's been reading a lot about the mommy wars online and

understands that there's no room for ambivalence. Whatever the case, working mom, or stay-at-home, one has to be loud and proud when it comes to one's choices.

"I make plenty of money. Em doesn't have to work," Ryan says. There's a patronizing edge to his voice that Charlotte doesn't care for and can't imagine Emily does either.

"But..." Charlotte is about to launch into a spiel about how there are reasons to work besides money. And about an article she just read in Glamour about how it can be hard to get back into the workforce after taking years off, but she stops herself, allows that maybe she's projecting because the thought of staying home all day with a baby makes her feel panicked. But Emily might...enjoy it? Who knows?

"Well, I am going to revisit down the line. Right now, I think I'll just take a year off and we'll see how it goes." Emily doesn't seem convinced, but Charlotte doesn't press. Though she can't quite figure out when this happened, as they slide into their thirties, Charlotte's come to understand that there are new rules now in her friendships.

Where once she and her friends used to quite freely comment on every dimension of one another's lives, give advice freely, even if it was unsolicited, tell each other exactly what they should (yes call him back) and shouldn't do (no, don't wear that to the interview), it now feels like they've started to erect some invisible boundaries around their diverging lives, like a plot of land they are nurturing and protecting. The fence says, stay out and let me do this and we'll see what grows. And also: what do you know of my life, anymore anyway. Come to think of it, she'd had that exact reaction when Mari tried to give her advice about Carlos. So Charlotte bites her tongue, live and let live.

Ryan's phone starts ringing and he gives Emily a sheepish look.

"Go, it's fine." Her exasperated tone is softened with a smile.

He walks away to deal with his work call with Owen still strapped to him, the picture of a multi-tasking dad, leaving Charlotte and Emily to watch the ducks float in lazy circles.

"You think I'm crazy for not going back to work right? I'm going to be one of those women whose brain turns to mush from baby talk day in and day out? Who has nothing to talk about but the Ferber method all day?"

Charlotte turns to look at Emily. "I think you have to do what's best for you," she offers as diplomatically, as supportively as she can, even though Emily all but read her mind, except for the Ferber part since she has no idea what on earth that is. "I think you have to do whatever makes you happy."

She says it like it's the simplest thing in the world, like figuring out what makes you happy, let alone doing it, hasn't proved to be harder than they all could have possibly imagined.

* * *

There really is a Starbucks on every corner of this city, Mari thinks as she finally, after two tries, finds the one that she is supposed to be at, the one on the east side of Madison and 44th, as opposed to the one on the west side of the street. It took her longer than she thought to walk down from Ryan and Emily's so she picked up the pace for the last five blocks and is now out of breath as she bursts through the door. First rule of a job interview—never be late. Not that this is an interview per se, but still.

She glances around and sees only one woman sitting alone surrounded by various sections of The New York Times. She calls to mind for Mari, "quintessential feminist activist;" she's in her early 60s, with a wild mess of long frizzy hair, flowy dress, a million silver bracelets climbing up her arm, no-makeup, no nonsense. Well, actually she doesn't just look the part, Frieda Stone is the part, being a pioneer as one of the first women to run her own law firm, Stone and Associates, and a legend for her work on Corning Glass vs. Brennan, one of the first equal pay for equal work cases to come before the Supreme Court.

Mari smooths her pencil skirt down with both sweaty palms and approaches the table. "Frieda?"

"Yes, yes, you must be Mari, sit." Frieda smiles warmly,

revealing deep, but becoming wrinkles all around her eyes, and begins stacking the various sections of the paper on top of each other.

"Thanks for seeing me. I'm such a...fan of you work." Did she really say that. A fan? "And Ted's really raved to me about you."

"I don't suppose he mentioned we were married? He usually leaves that part out." Frieda laughs and the wrinkles framing her eyes seem to move with her smile.

Mari is just glad she hadn't had time to get a coffee or she would have spit it out or spilled it all over in surprise. Ted was married!? She had always assumed Ted was a confirmed bachelor, married to his work, to the cause, in other words, a kindred spirit.

"Ah, it was just for a few years, way back in our twenties. It just didn't work out.

You might say, life got in the way. Anyhoo, enough of the girl talk." She places both elbows on the table and leans in. "Ted says you're the best young lawyer he's worked with and that means a lot coming from him. I don't have to tell you what a hard ass he is."

Mari is beyond flattered, but as usual, she's unsure how to deal with such an effusive compliment, so she just smiles and offers a too quiet, "That's nice to hear."

Frieda marches on. "A lot of lawyers come through the EJP and places like it and they want to do good and they have all this idealism but then they get burned out or realize they want to make money like everyone else, not that there's anything wrong with that. Ted says you have wherewithal though."

Wherewithal. Mari Castillo is a woman with wherewithal. She's pleased to think of herself this way. "I like to think so. I love the work."

"Well, he also doesn't think you should work there any more."

Again, Mari is glad she doesn't have coffee, because what? Ted doesn't want her? Now, she's thoroughly confused. Luckily it doesn't seem like Frieda wants, or needs, her to speak at all for this conversation to keep going.

"Relax, it's not like he's gonna fire you or anything. You're just like his baby bird.

He thinks you've done a lot of good the last four years and now it may be time for you to leave the nest. And I mentioned to him I was looking for someone sharp, hardworking, someone with wherewithal, to join my team and he told me about you. I have an opportunity if you want to hear it about it." She goes on without letting Mari answer.

"Basically, at my firm, despicable people pay us despicable amounts of money to get them off after doing despicable things. Mainly white-collar kind of stuff, which I think is the worst of the lot. I mean I'd take someone stealing for his family or an addict looking to score any day. Anyhoo, I'm starting to get nauseous every time we get one of these assholes off. And we're good, so we always do. So I want to take the money we're making off the bad seeds and start a robust pro bono operation, get back to my roots, to the work that mattered before I, myself, became a sellout. Thinking of a full-time team of three to four lawyers to start. I especially want to take on national, high profile civil rights cases, advising the legal teams on the ground because, hey even if it's pro bono might as well get the firm some big time publicity, right? I have a literary agent friend who said that all the crap books that sell millions of copies are the ones that subsidize the good books. This'll be the same idea, all of the horrible 'criminals of industry' I represent will pay for me to do the good work I wanna do. It'll help me sleep at night."

"So you'd like me to be one of the lawyers?"

Frieda looks at Mari like she's missed a very important point. "No, honey, I want you to run the whole shebang. Hire the team, find the right cases, make this work."

Wow, Mari thinks and then says. "That sounds like an amazing opportunity."

"I'll do you one better—like I said money isn't an issue. You can name your salary and I'll do my best to meet it. You seem like the type who might sell yourself short. My generation, we had to have balls to get what we wanted, since boobs were sort of a liability. At least in one sense." She chuckles. "So don't sell yourself short, huh? New York ain't cheap. case in point, I just paid five bucks for this latte."

New York City? A prestigious law firm? High profile pro bono cases? Naming her salary? It's a lot for Mari to process. She already got the one thing she wanted most this year, her mom's recovery, this seems too much, an embarrassment of riches she doesn't deserve. Or does she? She's worked hard, sacrificed so much, like for instance any sense of a life outside of work. Maybe, a little voice inside her that sounds suspiciously like her mother says, you do deserve this. Maybe it's exactly what you deserve. Her heart starts racing faster thinking of all the possibilities.

"I'm so honored and intrigued. When do I need to let you know?"

"End of the year good? I know you have to things to finish up with Ted. The Jenkins appeal, now that's an interesting case."

"That sounds great." Mari's relieved that she'll have some time to think on it.

Frieda nods and pulls the front page off her stack of papers. It's clear that Mari is dismissed.

"Okay, well, thank you again," Mari says getting up to leave. She finds her legs are trembling and steadies herself.

"A word of advice?" Frieda says just as Mari turns for the door.

"Sure, please."

"Take the job." She winks and looks back down at the paper.

Mari stands on the corner outside Starbucks slowing her heart rate, metaphorically pinching herself, trying to process what just happened, trying to comprehend the dizzying number of ways that life can change in an instant. Then ignoring the throng of strangers around her who look at her curiously, she breaks out into loud, giddy laughter and begins walking up Fifth, imagining that the City is hers.

After all, soon it may be.

* * *

Emily can barely breathe. It took two pairs of Spanx to get into this dress, but Ryan insisted she wear it, his favorite, and so here she is imagining the engineering feat it's going to take to peel off her shapewear if she eats even one more bite. The problem is the food is beyond delicious so she plans to have many, many more bites. Emily takes another sip of an exquisite crab bisque soup, which feels like velvet on her tongue.

Ryan has rented the much coveted, especially on a Saturday night, private dining room at the W Hotel in Union Square. It has all the hominess and intimacy of dining at home (a very, very nice home), but with a world-class chef, Todd English, cooking the food.

It's only too bad that Ryan also chose to invite Colin and Eric and their girlfriends, all of whom Emily finds incredibly pretentious and half hour into dinner can tell Mari and Charlotte do, too.

Colin has an annoying habit of mentioning how he went to school in New Haven at every opportunity, which Emily overhears him doing just now to Charlotte. Just say you went to Yale! She wants to scream, or better yet, does he really need to mention his Ivy League education at all? You don't hear them mentioning Harvard every thirty seconds.

Charlotte, having been to more dinners like this and rubbed shoulders with more snobby jerks of this sort than she cares to count, deftly banters about golf, Turks and Caicos, and sample sales, while all the while thinking, Really Ryan? You like these people? She's tried to give them the benefit of the doubt, but truly they're insufferable.

Charlotte and Mari exchange can-you-believe-this glances across the table when Colin leans over and asks Charlotte how on earth a "catch" like her hasn't been "snatched up"? The main course hasn't even arrived yet and he's already barely one disgusting step away from placing a hand on her thigh or rubbing a foot up her leg under the table, while his girlfriend grits her freshly whitened teeth and pours another glass of Merlot.

But Mari is still feeling so buoyant after her meeting with Frieda this morning, that nothing can bring her down, not even Eric's girlfriend, Elaine, making a truly hideous comment about how even though she supports our troops, it's a fact that it's mainly people who "aren't smart enough to have other opportunities" who join up, so it's no wonder Iraq is a disaster. And then seconds later asking Mari how on earth she can live in the South. "Isn't everyone so...backward and closed-minded?" Pot, kettle much, Elaine?

Fortunately, Ryan orders bottle after bottle of wine so by the time dessert arrives they can, with the generous blind spot that alcohol allows, almost—almost—convince themselves that they had a good time.

Actually, Ryan, for one, did have a good time and he's looking forward to keeping it going. "You guys ready to, go?" He tops off his glass as he asks.

"The check hasn't come yet, babe," Emily says patting his leg, though she is already counting down how quickly they can get home. Twenty minutes, she hopes; thirty if there's traffic up Madison.

"Oh, I took care of it," Ryan says and Charlotte wonders if she's the only one to catch the surprised look on Emily's face.

Mari quickly calculates. The bill was easily a thousand bucks, possibly more.

Charlotte is one thing, but Ryan has apparently jumped a tax bracket...or two. When did that happen? Granted Mari's not yet at their level where she can spring for dinner for eight, but she'll be glad to be at the point where she no longer cringes when the check comes and thinks about her share. Mari goes one step further and allows herself an exhilarating fantasy where she is the one picking up the tab, where she is the one buying $400 dresses at sample sales, where she is rewarded with her standard 80-plus- hour work week with a paycheck that per hour may amount to significantly more than minimum wage. Thanks to Frieda that day may well be within reach.

Mari shudders to consider that this line of thinking, that

leaving EJP, makes her a sellout. As her dad, whose dinnertime stories about his destitute childhood days often cast a guilty pall over any meal that was more than rice or beans, always said, "There's nothing inherently noble about poverty. Trust me."

"Well, thanks big spender." Colin slaps Ryan on the back. "Where to now?"

"There's a great lounge in the basement of the hotel here. We could check that out. Or go over to Lotus?" Ryan stands up, stumbling a bit, and misses the imploring look Emily gives him.

"Ryan, it's late and I'm exhausted. We told the sitter we'd be home by midnight." Emily hates the needy tone in her voice. Further hates that Ryan has put her in the position to be the nag. But there is no way in hell she's going to another lounge, let alone Lotus, a loud, packed nightclub in the Meatpacking District.

"We'll just pay her more money." Ryan shrugs as if it's the easiest solution in the world. "I'm sure she'll be happy to stay, make another $100 bucks. So, who's in?"

Everyone looks around awkwardly. It seems Ryan is the only one oblivious to the sudden tension in the room. Charlotte sees Colin and his girlfriend—Lisa? Lila? Charlotte can't remember— quickly confer.

"Sounds fun to us!" the girlfriend says and Charlotte suspects that she's just trying to one up Emily, and to remind Colin who moments ago was practically drooling on Charlotte, how fun she is, how she's the type of girl to go with the flow, the flow being whatever Colin wants. Charlotte has a feeling she's the type to pretend to like football as much as he does too, and that she plans elaborate snacks for "the big game." God, she probably even has a form fitting jersey. Charlotte decides she hates her.

Eric and Elaine quickly chime in that they're in too and Charlotte sees Emily is right on the edge, on the verge of losing it if someone, preferably Ryan but anyone, doesn't join team Emily stat so Charlotte does.

"Well, I for one am stuffed and exhausted. Emily, do you mind if we go home?"

Charlotte is happy to take on the role of the lame one if it gets them out of here as soon as possible. She plans never to see these people again.

"Me, too," Mari chimes in loyally, although tonight of all nights, given her exuberant mood she wouldn't have minded keeping the celebrations going and getting a preview of the city's hotspots. But then again, she also doesn't necessarily want to spend another second with E-Squared and the Snobersons, as she's taken to calling them in her head, so it's settled.

They make their way through the lobby and Ryan staggers out into the street to start hailing cabs.

"You guys first," he says to Emily chivalrously when a cab pulls over. When he leans over to kiss her, she turns her head and his warm, whiskey-soaked breath shoots into her ear. He still seems largely oblivious to the dynamics unfolding and cheerfully says he'll see them later.

Charlotte, Mari, and Emily pile into the backseat of the cab. It's clear Emily is seething and Charlotte and Mari aren't quite sure what to do or say, so they remain silent and let her stew.

"I don't know what's gotten into him. Seriously," she says after a minute, leaning her head onto the cool glass of the window.

"Well, tonight I think a little too much red wine got into him," Mari offers.

"It's just, all exhausting." Emily sighs and closes her eyes.

Charlotte and Mari aren't sure if she means the socializing, or the baby, or Ryan, or marriage, but suspect it's probably all of the above.

When they get home, Emily relieves the babysitter, quickly feeds Owen and asks if one of them can keep an eye on him while she takes a shower, which they are happy to do.

Mari sits at the kitchen island with Owen in her lap. She looks down at the baby with something like longing.

"You're a natural," Charlotte says, sipping water on the other side of the island.

"Really? I guess. I do love babies."

"Well, you know if you want to have one, you have to have sex, right?" The teasing is a risk given the strain between them, but Mari takes it in the spirit with which it was delivered: lovingly.

She laughs. "Yeah, think I heard that somewhere."

They're quiet for a minute while Mari strokes Owen's silky hair. It's the first time they've really been alone together all weekend and it's like they know the moment has come and they're both waiting for the other to speak. But it's not tense, thankfully. The wine has probably helped.

Charlotte breaks the silence. "Look, I'm sorry, Mari."

"Me, too," says Mari simply.

"Do you want to have breakfast in the morning? Just the two of us? Talk?" Charlotte asks.

Mari smiles. "Yeah, that sounds great."

"Good because something tells me we're not going to want to be here in the morning." Charlotte laughs. "We can get the hell out of Dodge."

And so, tomorrow there would be, for all of them, a lot of talking to be done, a lot of accusing, defending, explaining, apologizing, forgiving, repairing, the difficult but necessary calibrations that keep relationships functioning. But for now— Charlotte leans over and hugs Mari, kisses Owen's tiny forehead—it's time for bed.

Chapter Six
Paris, 2007

By the time Ryan hears the girls' giddy voices echo down the hall and then fade away, he is already sprawled out on top of the bed. It's too lumpy for his taste and the comforter is a threadbare sateen, but that's to be expected with a hotel that bills itself as "quaint" and "nestled off the beaten path." If Ryan had his way they'd be at the W, not a turn of the previous century hotel in the 3rd arrondissement with faded wallpaper and brocade drapes that have likely been hanging since Marie Antoinette ate cake. But someone had recommended the hotel to Mari, and to be fair she did all the planning for the trip to Paris, and so who was he to complain. At least out loud. And besides all he needs right at the moment is darkness, quiet, and a bed, any bed.

His eyes drift closed and he contemplates when was the last time he slept more than three hours in a row. Weeks, he calculates. Not since law school exams has he had a stretch with such little sleep and even then he somehow managed to carve out a few hours of sleep during the day after staying up all night to study. Not so the last few weeks. First he was pulling all nighters on the Henderson case, squeezing in quick 3 a.m. cat naps with his head resting in the crook of his arm on his desk like a fifth grader. He finally finished the extensive brief for the case—the case he had thought of as a reward when Tripper billed it as a "high profile opportunity," and then quickly realized, as the frustrations piled up, that it might actually have been a punishment for some unknown transgression. Tripper's passive aggressive antics get worse each year, and shuffling this case off to Ryan at the very last minute just as Tripper himself jetted off to spend nearly all of August in Nantucket was really not even passive anymore. Just aggressive.

Ryan feels his heart beginning to speed up as he fumes, though he's too wiped at the moment to get as worked up as he had in the last few weeks, including a low moment involving calling a rude cab driver a really rude name, because sometimes you fucking couldn't take it and who else was he supposed to lash out at?

But seriously, what the hell? He was supposed to have some measurable autonomy, his own team even by now, a condition promised him upon making junior partner (the youngest in firm's history) a year and a half ago. "You just need a little more mentorship," Tripper had told him at the time, unable to keep the condescension out of his voice, not that he tried very hard. But whenever Ryan tries to broach the subject there's another hurdle, another test, another crucible. case in point: Henderson. Which, of course, he rocked, no sleep and all! But he knows it still isn't going to be enough. He needs to figure out a way to get out from under Tripper's thumb once and for all, but at the moment he is too tired to mull over such machinations.

As if the work drama weren't enough, then Owen comes down with the croup, which Ryan had heretofore thought was one of those archaic diseases that had been safely eradicated, like polio or whooping cough. The poor little guy had a wheezing, phlegmy cough that sounded like an eighty-year-old man who smoked a pack a day, not a twenty-pound toddler. It also meant that Owen, who had just started sleeping through the night a few months before, now didn't sleep—at all. Emily insisted Ryan stay up all night, too, giving Owen steam baths to clear his lungs, or just pressing a cool compress to his head, which honestly didn't seem to do much beyond making Emily feel useful. And neither of these things was a two-person job to Ryan's mind, so he didn't understand why they both needed to be awake, especially when Ryan still had to get up at 6 a.m. for work. Each night he waited and waited for Emily to say the magic words, "It's okay, honey, I got this, you go to sleep." But he suspected Emily was probably punishing him for his week of all nighters, whether she realized it or not.

Punishing all around, that's what Ryan's life feels like these days. At work, at home, there was no break, no escape. Lately, the days blurred into each other in a relentless swirl of deliverables and meetings; diaper changes and midnight dashes to Food Emporium or Duane Reade for something Emily or Owen needs.

Ryan opens his eyes and stares at the plaster ceiling. An image has popped into his head. His father, sitting in his worn brown leather recliner, where he perched every evening that Ryan spent at his house (every other week by custody arrangement). After dinner (invariably something frozen and microwaved) his dad would collapse in the chair to watch the game—whatever sport that happened to be depending on the season—and then retire to bed to watch the ten o'clock news with a, "good night son." Ryan marvels: his dad likely got at least eight solid hours of sleep every night for forty years.

For all of the ways Ryan has wished his life to be different from his father's that seems pretty fucking awesome right now.

Now Ryan squeezes his eyes shut against a different memory: Emily's annoyed voice from moments ago when he told her he was going to stay behind and sleep.

"You guys go ahead. Have some girl time!" he said in an attempt to make the gesture seem generous.

"Ryan! We're only here for four days! And it's Paris." Paris said with nothing short of utter reverence even though Emily's been here several times before. But she had also spent the last week in a full panic that they would have to cancel the trip if Owen didn't turn a corner. And luckily he did, was almost good as new by Thursday, but Ryan had already decided that having shelled out $3,000 for their round-trip tickets they were going no matter what.

Emily's mom, who they flew in to stay with Owen, could surely handle a toddler recovering from a little cold, he'd rationalized.

Ryan lets out a big sigh, rolls over and punches the limp pillow in a futile attempt to add some buoyancy and as a small act of aggression. Emily could be annoyed; she would get over it. Ryan just needs a stretch of time where no one needs anything from him—not Owen, not Emily, not Tripper, not his paralegals, not his clients, not the homeless man next to his office who gruffly demands a dollar from him every single day.

And if he has to hole up alone in a dark hotel in Paris to make that happen, so be it.

There were worse crimes.

* * *

It's windy and there's a sharp chill in the air, the sun continually disappears behind thick clouds, but none of them mind. They all sport variations of the same outfit, jeans, trendy blazer and high leather boots, exactly the way each of them pictured themselves in Paris. Fall French chic.

Mari, Charlotte, and Emily wander down the sidewalk in a cheery gaggle, like school girls released on a field trip or at the end of the school year, all boundless energy for the unexpected adventures ahead. For a minute, the trio links arms and laugh as they walk side-by-side, Laverne and Shirley style, or like they're in a Playtex commercial.

It's affected and genuine at the same time.

They look up and all around them, the centuries old buildings, the wrought iron Juliet balconies, the laundry flapping in the brisk breeze. Mari says what they all are thinking: "This city is amazing." Emily and Charlotte enthusiastically agree, but for Mari it's extra special because she's here in the City of Lights for the very first time, a much dreamed of, bucket list trip just in time for her thirtieth.

Paris, so far, three hours after landing on a redeye and winding their way from the airport to the hotel, is just as she conjured from reading A Moveable Feast: charming sidewalk cafes; glamorous women, dressed to the nines, walking small dogs; old men painting water colors. Okay, so perhaps she hasn't seen any elderly painters yet, but it's just a matter of time.

"So what's our plan?" Emily asks.

"Walk, explore, make our way over for shopping, sightseeing along the Champs Elyse?" Charlotte says.

According to Mari's guidebook (consulted secretly since she doesn't want to appear like a total rube, especially after everyone teased her for reading Hemingway on the plane), the iconic street is about a fifteen-minute walk. Charlotte seems to know exactly where she's going; of course she does, she's been to Paris a million times, so Mari is happy to follow her lead.

"Perfect," Mari says, though she's somewhat distracted by the sight of the Eiffel Tower looming in the distance.

"Can we make a pit stop for an espresso?" Emily asks. She is exhausted. Beyond exhausted, though not so much so that she was going to stay back at the hotel sleeping (ahem). She's powering through on a rush of adrenaline and sheer will she hasn't harnessed since Owen was a newborn, not that she feels the need to be all dramatic about it like Ryan. And not that she would miss one moment of being out and about, and most important, childfree. She misses Owen, acutely, physically, especially after having his clammy little body nestled in her lap for the majority of last week. Seeing her normally vibrant one year old, who still marveled at his ability to get from point A to point B on two legs and loved the sound of his own voice with his every growing monosyllabic vocabulary ("bye-bye"), be so listless and vulnerable nearly broke her heart. But not coming to Paris for this much needed weekend away (her very first since having O) would also have broken her heart in a different (more selfish) way, so for many reasons she's glad Owen is better.

She intends to wring the weekend of every drop of delight possible. To savor not having a heavy diaper bag on her shoulder, to dress in a crisp white shirt she wouldn't dare at home, to leisurely eat meal after meal without a Cheerio in sight, to wander slowly through city streets and boutiques and museums. The museums! It feels like a miracle. So as much as she needs sleep, she's certainly not going to waste a day like Ryan. Besides having done the U.S. to Dublin trip more times than she can count growing up, she very well knows that when you take the redeye, the best way to avoid jet lag is just to power through. She'll be zonked by 10pm and Ryan is going to be up all night. Totally out of sync. She doesn't want to recognize the irony of this—that part of the point of this trip to Paris, for her at least, was the opportunity for her and Ryan to reconnect, to get back in sync. Only they would have to be awake at the same time for that.

"Yes, to espresso. I know a great café near where we're headed," Charlotte says.

"I wish I could spend the day with you all...and not have to meet Gabe's aunt for lunch."

"Wait what?" Emily says. "Gabe's aunt?"

"I told you this. Gabe mentioned to her that his 'girlfriend' was going to be here in Paris and she insisted on meeting me."

Now Mari is surprised. "Girlfriend, huh?" She smiles, nudges Charlotte.

"Oh please, don't start." Charlotte throws her head back dramatically.

"Well, you didn't tell me you guys were using labels now," Mari teases. "That's great." Then, tentatively: "Right?"

Since Charlotte met Gabe four months ago, Mari has had a tough time getting a read on this situation. In fact, she and Emily had an hour-long conversation about it just last week and ended up confused as ever about what Charlotte wants and why she seems so lukewarm about Gabe who is by all accounts is a great guy and crazy about her. But, Charlotte being unpredictable? What else is new?

"Yeah, it's good. Gabe's great. We're great." Charlotte says this as enthusiastically as she can manage. This is her reflexive response whenever anyone asks about how things are going with Gabe in the same way people say, "fine" when asked how they are, because no one wants to hear the convoluted truth of it, which in this case can be summed up as: Gabe is perfect on paper, a real stand up guy, and Charlotte should like him and so she tries, tries hard, but... Well, maybe it's not so convoluted after all.

When Gabe approached her, at a bar last May where she was treating her team to drinks as part of her ongoing but futile campaign to convince them she's one of them and not the "the CEO's daughter," she'd sized him in up in milliseconds: recent SF transplant via the Midwest, working in tech, not a start-up but someplace more established, has a dog, probably a lab, goes to Muir Woods to hike on the weekends, owns more than one Patagonia fleece vest. Turns out she was right on almost all counts. His dog is actually a boxer, named Bailey.

In the absence of electric attraction, Charlotte agreed to go out with him for a few reasons. One, because he's generically attractive in the way that reminds her of every guy cast as the "nice" guy in every Lifetime movie ever made: sandy blonde hair, pleasing symmetric features, unassuming smile complete with dimple. Also because he seemed exceedingly pleasant, cheerful...safe. In other words, like he didn't have an addiction, massive debt, or secret fiancée. And lastly, and mainly, because after chatting for just a few minutes about what she can't even remember, he'd actually said, "You seem great and I'd love to take you out next Saturday night." The aw shucks straightforwardness of that was so disarming, "sure" fell off her lips before she even quite realized it.

There was another reason: other than one unwise, drunken, protection-less, one-night stand in the spring that left her racing to the gyno for a full work up and all clear (which, phew!), she hadn't slept with anyone since Carlos, her longest dry spell ever.

Leaving her to wonder, how the hell does Mari do it? Turns out celibacy doesn't suit Charlotte, at all, and she wanted to get laid—albeit responsibly.

So she agreed to go out with Gabe. First, to a Giants game (nosebleed seats, she didn't mention her family owned a box) and then again (to see Ocean's Thirteen) and again (a Saturday hike in the Muir Woods, no surprise), until before she knew it she overheard him referring to her as his girlfriend. And this, Charlotte found, was actually a quite enticing development, especially that it happened without any sort of coercion, manipulations, or ultimatums. And Charlotte liked the idea of being someone's girlfriend, being claimed, of knowing exactly where she stands with a man, even if she isn't sure about her feelings for Gabe himself. So she's doing her best to ignore the fact that some days she feels like she's dating a labrador puppy.

"Well, I'm so glad you're bringing him out for my party. We can't wait to meet him," Mari says, oblivious to Charlotte's mulling.

"Yeah, Ryan has mentioned a few times that he's ready to grill him, make sure he's good enough for you." Emily laughs.

Charlotte is touched by that, relishes imagining Gabe sweating under Ryan's scrutiny. Though the truth is, Gabe, like a labrador puppy, is pretty impossible not to like. Which is why Charlotte didn't plan to invite him in the first place; everyone is bound to get way too excited about "their future." Gabe, though, had just assumed he was coming when he heard her talking about the trip and Mari's thirtieth birthday party.

Charlotte had, in fact, already booked her ticket, and further, had already starting wondering if she might meet someone new at the party, you never knew. But she quickly called American and booked Gabe a ticket, lucking out and getting two seats together as if it were her plan all along. He was actually hinting at coming on this trip, too, but she drew the line.

She understands that Mari and Emily are just happy for her, but she also finds it slightly cloying. It's almost as if she's a child learning to ride a bike, *Oh look Charlotte, look at you, you're doing it, a healthy relationship!* This is unfair, she realizes; they mean well and want the best for her, but she just wishes she didn't feel like the subtext of every conversation about Gabe wasn't, *he's SUCH a nice guy, you're crazy to mess this up.*

Case in point: "He seems perfect for you, Charlotte...smart, successful, tall.

Adorable," says Mari now. "You deserve a nice guy like

that."

Charlotte silently bristles at what she suspects Mari's generously left unsaid: *and not like the other assholes you've dated.*

"Yeah, I know. I can't say it's love at first sight but he's growing on me." She smiles. It's a stretch, but Charlotte at least knows enough to at least wish this were true, and if she continues to try hard enough, it might be.

"Well, we can't all have love at first sight like Ryan and Em," Mari says and Charlotte can't quite understand why she's perpetuating this fairy tale when it was pretty clear that Ryan wasn't in love with Emily at first sight. But he did fall in love, so perhaps the specific point at which that happened doesn't matter. Still though, Charlotte finds it a little ridiculous.

"Well, love or not at this point, it's just nice to wake up with someone on Sunday morning." Charlotte thinks about all the lonely Sundays she endured before she met Gabe, when after her morning run or occasional brunch the empty hours stretched before her. Hours she filled with fantasies of what her ideal Sunday would be like (grocery shopping and preparing lavish dinners with her partner, sex marathons, snuggling together on the couch re-watching The Notebook), and then becoming increasingly demoralized at how much her actual Sunday (organizing closets, reviewing spreadsheets, dinner with her parents as a last resort) diverged from said fantasy. So that by 9 p.m. she was climbing into her pajamas eager for the day to be over.

"And I bet it's nice to go to bed with him on Saturday night, too!" Mari laughs.

"Wouldn't you like to know..." Charlotte plays coy, but only because the reality is the sex is really nothing to write home about. How she wishes she had some juicy details to share but they've barely moved past missionary; Gabe fucks her respectfully, kindly, as if they were thirty years older and might retire to side-by-side twin beds afterwards. But is that a reason to break up with someone? Especially someone who asks you about your day and listens to your litany of trivial complaints about it and who remembers your little quirks, like that you hate mint. Is mediocre sex better than no sex? In Charlotte's current calculations, yes.

"At least you're having sex." Emily doesn't mean to say this, instantly wishes she could take it back. She's open with her other girlfriends, her mom friends, about her sex life, or lack thereof, because they get it. But since Mari and Charlotte are Ryan's friends first and foremost, she feels disloyal and oddly embarrassed. She quickly adds: "I mean, we've just been busy lately, with Owen, and Ryan has been on this insane case..." She hopes she's made it sound like it's only been a few weeks since they've had sex, not months. Or to be exact—Emily quickly calculates—not since after her friend Brie's thirtieth birthday party in May, a full five months, almost half a year, she realizes with horror.

Last week she met up with some moms from Owen's music group for coffee. Emily's by far the youngest one in the group, by at least five years (and more than one woman has hinted that Owen must have been accident), but finds that even if she considers herself a young hip mom, the experience of motherhood is pretty universal despite one's age and that, sadly, all of the clichés that she thought she would avoid by virtue of her age ("we won't be those people who never go out!" and "we'll still have sex all the time!") are fairly unavoidable.

Over donuts and croissants, universally consumed with requisite regret ("I really shouldn't be eating these! The calories!"), the conversation quickly took the typical turn to the inadequacies of their partners and then to sex and how everyone was too tired (or busy or bloated) to do it. One of the women, a self-proclaimed "renegade single mother," who at forty-two is pretty clearly still trying to hang on to twenty-nine by way of skinny jeans and graphic tank tops from Forever 21 said, "Well, ladies if you don't fuck your husband, someone else will. Guaranteed."

Remembering this, Emily cringes. The messenger notwithstanding, Emily has heard enough horror stories to know that there's some truth to this cruel calculation.

Not that she doesn't trust Ryan, she does, completely, but she still she has to do her part and if she's honest, she's probably rolled over in bed one too many times in the last few months. Well, not tonight. An exciting idea grows: she will seduce her husband this weekend. Big time. Like blow his mind. She can even find some sexy lingerie while they shop today.

"So here we are," Charlotte says as they come to a circle that opens onto the wide avenue of the Champs-Élysées, the Arc de Triomphe rising at the distant end. Mari is a tad disappointed to see that it's mainly populated with pudgy tourists with fanny packs and guidebooks, and dotted with American retailers (a Disney store? Really?), but she can still, if she squints, picture it the way she had imagined as she read A Moveable Feast, with men in bowlers and women with parasols strolling on a sunny day.

"I told you it's a little touristy, but I know some great, local places," Charlotte assures them. "We'll make our way to a fabulous boutique nearby. And have the best chocolate you've ever had. And Ladurée for macaroons!"

And so they explore, sampling sweets, caffeinating, window-shopping, people watching, and in Mari's case, thinking with astonishment, over and over, I'm in Paris!

They've made their way to a less crowded side street now and Charlotte leads them into Coquette, a tiny boutique. "This is the place I was telling you about. You'll love it." A bell above the door jingles as they enter.

"Charlotte, quelle surprise! Que fais-tu ici?" The owner, a petite woman in her seventies with a glossy, blunt bob, greets Charlotte enthusiastically. The two exchange pleasantries in French that Mari, despite two years of studying it in high school and some recent cramming, can't understand at all.

Charlotte turns to them. "This is the fabulous, Martine, you guys. She was a big time fashion designer and then retired and opened this shop where she features the best up-and-coming designers in France. My mom bought the dress for her rehearsal dinner here."

"I'm so pleased to meet you, ladies," Martine says, in her lyrical French accent, which sounds to Mari, impossibly sophisticated. "Welcome to Paris. Please look around.

I just got in some exquisite new items. Charlotte, you'll love this." She leads her over to a nearby table and holds up a blush pink cashmere sweater with delicate beading along the collar. Charlotte clasps her hands to her face like a little girl presented with an ice cream sundae. "Omigod, it's fabulous!"

Emily and Mari smile, used to seeing Charlotte transform into a giddy mess when presented with an object of affection up for sale, familiar with her actual squeal of delight at the feel of a leather bag, or a new pair of shoes on her feet.

"And I just got this. Is beautiful, no?" Martine holds up an emerald green silk dress that flows on the hanger. Mari doesn't realize it, but she's squealed Charlotte-style. She tentatively reaches out toward it as if it's too precious to be touched. The fabric is so light, so smooth.

Seeing Mari's uncharacteristic reaction, Emily and Charlotte look at each other.

"Mari, you have to try it on. It would look so good on you."

Martine senses the spell and the potential sale. She hands Mari the dress nudging her to the small fitting room—essentially a curtain on a circular rod—at the back of the store.

Mari takes the dress, carefully, and discreetly tries to find the non-existent price tag as Martine waves her on. She chooses not to even imagine how much it costs as she slips it over her head and the fabric streams down her body and settles in all the right places, framing her collarbone, tapering at her waist, ending just above the knee. She's been looking down at the dress, but when she looks up, in the dressing room mirror, when she takes in her reflection, she hardly recognizes the thin, glamorous, beaming person smiling back at her. It doesn't feel like a dress, it feels like a magic trick. She sweeps the curtain back, perhaps too dramatically, but she gets just the reactions she hoped for, oohs and awws all around.

"Wow, just wow." Charlotte has honestly never seen Mari look better. Mari has been transforming, Charlotte thinks, since she moved to the city—she's noticed the subtle way being in the city (and out of godforsaken Montgomery) has changed Mari by way of sleek haircut, arched eyebrows, trendy clothes. Mari would never cop to it, but she's clearly, if not entirely consciously, adopting New York's maintenance rituals and costumes: massive leather totes, Tory Burch flats, blowouts, weekly manicures because, hey it's only seven bucks. Even Mari, who proudly goes years without buying a new pair of jeans (much to Charlotte's horror), and who has been known to trim her own hair, has succumbed to the city's fashion and beauty de rigueur, made a thing by the models, fashion editors, actresses, hedge fund wives who wander the streets of New York as if they are always on the way to a Vogue shoot and not Starbucks. Or at least that's what Charlotte thought when she saw Chanel's Hydra Beauty Crème in Mari's toiletry case.

Martine nods her approval. "The designer is only twenty-six, a genius. She made three of these dresses only. See this?" Martine points to the lace hem. "Eight hundred stitches, by hand. All perfection." She sighs as if she can't believe the feat. "I've already sold the other two, but this one is for you."

"How much is it?" Mari asks tentatively, fearfully even. Her heart is actually racing.

Martine tsks like this is an inconsequential consideration. "A steal—600 U.S. Dollars."

Mari's stomach plunges. That's basically her rent for a week, for a dress. Even if she can afford it, it's not practical.

"You have to get it, Mar." Charlotte says, meeting her eyes in the mirror.

"Are you kidding? No way, this was just for fun." But a part of her...

"Then I'm buying it for you." Charlotte interrupts before Mari can even finish her thought. "You have to have that dress. Everyone has to have one piece of couture."

Mari isn't so sure about that rule in general, but she does have to have this dress.

She sees it now, clearly.

"Me, too!" Emily chimes in. "It will be from both of us. For your birthday! You can wear it for your party!"

Mari does another quick spin, considering. On one hand, it's too much. Even them splitting it, it's too much, too generous. On the other hand, it is gorgeous and she somehow likes the idea that this dress will be from the two of them. The sisterhood of the magical dress. And she feels something, a certain electricity coming off it, as crazy as that sounds, that makes it seem like this dress could be more than a dress, but a talisman. Perhaps she'll be wearing it when she meets her husband, or for her first Supreme Court appearance, or when she accepts some sort of global humanitarian award. This is a dress that makes her feel anything, and, everything is possible, and so she says, "Yes, okay! Omigod thank you guys so much."

Charlotte and Mari stand up to embrace her and the three friends smile at each other in the mirror. Martine looks on gleeful, because she's made a sale and also because these girls remind her of something, of herself thirty years ago, of her friend Vera who she hasn't seen in too many years, of the slim body she once cursed but now longs for. She basks in their refracted delight. Oh to be young again.

As Martine is ringing up the purchase and lovingly wrapping the dress in bright pink tissue paper, Charlotte looks at her watch. "Shit you guys I'm going to be late! I gotta go. My only hope is to pretend that I don't speak French. Maybe the visit will go that much faster?"

"You're terrible! I'm sure she's nice. She could be your future aunt-in-law. Be nice."

"On that note..." Charlotte air kisses Martine and quickly hugs Emily and Charlotte. "Enjoy the day! I'll see you back at the hotel," she calls as the door closes behind her.

"So what now? What do you want to do?" Mari asks Emily, knowing very well that though the rest of the day will be lovely, she's already experienced the best part.

Emily knows exactly what she wants to do. Even more inspired now by Mari's purchase, or more specifically the way that

Mari was transformed into some sort of confident super model when she put it on, Emily wants to shop for lingerie. She wants to wear the sexiest, skimpiest, most delicate bra and panties she can find—garters even!—and feel like a...nineteenth century courtesan. She is suddenly feeling desperate to do this, but she's also too mortified to tell Mari of the plan, much less have her come along on this intimate quest. So she lies, a small one.

"I think I'll head back to the hotel actually and check on Ryan, wake him up so we can have a late lunch. Is that cool?"

"Yeah, yeah, no problem. I think I'm going to explore a little bit. Meet back at the hotel around 6:00? Go to dinner?"

"Sounds good to me." Emily is already over the lie and wondering if she can sneak back in the store and ask Martine where she should go for lingerie. No doubt she would have a spot-on recommendation.

"Since you're going to the hotel do you mind taking the dress back so I don't have to carry it around?" She hands the bag to Emily reverentially. It is, after all, now the most expensive thing she owns.

"Of course!" The two do the two cheek kiss to say goodbye like true Parisians and Mari takes off down the street, happy actually to be on her own. The question is where to? She's already shopped out at this point (and subsequent experiences or purchases couldn't compare), and tomorrow they were spending the day at museums, mapped out by Emily, their resident art expert, so Mari stands in a doorway, consults her map and makes a tough decision. So much Paris, so few hours, but the Sacré-Coeur is on her list and by her estimation a manageable hour or so walk away, and so this is where she heads.

She has grown to love walking more and more since she moved to New York City.

Even on the coldest, rainiest days, she bundles up against the weather and makes her way wherever she needs to go. Partly it's because it makes her feel intrepid and partly because she very quickly developed a strong aversion to the subway that her new friends—especially Julia—chides her about all the time. ("It's part of the charm of the city!"). Mari sees nothing charming about being packed like sardines in a steamy hot car, down in the bowels of the city, with her nose pressed against someone's smelly armpit, which has happened more than once. She knows the rules: don't make eye contact, don't engage, wear headphones to tune out the litany of people spreading the word of Jesus at the top of their lungs, but still, just last week when she needed to take the subway to a meeting, a guy came up to her, within inches, and told her that he wanted to cum all over her face. And he is not the first, or even the second guy to say this, leaving Mari to wonder if there is something about her face in particular.

But worse even than the creeps, are the sob stories. The man with no arms and legs, the pregnant woman with no teeth, the guy with a bloody gash across his eye, who all start with, "Please excuse the interruption." Mari knows she has to ignore these people, that she can't help every one of them, and besides Ryan told her it was even illegal to give people money on the train. But she's not like the other riders she sees who continue to read their book or stare off into space. Mari found that she was unable to steel herself in such a way, unable to look away, even when Ryan told her that at least 75% of the beggars are "faking it." "You can't fake having no legs and arms!" she'd argued, but he just shrugged. And so she walks.

Mari leisurely winds her way through the streets of the eighth and ninth arrondissements, letting her eyes linger on every detail and landmark. Maybe she's still on the high from the dress, or that fact that she's in Paris, or the fact that she's about to experience a big milestone: thirty, but she feels so...alive. And filled with gratitude for her new life. That's how she thinks of it, when she compares where she was at this time last year—living in a creaky, old apartment in Montgomery, working eighty-hour weeks, far from her family and friends, with no social life to speak of beyond the occasional dinner with Ted—to her life now. Now, she lives in a spacious brand new studio in the Financial District, where she walks to the plush offices of her prestigious law firm in a gleaming skyscraper, where a team, a small team, but still a team, of smart, interesting people report to her. Granted, she still works eighty-plus hours a week, but that's okay.

She also now has new friends she adores, including her new bestie Julia, who she met, strangely enough, waiting in line at a Barnes and Noble. Julia struck up an instantly intimate conversation, as Mari understands now she is wont to do. At first, Mari worried that she was a crazy; it might have been the magenta pants and the felt hat and the stack of books she was buying, which was heavy on the self-help. But Julia suggested that they go up to the café for coffee after making their purchases, where they talked all through the afternoon and from there it somehow felt to Mari like she'd known her since first grade, not just since February. That this adventurous, creative, wacky (she does comedic improv for a living) person is her friend and is constantly pushing her outside her comfort zone (drumming lessons!) is a marvel.

Here's what scares her though. As grateful as she is for her new life, she didn't really realize that anything was missing in her old life. If you asked her a year ago, she would have called herself content with her small world. It's as if her ears were plugged and now that they're not she is only realizing the degree that everything was previously muddled. Here she thought that she had everything she wanted, but only because she didn't know to (or didn't dare?) want more. Not that she didn't love her work with EJP and with Ted—but if the opportunity with Frieda hadn't fallen into her lap, Mari knows she could have (easily) worked at EJP day after day, year after year, struggling with the toughest cases and scrounging for funding to keep their grassroots operation going, and never looked up to see what else was out there. That she could have missed out on New York, on working at Stone and Associates, on her vibrant circle of new friends, because she had become complacent, fills her with a cold dread. She vows to never have the same blind spot again, to always, always reach for more. This, she decides as she walks, will be the guiding principle of her thirties.

The Sacré-Coeur comes closer and closer into view, gorgeous and gleaming and perched on the highest point in the city, until she is standing at its gates, which are surrounded by vendors selling souvenirs, food, maps. She orders a butter and sugar crepe—all in French, thank you very much—and is pleased when she understands what the vendor says to her as he hands her the paper-wrapped crepe. "Pour la jolie fille." He smiles revealing a snaggled string of teeth.

"Merci," she says confidently. It's easy to speak French as long as she sticks with five words or less.

She finds a spot on the pristine lawn, which looks as if it's been draped in a blanket of perfect grass, and is dotted with friends chatting and journal scribblers and right by her two men concentrating intently on a game of chess. She takes a bite of her steaming crepe and the butter and soft dough oozes into her mouth. Surely she's never tasted anything so good, she thinks, as she takes in the panoramic views of Paris, which from her vantage point atop the city appear to be laid out at her feet. And in front of her, the bright white basilica looms, and she feels its imminence. She looks forward to touring it, seeing one of the largest stone mosaics in the world in the apse and the giant organ, billed as the most impressive in Europe. She looks forward to the quiet, grateful prayer she will offer.

* * *

They all agree, it has been one of those rare, charmed days. Everyone and everything cooperated, especially the weather, which was another gorgeous fall day. As dusk falls, they walk along the Seine to dinner, reminiscing about their favorite highlights. For Charlotte, it was hands down her dawn run along this very path and up through the grounds of Notre Dame. Mari can't stop talking about Luxembourg Gardens, and the decadent picnic feast of breads, tartines, cheeses and Jacques Genin chocolates they brought there. Ryan loves the Hermes wallet he bought. It's made of the exact same butter yellow leather as the seats of the '08 Bugatti. If he can't have his dream car (yet), he might as well have the wallet. Even though, granted, he could pretty easily get a Hermes wallet in New York, and maybe for cheaper, given the exchange rate, he'll know where it came from and expects to get a lot of compliments.

For Emily, it was, of course, the art. She had taken the group to her very favorite museum, the Jacquemart André. She loves the backstory of the museum almost as much as the collections it holds. In the late 1800s, it was once the private home (Belle Époque mansion designed by Henri Parent) of Édourard Andres, heir to a huge banking fortune, and his wife, a painter, Nélie Jacquemart. The two shared a passion for art and dedicated their lives to travelling the world, amassing one of the finest collections in the world, which they displayed in every inch of their massive home. They'd agreed that when they died, they would bequeath the house and the entire collection to the Institut de France, which opened it as a museum in 1913.

Though Emily did her undergrad thesis on Victorian Portraiture, she's always been promiscuous in her tastes and interests so the Jacquemart Andre is perfect for her—all of the range of the Louvre, with everything from the Dutch masters to seventeenth century Italian frescos, but a quarter of the size, and the crowds.

"The Jean Marc Nattier? Brilliant." Emily sighs wistfully as if she's talking about an old lover and not the work of a long dead painter who none of the rest of them can remember in the sea of exhibits anyway.

"Maybe you could do some volunteer work at your old gallery, Em?" Charlotte suggests. What she wants to say (yet again) is, what a waste, go back to work, you love this! Seeing Emily fawn over the paintings today, her passion, her depth of knowledge—Charlotte had no idea that Emily had studied in London for a semester and gotten a prestigious internship at the Tate Modern—it was obvious, to Charlotte at least, that Emily misses the art world. Something tells her that finger painting with Owen isn't quite cutting it.

"Maybe...we'll see," Emily says. But the wheels churn in her head. Maybe she could do some private tours here and there for big donors? Nathaniel, her old boss, would probably be open to that. It would be after Owen goes to bed. It wouldn't hurt to ask. Suddenly excited by the idea, she grabs Ryan's hand, squeezes, looks up at him.

"Maybe I could, right?"

"Sure, babe. Owen's older now. Why not?" Ryan is happy to indulge what he suspects is a passing fancy.

He leans over and kisses the top of her head and a chill goes down her spine.

Buoyed by the great day they've had, she's all the more excited for later and the special surprise she has for Ryan. Under her dress, unbeknownst to any of them, is a set of the most gorgeous French lingerie; a blush rose lace bustier with black piping and pair of matching sheer panties with hand sewn floral embroidery.

After she said goodbye to Mari yesterday, she'd dashed back into Coquette and bashfully asked Martine where to go.

"Is easy. Aubade. The best." Martine gave her directions to the store and not only that, she called ahead so that Emily found herself getting personal attention from a woman named Estelle, who approached her search for lingerie with the same seriousness and sense of purpose she and Ryan had had when they searched for Owen's car seat.

Though Emily had fretted about all the options, and specifically which one would best hide her lingering baby pooch, Estelle had proclaimed the set she wore now, "divine." "It's innocence waiting to be ravaged," she'd said, nodding approvingly as Emily stood before her feeling more than a little exposed. But "innocent waiting to be ravaged," sounded exactly right, and very hot and so she plopped down her credit card, trying to ignore the fact that the lingerie probably cost more than an entire weekend with a high class escort.

She had been a little unsure of lingerie protocol. Was she supposed to change into it later, right before the action, under the guise of "freshening up" or was she supposed to wear it and be ready for anything. Emily chose the latter, dressing in the hotel bathroom, and is glad she did, because somehow the wearing of it in public, under her black cocktail dress, her own little secret, makes her feel like a hotter, sexier version of herself, which was exactly what she was going for. And thus the chills and the fluttering feeling between her legs.

"You okay?" Ryan asks. "I've never seen someone get so hot and bothered over some paintings." He laughs.

Emily smirks. "You have no idea."

"All right, save the sexy painting talk for later guys. We need to pick up the pace. We gotta be there at 8 p.m."

"And where's that again?" Mari asked, eyebrow raised.

"Nice try! Still not telling."

Charlotte was more than a little excited about the surprise she'd arranged for the evening. An old friend of her mother's, Vivian Joly, had retired to France and met her husband (number three but who's counting), Michel. Five years ago they bought a small houseboat, refurbished it, including adding a full chef's kitchen, christened it Le Petite Bateau, and started doing boutique dinner cruises for up to eight people. Michel makes all the food and Vivian plays sommelier, showcasing the best French wines. The result was an impeccable floating dinner party with breathtaking views.

Charlotte and her brother had joined her parents here a few years ago for their thirtieth wedding anniversary, a rather strained affair all around but for the effusive warmth of the Jolys and the amazing food. And the even more amazing wine. Thank god for the wine.

Charlotte had hoped to have the boat to themselves tonight for a special early birthday dinner and celebration for Mari, but as it turns out one other couple had already booked Le Petite Bateau way in advance to celebrate their fiftieth wedding anniversary, so they would be two parties, two generations, celebrating together.

"Here we are!" Charlotte says, looking down at the adorable little bright white boat, which she is touched to see that Vivian has decorated with a tasteful selection of balloons and votives and a small hand printed wooden sign that says, Bon Anniversaire, *Mari,*

30! There's also one that says Bon Anniversaire Rothschilds, 50!

Vivian and Michel stand on the deck, waving. "Hello! Bienvenue!"

"Wait, is this for us?" Mari asks. This boat is the most charming thing she's ever seen.

"Yes! We're going on a private dinner cruise up the Seine to celebrate. Come on." Charlotte charges down the stairs that take them from the pathway down to the river and the dock. She practically leaps onto the boat, despite her four-inch heels, and is met with hugs and kisses from their hosts. Introductions all around as the others, excited, dazzled, surprised, climb aboard.

The Rothschilds, grey haired, liver-spotted and adorable, are already onboard, sitting at a table for two on one side of the small glass enclosed deck. It's clear that they don't speak much English, but everyone acquaints themselves using the international language of smiles and gestures.

On the other side of the deck is a table set for four, where they sit down to full wine glasses and warm, flaky bread.

"Okay, this is amazing," Ryan says.

"Seriously. Thank you so much Charlotte for arranging this. Just wow." Mari says.

Vivian and Michel bustle around the boat and pretty soon they've pushed off and are floating down the river, as the lights of Paris shine on either side of them. If Paris by day is magical, Paris by night has a radiance and mystery all its own, Mari thinks. Ryan raises a glass, looks around at "his girls." He's never seen Mari look better.

And Charlotte, always beautiful, looks especially radiant in the soft flickering light. And then Emily. There's something different about her tonight. And not just that she's wearing makeup and heels for the first time in as long he can remember. She just seems...happy. Ryan feels a surge of tangled emotions looking at Emily and around the table—affection, pride, gratitude, and something else. Something harder to place, and completely unexpected, the tiniest edge of fear.

He shakes his head, raises his class higher. "Cheers to Paris!

This has been a truly amazing trip. Maybe our best ever."

This gets a "woot woot" from Charlotte.

Ryan continues, "And to the first of us to turn thirty. Show us how it's done, Mari!"

"Need I remind you, you guys aren't far behind," Mari says, as they all clink classes around the table and then sip what Mari believes to be the best glass of wine she has ever, ever had.

Michel arrives with the first course, small plates for each of them of duck liver mousse, smooth and rich tasting. He waits expectantly as they all dive in, explaining how he had a career as a mortgage broker, sold his company and decided to come to France to train to be a chef, which is where he met Vivian. Somehow he convinced her to buy this boat, which was destined for the scrapyard, and now they spend their days cooking, drinking, and sailing, and couldn't be happier.

The group, their level of festivity rising with each glass of wine, enthusiastically toasts to that. "To living the dream!" And as they scrape their bowls, Michel disappears to get the next course.

Mr. Rothschild leans over to their table. "Good, yes?"

They all effusively agree. Ryan raises a glass again towards the older couple. "To you, to fifty years, congrats!"

It's clear they get the gist of the toast, raising their glasses. Mr. Rothschild reaches across the table and picks up his wife's hand, kisses it dramatically.

"Lucky man, me."

At this gesture Mari is flooded by wave a hopefulness, Charlotte by an intense longing, as they, without realizing it, have the exact same thought: This. This is what I want. One day.

Ryan grabs Emily's hand, holds it to his heart. "Me too."

"Children?" Mrs. Rothschild asks.

Ryan eagerly digs in his coat pocket to pull out the gadget he is completely obsessed with and is never more than four inches away from. A few months ago, in June, Emily was dismayed when he came home at 6 a.m.—after spending all night waiting in line at the Apple store—with a $700 cellphone. ("Emily it's not just a phone, you should see what it does!") She's still not impressed, other than the fact that it does mean that they have photos of their boy with them at all times. She lingers over the picture Ryan pulled up, of Owen grinning like nobody's business, before passing it over to the Rothschilds.

"A good boy." Mrs. Rothschild says, smiling and nodding.

"He is," Ryan says, suddenly missing Owen with an unexpected intensity.

Michel returns with the next course, a cold lobster soup. And the next and the next until Emily is seriously rethinking wearing what is essentially a corset, an ever- tightening corset, under her dress. Vivian has made sure they've never had an empty glass, and by the time the boat makes a wide arc to return back to the dock, they are past tipsy.

"Omigod!" Charlotte says, too loudly, while the much more sober Rothschilds, smile indulgently. "We haven't played best and worst in forever! We have to do the obvious one. Best/worst, turning thirty. Mari."

"I have to remind you again. You guys are like, what? Four and six months younger than me!"

"Hey I have pretty much a whole year!" Emily says, though ever since she had Owen, she feels leagues older than Charlotte and Mari.

Mari thinks. "Okay, I think for me best is knowing that I really like my life right now, so it feels good to be thirty and in a good place." She pauses, thinking again and then starts laughing. "The worst is, I may now be too old for the Pussycat Dolls?"

"You are NEVER too old for girl groups!" Charlotte says, emphatically. "Long live the Spice Girls!"

"Or boy bands! Long live 'N Sync!" Emily laughs. "They're going to make a comeback one day. Mark my words."

"Ryan? Your turn," Charlotte says.

"Hmmm. Best is my five-year plan is pretty much on track. The worst is...I need another five-year plan. Gotta get on that." An image of Tripper's smug smile pops into Ryan's head and then an image of his fist connecting with Tripper's smug smile.

Emily pipes in. "Well along those lines, I feel like the best thing about turning thirty is that I can have another baby and maybe people won't think, but you're soooooo yoooouuung."

"Whoa, babe. Another baby?" Ryan says. And then to himself: No way in hell *right now.*

She mock glares at Ryan. "We are giving Owen a sibling. Anyway. The worst thing is that, once your twenties are over you stop being able to get away with stuff.

Like you get a pass to be reckless and stupid and now it's over and it's time to be a grown up."

"Yeah, I didn't take advantage of that pass nearly enough!" Mari says, trying to think of the most "reckless" thing she ever did in her twenties. Getting an open container citation by the Boston police? And that was really Ryan's fault since she was holding the drink he insisted on leaving Fenway with, while he ducked behind a car to piss.

"Charlotte's turn," Ryan says.

Charlotte has been thinking, struggling to come up with a best since the truth is she is sort of dreading turning thirty. It feels like time is running out, like the path forward gets more narrow and more obscure, like feeling her way through a dark room to find a light. But obviously there's no way she's bringing down the group. So she goes with sentimental, which is always a winner.

"The best is all of you! Who could face thirty without best friends like you?"

Awwws all around as they clink glasses.

"And the worst? All of you! You drunk assholes drive me crazy sometimes."

Ryan takes a finger full of frosting from their dessert, streaks it across Charlotte's cheek and then licks his finger. "You're lucky we put up with you."

"Seriously though, you guys, this trip has been amazing. And I just...I am so grateful...I don't know what I would do if..." Mari stumbles along, fighting the lump in her throat.

"MAUDLIN MARI!" Ryan and Charlotte both scream at once, and everyone, including Mari, breaks into hysterical laughter.

They've pulled up at the dock and rave endlessly to Michel and Vivian about what a wonderful time they've had. Mari pulls out her camera, forgotten until now, and insists on a full slate of pictures.

"Okay, guys come on," Charlotte says, ever the tour guide. "Time for Eiffel Tower!"

That morning they got tickets for the 11 p.m. lift to the top, the last ride up, with a hazy plan to do a midnight champagne toast on the observation deck. In the cab, Mari has a momentary worry that she may well vomit at the top of the tower, which is not how she pictured her first visit. But Ryan directs her to chug water and she feels better.

Now, though, she's worried she'll have to pee as soon as they get to the top.

Fortunately she doesn't vomit...or have to pee at the top. Probably because she's too distracted by the amazing view, of all of Paris stretching out, twinkly and dazzling, that she forgets mundane things like bodily functions. All she can think is: I can't believe I am here. For as drunk and giddy as they all are, the heights and the breathtaking views have a sobering quality, demand a certain reverence. A cathedral in the sky. For a minute they are quiet, taking it all in.

Mari looks out over the city and then up at the inky sky, "earth's ceiling" she used to call it when she was a kid. A few stars are scattered like freckles. What strikes Mari most is how many people have enjoyed this view, have walked in the streets, and before that fields, below them for centuries upon centuries. It makes her feel inconsequential, in a good way. Her job is just to keep the tide of humanity rolling along, to live (well and long, she hopes) and to die—and then someone in a hundred years from now will be on this very tower, having this very same thought, and so the universe stretches towards infinity.

A bright flash snaps her out of her reverie. "Smile!" Charlotte has her camera and is taking pictures of anything and everything.

They begin to pose in various configurations. Ryan grabs Emily, kisses her passionately and Mari catches the shot, makes a note that this could be the perfect anniversary present.

Somehow the energy of their little group is effusive among the smattering of tourists remaining atop the tower. Even the guards, clearly ready to close down for the night and clock out, smile.

Another American tourist approaches them. "I'm Barb...from Tennessee," she says cheerfully. "Ain't this amazing? Here let me take a picture of all y'all."

"Yes! Thank you." Mari hands her the camera and the four stand together, smiling manically.

"That was a good one." Barb hands the camera back. "You guys sure look like you're having the time of your lives."

And it was true, they were.

Chapter Seven
Sag Harbor, 2008

Mari wakes up with an uncomfortable crook in her neck, a bead of sweat rolling down the back of her entangled leg, and slightly sour breath in her face. If it were up to her, she would wake up like this every single day for the rest of her life, nestled under Christopher's right armpit.

Without moving, she glances at the clock over his shoulder. She has two hours until her train and she's already packed so she snuggles in a little deeper as Christopher snores softly—a sound that reminds her of a cat purring—and closes her eyes. It's only been a few months, so she's really, really trying not to get ahead of herself, but every day, sometimes multiple times a day, like now, she'll still get that stomach flip-flopping feeling. Her breath will catch and she'll think: holy shit, I'm in love.

She gets it now, completely, the greeting cards, the poetry, the pop songs, all of it, all of these writers and singers trying to capture what this feels like, the drug-like rush and joy. She herself hasn't been able to find the words to properly sum up this feeling, she's a lawyer, not an English major after all. But Christopher, who was an English major, and is a successful book editor, left her a note a few weeks ago that said, Love is *the emblem of eternity; it confounds all notion of time; effaces all memory of a* beginning, all fear of an end. And well, that pretty much nails it.

She's tried to figure out the exact moment she realized she was in love, but it was almost like falling asleep or waking up, one moment you're in a different, completely opposite state, and have no clear memory of the process.

But if she had to pinpoint a time, she would say it was at the end of their second date, even though that sounds ridiculous because she barely knew him. But somehow she felt that she did know him on some sort of primal level that her rational lawyer brain struggled to accept. That night, after eating mussels and frites in the garden of Three Owls, an adorable restaurant deep in the West Village, they'd wandered around the neighborhood, Mari's favorite thing to do in New York, talking about books and family, their jobs, places they've travelled. Out of nowhere, but like it was the most natural thing in the world, Christopher reached down and grabbed her hand and though she would never admit it, to anyone, not Charlotte, not Julia, not even her mother because she realized she sounded like a ridiculous school girl, she felt it.

It was a jolt of surprise, a sense of relief, and a warm buzz deep in her center, that hit her all at once, accompanied by one thought, an epiphany really: this is it. It was such a cliché, but overwhelming feeling that she'd involuntarily laughed out loud, overcome.

"What's so funny?" Christopher had asked, looking amused but perplexed.

"Nothing. I just thought of something, that's all." Mari may have been inexperienced but she wasn't an idiot and understood that there were "rules." It was, after all, only their second date and only a week after they'd met at a reading Julia had dragged her to—by Jake Wallace, whose debut novel, To Speak Ill of the Dead, was being heralded by critics as a "groundbreaking literary achievement."

Funny to think now how much she truly hated the novel. Pretentious, overly stylized and a tad misogynistic is how she would have described it, how she did describe it actually to the man standing next to her at the reading when he asked what she thought of the book. Turned out that man was Christopher, who then introduced himself as the editor of the book.

"Well at least you bought a copy," he joked, while Mari struggled to form words given that her mouth was so full of her foot. After the event, he invited her and Julia to join him and Jake for a drink. "You'll see he's not so bad. And neither am I, for that matter," he joked.

Halfway through their second round of martinis at Citrus, Julia kicked her twice under the table, their signal to escape to the bathroom where Julia gleefully announced that Christopher couldn't take his eyes off Mari. This was something Mari had, too, noticed, but had convinced herself was a figment of her imagination, because how could Christopher, with his navy blue eyes and jet black hair (Mari's favorite combination), and his glamorous career—if Mari wasn't a lawyer she'd dream of being a book editor for sure—be interested in her?

Sitting there listening to Jake and Christopher gossip about writers and celebrities they'd met and trade tales of exotic travels and exclusive writers conferences had never made Mari feel more like a boring corporate lawyer, though they did seem quite fascinated by some of her death row cases, and when she'd told them about the execution she'd witnessed. And there was the fact that Mari and Christopher seemed to share the same taste in books (Jake's notwithstanding). And Christopher had reached over to touch her a few times, and laughed—genuinely—at her jokes. So later in the evening when he said he'd like to see her again, she was already prepared to say yes...and to ignore Julia's I-told-you-so smile.

Christopher stirs, sleepily kisses the top of her head. "Mornin'. You up?" he says in his husky morning voice, her favorite.

"Yep. Just lying here. Thinking," Mari says.

"Hmmm, about what?"

"The day we met actually."

"Oh yeah? When you called my author a pretentious asshole?" he teases, sleepily.

She hits him playfully. "I don't think I said asshole."

"And you still can't admit you were wrong, even now that Jake's made the NBA short list?"

The announcement that To Speak Ill of the Dead had received a National Book Award nomination had come just last week. Mari and Christopher, along with Julia and Jake (who had been nursing an unrequited crush on Julia), had celebrated with more martinis at Citrus. Mari was looking forward to dressing up and hanging out with the fancy literati as Christopher's date at the ceremony next month.

Mari turns over onto her back, reluctant to leave Christopher's embrace, but her neck can't take anymore.

"Nooo, don't go." He reaches over to spoon her, begins kissing the back of her shoulder and up her neck. "What time's your train again?" he mumbles, his lips pressed to her skin, which is now tingling with pleasure.

"9:40. I still wish you could come," Mari whines playfully. "It's our first weekend where Charlotte's bringing a guy and I have someone to bring, too, but I'm still going to be the fifth wheel."

"Believe me, I would rather be with you than at this writer's conference all weekend. Being trapped with forty eager writers in a stuffy conference room hotel for forty-eight hours won't be nearly as fun as hobnobbing with Ryan's fancy friends at the In the Black party."

"Ugh. Don't remind me. I'm still annoyed about having to go to this."

This "In the Black" party pretty much goes against everything Mari stands for: specifically wealthy people celebrating how wealthy they are. And given what's happened this week, that Lehman suddenly and dramatically imploded—it seems especially distasteful and ridiculous; the economy is on the brink of collapse. But, Ron Greenberg, Fortune 500 Hedge Fund Manager of the Year, apparently was taking a the- show-must-go-on approach. He held the party every year, the first weekend after Labor Day, the last before he "closed his house" for the summer, and invited all of finance's who's who to wear black, drink a lot, and Mari imagines, count gold bars or something.

Apparently invites are all but impossible to score but Ryan's friend Colin (who Mari thinks of as "Colin the Terrible" ever since their very first dinner at the W a few years back) somehow got an in, right when they, well Mari really, was in the middle of planning Greece as a destination for this year's trip. So Ryan suggested— insisted, really, much to Mari's annoyance—that they go the Hamptons instead where they could stay at Colin's for the weekend. He and Emily also announced that they were three months pregnant in the same conversation, which supposedly would make it hard for Emily to travel beyond New York, though Mari knew Ryan was just using this as a convenient excuse. But, again, the whole point of their tradition was that they get together for the weekend, wherever it was, so Mari was game to change the plan, especially when she realized this would be the perfect opportunity for everyone to meet Christopher, until the writers conference foiled that plan, too.

"Well the timing for this party really couldn't be worse. It's going to be more like a funeral, which I guess is perfect since everyone will already be wearing black."

Christopher laughs. "I'm sorry, I know it's terrible and our economy is basically imploding, but these hedge fund guys are getting what they deserve."

"I know. I don't know how festive everyone's going to be, right?"

"What time do Charlotte and Gabe get in?" Christopher asks.

"They took the redeye so they land anytime now. They're going to head to Ryan and Em's and then they're all going to hit the road."

"It's sucks you have to take the train solo. I really do wish I could come."

"Exactly, see what I mean. I am literally the fifth wheel," Mari groans dramatically, but it really does sting.

When they'd made the plans to get out to East Hampton, Ryan had offered to drive, which made sense, but Ryan's car could only fit Ryan and Emily and then Gabe, Charlotte, and Owen in the back so Mari generously volunteered to take the LIRR, assuring everyone it was "totally fine" and "not a problem at all," but honestly, she had expected Charlotte to at least volunteer that she and Gabe would take the train with her. Then again, that would have meant three hours on the train with Charlotte and Gabe, which is not exactly at the top of Mari's list of fun things to do. Though she's only been around them together once or twice, it was enough to witness an uncomfortable ongoing dynamic wherein Charlotte "playfully" mocks Gabe, and Gabe plays the role of beleaguered lapdog, which infuriates Charlotte, Mari knows, and inspires her to mock him even more. Mari remains more confused than ever by this relationship. She was convinced Charlotte was going to break up with Gabe over the summer, but then low and behold she announced that he was coming on their annual weekend.

"No chance you can bail on the writers conference?" Mari pleads futilely. She understands the demands of work more than anyone—just last week she had to bail on Christopher, twice, to finish a brief but still, she wishes.

"I wish. I'm going to miss you. We can have phone sex though. How about that?" He laughs, but Mari knows he's only sort of joking. The first weekend after they'd had their very first sleepover (amazing), Mari had to travel for work, to speak at a conference of the International Refugee League, which she had been very much looking forward to, but that was before she had the possibility of a sexy man in her bed, versus an empty one at the Radisson. She and Christopher had stayed on the phone for hours after she got back to her room after the very stuffy opening reception, and at one point the conversation took a turn to the dirty—the very dirty. And Mari, though a complete phone sex virgin, loved it. But it's still nothing like the real thing, which Mari also being something of a novice, is too getting really good at. This also has been a revelation: she loves sex. Her previous encounters, limited as they were, we're pretty flat. With each of her previous partners, a dismal three, it was mechanical, forced, and more than a little awkward. Particularly the time when she'd unexpectedly got her period with Ian and he jumped out of bed, screaming, "oh, god, gross," like an eighth grader. But with Christopher, with Christopher it's just so natural. She is wholly in her body and in the moment at all times and not the least bit self-conscious, which is something she, frankly, never thought possible, no matter how much in love she was.

"Phone sex could work," she says, lowering her voice, turning to kissing him. "But why wait? We could also make good use of the next hour before I have to go." She reaches down to stroke his penis, which is already semi-hard. She kicks the covers off of them so she can see what she's doing. She doesn't in general find penises very attractive, except for Gabe's, which is long and smooth, and the perfect girth.

He lies back, moans softly. "Yes. I love this plan...a lot."

He quickly rolls over on top her, then whispers in her ear, his breath as warm on her as his dick, which is pressing against her. "And I love you...a lot." He leans down and kisses her forehead.

* * *

A cascade of Cheerios hits the back of Emily's head, gets tangled in her hair as she tries to brush them off; all the while Owen continues to scream at the top of his lungs. His piercing wails bounce around the inside of the car. It feels as if someone has a put a metal bowl over her head and is hitting it with a spoon.

"Emily, can't you do something?" Ryan grips the steering wheel, is gritting his teeth. It's impossible they've only been in the car two hours. This has easily been the longest fucking two hours of his life.

Emily takes a deep breath, fights back tears. Ryan has been so unpleasant this whole trip and they were on vacation for godsakes. "I'm not sure what exactly you want me to do. He's a toddler, trapped in a car seat for hours."

She turns around to the backseat, takes in Charlotte and Gabe's horrified, overwhelmed faces sitting on either side of the car seat, along with Owen's bright red one. Their expressions, the overall tableau, could almost be funny, if Emily were watching it on TV, some zany sitcom and not actually living it.

"I'm sorry, guys. He's not usually like this." They don't look convinced. "Owen, buddy, what's going on?" she says, as gently as possible.

"I. Want. Out!" he demands, kicking his legs and tugging at the straps of the car seat with his chubby hands.

"You can't right now. But soon, honey, okay." Emily summons her most soothing, placating voice. "Here do you want this?" She hands him a bottle of milk. She'd hand him just about anything at this point—a giant chocolate chip cookie if she had one—just to make him stop screaming.

"Nooooo!" He swats the bottle away. "I want out nowwwwww," he yells again.

Emily turns back toward the front seat defeated.

Gabe leans over and tries to engage Owen with a counting game, then by pointing at things out the window ("A big truck!"), and finally, much to the collective surprise of everyone in the car, by suddenly belting out "The Wheels on the Bus" at the top of his lungs. Owen is shocked into silence and then giggles. Everyone collapses with uneasy relief, marveling at the split personality of toddlers.

Emily passes Owen the bottle once again and he lays back and sucks it as if he doesn't have a care in the world, as if he wasn't, moments ago, possessed. He has clearly tired himself out.

Emily turns to Gabe. "Thank you," she mouths. Gabe is really good with kids.

This is something that's stood out to Emily in the few times she's been around him, which she's pointed out to Charlotte encouragingly, so as to put some "pros" in that column for the ever-wavering Charlotte. Meanwhile, Charlotte—who goes back to flipping through Vogue (the September issue!) in the backseat—is not, Emily has found, the best with kids. She knows Charlotte loves Owen in a general sort of way, but prefers the Facebook version of him to the real live, crying, sticky-handed toddler, who last visit smeared chocolate on Charlotte's silk blouse causing the adult equivalent of a toddler meltdown ("It's Derek

Lam!").

Charlotte, fed up with having to endure Owen's tantrums, also has a flashback to this very incident at this very moment. The dry cleaner said there was no hope for the shirt and it was one of Charlotte's favorites. Today, knowing she'd be within easy reach of Owen's grubby hands, she made sure to wear a black cotton t-shirt. Fool me once, as they say. Charlotte's next thought is one she's not proud of, is maybe even a little horrified by: Thank god I had an abortion. Because if she had a bratty toddler right now, screaming and throwing cereal at her, if she was relegated to wearing dark cotton every day of her life, she would lose her mind. Being on the receiving end of a major toddler meltdown is not her idea of a vacation. She and Gabe should have taken the train with Mari. Actually, they should have insisted Ryan and Emily get a babysitter—so what their moms weren't available, they could afford a nanny—because this weekend was, is supposed to be for grown-ups. But rather than scream and a throw a fit like Owen, Charlotte takes deep calming breaths and transports herself to St. Bart's via the pages of Vogue and a divine sixteen-page tropical editorial spread.

The silence in the car feels deafening in the wake of Owen's screams, but no one dares speak. It's as if talking will break the spell of silence and set Owen off again. Emily lays her head back and closes her eyes, fights another wave of nausea. She never had morning sickness with Owen but now she's consumed by it and not just in the morning but all day long, so that she subsists entirely, if barely, on ginger ale and saltines. She secretly worries that this is her body's way of telling her she's not ready. This whole car ride is a way of telling her she's not ready. She can barely handle one active toddler, how can she manage two kids? The rest of the weekend fills her with dread. It was such a mistake to bring Owen, but Ryan had insisted that they had to be there for this stupid Black Party. She can only imagine just how un-child friendly Colin's house is, a ten- bedroom estate that he took over from his parents when his dad was re-located to Europe for work, and then apparently transformed into some kind of over-the-top bachelor pad complete with a video game room and "beer lounge," whatever that is.

The robotic voice of the GPS abruptly breaks the silence. "In three quarters of a mile take exit 70 toward NY-27/Alt Route/Montauk."

"Looks like we're close!" Gabe says, perennially cheerful, a state of mind none of the rest of them shares at the moment, thus no one responds.

Ryan exits, follows the directions through a maze of gorgeous streets and massive estates until he turns into a long hedge-lined driveway, announcing, "King's Castle."

Charlotte almost bursts into laughter. Are you kidding with this, Colin?

Meanwhile, Ryan looks up and around in absolute awe. He knew the house was going to be sick, but this? This is insane. Guess it pays to be born with a silver spoon. Obviously.

Colin happens to be standing in the driveway next to a bright red Porsche tapping furiously into his phone as they pull up. He jogs over to greet them.

"Hey guys, how was the drive?"

Hell they all think, but don't say.

"This place is...amazing," Emily says dutifully, trying to ignore the Cheerios that fall from her lap as she gets out of the car.

"Well, I may have to sell it if the market keeps going like it is so we better enjoy the fuck out of it this weekend!" He laughs loudly and then looks at Owen who's woken up, blinking his eyes at his new surroundings. "Oh sorry. Kiddos present."

"Nothing he hasn't heard before," Ryan jokes.

"You guys go in. Make yourself at home. Take any bedroom upstairs. I actually have to run out, pick something up, but I'll see you back here later. Hit me on the cell if you need anything." He climbs into the Porsche, starts the engine and Kanye West blasts from the stereo. Charlotte takes a wild guess that this errand involves meeting his friendly local drug dealer for some blow.

Gabe has taken all of their bags from the trunk and carries Owen's diaper bag and Pack 'n Play. "Let's get you guys situated.

Where to?"

Ryan leads the way up the flagstone steps and into the house.

"I gotta hit the bathroom. Em, can you get us a room?" He points vaguely up a massive curved staircase as he takes off down the hall to find a bathroom, which he sees right off the kitchen. He closes the door behind him and presses himself against the back of it. Hold it together, man. Hold it together. He steps forward toward the marble pedestal sink, hanging above it is the silhouette of a voluptuous naked woman sculpted out of iron. Classy, Colin. Classy.

Ryan splashes himself with cold water from the tap, looks up to find a pale face with dark circles around the eyes staring back at him. He's reaching to pat his face with a hand towel that he guesses did not come from Bed Bath & Beyond when there's a knock at the door. For a split second, he has the ludicrous thought that he could hide in here. If he just doesn't answer...

"Ryan, open the door it's me."

He feels a mix of relief and apprehension hearing Charlotte's voice. He opens the door and she squeezes in and closes it behind her.

"What the fuck, Ryan?" Charlotte's perfume envelopes the small bathroom and she's standing close enough that he can feel her breath—and her annoyance—in the close quarters.

"What are you talking about? What?" When in doubt, play dumb.

"You know what. You've been a total asshole all day. First you snapped at me for packing too much—and what the hell do you care what I pack—and then with Emily in the car? What the hell? We're on vacation, remember? At the place you demanded we all come, remember?"

"I know. It's going to be fun," he offers weakly. He takes the towel off the rack and pats his face, buying time. He hates the way Charlotte can make him feel instantly chastened, he much prefers irritation, as when Emily calls him out on his shit.

"Not if you keep acting like this it won't. I mean, I told Gabe these trips are a wild good time. It's his first time. I'd like to make a good impression, you know."

Ryan scoffs, loudly.

"What?"

"Come on, Char. A good impression? Give me a break. You could care less about Gabe. You know it, I know it. The only person who it hasn't dawned on yet is the poor sucker, Gabe. So do me a favor and stop pretending you give two shits about Gabe. Why are you even still with him?"

It's the height of hypocrisy for Charlotte to pretend she hasn't asked herself that question a thousand times, but she's outraged at Ryan nonetheless.

"You've got a lot of fucking nerve."

Just then the door opens and Emily pokes her head in. "Oh, hi? I was looking for Ryan."

Emily looks uncomfortable. The air suddenly feels think with a vague unease.

"Um...am I interrupting?" Emily says, hesitantly.

"No, no. I was just trying to convince Ryan here to be less of an ass for the rest of the day." Charlotte realizes she sounds guilty, feels guilty, though there's no explicable reason.

"Yeah, that would be nice," Emily says, quietly backing into the hall.

"No, you come in..." Charlotte maneuvers around Ryan to step out of the bathroom.

"I just came to say that Owen's asleep in the Pack 'n Play in the third or fourth room to the right down the upstairs hall. Do you know if we have the monitor? I couldn't find it."

Damned if Ryan knows if they have the monitor, but he knows better than to say this.

"I don't know. I'll look for it. Hey, why don't you two girls go to town, grab some lunch or something. I'll stay here with Owen." A peace offering. "Give Gabe and I a chance to hang out," he adds, looking pointedly at Charlotte, which she pointedly ignores.

"Let's do it, Em. Let's get out of here." Charlotte links her arm through Em's in an exaggerated show of sisterly bonding.

"Not sure if I can eat anything, but it will be nice to walk around," says Emily.

"Well, we also need to get you a manicure stat." Charlotte says, taking in Emily's chipped nails. "Come on." She leads Emily down the hall then turns around. Be good, she mouths back at Ryan.

He smiles and flips her the finger.

* * *

"Hello?" Mari calls out. Her voice echoes across the massive foyer. She's pissed, seething really. Ryan, Emily, Charlotte...someone was supposed to be at the train station to pick her up an hour ago and no one showed up. Worse, no one is answering any damn cell phone. Luckily she had the address for Colin's house written down, because she wanted to send a hostess gift.

She drops her bag in the foyer and makes her way to the living room. She finds Ryan and Gabe both sprawled out on ridiculously oversized leather couches, sound asleep. Owen's sitting quietly in his Pack 'n Play, moving a toy car round and round. She goes over to pick him up.

"Hey, little guy!" She loves Owen and feels instantly less angry as soon as she has his chubby little body in her arms.

"Mar-Mar!" He reaches up and grabs at her cheek.

"Oh Mari, shit. What time is it?" Ryan sits up on the couch.

"1:30. You were supposed to pick me up thirty minutes ago. What the hell?" She plops down on the couch with Owen on her lap.

"Sorry, sorry. We just went to lay down for a minute..."

"Sorry, Mari," Gabe adds sheepishly. "No one told me we were picking you up or I would have come."

"Where are Charlotte and Em?" Mari asks.

"They went into town. Em's phone is dead. She left it here to charge. I don't know why Charlotte wouldn't have answered."

Mari continues to bounce Owen up and down as much to

entertain him as to soothe herself as she feels her level of anger rising again. I mean, yes, shit happens, but just forgetting about her all together? Then again, she knows she can't spend the entire weekend pissed off. But God, she's pissed.

"I'm starving." She gets up abruptly. "Assuming there's food somewhere around here." And a drink, she thinks. She could use a drink. That will help.

"Check the kitchen. Pretty sure it's fully stocked."

She passes Owen to Ryan and makes her way to the kitchen. The subzero is massive, and as promised is brimming with food. She shifts around bowls of fruit and blocks of cheese to survey all the offerings.

"Oh, hey there—I wasn't expecting you until tomorrow morning?" She hears Colin's voice and abruptly closes the refrigerator as if she's trespassing.

"Excuse me?" Mari is confused. Was no one expecting her today?

"I thought you were scheduled to come tomorrow. Was hoping you could be finished by the time my guests and I are up— like by 8 a.m.? The laundry is piled by the pool house door."

It dawns on her, slowly, sickeningly. Not only does he not remember meeting her before, but he thinks she's the cleaning woman. This feels like one of those things that couldn't possibly be happening, but yet, to Mari's horror, is very much happening.

"Um, we've met before? I'm friends with Charlotte and Ryan. I know them from Harvard Law." She hates that she's added this last part, like it gives her some sort of legitimacy, as if she's screaming, see I am one of you, when the last thing she wants to be is one of him. Fuck. Could this weekend have started off any worse? "Mari," she adds lamely.

"Oh! Yeah...hey Mari, sorry about that."

He doesn't seem the least bit sorry, actually. Or have the decency to be as embarrassed as he should be. Of course, he would confuse a Latino woman in his kitchen for the maid. Honest mistake. Mari doesn't know if she's ever felt more rage. She has got to get away from him. NOW.

"Um, I'm gonna go put my stuff away." She brushes past him and out of the kitchen as quickly as possible.

"Okay, cool. Take any room upstairs. I'm staying in the guest house, so this place is all yours."

The guesthouse, which she can see through the French doors off the kitchen, isn't far enough away for her liking. It's also as big as most people's regular houses.

She grabs her bag from the foyer and makes her way upstairs, picks the room farthest down the hall with a view over the marshes surrounding the side of the house.

She dials Christopher, desperate to hear his voice and lament to him about this total train wreck of a day but she gets voicemail.

Just as she's starting to unpack she hears the front door open and Charlotte bounding up the stairs. "Mari! I'm so sorry! Where are you? I just got your messages! I feel so bad!"

Mari doesn't bother calling out, just lets Charlotte try door after door making her way down the hall. Finally she reaches Mari's.

"There you are!" Charlotte runs over, throws herself on the bed next to Mari.

"God, I'm so sorry. Seriously." She produces a bag of cookies from behind her back.

"Here. Peace offering. They're your favorite, snickerdoodles! From a bakery downtown. You don't understand, the trip here was so horrific. Owen screamed the whole way and Ryan and Emily bickered and...we were just all out of sorts. I left my phone in the car when we went to lunch. Forgive me?"

Charlotte finally stops talking and Mari just smiles and takes the cookies, which are delicious. It's impossible to stay mad at Charlotte.

"Is the coast clear?" Emily calls from the hall.

"Yes, we're forgiven!" Charlotte calls. Em enters the room and goes over to hug

Mari. "Sorry, girl. It's been one of those days."

"The snickerdoodles helped," Mari says, smiling.

They're startled by a voice on the intercom.

"Of course, there's an intercom," Emily whispers, rolling her eyes.

Colin's voice fills the room. "Ladies. Gents. Get dolled up and then get down here. I got a bartender making us drinks for happy hour and then a chef for dinner. Dress code is grown and sexy."

"Holy shit, that guy is an unbelievable ass," Mari says, almost wondrously, as if it's not possible for one person to be so terrible and yet...

"No kidding." Charlotte raises her cookie in agreement.

"Why on earth is Ryan even friends with him, Em?" Mari asks.

"I really have no idea. Supposedly he has all these connections. At least he broke up with Lisa. Talk about the worst—well, you met her. Ryan had this grand idea that we should be couple friends so I was forced to hang out with her. Now that she's out of the picture at least I don't have to see Colin as much."

"Why'd they break up? Let me guess, she caught Colin with a hooker?"

"I don't know but I wouldn't be surprised," Emily says, laughing.

"Well, whatever, look at this place. And a private chef? I'm willing to bet he has a stockpile of amazing booze. Let's just ignore him and milk the shit out of this," Charlotte says, fully intending to do just that.

"Yeah, I could use a drink," Mari says. "Big time."

"Ugh, I am so jealous." Emily groans.

"Oh come on, you can have one drink. It's not going to hurt the baby, which isn't even a baby yet," Charlotte says. "I'm going to get dressed." She turns to Mari as she makes her way to the door. "And when we get down there, I'm going to need a full Christopher update! Dirty deets and all. Like you still haven't confirmed dick size for me."

Ever since Mari's been dating Christopher, Charlotte has seemed to make it a campaign to shock her with explicit question after question.

"Get out of here!" Mari laughs, throws a shoe at her, hitting the door frame instead.

Charlotte picks it up. "Hmmm. Jimmy Choo Mary Janes?" she says, surprised.

"I'm impressed, Maribel Castillo. Wear these tonight." She winks and disappears out the door.

* * *

There are three things Charlotte hates more than anything in the world at the moment: Ginger, which (inexplicably) seems to be the "exotic" key ingredient in every damn drink this bartender makes; Gabe's shirt, which is flannel and which she was almost positive she threw away in her attempt to obliterate flannel from his wardrobe entirely; and Colin, who's been droning on and on about his famous neighbors and who is clearly high as a kite.

"Anyway, I'll introduce you guys at the party tomorrow," Colin says, about some Goldman exec whose name Charlotte didn't catch.

"Can't wait to meet him," Emily says politely, struggling to stay engaged in the conversation and fighting her envy as everyone gets pleasantly tipsy around her.

They're gathered in Colin's "man cave," which is exactly how Emily would picture it: lots of leather, chrome, wood paneling—it's like drinking in the inside of a Rolls Royce, which is probably the direction he gave the designer.

Colin looks confused. "Wait, you're not—you guys—aren't coming to the party tomorrow," he says bluntly. "I was only able to get one plus one and Ryan here's it."

Charlotte turns to Ryan, voicing the surprise of the entire group. "Ryan, you said you got an 'in' to this fucking party so I assumed we were all going?" It's unclear whether Ryan knew very well he was the only one going or is saving face in front of Colin but either way this is beyond fucked up and Charlotte is outraged.

"I wasn't sure what the deal was..." Ryan offers lamely. "But it's cool, we'll figure something out." Colin looks dubious.

"So let me get this straight. You dragged us all out here for a party tomorrow night we can't even go to? Unbelievable." Charlotte downs the rest of her drink, ginger be damned and hands her empty glass to the "private bartender," who's really just a college kid, who looks increasingly uncomfortable with the mounting tension in the room.

No question Emily, too, is outraged, but also secretly relieved. Now she doesn't have to try to fit her growing baby bump into her fitted black dress nor do they have to leave Owen with some strange babysitter she'd found through Nannies Now, East Hampton's elite babysitting service.

"Well, look, I'm just going to go for like an hour..." Ryan says, realizing that even to his ears it sounds like an empty promise.

Colin lets out a bark of laughter. "Um, no way man. This thing rages all night.

The good stuff doesn't go down until after 2 a.m." He winks and Charlotte immediately wants to shower.

"Well, let's just worry about tomorrow, tomorrow. We don't need Ryan to have a good time," Mari offers. And we definitely don't need Colin, she adds to herself.

"We'll find something to do while Ryan goes and hobnobs."

"Good, that's settled. Come on, let's eat," Colin says.

Dinner is a rather strained affair, monopolized, to no one's surprise, almost entirely by Colin. Mari has never met anyone who can talk as much as Colin can, about nothing or himself, which essentially amounts to the same thing. But at least the food is absolutely delicious and he didn't accidentally ask her to serve it, she thinks ruefully.

Ryan leans over and lovingly feeds Emily a bite of dessert, a triple layer cheesecake, and Mari feels such an intense longing for Christopher that she has to fight the urge to leave the table and call him.

"Let's go Caleb, Ryan. Cigars in the library," Colin says as the chef clears the last plates.

"Um, it's Gabe actually," Gabe says. He prides himself on

having a lot of tolerance for people and on his ability to get along with anyone, but then he's never met anyone like Colin before. Jesus, he does not want to have cigars with him, not least because smoking is a terrible habit.

"Really? The men are retiring to the library? What is this, an Edith Wharton novel?" Charlotte says.

"Actually, I'm going to head to bed," Emily says, grabbing one more bite of cake.

"Me, too, actually. Night guys!" Mari says, but by bed she means a call with Christopher, and by call with Christopher she means some hot talk, after she gets a chance to do some serious venting about the day.

"Well, I'm joining your little boys club then," Charlotte says defiantly, and follows the guys down the hall.

Colin pours them all bourbon ("Elijah Craig twenty-one-year-old single barrel") then immediately traps Gabe, too polite to say no, into watching a video of his last skydiving trip ("What a rush, man!"), while Ryan and Charlotte collapse on the sofa in front of the fireplace. They're surrounded by books but Charlotte is willing to bet that Colin hasn't read a single one of them. In fact, they're probably all fake.

The culmination of annoyance, fatigue at the long day, and a general anxiety she can't quite place, leads Charlotte to make the decision that she's just going to get as drunk as she can over the next hour and then pass out. Tomorrow's another day.

She downs her drink and leans over to Ryan. "You know he's a full-on asshole, right?" She looks across the room at Colin who's now showing Gabe pictures from a trip to Dubai. "I mean, he's almost a cliché of himself. Why the hell do you hang out with him?"

"Ah, Colin's all right. He's just insecure. He overcompensates. But he knows everyone in the city. His dad is VP at UBS and on a million boards. He's also head of one of the big Republican Super PACs. He's got his hand in everything. And that's the way the city, hell, the world works. All about who you know and who can open doors. You know that," Ryan says.

"Damn. Cynical much? What happened to actually having friends you actually like, over who can get you somewhere?"

"I have enough friends I actually like." Ryan smiles at her. "But I also have a wife and two kids to support." Not to mention a truly staggering pile of debt under which he is sinking.

"And what, pray tell, is Colin doing for you?"

"Eh, I don't want to get into it. Just some business dealings."

"I don't know that you want to get involved with that guy at all. There's got to be a better way."

Ryan shrugs. "Easy for you to say, you don't have to worry about these things,

Ms. I've Got Keys to the Empire. You've had everything handed to you."

This comment comes out of nowhere and stings Charlotte, especially the matter- of-fact way Ryan says it and the fact that he, he of all people, should know better.

"Well, that was uncalled for."

Ryan sees he's hit a nerve. "Sorry, sorry," he says genuinely. "I know you work hard. It's just different, Charlotte, when you have no backup plan. No trust fund. Do you know how much private school in NYC costs? Diapers? UPPAbaby strollers."

Ryan reaches up to loosen his collar. He feels the familiar tightening of the throat, throbbing in his head, as the ticker tape of his expenses and debts passes through his mind, with all of those zeros. He thinks about the letters from the bank secretly piling up in the locked drawer of his desk. He can turn things around, he reminds himself, he can fix this before Emily or anyone is the wiser. The markets are bound to stabilize soon and then he'll... Charlotte's voice brings him back.

"Did you hear me? What's an uppa?"

"Never mind, it's basically a car for a baby."

"I totally get it, life's expensive."

She doesn't get it at all, Ryan thinks. Not one bit. Charlotte has never ever had to think about money in her life, for her it's just a resource that appears, like water from a tap. He can't begrudge her for her naïve sense of privilege though, she doesn't know any better.

"Yes it is." Ryan sighs, heavily.

"You know if you ever..." She pauses. "If you ever need help... I'm here."

"Thank you," he says sincerely, but the truth is, he's well beyond Charlotte's help.

Charlotte doesn't know if she's ever seen Ryan look so defeated. Granted he's had a lot to drink, but he looks like he's carrying the weight of the world on his shoulders.

She lays her head on his shoulder. Gabe glances over, his look hard to read, or rather Charlotte doesn't care to read it. She should rescue him from Colin, that's what a good girlfriend would do, but she doesn't. Instead, she closes her eyes and listens to Ryan's heartbeat.

"I miss it," Ryan says out of nowhere.

"Miss what?" Charlotte mumbles into his shoulder.

"I don't know. The good old days?"

"Like what, college? Law school?"

"Yeah, like when we thought finals were hard. When our problems were figuring out the curve. I don't know—I guess I'm just feeling nostalgic or something. Ignore me."

She opens her eyes, turns to look up at him. "I liked cynical Ryan better," she says.

"We can't all be sunny optimists like your Gabe." Ryan smiles, pinches her arm. Charlotte gives him a look. "Don't start." She turns her head back down. She notices something; a new little paunch is visible underneath Ryan's shirt. She fights the urge to put her hand on it, thinks about all the ways her own body has changed. Or more accurately how much harder she has to fight to get it to stay the same. Her dermatologist recommended a wrinkle cream on her last visit, which was bad enough, worse was that it was the same one her mother's uses.

"You know you have to break up with him, right?" Ryan says quietly.

She's quiet for a moment, then sighs. "I know." A beat. "But I don't want to be alone again, Ryan."

"Give me a break, Charlotte. Lose Gabe and you'll have another guy in a hot second. Maybe Christopher has a friend?"

"Do you think that's going to last? Christopher and Mari?" Charlotte is horrified to find that she sort of wants Ryan to say no, that it would be nice that if she were going to be single again, not that she's making any hasty decisions, Mari were too.

"Yeah, actually I do. He's cool to hang out with for sure. Not sure how much he likes me," Ryan laughs. "But I like him a lot. He seems like a cool dude. He's good for Mari."

So basically Ryan loves Christopher, hates Gabe. Charlotte feels irrationally betrayed by this assessment.

"I've seriously never seen her this happy. Do you see how she keeps bringing him up in conversation? Christopher this and Christopher that," Ryan continues. "Kinda cute. For now... It's going to be hella annoying in three months," he jokes.

"Don't worry, the magic will have worn off by then, just like you and Em."

"Um, ouch?" It's Ryan's turn to be stung.

"Sorry. I was just kidding..." She was, mostly. "But you guys were sort of intense today in the car?" Truth be told it reminded Charlotte of her mom and dad, biting and bickering.

"Eh, Em and I are good. Marriage is just wild. There are good days, bad days. It's just...hard to understand, I guess."

Charlotte cringes at this. Hard to understand. Meaning hard for lonely, unmarried people like yourself to possibly fathom the realities that we complex married people face. It's like when people get hitched they're suddenly, smugly on the other side of some fence, or on some other (higher) plateau, that other people (lesser people is the subtext), are too naïve or immature to understand. It's annoying as fuck, and for a split second she thinks about saying so, but instead she gets up to get a refill and to save her boyfriend.

* * *

"Dude, you're coming down that staircase like Cinderella

going to the ball. Come on, we're late." Colin stands in the foyer in a shiny black Paul Smith suit.

"Shut up, man. I'm coming. You driving or am I?" Ryan bounds down the stairs, still fastening his cuffs.

"Um, you mean are we taking the Porsche or your Acura? I think you know the answer," Colin says. "Anyway, I think Charlotte and Gabe took your car. They went to dinner in town."

Ryan left Mari and Emily giving Owen a bath in a giant whirlpool bathtub, which Owen called a swimming pool with bubbles. They'd all spent the day exploring town, going to pick apples at a nearby orchard, and then hitting a nearby winery, which had horses much to Owen's delight. Everyone seemed happy to go their separate ways for the evening so Ryan feels much less guilty leaving to go to the party. Besides, he'd reminded Emily, this was work, these were very important connections for him to make and she seemed convinced.

"Honestly Ryan," she told him when they got back to the house. "All I want to do is put Owen down and watch a movie with Mari on that giant TV screen. It's all good, have fun."

Indeed, less than an hour after Ryan and Colin leave, she and Mari are ensconced on the couch where they ordered 27 Dresses on Colin's Pay-Per-View, because why not, and Emily is a happy camper. She's even managed to keep down a little bit of the popcorn Mari microwaved.

She hadn't realized she'd nodded off until she feels Charlotte frantically shaking her awake. The cable box glows in the dark room with the time: 2:45 a.m.

"Em? Em? You have to get up. There's been an accident."

Emily's first thought is Owen. She springs to sitting. "Oh my god, what happened?"

"Ryan and Colin were in an accident. We have to get the hospital. Don't worry, Ryan's okay. I spoke to him."

"Wait, what?" Emily is having trouble processing.

"I don't know much yet—only that they got in a wreck on the way home from the party. They're at the hospital. It's not far. Gabe will drive us."

Emily is more alert now, focused. "Where' s Mari? Can she stay with Owen?"

"I'm here, Em," Mari says, coming in from the hall with Emily's sneakers and jacket. "Here you go. Gabe's already in the car. Call me as soon as you guys know something."

Gabe drives cautiously but somehow seemingly swiftly through the dark streets to the hospital, which is mercifully only a few miles away.

"You guys go in. I'll park and find you." Gabe drops Charlotte and Emily in front of the Emergency Room and they race through the doors to the information desk. A nurse sends them down the hall to a row of curtains. Emily's knees buckle with relief when she sees Ryan lying on a bed. She races over to him, collapses into his chest, bursting into tears. Even though the ride to the hospital was short, and Charlotte said he was okay, she had plenty of time to imagine every terrible scenario: Ryan in a coma, Ryan paralyzed. Worst of all: Ryan lying in a coffin.

"Are you okay? What happened?" Emily asks as she holds onto him. Charlotte comes up on the other side of the bed and grabs his hand, squeezes, which is a completely inadequate way to communicate the depth of which she is feeling, looking at him lying there with a black eye and dried blood all over his clothes.

"I'm okay. Just cuts and bruises, hurt my arm. I don't know what happened. It was all so fast. We left the party and we're driving on Route 114. I remember Colin was complaining about how lame the party was—everyone was on edge, talking about lost jobs and shrinking portfolios." Ryan is staring off into space, speaking in a monotone.

Charlotte suspects he's still in shock.

"The next thing you know, I just remember the loudest sound I've heard and then a thud. Glass everywhere. I guess Colin lost control of the car. We hit a tree. But it was all on his side. There was so much blood..." Ryan trails off, slumps back in his chair. "I can't believe I'm alive," he says with wonder.

"How's Colin?" Charlotte asks.

"The doctors won't tell me anything. He was unconscious in

the ambulance.

They took him to the ICU, I guess? I have no idea how to reach his parents in Zurich. Or any other family. I called Lisa. I didn't know what else to do." Ryan looks helpless.

"That was the right thing. Colin will need someone," Emily says.

"Yeah, she's on her way from the city," Ryan says.

A cheerful nurse arrives to take him for an X-ray of his arm. "Just to be on the safe side," she assures them. "We'll come get you when we're done. He can probably go home in a couple hours." The nurse directs them to the waiting room. Emily is loath to leave Ryan's side. She kisses him and then again. Charlotte holds his hand, fortifies herself to let go.

Charlotte and Emily find the waiting room and settle in on the stiff vinyl chairs.

Charlotte calls Mari, who's been waiting by the phone, praying fervently, and gives her a quick update.

Fueled by adrenaline and hormones, Emily hasn't stopped her steady stream of tears. Charlotte drops her phone in her bag and puts her arm around Emily.

"It's okay, Em," Charlotte reassures her. "Ryan's fine."

"But what if he wasn't?" Emily wails, unconsciously putting her hands on her belly.

"But he is. That's what's important." Though Charlotte, too, feels a cold and sick sense of dread having imagined the worst. She thinks back to the ringing phone jolting her awake, knowing instinctively that something was wrong and thinking, anyone but Ryan. Please God, anyone but Ryan.

"But only by a small twist of fate," Emily whispers. "It could have been his side of the car that hit the tree."

"We're all spared or screwed by a small twist of fate. That's the way life works. Ryan was spared."

Emily's sobs escalate as if contemplating this small sliver of fate, the capriciousness of life and death, has made her feel worse. Charlotte pulls her head into her lap, strokes Emily's hair. "It's okay, Ryan's fine. We're all okay." She repeats again and again, in a soft voice, Emily's tears leaving a wet patch on the thigh of her jeans.

We're all okay. We're all okay.

Chapter Eight
Hallandale Beach, 2009

Aug 5 (10:10 pm)
To: Emily <artgirl1@gmail.com>;
Ryan <lawman02@gmail.com>;
Charlotte <CMayfield@gmail.com>
From: Mari <MaribellaC@hotmail.com>
Re: News!

Sorry for the group email guys...I couldn't decide who to call first so I figured I would just tell you at the same time...so, well...here goes: I'm pregnant! I know, I know.

Crazy, right? I'm sure you're as shocked as I was looking at that stick. Turns out you really can't miss a pill (or, er, two.). So, obviously, this was a little...unplanned BUT I have to say, initial shock aside, we're happy. Really happy actually. Christopher has already called all of his editor friends and got me just about every book ever written about pregnancy—let me tell you there are a LOT of books about pregnancy out there. Anyway, I thought my parents were going to freak out—we told them this past weekend—but they were actually cool about it. Though, poor things, they were just getting used to the idea of us living in sin. Of course, their first question was when we're getting married. Meaning how soon can we make that happen. Sooooooo more news: We're getting married! ASAP.

Next month actually (before I start showing, which is my mom's one weird request, I guess so she can forever be in denial when she looks back at the pictures? Haha.) We're going to keep it super small, just close friends in my parents' backyard. So I wanted to run something by you guys. How would you feel if we did it on our weekend? The second weekend in Sept. Labor Day weekend doesn't work, and we could do the weekend after but that means a lot travelling back to back for everyone if we still go away for our weekend. So this is...efficient? If selfish, I realize. But the truth is, our weekends mean so much to me so it's also fitting to celebrate that weekend, no?

Essentially it'll be just like a regular fun weekend away, in sunny Florida, except C and I will quickly exchange vows somewhere in the middle of it (and his family and my family will be there, and a few other friends, and my sis... and feel free to bring the kids obviously) but otherwise, exactly the same! ☺ What do you think?

> Aug 5 (12:20am)
> To: Ryan <Lawman02@gmail.com>;
> Charlotte Cmayfield@gmail.com;
> Mari <MaribellaC@hotmail.com>
> From: Emily <artgirl1@gmail.com>
> Re: re: News!

OMIGOD. OMIGOD. OMIGOD. YAYYYYYYY! We're so happy for you, Mar. As I write Caroline just nursed and is lying in my lap and I'm having one of those moments where I think, I want to do this again and again and again. I'm sure the feeling will pass (ha), but motherhood really is bliss (most of the time) and you're going to LOVE it, and be so good at it. Ah! I'm so happy. And absolutely next month works. Ryan and I would NOT miss this for the world. I can't believe it! YAAAAYYYYY!

Love you! Xo Em

PS: Ryan just called me from work and said, "I knew it!"—

he's a trip. He's very happy for y'all.

PSS: In terms of pregnancy books-can't go wrong with What to Expect When You're Expecting, a classic. I can send you my copy (with my neurotic notes in the margins!) if you don't already have it. Much love!

> Aug 6 (6:05am)
> To: Ryan <Lawman02@gmail.com>;
> Mari <MaribellaC@hotmail.com>;
> Emily <artgirl1@gmail.com>
> From: Charlotte <CMayfield@gmail.com>
> Re: re: News!

> Holy. Shit.

* * *

The large piece of spittle flies through the air as if in slow motion, and arrives on Charlotte's cheek like a slap. Talk about further insult to injury.

"Er, sorry, um...," the spitter says, looking more flustered than even seconds ago.

"And about the luggage...I'm sure we'll be able to track it down."

Charlotte makes a disgusted show of wiping her face. She almost feels sorry for this guy—almost, because she does realize this is not his fault, the fact that her luggage somehow didn't make it onto her flight to Ft. Lauderdale. And the unfortunate spitting also seems to be out his control, too, owing to some sort of speech impediment but the fact remains that both of these things are unacceptable.

"Look, I want to make you understand how much I need this bag. I need you to find it and get it on the very next flight here." She uses her most authoritarian voice, which fortunately comes naturally. "I want it delivered to my hotel room, The Crown Plaza, Hollywood Beach, tonight."

"Yes, Ms. Mayfield. Like I said, we're going to do the best we can." His blue Delta sweater vest is too tight, and his name plate, "Tom," is slightly askew; he seems pathetic, nervous, and weary, probably from a lifetime of being trapped in this suffocating tiny office near the baggage claim carousels, being screamed at by angry passengers, not unlike herself.

"You have until midnight." Charlotte looks at her watch for effect. "If not..." She lets the threat hang there, accompanied by an icy stare, and Tom actually cowers.

Jesus, Charlotte thinks, they really need someone with more of a backbone in this job, a worthier adversary. Or maybe this is part of Delta's strategy; disgruntled customers lose their steam upon encountering the sad customer service worker, classic de-escalation.

Well, not Charlotte Mayfield.

"Charlotte, come on. It'll get here," Gabe grabs her arm. He has the audacity to be annoyed, she can tell, with her. She can recognize the look in his eyes: I wish she would just calm down. As soon as they walked into this office, Gabe, she knew, would be on Team Tom, since he has an inexplicable affinity for service workers the world over and an infuriating immunity to feeling inconvenienced by anything. Gabe's philosophy?

Shit happens. Roll with the punches. Life's too short. Blah blah.

Sure enough, as soon as she marched into the office and started her initial rant ("We have a big problem here, Tom") Gabe had told her to calm down. To calm down. You never tell a woman, especially an irate one, to calm down, so this actually only served to increase her fury, which she directed at poor Tom.

She pulls her arm away from Gabe and marches out of the office. "I'm going to the bathroom, be back," she says over her shoulder, not giving Gabe a chance to respond.

She knows she's skating on thin ice. This is something they talked about when they got back together after their three month "break." The irony is, it was Charlotte who broke up with him, but somehow Gabe felt entitled to have demands—this is how

Charlotte thought of them—for what they (and "they" really meant Charlotte) would need to work on, if this second chance were going to work. Charlotte found this absolutely audacious—after all, it was she who broke up with him, and she who initiated them getting back together, so if anyone were going to have demands...

Charlotte had realized immediately it was a mistake to have called him, but after she got Mari's email—that she was pregnant and getting married—all Charlotte could think was, I can't be alone, I can't be alone. It was a visceral feeling, almost like a survival instinct, something beyond her control, something more powerful than she could fight or ignore, so almost without even realizing she was doing it, let alone thinking through the consequences, she'd called Gabe at midnight and asked him to come over, said she'd been thinking.

This thinking that she'd been doing, in the wake of Mari's email and lying in the dark while he drove over, was really a panicked ramble about how lonely she'd been since breaking up with Gabe; how tired she was of feeling like the third or fifth wheel all the fucking time as all of her friends seemed to be getting married and engaged in a sudden deluge such that she practically had a standing gift order (the cheese plate set) at Pottery Barn. How she'd signed up for Match (the worst) when she broke up with Gabe and gone on three truly terrible dates. How she was going to show up to Mari's wedding alone and sit there with blissful couples and drink champagne and go back to her sad lonely hotel alone. And how she JUST COULDN'T TAKE IT. So by the time Gabe arrived thirty minutes later, that panicked ramble had crystallized into one thought: "We should get back together."

It was a mistake, impulsive and selfish, but as Charlotte strides down the long drab hallway of Ft. Lauderdale-Hollywood International Airport and enters the beige bathroom that smells of diapers and disinfectant, she is still glad, or maybe the word is relieved, that Gabe is here. That he's waiting for her 100 yards away, annoyed but forgiving, and that he'll dance with her this weekend at her best friend's wedding and sleep next to her, and rescue her from herself, which had been the point after all.

She shuffles into a tight stall, as clean as can be expected of a public bathroom—a small mercy—and pees as quickly as possible. She sees there's a dark dot of blood on her underwear as she hasn't changed her tampon since getting up this morning, before getting on her six-hour flight. Great.

Well, at least new underwear is easy enough to buy, but what about everything else in her suitcase? The fuchsia Marc Jacobs dress she bought and brought just for the wedding. Her brand new floral platform heels also procured for the occasion. What the hell would she wear if her luggage doesn't come? She can't borrow from Mari. And the thought of rifling through the racks of the dress department at some Macy's or Dillard's in a dreary Ft. Lauderdale mall makes her cringe. She'd rather wear what she has on, she thinks, pulling up her black leather leggings and flushing the toilet with her knee high red boots. Maybe she could pull it off.

She gingerly places her leather tote on a dry spot on the counter and washes her hands, rakes a hand through her new "wispy" bangs, which her hairstylist had convinced her were a good idea. She's not so sure because the image looking back at her now looks an awful lot like her mother, which makes her nervous in all sorts of ways.

Charlotte wants to splash cold water on her face—it always looks so refreshing and pleasingly dramatic when people do it in the movies—but her makeup has lasted this long (though a touch up would be welcomed) and she has no idea when or if she'll ever be reunited with her make-up bag.

Her phone buzzes in her bag. Two new texts.

From Gabe: You coming back? I got you a soft pretzel. ☺

From Mari: Have you landed?? Girls and I are going to get manis and then have lunch. Meet us whenever you can!

She drops her phone back in her bag, without responding to either, where it hits something hard, the velvet box. Thank god, even though in thirty-one years of air travel she's not once had a lost bag (until today), she still wasn't idiot enough to pack these away in her checked bag.

She pulls the box out and opens it. The earrings sparkle in

the florescent lights of the bathroom.

"Oh wow, those are beautiful. Sapphires? " A woman Charlotte didn't even realize was standing next to her at the sinks, peers over.

"Yeah. My mother wore them for her wedding. I'm lending them to my best friend. Something borrowed and something blue." She shuts the box and places it back, deep in her bag. Gets out her lip gloss and starts to re-apply.

"Lucky girl. You're a real good friend."

"Thanks. Yeah...I'm excited for her." Charlotte drops the lip gloss in bag, in no mood for small talk, which clearly this woman doesn't realize.

"And what about you? You got a boyfriend?" She's staring at Charlotte in the mirror, smiling, like they are old friends reunited, catching up.

Is it any of your business? is what Charlotte thinks, but what comes out is: "Uh, yeah, I do, actually. Here's here with me."

"Well, maybe you'll be next then?" The woman smiles and winks at her as she grabs her rolling suitcase and walks toward the door.

Charlotte plasters on a smile. "We'll see."

She doesn't bother to tell the woman about the stream of toilet paper, trailing behind her, stuck to her shoe. Because, really, is it any of her business?

* * *

When did there get to be so many nail polish colors, Mari wonders. It's like there's been an explosion the last few years and the shelf for just "pink" overflows with more than thirty bottles of various hues. A Korean woman stands next to her expectantly as Mari holds bottle after bottle up to her nails.

"I'm going with red. I never wear red." Emily turns the bottle in her hand over to read the name. "Red Hot Diva. Perfect," Emily says.

Mari finally settles on her usual color, Ballet Slippers, just as

Julia looks over and says, "Let me guess, Ballet Slippers?"

"What can I say? I am a creature of habit." Mari smiles and hands the bottle to the nail tech.

"But it's your wedding! That calls for going a little nuts," Julia says, selecting an electric green for herself that only Julia could pull off.

"All the more reason to go with what I know will look good."

"Always so practical." Julia teases affectionately.

They have the place to themselves and all settle in side-by-side chairs at Kim's Nails, in a strip mall just down the street from Mari's parents house. It's so different from the "fancy" salon that Mari goes to in New York—there are fake orchids instead of fresh ones and no fruit-infused water. This is where Mari got her very first manicure for prom fifteen years ago. And the owner Kim, who's been here since way before even then, has been fussing over Mari and her friends since they walked in, which is VIP treatment she doesn't get in New York.

"So is Charlotte here yet?" Emily asks.

"Yeah, she landed a little while ago. I guess they lost her luggage. So she's not a happy camper."

"Oh no, all her precious couture," Julia cries with mock outrage.

"Hey! Be nice. You promised." Mari has come to accept the fact that Charlotte is not Julia's favorite person and Julia is not the type of friend who can pretend otherwise.

Mari should probably be annoyed by this— after all, the unspoken friendship code is that everyone in various circles is supposed to at least pretend to like each other—but one of her favorite things about Julia is that she's unapologetically opinionated, a real "straight shooter" as Mari's dad called her, so Mari gives her a pass and allows the occasional snarky comment, which she has to say usually aren't totally off base. Mari is just glad she didn't push her luck with a bachelorette party, which would have seriously strained the fragile diplomacy on both ends and probably have ended in disaster.

"I just still can't believe Gabe is coming. I really thought they were through in May," Emily says.

"Me, too. But Charlotte says he begged her to come back and she just felt like he deserved a second chance. So who knows?"

Emily, for one, has always been on team Gabe, feels he's exactly the sort of calming influence Charlotte needs. "He's a nice guy, I like him. I mean, a little...straight-laced. But—"

"Oh my god, are you kidding? He's boring as paint." Julia cuts Emily off, laughing.

"But he seems to worship Charlotte and by that I mean, put up with her shit."

"Julia, you've only been around them together once," Mari reminds her.

"What can I say, I'm a good judge of these things. And besides, when I was around them she demanded that he leave the bar and go get her that ginger juice or whatever it was, because her poor stomach was upset. So, I rest my case. I mean, have a ginger ale. It's right there. You've even said it's like she creates hoops just for him to jump through. I don't know how he deals." Julia shakes her head sympathetically. "Oh yeah, must be the trust fund!"

"So anyway, what's the plan for today?" Emily navigates a subject change because she knows full well once Julia gets on a kick—especially a Charlotte kick— there's no getting her off it. She likes Julia, she does, but it's pretty obvious to her that she's jealous of Charlotte, or at least Charlotte's relationship with Mari. Those two together are like lionesses lazily eyeing each across the savannah, each ready to stake a claim. Or maybe Emily has been watching too much Animal Planet with Owen. Either way, she has secretly appointed herself peacekeeper for the weekend.

"After this, we can grab some food if you guys want. And then everyone can just nap and regroup back at the hotel. Christopher's parents and his brother get in at like 4, so we're going to go pick them up at the airport. Then dinner at Sal's at 8 p.m."

In lieu of a traditional rehearsal dinner, Mari and Christopher and guests are going for pies at her local and beloved pizza joint, complete with orange Formica tables and a defunct, dusty jukebox in one corner. Mari had tried in vain to explain to a perplexed Charlotte that no, they weren't going to Sal's because they couldn't afford any place else; her parents were willing to splurge on anything wedding related, as they did when Carmen had a hundred people at the Harbor Beach Club. But Mari honestly just wanted to have pizza with everyone she loved tonight, and beers and champagne in the backyard, and have all of this wedding business be no big fuss at all. Beyond the location, though— Mari's parents' backyard—tomorrow evening's reception plans were taken out of her hands. Julia, leading the charge, insisted that she and "the crew" would take care of all the decorating and party details.

So the plan is that Christopher and Mari will go to the courthouse in the morning and make things official. Since Hallandale Beach doesn't require witnesses for weddings (much to her mother's dismay and Mari's delight) she and Christopher can go, just the two of them, which Mari loves. It's like the best of both worlds—eloping during the day and having a reception at night. After City Hall, as a wedding present from Christopher's parents, they're going to the Acqualina Spa and Resort down in Miami, where they are to stay occupied with lunch, massages, and otherwise unwinding in their suite (ahem) until a car returns them to Mari's parents' house for the reception at 6 p.m., and whatever surprises await.

Mari feels a surge of child-like giddiness as they all move over now, with bright, shiny wet nails, to sit with their hands under the UV dryers. She feels a flutter in her stomach and wonders if it's the baby, or her excitement. It's almost as if so many things have been happening at once and so quickly, that the momentum and busyness of work and planning has carried her like a wave to this moment where it's suddenly sunk in: tomorrow, she is becoming someone's wife and in six months, she'll be someone's mother. Isn't that just like life, to go along business as usual for tedious stretches and then BAM, like that, everything changes in the blink of an eye. Mari has become accustomed to this fact, but what surprises her is how calms she feels in the face of this dramatic change; how confident in her choices and the direction of her life. She has such a powerful sense that the universe is unfolding exactly as it should and all she has to do is sit back and go with it. Or maybe Julia's woo woo ways, as Mari jokingly calls them, are rubbing off on her.

Emily feels her boobs start to tingle, she looks at her watch and realizes she'll need to get back to nurse soon. "I don't think I can do lunch guys, I actually need to get back and feed Caroline. And relieve your mom. Do you think she's okay with kids?"

Emily feels terrible that she left a three-year-old and six-month-old with Mari's parents, while Ryan went off with Christopher on some secret errand and the three of them got manis, but Mrs. Castillo really had insisted.

"Are you kidding? She loves it. I'm sure she's fine. She wanted to have a full house this weekend, and the more kids the better, which is good since Christopher's brother is bringing his three boys, all under five."

"Three boys. Jesus." Emily can only imagine. Actually, it's stressful to even imagine.

"Christopher's mom has made it no secret that she absolutely wants her next grandkid to be a girl. No pressure!" Though she's always ready with the required neutrality—"whatever the sex is fine, so long as it's healthy"—Mari, too, desperately wants a girl. She fantasizes about her daughter's dark curls, the sweet gap in her teeth, her round chubby tummy toddling towards her, arms reaching. She can picture her baby girl in such detail she can't imagine it any other way.

"I still can't believe you're not finding out. I need to know," Julia says. "I have a mural to design for the nursery!" Mari is re-thinking the idea of letting Julia loose in the nursery with a paintbrush, but she'd insisted. Something tells Mari, based on the art Julia's created that adorns her Bushwick apartment, that they aren't getting cute giraffes or adorable frolicking monkeys. Instead it's probably going to look like the side of an NYC subway car circa 1974.

"I just have a feeling it's a girl," Emily says. "She and Caroline can be best friends.

I can't tell you how excited Owen is to go to a wedding, by the way. He keeps telling everyone he's the bestest man and he threw a tantrum when I wouldn't let him wear his suit to preschool this week. Finally I let him bring the bowtie for show and tell."

Mari thinks of adorable Owen, what a character he is, all devilish energy and precocious charm. Maybe a little boy would be nice, actually, with Christopher's dimples and blue eyes.

Mari takes her hands from the dryer and rests them on her belly with a contented sigh. "I'll be fine either way, as long as he or she is healthy."

* * *

"Sorry, I'm sure you'd rather we be golfing right now," says Christopher. "But thanks for coming with."

Ryan would rather be anywhere than this dusty dark "rare" (read: used) bookstore, even getting manicures with the girls. When Christopher asked him to come along to pick up a present for Mari, Ryan never would have imagined a two-hour road trip, passing god only knows how many signs for alligator farms, to middle of nowhere Florida, (it ain't Miami that's for sure) to get here: Isadore's Rare Books.

"No problem, man. Mari's going to love it." Though granted it's not necessarily the direction Ryan himself would, did, go as a gift for his bride. He opted for three-carat diamond studs for Emily—classic and timeless. Not to mention had Christopher opted along those lines they'd be at Zales or someplace right now, in civilization. But Christopher had tracked down a first edition of The Age of Innocence right here at this rare bookstore. How this is possible Ryan can't even imagine because something tells him Isadore's doesn't have a robust Internet presence, but here they are.

"On our first date she told me it was the most romantic book she's ever read," Christopher says.

Ryan likes Christopher but, Jesus, sometimes he's more of a girl than the girls.

"She obviously hasn't read, Don't Hate the Playa?" Ryan laughs.

Isadore, the shop's owner who is easily pushing one hundred according to Ryan's estimations, slowly makes his way back to them from retrieving the book from the back room.

"Here it is." Isadore lays the hardcover wrapped in cellophane on the counter reverentially.

"Can I?" Christopher asks, nodding at the book.

"Please, yes, have a look." Isadore nudges it towards him.

Christopher delicately removes it from the plastic sleeve and carefully opens the front cover. "Look at this Ryan." He points to the copyright page. "First edition, 1920.

Wow." He closes the cover and runs his hand over the embossed type. "It's amazing, isn't it?" Gabe seems truly awed.

"Sure, I guess? Yeah." Amazing isn't necessarily the word that would come to mind for an old book, but Ryan can't deny that it's pretty fucking thoughtful.

Christopher goes to pull out his wallet. "$1200, right? He starts counting $50 bills out. "I brought cash, like you asked."

Ryan almost chokes. "Wait. A G? For a book?" Ryan is one to talk, but really, a thousand dollars for a book?

Thinking about financial excess, money in general, brings with it the sickening feeling and suffocating anxiety that follows Ryan everywhere now like a cloud. Not now, he admonishes himself. It's all going to be fine. This is a fiction he tells himself to get through the days, until...until what he doesn't know.

"Oh, it's not just any book, young man," Isadore tells Ryan. "It's very special and valuable. A collector's edition. My mother bought it for me. Gave it to me when I was sixteen. She always wanted me to read more. I took very good care of it."

"My girlfriend—wife, will cherish it. Thank you, sir," Christopher says, leaving the thick pile of cash on the counter.

Isadore reaches across the counter and puts his liver-spotted hand over Christopher's. "Good luck with your wedding, young man, and remember, women are meant to be loved, and not understood."

Christopher grins. "Oscar Wilde right?"

Isadore pats Christopher's hand affectionately. "You're smart, smart people know how to be happy."

"Thank you and I will. We will."

Ryan is getting a little worried that Christopher is going to hug this guy. They need to get out of here before Isadore invites them for tea and stories about the Depression.

"Well, we better go, thanks man!" Ryan starts backing toward the door, nearly knocking over a towering stack of yellowing Life magazines.

Back in the car with their precious cargo secured safely in the trunk of the rental, they make their way down the sparse two-lane highway.

"Hey, how about we stop?" Ryan points up ahead to a bar, a shack really on the side of the road. There's a decrepit placard that reads: Dive Bar & Bait, and a sign right at the roadside with black plastic letters announcing two for one drafts all day. Ryan appreciates the all around directness of the place, and though he's alarmed by just how often he has this thought these days (or years): he needs a drink.

"Sure, I guess we have time for a beer." Christopher pulls into the parking lot, spraying gravel.

Dive Bar & Bait is just as advertised, just how Ryan hoped it would be: dark, rank with the smell of old beer, with peanut shells on the floor, a sticky bar top, and a dart board. No false advertising here. Ryan can't remember the last time he'd been in a true dive; this is so different from the glossy bars and clubs he frequents in Manhattan with aggressively curated decor and $20 cocktails in thimble-sized glasses.

Just last week Colin took him to opening night at Blue, the newest celebrity club du jour, where Colin slipped the bouncer $100 to get in; at which the bouncer laughed.

("Um, try again, man.") Turns out $500 dollars and bottle service is what it took to get you to the front of the around-the-block line and to a VIP table (next to Usher). Ryan found this extortion outrageous and wasn't about to co-sign or contribute for various reasons, but Colin happily coughed up the cash.

After six months of intense physical therapy following the accident last year and two months of relative sobriety, Colin was back hitting it as hard as ever, harder even, as if tempting the fates made him braver. "Yolo," he was always saying, or rather screaming at the top of his lungs, usually before downing his next shot, not quite realizing that the YOLO plus shots scenario belonged to another, slightly younger, generation; or that he was just short, like maybe two quick years short, of being a laughing stock.

Some, Ryan included, might have had a near death experience and decided once was enough. Colin's approach was to say, F-you, universe, and try to prove just how invincible he really was. That meant more drinking, late nights, and a brand new Harley.

The irony was if he didn't have a death wish before he sure seemed to now. But then again Ryan can't argue with Colin's philosophy, you only live once is right, but lately he's been thinking that's more than enough actually.

The bartender leisurely finishes his conversation with the only other people in the place, a couple of guys not that much younger than Isadore, with thick red wrinkles suggesting a lifetime in the Florida sun.

He comes over to them, clearly sizes them up as out of place. Ryan feels like he has "rich New Yorker" written all over him. "What can I get y'all?" He sounds suspicious, like you can't trust rich New Yorkers, which was probably a little true.

"I'll take a Bud Light." Because when was the last time he had one of those? And he knows damn well not to ask for a seasonal IPA.

"Same," echoes Christopher.

When Ryan takes his first sip he's instantly transported back to college and law school; that dirty place they used to go to in Back Bay where you could make your own Bloody Marys all day on Sundays. What was the name of that place? He's disturbed he can't remember.

Ryan holds up his beer, already half empty. "Well, here's to your wedding weekend. You ready man?"

"Yeah, actually I am. More than ready." Christopher has, in fact, never been more sure of anything in his entire life; a certainty he never would have imagined he would feel about such a big decision, considering he had trouble committing even to paint colors.

"Mari's a great girl. I guess that's stating the obvious to you."

"I'll drink to that," he lifts his glass and takes a long pull. "So any advice for me?"

Christopher asks when he's done.

"Nah, you don't want to ask me." A dark cloud passes over Ryan's face.

"But you've been married—what five years now? You're a veteran." Christopher laughs.

"I'm no expert. At all. Just be good to her, okay." Ryan downs the rest of his beer and motions to the bartender for another, changes the subject. The last thing he needs to be doing right now is giving marriage advice. "So, who else in your crew is coming?"

"My parents and my brother and his wife and kids. They have three boys, one of them Owen's age so that'll be fun. And my buddy Sean from growing up and Jamal, I think you met him before? Jake couldn't make it. He's at Yaddo."

Christopher elaborates when he sees Ryan's look of confusion. "It's a fancy writer's retreat in upstate New York."

"He's missing your wedding to write?" Ryan asks, but then again it's not like he hasn't missed many things because of work.

"Jake would miss his own wedding for his art. I don't mind. He's way behind on his next book. I'd rather have that...my boss would rather have that...than his presence here. But he sent down a really nice bottle of scotch, which we can get to later."

"Sweet. And this is the way to go man. Keep it small. Emily and I did the same thing. Small wedding in Ireland and then about fifty people for a reception in New York. It was a fun night." From what he can remember, somehow it already feels so long ago.

Sometimes he looks at his wedding photos and it's like someone else is standing in as him. It feels like it's an entirely different person besides Emily, there in a white suit (the one Charlotte rightfully tried to talk him out of, he sees now) and the I've-conquered- the-world smile. That guy really had no idea.

Christopher polishes off the rest of his beer. "We ready to head back? I gotta pick up my parents at the airport soon."

Actually Ryan wouldn't mind staying a few more hours, talking to the bartender about l-i-f-e, chatting up the grizzly old timers in the corner, hearing about their biggest catch, or how their boat got to be called "Della's Dream." If he's lucky maybe one of them would have a good war story about bravery and survival and Ryan would think, damn that's some shit, and he would have a completely new perspective on his own life.

But instead he downs the last dregs of his beer and kicks back from his metal stool.

"Yep, let's go."

* * *

Mari has tears in her eyes as the driver pulls away from the house. She turns around in the back seat of the town car to wave again through the rear window. Her parents, Christopher's parents, and Carmen are still standing on the sidewalk in front of the house, smiling and waving manically. They had come over early this morning for breakfast and then gathered outside and thrown rice at them in a sort of a reverse receiving line as Mari and Christopher walked down the driveway and into an awaiting limo with the words, Going to the Chapel across the back. Carmen's brilliant idea. "I feel bad now. Are we selfish to do this alone?" Though this is exactly what she wanted—just her and Christopher and the clerk at the courthouse—driving away from her family has left a lump lodged in her throat.

Christopher grabs her hand. "I don't want to share you with anyone this morning. We'll get to celebrate with them later. For now, it's just you and me." He lifts her hand and kisses it. As usual, Christopher talks her off the ledge and she's flooded with reassurance.

"You're right. No one wants to sit in a hot church anyway and through a boring ceremony." Well, except her mother who would be reassured by the fact that the most important guest was there offering his blessing: God. The two of them going alone today wasn't as much of a sticking point for her mom as was the fact that they wouldn't be married in the Catholic Church (a deal breaker for Christopher), but Mari hoped in time to be forgiven by her mom—and God.

"You nervous?" Christopher asks.

"No, excited. And maybe just a little tired, too, actually." She lies on him, rests her head in the crook just under his arm, where she knows from practice she fits perfectly.

Mari hadn't slept at all the night before—a combination of excitement, adrenaline, and the hormones coursing through her veins kept her tossing and turning.

She felt like it was a combination of Christmas Eve and the night before the bar exam. At 2 a.m. she finally gave up on sleep and got up. She'd peek in on Christopher asleep next door in Carmen's old bedroom, where he slept soundly in a twin bed under Carmen's old Menudo posters still hanging above the bed, a hilarious sight. And then she went to find her mom exactly where she knew she would be. A chronic insomniac, ever since Mari was a little girl, her mother could reliably be found bustling around the kitchen at all hours, which if Mari had been the type of teenager to sneak out, would have proved challenging.

Her mom stood at the small butcher block island, speckles of bright white flour dotting her dark hands and arms. Mari watched her for a minute, she looked thin and tired, and every bit her fifty-nine years. Even though Carmen and her father both insist that she's doing okay, that she's going to her check-ups and she's healthy, Mari worries, how can she not?

"Hey, Momma."

"Hey, honey. What are you doing awake?"

"Couldn't sleep."

Her mom was already putting on the teakettle as Mari settled on a chair at the small kitchen table. "I'll make you some chamomile."

"Thanks. What are you doing?"

"Cooking! I have dozens of pasteles to make by tomorrow afternoon, because my beautiful daughter is getting married." She reached over and put her warm hand on Mari's cheek leaving flour fingerprints.

"Thanks, Mom. I appreciate it." It was then that Mari realized something: she was nervous. She hadn't been face-to-face or alone with her mother since she'd called last month with the shocking announcement that she was pregnant. Good Catholic girls don't get knocked up out of wedlock, so this is the call that parents of good Catholic girls never want to get. And though Mari senses that her parents like Christopher, they barely know him. A case could be made that Mari herself barely knows him; it's only been a little over a year, after all. And her mother already worries about so much: is Mari eating enough, praying enough, sleeping enough. Mari can only imagine how much she'd been worrying about her unexpectedly pregnant and as yet unwed daughter. She wondered what unvoiced recriminations were floating through her mom's mind at the moment: that Mari is making a mistake, that Mari is moving too fast; the she's being reckless and irresponsible and ruining her life. Mari decided to head her mom off at the pass, to get ahead of the lecture that was no doubt inevitable now that they were alone.

"Look, mom, I know it's...this all..." She waves her hand loosely in the air over her belly. "It isn't happening like you would want—we aren't getting married in church and well, I'm pregnant and all but—"

Her mother put her hand up mid-sentence. "Hush, Mari." She came over, pulled a chair close to her and leaned in. "You're happy, Mija. I can tell. I don't think I've ever seen you this happy."

"I am," Mari let out the breath she hadn't known she was holding. "So happy."

"That is all I want for you. You've always been a smart girl, sometimes too smart.

And a good girl. Sometimes too good," she winked. "You've made me and your father so very proud with all of your accomplishments and your hard work, but this, this is what we want for you. A good husband and a family. This is what we're proud of." She pulled her close and Mari was enveloped by her familiar scent, cinnamon and Estee Lauder. "Now come, help me make cook."

They work side by side, quietly, rolling out dough, assembling the filling of onions, ham, cheese, which they will bake tomorrow. "You'll do this with your little girl one day," her mother said, perfecting a crease in the dough Mari had overlooked.

Mari stopped what she was doing. "Do you think it's a girl?" A hopeful question.

"I know it is," her mother said. "Una niña bonita."

In the car, Mari turns her face up towards Christopher's. "You know, my mom is convinced it's a girl?"

"Well, she has a 50/50 chance of being right," he jokes. She slaps him on the thigh and nestles back into her favorite spot.

They're oddly quiet the rest of the short way to the courthouse, lost in their thoughts, fully aware that these are their last minutes as single people, that they are leaving a phase of their lives behind and starting another. When the car pulls up in front of the courthouse, Christopher sits up straight. "It's go time!"

Mari laughs. "Um, we're not being dropped off at the front lines."

"Well, love is a battlefield."

"See, that corny sense of humor is exactly why I am marrying you."

"It's not my money?" He laughs and grabs her hand to help her out of the car.

They both squint in the brilliant sun; it's almost cliché how beautiful it is out. Mari feels a stab of love for her hometown; New York is great, but part of her will always be a Florida girl, who grew up with sand always in her shoes and the smell of Coppertone on her clothes.

Mari straightens her dress as they walk down the marble corridor. It's the dress Emily and Charlotte bought her in Paris, one of her most prized possessions. But between pizza last night at Sal's and the fetus seemingly expanding by the minute inside of her, it's now a little tight, but not wearing it today was not an option, it was her lucky dress and to use a cheesy expression, she feels like a million bucks.

"You look beautiful, Mari." Christopher stops, stares for a moment, and then grabs her hand and leads the way into City Hall.

The ceremony is swift and efficient. They've saved their vows for later so they just have to answer a few simple questions ("we will"), asked by an all business bureaucrat. In fact, it's over so fast and with such little fanfare, Mari isn't even sure it really happened. It took longer to renew her driver's license.

"So, we're married?" Mari doesn't mean it to sound like a question, but it's just so surreal.

"Yes, we're married!" Christopher yells this, loudly, his voice echoing off the marble walls of the courthouse, catching the eyes of surprised and delighted onlookers who smile at them and offer congratulations as they make their way down the hall.

Christopher grabs her hand as they as the spill out onto the street where Hector, their limo driver, is waiting for them.

He opens the door. "Here you go Mr. and Mrs. Victor."

Mari beams. "That's the first time anyone has called us that. It's nice." Then she turns to Christopher and whispers, "But you know I am not changing my name, right?"

"Big surprise there. Frieda would probably fire you."

They go to the resort and check into their suite. Carmen had brought their stuff last night, their bathing suits and their outfits for the reception.

"So what now?" Mari flops down on the king-sized bed.

"Well, we have an hour to kill before our lunch rez and massages." Christopher takes two fast steps and then jumps on the bed next to her. "So I could think of a few things."

Mari lies on her back and he scoots himself towards her so

he's inches away, facing her. He pulls her face towards him, looking into her eyes.

"Hi there, wife."

"Hi, husband." She smiles, beams really. He leans over and kisses her deeply, slowly, like time has stopped. And just for a moment, it has; everything as meaningless as time and space has fallen away and it's just her and Christopher and this moment, which Mari doesn't want to end. Christopher has kissed her hundreds, thousands even, of times, but this feels different; it feels weighty, it feels as if—here Mari doesn't even want to allow herself to finish the thought because it's admittedly so melodramatic and ridiculous—but it feels like they are two souls as one; like they are connecting on some deeper level that goes beyond the boundaries of their physical bodies.

Still kissing her, Christopher trails a hand slowly down her neck, over her clavicle, and then circles her right nipple and then her left, hardened now, they make an imprint through the soft fabric of her dress. He moves on, pulling her dress up to reveal the soft slope of her pregnant belly. She feels a fluttering, which is too early to be the baby, is something else all together. By the time he gets to the warm spot between her legs, Mari is panting and flushed, every inch of her tingles. She's desperate for him, yet also wants to prolong the moment, and knowing she has no control over how fast or slow whatever happens next will unfold—how long will he tease her?—makes her dizzy with anticipation.

Christopher whispers in her ear, his voice husky with desire. "How does that feel?"

Mari intends to say, good, or amazing, but she's lost the capacity for coherence, so what comes out instead is a slow moan, as she clutches him to her.

He slowly pulls away, quickly undresses. Just as frantically Mari shimmies out of her dress and within seconds, which is still too long, they're back in each other arms, desperately kissing, licking, sucking, exploring. It's as if they've never done this before, such is their eagerness, curiosity, and hunger; and yet it's as if this is all they've ever done, such is their ability to find their rhythm and fit together.

Afterwards, sweaty and spent, Mari lies quietly, spooned against a dozing Christopher, his warm, steady breath like a metronome on her back. Her first hours as a newlywed have been perfection; she tallies her emotions: happiness, contentment, excitement, but there is something else, a sensation that's more telling and somehow more satisfying than the others. Above all else, she thinks as she closes her eyes, and drifts to sleep: she feels safe.

* * *

When Mari walks into her wedding reception six hours later, still flushed and satiated, she bursts into tears, which was not the reaction, she (or anyone) was expecting. But it's all too much, too much joy, too much happiness, too much love (perhaps too many hormones); it's like she's short-circuited.

There's just so much to take in. Her parent's backyard has been completely transformed into what looks like a whimsical garden from a fairy tale or a magical circus.

There are tea lights scattered everywhere and twinkling lanterns strewn throughout, giving the illusion that they are submerged in a cluster of stars. And the flowers!

There's a braid of flowers through the wooden fence, petals scattered throughout the grass and huge centerpieces of lush blue hydrangeas—the only flower Mari can name—anchoring each of the four tables. Someone has had the ingenious idea to construct a small dance floor out of reclaimed wooden planks, which are framed with lights and flowers. Next to the dance floor is a long table overflowing with food like it's the last supper, including the pasteles. And perhaps her favorite part: a trio of vintage machines in the corner: an old time popcorn maker, a soda fountain, and an soft serve ice cream machine, which she sees the kids are already stalking. It's almost as if Julia has also managed to decorate the sky itself, which is the perfect shade of violet to compliment the flowers.

"You guys! This is too much." Mari wipes her eyes with her hand.

"Well, tears weren't the reaction we were hoping for." Julia comes over and hugs her. "Don't. You'll ruin your make-up and you look perfect." Then everyone is upon them, hugging them and saying congratulations, and it's a blur of faces of all the people she loves. Her dad at one point hands her a handkerchief, which is already damp, apparently with his own tears.

"Thank you. Thank you everyone so much. We're so glad you could be here."

Mari says as everyone forms a natural semi-circle around her and Christopher.

"Well, as you know, we're already married. Five hours! And so far so good,"

Christopher jokes and everyone laughs. "But we want to exchange vows and rings in front of you. So let's just do that part now and then we can get to the drinking and the dancing. Though I'm guessing you guys have already gotten to the drinking part."

"Here, here!" Ryan calls out, holding up his glass.

"So here goes," Mari says.

Christopher and Mari turn and face each other, hold tightly to each other's hands. Christopher squeezes once and then again. There's a beat of silence while each of them waits for the other person to start.

"Oh, me first?" Christopher laughs.

"Or I can go," Mari offers.

"Clearly we didn't rehearse this," Mari says to the laughing crowd.

"Okay, I'll go," Mari says. Another beat. A deep breath. "Sorry, I just want to try to make it through this without crying."

"I have plenty of Kleenex," her mom calls out. "The kind with lotion!" More laughter.

Mari focuses, zeros in on Christopher, and like a camera going in for a close up, everything else fades. She feels steady, like the beating of her heart.

"Christopher." At that he smiles such a big smile she almost feels like she doesn't even have to go on, enough, everything has been said with that one word. But she does.

"A wise woman, my mother, once told me to marry a guy who loves you just a little more than you love him."

"Amen!" her mom calls out, playfully hugging her dad.

"And when I told you about that a few weeks ago, I confessed I messed up because there is no way you could love me more than I love you. And unbelievably we actually argued about this—with my legal training, I feel like I made the best case, of course—but I think the fact that we're competitive on this score says it all. That we are both very much in love with each other. But more than that, that we both exalt the love we have for each other; we are proud of our zealousness on this front; and if this is one area where we're going to try to out do each other, so be it."

Mari pauses here.

"I never thought I would be in love actually. Well, I looked ahead and saw the practical aspects of life; I pictured a kid or a husband, one distant day. But I never imagined, could not have imagined really, the feeling that would go along with this. I feel a lot of things; but mainly, and most surprisingly, is humbled. That God saw fit to deliver you to me; that everything would align in such a way that I would meet you, the only person in the world I could imagine spending the rest of my life with. And then that you and I are the only two people who could make this particular baby." She puts a hand on her belly. "I don't want to ever take it, you, our baby, for granted, because it's astonishing that we could be so lucky, that we are somehow deserving of such bounty.

So I vow to you that I will always feel grateful for you—even when you're annoying me, reading out loud from books when I am trying to work or watch TV. And I vow to you that I will work hard, compromise, sacrifice to make sure that we always stay in this place together; happy, connected, optimistic, joyful.

"It's one thing to be in love; but I also respect you, Christopher; your integrity and how each and every day you really try hard to be the best man you can be. I also admire you; your relentless curiosity and the way your brain works, how creative you are. And mostly, I like you. You make me laugh and you're so easy to be around and also you always let me order for both of us even if it's an entrée you don't particularly want and you know I do; which probably shouldn't be one of my favorite things about you, but it is.

"You always see the good in people, especially in me, and you make me want to be a better person. At the end of the day I don't know who loves who more here, but I vow to spend a lifetime trying to win that argument. I love you."

A single tear falls from the corner of Christopher's right eye, though no one else can see it. Mari hears sniffles from the crowd but doesn't break eye contact.

"Okay, wow, so..." Christopher pulls his hand away from Mari's and quickly wipes them down his pants, grabs them again. "Mari. Earlier this week we signed a legal paper binding us together and earlier today we stood in front of a public official who said the State of Florida finds our union legit. All that's important. I am counting on that tax break."

Laughter rises around them.

"But this here is far more important, the most important step, because this is when we pledge our love to each other in front of everyone we love. I want to stand here in front of all of our family and friends and make you three fervent promises with them as my witness. One, I will cherish you each and every day. I, too, realize how lucky am I, how lucky we are to have this, this beautiful and boundless love between us.

Two. I will always be Team Mari and have your back. Today, we feel invincible, like nothing could ever go wrong, but we're not going to be immune to misfortune, sickness, money issues, that failed screenplay I haven't even started writing yet. Who knows what will happen. But I want you to know that whatever comes our way, good or bad, we will celebrate or commiserate together, and anything I can do, big or small, to make your life easier or better, I will do.

"A lot of you here know how much I love my quotes; and I wanted to read something here that captured my feelings, that articulated better than I ever could how I feel. Shakespeare? Tolstoy? Dr. Seuss? Finally, I asked one of my best friends Jake, who I wish could be here today, since he's an award-winning writer after all, and a genius and not to mention the person who happened to bring us together. And Jake told me he'd write something for me and send it to me. So last night an email from him pops up—just like Jake to get down to the wire— and I was expecting poetry, profundity. So I open this email, and all it said is:

Sometimes there just are no words.

I'm very worried that this is a reflection of his writer's block." Christopher pauses for more laughter. "But then I got to thinking that this is poetic and profound, because actually Mari, the way I love you, can't be put into words. It's too big, too powerful, too infinite to be captured by something as inadequate as language. It's like trying to describe the sun or the ocean or the stars...okay, that sounded a lot less cheesy in my head... But it brings me to my third promise to you: I will be here for you and with you, reliable as the sunrise, faithful as the stars to the earth, with a love as relentless as the sea. I love you."

As Christopher speaks, Gabe, clearly moved, reaches over for Charlotte's hand and she has to fight the urge to pull it away. Charlotte feels sick to her stomach, like a caged animal. Every single emotion she's having while listening to these vows—anger, panic, envy—is so horribly out of step with what she should be feeling—happiness, joy, warmth—that it in turns causes another spiral of emotions—guilt, self loathing—and the swirling cauldron of all off this makes her feel as though she might, right here, shatter into a million pieces. She wishes she could blame her period but this is far beyond PMS. What is wrong with her?

This is Mari's special day, her big moment, and all Charlotte can think is: I want that, what she has. And also: I don't love Gabe. And then: I've wasted nearly three fucking years of my life. She's never loved Gabe. The simple fact of this is something she's always known, but seeing this display in front of her, seeing this love, authentic and effusive, pouring out before her eyes, so real that she almost feels like she could reach out and touch it, presses this realization into stark relief. Gabe was a placeholder at best, a crutch at worst. This relationship was only supposed to be temporary, until something better came along.

Charlotte remembers very clearly a feeling she had when she was little that time moved so slowly. When her brother got to do things she couldn't (ride a bike, go to school, sit in the front seat of the car) it seemed like forever until she would catch up.

Oliver is only older by two years, but it might as well have been a lifetime. But now time goes by in a flash, faster and faster. The last few years has passed her by and she has nothing to show for it. It's like an impossibly cruel trick; that time is gone. Poof! And if that happened with three years, it could easily happen with five or ten. She was already closer to forty than twenty, she didn't have years to lose.

She pulls her hand from Gabe's to pretend to wipe her eyes, but finds they are actually wet with tears. Mari's dad had started talking at some point while Charlotte was lost in thought and she snaps back to the moment in time to clap at the end of his speech. Mr. Castillo raises a glass, which gives Charlotte a way to occupy her hand, lest Gabe dare grab it again, and then everyone takes a sip of champagne. Or in Charlotte's case, guzzles it as quickly but as subtlety as possible. And then she runs. "Gotta pee, be right back."

She dashes off to the bathroom (this is becoming a theme this weekend) to try to collect herself. It will require all sorts of forces of will to pull it together so that she can be happy for her friend and so that she can enjoy the rest of the evening with Gabe and dance and laugh, all of which feels utterly impossible when all she wants to do is sneak back to the hotel—or better, the airport. And so she looks at herself in the mirror, steadies her breathing in and out and, in a particularly, but appropriately, desperate move, starts talking to herself. "You can do this Charlotte. Pull it together."

And then at some point, maybe three or so minutes in, she does. She feels better. In fact, she feels a sense of relief that comes from knowing what she has to do.

Break up with Gabe, for good this time. Actually, she decides, generously, that she will let Gabe break up with her. But that will come later and she'll deal with it later.

Tonight, she'll go hug her friend and tell her she's happy for her and mean it.

Then she'll kick off these shoes, which are gorgeous and thank god were found by Delta in time, but have left a huge welt on her right toe. And then she'll grab Gabe and dance with him and pretend to be delighted by his mortifying moves. She will not, under any circumstances, think about the future, think past the next champagne refill and the next song. And so, fortified with her plan to get through the next few hours, she washes her hands and follows the music back out to the dance floor. And, no joke, "I Will Survive" is belting out of the speakers and Charlotte lets out a genuine laugh. The universe is either mocking, ironic, or a hell of a cheerleader.

Ryan sees Charlotte pass in front of him, just as he's having an epiphany of his own. He has to tell Emily. Not tonight, obviously not tonight. But when they get home, he'll sit her down and pour her a glass of wine and he'll tell her about the money and the mortgage, and well, everything. He has no choice. He has to believe she'll understand...eventually. And she'll have his back, just like Christopher talked about in his vows. Having made this decision, more than fear, though there's that, he feels a sense of relief.

He leans over and takes Caroline from Emily's arms. She's tiny and perfect and sometimes when Ryan looks at her he can hardly bear it. With Owen it's different; he feels proud and cocksure, this is his son, he knows what to do. With Caroline the only thing he feels is awe. She already brings him to his knees.

Gloria Gaynor gives way to Michael Jackson on the playlist Julia has obsessed over for the last month and "P.Y.T." flows from the speakers.

"Come on baby girl, it's time for a father, daughter dance," he says to Caroline who coos in response.

"Can I come, too?" Emily grins up at him and he grabs her

hand, spins her around when she stands.

They join the small but mighty group dancing with abandon. Christopher's brother is doing a laughably bad but wholly committed impersonation of Michael Jackson.

Ryan watches Charlotte dance with Gabe with a huge smile on her face. Who knows, he thinks, maybe they have a chance after all. Because it's a wedding, the start of a new life, a fresh chapter; and that has given Ryan the sensation that anything's possible, including Emily forgiving him.

Julia appears with a camera. "Let me get a picture of you guys!"

Emily, Mari, Christopher, Gabe, and Charlotte dance towards each other, pose in a tangle of arms and smiles, blink against the bright flash.

"It's going to be hard to top this next year!" Mari says over the music while they're still huddled.

"I know! Where are we going to go?"

"I just realized something—every year our anniversary is going to be on your weekend," Christopher says.

"Oh great," Charlotte jokes.

"That's too funny. First your birthday and then your anniversary—these weekends are all about you, huh, Mari," Ryan teases.

"So where to?" Charlotte says, fantasizing about doing something daring, exciting, like when she up and travelled through Europe out of nowhere! There were still so many adventures she's somehow put off, like driving up the PCH and climbing a mountain. Not Everest or anything, but something. "Oh! How about Thailand?"

Charlotte suddenly has to go Thailand.

"Um, that might be hard with this one," Emily says, holding up Caroline in her arms. "And that one." She nods over at Owen who is chasing fireflies and trapping them in a mason jar Mari's mom gave him.

"And don't forget this one." Mari puts her hand on her barely there baby bump.

"Maybe a house in the Caribbean?" Emily suggests.

"That could work," someone says.

"We'll figure it all out," another voice carries over the music.

Right now, though, there's a more pressing concern: the electric slide.

Chapter Nine
Bermuda, 2010

She should not have come. This is the thought that has plagued Mari since landing in beautiful Bermuda hours ago. The sun is shining brilliantly, it dances on the crystal blue water of the resort's lagoon style pool, which is surrounded by tanned tourists, laughing, drinking, having the time of their lives. Mari watches them from the perch of her poolside lounge chair with a clinical detachment, as if she's observing animals in the wild. Oh look at them, happy people enjoying festive vacation rituals.

The cheerful scene before her is so opposite of her state of mind she almost feels like a contaminant, sure that the misery is coming off of her like heat waves, yet the revelers around her remain completely oblivious. This feels like an affront to her. Can't you see I am suffering over here, some desperate part of her wants to scream. How dare you...frolic?

"Get you something else, hon?"

Mari looks up, squinting in the sun, to find a pretty rosy-cheeked waitress standing above her lounge chair.

"Sure, another." She waves her empty cup, the last dregs of watered-down margarita drying at the bottom. "Thanks." What's another one, she thinks, calculating; her third? Her fourth?

The "old" Mari never would have done this: three drinks in the middle of the day, getting drunk alone. But when you lose your baby at twenty weeks and your mom's cancer comes back with a vengeance and your life, in general, becomes a tragic farce, you become a new version of yourself. The new Mari does all sorts of things that she normally wouldn't, like cry at work, or stay in pajamas all weekend, or sit by the pool at a five-star resort and wish she were anywhere but here, even though she knows full well there's no place she can escape to where her grief and anxiety and anger can't follow, not even sleep.

The one small mercy: strangers around her notwithstanding, she's all alone for the next few hours after insisting that Ryan, Charlotte, and Christopher go jet skiing without her. So there's no need or requirement to "buck up," or to "put on a happy face," to even speak at all beyond, "sure another." Some days, the bad days, the herculean effort required of her to maintain even the barest minimum of social graces saps her energy such that by the evening she can barely mumble "good night" to Christopher before falling into a trance-like sleep.

The waitress arrives with a sweaty plastic cup filled with electric green slush. Mari takes a long, hard sip that instantly gives her killer brain freeze. But the respite of physical pain, the sharp waves going up the back of her skull, is actually a pleasant, but too brief distraction. The tequila rushes to her head, which she's counting on to ward off the memories, images, and realities that flood her when her mind is left to its own devices.

But no, here they come: the face of the radiologist who went from smiling to pale white as she looked at the ultrasound. The doctor's calm reassuring tone, "We don't know why this happens, especially this far along. I'm so sorry." The wails that echoed through the exam room, which turned out to be her own. Coming to in the recovery room convinced she could feel the emptiness of her womb. Finding Christopher crying in the bathroom. Her father's voice, small and distant, on the phone,

"Mija, I have some hard news."

Her mother's bald head and frail frame.

Despite the tequila (or maybe, she now wonders, because of it?) these images run through her head in a more or less constant loop, unwelcome but as familiar to her now as her own reflection, and so she just surrenders.

The counselor in her miscarriage support group—who knew there was such a thing—told her and her fellow heartbroken almost-mothers that some women start to feel noticeably better when the birth date of their baby comes and goes. For Mari, that was April 16th, a day that she only managed to get through with gritty determination and two Valium. But she didn't feel better the next day as she hoped, or as an entire summer passed, and now here she was full circle, on the anniversary of one of the happiest days of her life, and yet she still feels numb on her best days, despondent on her worst. At least she doesn't cry when she sees babies in commercials anymore, so that could be taken as progress. Then again, she always turns the channel when those commercials come on, so maybe not.

The counselor had also told her she might feel better when she had another baby. The feeling of loss wouldn't go away, she'd said, but it would be replaced by the joy and the "beautiful diversion" (as she put it) of another child. This sounded promising in theory, but her and Christopher's half-hearted attempts to conceive again had so far been unsuccessful, which was actually okay with Mari since she was terrified, phobic really, of losing another baby and also because it felt oddly disloyal thinking of conceiving again. Like she was trying to replace the (irreplaceable) baby she'd lost, the baby girl she'd dreamed of.

But it's not like Mari doesn't want to feel better, that she isn't ashamed that she's allowed herself to settle in this dark place for weeks and months now; she had always prided herself on being a "strong" person, felt that she could deal with anything life threw at her, but that was an easy belief to hold so long as it remained largely untested.

Unlike Christopher she doesn't have the capacity for remembering quotes, but she knows there's a famous one about how character could be measured by how one dealt with adversity, or something to that effect, no doubt said by some sort of inspirational public figure? Lincoln? Oprah? Bobby Knight? She has no idea. But what did they know really?

And at least Mari wasn't a hypocrite. She has always tried, and hard, to be humble in the face of God, to be grateful for the many blessings she didn't deserve, but didn't it also follow then that she could feel resentful of the misfortune she also doesn't deserve; that she could fairly ask, why me? Mari recalls the stern pep talk from Frieda that disabused her of this notion.

Frieda had found Mari in the bathroom crying, this was her first week back to work "after"—that's how she now classifies her life since losing the baby. Frieda locked the door and leaned against the countertop watching her silently, as Mari tried in vain to pull herself together since even in her desperate state she was still mortified to be crying at work and in front of her boss. "I just...I don't understand why? Why me?"

Mari had whispered, hoarse.

Freida looked at her for a long minute. "I had a stillborn baby. Gave birth to her, held her, buried her in the dress we had planned to take her home from the hospital in."

She was staring off in the direction of the white wall behind Mari, as if seeing the memory, and then she turned to Mari, who had been so shocked by this confession, she'd stop crying. "Six months after that," Frieda continued. "My younger sister dropped dead of a brain aneurysm. She was thirty-one. And then Ted and I split up. That might have been my fault because the grief turned me into a crazy person. Something tells me you can relate." She looks down at Mari crouched on the tile floor. "So yep, honey, life can sure suck. But see, you aren't exempt from that. You're not special. Bad shit, even worse shit, happens to people all the time, so the question isn't really why you? It's why not you? And the next question is: what you are going to do about it now?

Spend your life crying in the bathroom? I don't think so. You just gotta deal. Simple as that."

Mari had stood up then, a move in the right direction at least.

"I want you to take the rest of the day off. Go home, cry, scream in your pillow. Get it all out. Then each and every day, I want you to fight like hell to feel a little bit better. Some days this will work, some days it won't, but you gotta try each day, okay, buttercup?" Frieda leaned over and rubbed her back, a gesture so uncharacteristic but so touching Mari had broken out into a fresh wave of grateful tears.

"Oh hell. Enough of this," Frieda said, but kindly. "Get out of here. And don't let anyone see you. You know I have a no crying at work policy." She grinned and gave

Mari another quick hug. "Oh and never tell Ted I told you about the baby. It's just...something he never talks about."

Mari stopped at the door, turned back around, paused. "What was her name?"

She had immediately worried she'd overstepped.

Frieda didn't say anything for a beat, as if answering was going to cost her something.

And then, quietly, "Sarah. After my grandmother."

Frieda's words resonated with her that day, and though they didn't have the magical effect of instantly curing her heartache, she does still think of that conversation and draw strength. When the darkness threatens to consume her—like three weeks ago when her dad had broke the news to her that her mother's last round of chemo didn't work and they were running out of options, and she'd understood with a clarity that pierced her through and through what that meant: her mother was going to die, and probably soon— Frieda's words echoed in her head. You're not exempt. Deal.

She's trying. She's been doing yoga, journaling, and reading a lot of Anne Lamott.

Right now she has a copy of Joan Didion's The Year of Magical Thinking in her bag. Not exactly a beach read, but it's inspiration she needs, not escape. She needs someone to show her how to do this, how to come out on the other side. She's already begun grieving her mother, which in one way is sick, but in another way gives her the comforting allusion that she'll be more prepared when the day comes. That if she has some sort of head start on the process, she'll be that much farther along. Mari has always been an overachiever.

She hears giggles and her thoughts are interrupted. They stand, tummies protruding in fluorescent bathing suits, at the lip of the pool, a few feet in front of Mari, holding hands and staring into the water. Mari tries to understand what they are saying but they're speaking another language, maybe German. It's clear though that they're trying to convince each other to jump in here at the deep end. Mari is just close enough that she could give each of the girls a little push with her extended leg. But she doesn't, obviously. Finally, the one who looks a little bit older, maybe eight to the other's seven, firmly grabs her friend's hand and yells, "jetzt!" And they disappear into the water, sending a vigorous splash of water shooting into the air, a few drops of which land on Mari. Seconds later their heads bob up and they are laughing, ecstatic, proud they did it. Together.

Between watching the little girls, best friends, and tucking into her now fifth cocktail, Mari knows it's only a matter of time, seconds, before her thoughts turn to Charlotte, a subject she's been trying to avoid and another reason why she didn't want to come on this trip. She's still trying to make sense of her feelings, of her anger, of why when she saw Charlotte's smiling, sympathetic face when they arrived at the hotel today, Mari, unbeknownst to anyone, wanted to smash it. Just one satisfying slap right across her cheek. Maybe it's the alcohol, or the sun, or the guilt over having this strange flash of rage, but Mari's cheeks burn and she holds her cold cup to them.

Mari has spent a lot of time trying to pinpoint the source of her anger. At first she thought it was obvious. That it had begun when Charlotte found out that Mari had miscarried (Christopher had sent everyone a text, she was too shattered) and Charlotte waited days to call her. Almost a full week. And what supportive words did she have to offer when she finally reached out? "You can try again, Mari. On purpose this time."

Mari knew that people could resort to some ridiculous platitudes in times like these, sometimes you just didn't know what to say, but her best friend? Charlotte was so glib, so indifferent, so distant, especially compared to others; to Emily, who stayed on the phone with her for hours, silently, while Mari just cried; or to Julia, who painted her a small abstract picture of baby footprints and handprints with a perfect Mary Oliver poem, and arranged for the most obvious baby paraphernalia to be packed away before Mari and Christopher came home from the procedure. That was friendship. What the hell was, You can try again? And if that quote about your character being tested in adversity is true, then so are one's friendships.

And then it occurred to Mari that the source of her anger could actually be traced further back, to last year. The night Mari had sent Charlotte the email that she was pregnant—the one that clearly indicated how happy she was—Charlotte had called the next day and immediately said, "you know you don't have to have it, right?" Mari was too surprised to say anything. She was having a baby with the man she loved; granted the timing wasn't perfect, but get rid of it? And also though she believed in a woman's right to choose, was a card–carrying member of Planned Parenthood, she would never herself have an abortion. It was a sin to her, as provincial as it may be, which she would have thought Charlotte understood.

"I'm just saying." Charlotte had plowed through Mari's uncomfortable silence.

"You barely know this guy. So you could wait until you're sure you want to marry him and then if you do, get pregnant then."

Is she kidding? Mari wondered. When did her boyfriend of almost a year become "this guy"?

"Charlotte, I am sure, very sure, I want to marry Christopher and I would never have an abortion. So, um, it's happening."

Charlotte was quiet, long enough for Mari to remember (of course) that Charlotte herself had had an abortion all those years ago and she wanted to explain that she didn't mean that there was anything wrong with it, that she didn't judge it, but that it was a personal choice, but before she could Charlotte was speaking, snippily. "Okay, well I just don't want to see you make a mistake. That's all."

Then, as usual, Charlotte turned the subject back towards

herself with big news of her own: that she and Gabe were getting back together. Talk about a mistake, Mari had wanted to scream. It wasn't until well after they hung up (after another thirty minutes of dissecting every detail of this ill-advised reunion) that Mari realized something: Charlotte had never said the words, "I'm happy for you" or "congratulations."

These two events, taken together, have morphed and meshed into a terrible conclusion in Mari's addled mind: that Charlotte never truly cared that she was pregnant, had in fact, thought it was a mistake, so it follows then that she never truly cared that she miscarried. And an even darker, cynical, awful part of Mari's mind took it further: Charlotte rooted against her, her wedding, the baby because she was jealous.

She allows for the possibility that this is an irrational feeling, given her current state of mind, but still, once she opened this door, to consider that Charlotte wasn't the friend she thought she was, she hasn't been able to close it. This open door meant other thoughts could leak in, like the realization that there has been a sticky web lingering just beyond the edge of her concrete awareness these last few years, a disconnect, a distance, certain flaws and fault lines in her friendship with Charlotte that she had ignored, or rationalized, or even missed, until this reckoning.

It's like last summer when she and Christopher got their first piece of art for their apartment, real grown up art, from a gallery. When they went to hang the giant abstract on the wall, a piece in the corner snagged on a nail, leaving a tiny tear. Mari probably wouldn't have noticed it at all if Christopher hadn't pointed it out, but now whenever Mari looks at the artwork, all she can focus on is that crack in the plaster canvas and wonder when it will inevitably spread and ruin the beautiful painting.

So the only thing Mari can do is try her best not to look too closely.

* * *

"I just don't understand. Why did they even come if they

didn't want to hang out?" Charlotte says. First Mari bails on jet skiing today, which fine, but then she and Christopher opt to have dinner just the two of them back at the resort. "I thought these weekends were about all of us hanging out. Together. Wasn't that the point?"

"And look what they're missing?" Ryan says sarcastically waving an arm around the restaurant. According to the concierge, this local place, walking distance from the resort (though a treacherous, long walk on a dark curvy street with no sidewalks), is one of the most popular spots on the whole island for tourists and locals alike. Ryan didn't know what he expected, but not someplace that's a dead ringer for a T.G.I. Friday's, complete with appetizer sampler platter.

The waiter arrives with their drinks, a pitcher of the house (and island) specialty, Rum Swizzles.

Charlotte continues, "But seriously, it's like she's been avoiding me. And I'm not being paranoid. I called her like three weeks ago and she just never called me back. I got some vague text like, sorry, things are hectic, catch up in Bermuda..."

Ryan swallows a big swig of the sweet fruity concoction. Okay, now he sees the appeal of this place: this drink is amazing. And strong. Holy shit.

"Charlotte, she's just having a tough time, maybe she doesn't feel like talking. I mean this year has sucked for her big time." And how Ryan can relate.

"Well, we've all had tough times this year. Breaking up with my boyfriend of three years was no walk in the park, you know." On some level Charlotte can see that this is a rather bold comparison, Mari's late term miscarriage with her breaking up with Gabe, but a loss is a loss. And the true trauma is being alone again and facing the prospect that she may never have a husband or a family and isn't that, in the end, the same heartbreak? Which is to say, she gets it, it sucks when you don't get to have the things you want most and so she stands by her original thought: they are all battling their demons. Speaking of... Charlotte notes that Ryan has already gulped down his drink and is pouring another.

She raises her eyebrows. "I thought you were cutting back? Project Make Emily Happy?"

"Well, first of all, she's not here is she? Second, I have been drinking much less at home. But third, we're on vacation, so sorry, but I'm getting hammered." He guzzles from his glass as if to underscore this point. "Jesus, we used to go on these trips and drink all damn day. When did it become a crime to drink?"

"Um, maybe when your marriage blew up?"

Ryan, ruefully: "Oh yeah, that's right."

Normally when reminded of his troubled marriage, in one way or another a daily occurrence, he got a pinching at the back of the eyes, and a tight painful feeling in his chest like an elephant was sitting on him, or like an elephant was inside him clawing to get out. He had even gone to see the doctor about it, convinced that he was having some sort of slow heart attack, or maybe lung cancer, something was eating at the muscles and fibers and what not inside of his chest. But the doctor chalked it up to stress, which is not a condition you get much sympathy for, especially from your aggrieved wife, so a small twisted part of him wished it were lung cancer after all. Then he had thought of Mari's mom and felt very guilty.

But right now he doesn't feel his chest tightening, rather with each sip he feels lighter, looser than he has in days or weeks. What's in this stuff?

"How are things, anyway?" Charlotte asks, silently deciding that she, too, will get hammered and picking up the pace.

"The usual."

"Gonna need a little more than that."

"I don't know. It feels like two steps forward and two steps back. She's still mad.

Still. And I mean, I get it. I did secretly take a second mortgage out on our apartment without telling her and then the market fell apart and I basically bankrupted us, so yeah she's working through her feelings of betrayal."

The process of which involves an awful lot of tears and passive aggressive punishments and tedious weekly sessions with

Sheila, a condescending couple's therapist Ryan has come to despise, though he's well aware that he's forfeited the right to complain about any of the above. He's concluded that the only thing to do here is allow himself to be hazed until either Emily forgives him or until he just can't take it anymore. He's giving himself until the end of the year to see which way that particularly cookie is going to crumble.

"How's counseling?"

He sighs. "Still the two of them spending an hour a week ganging up on me. I mean this chick makes no attempt to even pretend to be impartial. It's all, Ryan can you see how Emily feels hurt that you did this or that... Ryan can you see how it's your responsibility to win her trust back? Ryan, shall we re-examine all of the ways you've failed as a husband? It's seriously the worst. I feel like I have to win over two people, her and Emily and one is hard enough!"

He grabs a quick sip and then blows on, getting worked up now. "Get this, day before yesterday, Emily wanted to spend the entire session talking about how mad she was that I was going on this trip without her."

"But she's the one who changed her mind last minute when her boss asked her to work at the Delgado exhibit?"

"Exactly! She tells me that she really needs to work because since she's just gone back to the gallery she has to prove to Nathaniel that she's back in it. Mind you, I also got a whole thing about how hard it was for her to go back after taking four years off to raise the kids, as if that's my fault... And then also a whole thing about how she really doesn't have a choice now but to work given our finances. So it's my fault she left and it's also my fault she has to go back, even though she's been talking about wanting to go back for years. But then she tells me since we already got plane tickets and prepaid our hotel room there's no point in forfeiting both and that I should go. So I'm like, okay. Well apparently that was the wrong answer. I was supposed to know that even though she told me to go that meant I should really have insisted on not going. I really can't fucking win."

Does he want to even win? Just when he thinks he's gone through every hoop, faced every test, another one appears. He's beyond exhausted. He just wants things to be easy again, though he's starting to wonder if they ever were.

"Brutal. But can I ask you something?"

"Yeah, but first can we order? I need food stat to absorb at least some of this rum." Ryan collapses back in the booth realizing that he has officially reached inebriation while Charlotte waves down the waiter and orders them a plate of nachos.

"Okay, so why didn't you just come to me, Ryan? I would have given you the money."

"I needed $250,000 because I was going to bribe a federal judge! I wasn't going to get you involved in that!" Charlotte is the only person in the world who knows that.

He told Emily he needed the cash because he was planning to start his own firm. And even though every week the damn therapist reminds him about honesty, it's too late to tell Emily the truth now and anyway he didn't do it so doesn't that make it moot?

"But you didn't go through with it." Not that Charlotte would have judged if he did. Five years at Mayfield Construction and thirty-five years being Jonathan's daughter, she knows of slicked palms, tax shelters, fuzzy accounting, and shady backroom dealings.

"Not because I came to my senses. I don't even have that going for me. I destroyed Em's and my finances and fucking Vince left the firm anyway."

"It's good he left; a silver lining. It spared you from doing anything illegal. And Vince found another shady schmuck—not that you're a shady schmuck, but you know—to do his bidding and that guy will be kicked out of the bar, or go to jail and not you."

"But I also lost more than a million in a year in billings when Vince left, and with that my bonus. Oh and also my dignity when Tripper called a partner review." This was a tortuous exercise unique to Barker Jones and Simon in which any partner (in this case, Tripper, of course) could call a meeting where all of the partners got to together to evaluate or reprimand a colleague who was losing business, not bringing in enough business, or for some other misconduct; the whole point was to put you on notice...and to publicly humiliate you.

"All those fuckers raking me over the coals." Ryan is going to lose it thinking about their smug faces, their concerns about Ryan's "commitment," their decision to dock his bonus after he put in damn near ten (ten!) years, and Tripper's self-satisfied face: "Now may be the time to ask yourself if BJS is the best fit for you after all?"

"I seriously can't talk about this anymore, Charlotte." Ryan starts stuffing his face with nachos, even though along with not drinking as much, he's supposed to be eating better, too. This is all part of Emily's Ryan Improvement Plan—that its acronym is RIP is not lost on him. Her theory being that he has gotten off course and lacks discipline in all aspects of his life and that this is the root of all of his "self-destructive choices." So running again and eating kale is supposed to shape him into a better person. But this is what kills him. He is already a good person! Why can't Emily see that? He may have made one mistake, but it was all because he was trying to build a good life for them!

Your personal trainer isn't volunteering his time, Emily. He knows he fucked up—big time, and that it could have been so much worse, but he still feels like the punishment should fit the crime. He also needs her support to rebuild, or at least for her to ease up on him a little bit so he has some energy left over to figure out how he's going to dig them out of this hole.

The waiter comes over to collect the empty plate from the nachos they devoured and brings along with him two large shots. "For the happy couple, on the house."

Ryan and Charlotte graciously don't bother to correct him, they down the shots.

Within seconds Charlotte feels the room start to spin. "How many drinks did we already have? We should not have done that."

"Tell me about it, but too late now. Let's get out of here—walk to the beach?"

"It's pitch black?"

"So? Come on." Ryan drops a wad of cash, enough to more than cover the bill, on the table and gets up. Charlotte picks up the money and hands it to him. "Lemme.

You're broke, remember?" She smiles.

"Thaaass right," he slurs, also smiling. "I almost forgot."

They stumble along the same dark road that leads back to the resort.

Occasionally a car comes whizzing past, dangerously close, so they stick to the far shoulder, which is rocky and pockmarked. Charlotte trips in her wedges and Ryan grabs her hand to keep her from falling. He doesn't let go.

They see a small alleyway off the road that Ryan guesses will lead to the beach.

His navigational abilities are questionable at this point, hell he can barely stay upright, but they luck out and end up by the ocean's edge where they collapse in the cold sand.

"Jussss us." Charlotte is aware she's slurring her words. For stretches up and down the dark beach, they are the only people. In the distance, the waterline curves and they can see their resort about a half-mile down dotted with lights and overturned kayaks, but here, it's secluded.

"I love that sound."

"What sound? There's nothing."

"The waves."

"Oh that. Yeah, it's nice."

They lie back and listen, looking up at the sky, the thin streaks of grey clouds against the ink stained sky.

Charlotte rolls over so she is on her side, facing Ryan. "You know, I would have done it no matter what."

"Done what?" He turns to face her.

"Given you the money. Even if it was to bribe a judge."

Ryan is touched. This is what he loves most about Charlotte, she never judges.

She always has his back no matter what. When he needed money all those years ago, she was there. When he's needed a laugh, pep talk, drink, advice, anything, Charlotte's been there. And Charlotte gets him, understands who he is, a fucking good person, flawed maybe, but that fundamentally he's a rock star, okay not a real rock star, but like special. Bottom line: Charlotte believes in him.

And so because of all of this, and because it's a beautiful night and because Ryan is lost, and defeated and lonely and if he's, honest, a little horny, and he doesn't want to be any of those things, if only for an hour, he does what he does next. Which is lean over and kiss Charlotte. He's half-expecting her to push him away, to express shock or outrage, to remind them to come to their senses because someone should but he knows it won't be him. He decides he will kiss her until one of those things happen, but it doesn't. And pretty soon, he's not deciding at all, it's ...this...is just happening.

He slips her dress over her head. Pulls her hair back and thrusts his face in her neck, inhaling the scent of her, which is so familiar but suddenly so intoxicating at the same time. He moves to her chest, slightly warm with sunburn from being on the water all day, buries his face between her breasts, which are smaller than he remembered or imagined, but pert and perfect. He tugs at her bra now, desperate to get her nipple in his mouth and when she grips his hair and throws her head back and moans, loudly, it sends such a wave of pleasure through his own body that it's almost as if he's just come alive.

Urgently now, Charlotte takes off his shirt, pulls him on top of her. Lost in the moment, she shimmies out of her underwear and feels the cool superfine sand trickle into all sort of warm places, realizes that she's never had sex on the beach before. How it possible she had never done this? How is it possible they had never done this? How is it possible that her body can feel this good?

Ryan plunges inside of her. She feels almost like she did when she lost her virginity to David Dural, not in the sense that this is awkward or fumbling at all, it's the opposite, but in the fundamental sense that a line has been crossed, new territory has been entered, the world has tilted.

At one point Ryan pulls away from her, looks in her eyes. Charlotte wishes then she weren't so drunk so that she could clearly decipher his expression and what she sees there: longing, pleasure, desire...and love, that too.

Charlotte closes her eyes, her hips rhythmically rising to meet his as Ryan glides in and out of her. He's whispering her name in her ear with desperation. With each hot-breathed exhalation: Charlotte, Charlotte, Charlotte. She wants this to go on forever, but she feels the heat building between her legs, she knows she's going to come soon.

This is her favorite moment, reaching this precipice where it's clear to her that it's going to happen, in one minute, or maybe five and all she has to do is relax and wait for the ripple and waves to overtake her.

It is then that Charlotte has a thought as brazen, as exhilarating, as scary and as wild as the very scenario playing out: maybe, maybe it was Ryan after all.

* * *

Someone is waking Ryan up by stabbing him in the eye. How else to explain why he feels like his brain is being split open? He blinks, attempts to sit up, and then realizing that's going to require way too much effort, lies back down. Not that he remembers but thank god he had the presence of mind to close the blackout shades when he came back to his room last night, or rather this morning. He recalls seeing the light purple shadows of dawn at one point. And then, like a flood being released, he recalls everything else, too: sex with Charlotte. The delicate underside of her breast, her strong legs wrapped around him in a vice grip, her screaming his name. Regret, swift and intense, rises at the exact same time as an erection, which says pretty much everything about how utterly fucked up this is. A wave of guilt hits him so hard he rolls over and gags over the side of the bed. He dry heaves and a viscous reddish stream drips to the floor. One thought over and over: How did this happen?

He hears his phone vibrate in the pocket of his pants on the floor, but that is absolutely more than he can deal with. Especially, if it's Emily. Emily. This brings a fresh wave of dry heaves. He stumbles to the bathroom this time, hovers over the sink.

He stands up straight with his eyes closed waiting for the throbbing in his head to subside. When it deescalates from a jackhammer to more like the steady bass of a rap song, he opens his eyes. No surprise, he looks about as bad as he feels. Dark circles under his eyes, greenish tint to his skin, thick film on his teeth. He looks like a junkie after a week-long binge, this is what one night of overdoing it does these days.

Splashing cold water on his face helps, brushing his teeth is damn near transformative.

But not quite transformative enough because he is still the person looking back at him, a person, at the moment, he does not wish to be.

He has a series of visions, all of them unwelcome, in rapid succession. Emily finding out. Emily divorcing him because she would never forgive him for this, not for sleeping with Charlotte about whom Emily has always nursed a not so secret (and apparently justified) insecurity. Him sitting alone in his pathetic bachelor pad, where his kids come visit every other weekend. This is the one that hits him to his core, because he's always vowed he would never be that person, aka, his own father.

The horrible visions are followed by an equally daunting series of questions:

What kind of person was he? How did things get so out of control? How could he do this?

And of course, why? This is the one that will haunt him for years to come.

Now, he needs breakfast. A little fortification, coffee, and bacon and then (maybe) he can face today, tomorrow, his life. He goes to throw on his khakis from last night, but a handful of sand falls from them and there's a stain on the front of them he'd rather not think too much about. He takes his phone of the pocket, drops the khakis back on the ground, and digs in his bag for a pair of jeans and a t-shirt. Takes a deep breath and looks at his phone. Two missed calls from Emily, which bring more nausea, and a text from Mari: Headed to breakfast downstairs.

The Rusty Pelican, one of the resort's many restaurants is packed with bright-eyed couples and families ready to take on another day in paradise. Ryan spots Christopher and Mari at a table in the far corner. And then Charlotte, too, sitting with her back to him. He should not be surprised that she's here, but her presence, her proximity bowls him over. A surreal and all too vivid image flashes in his mind: his face buried between her legs, the soft dark brown fuzz of her pubic hairs. He can't do this.

But then he is, walking over to the table.

"Hi guys!" His voice is two levels louder than it should be.

"Whoa, you look terrible," Mari says. "And you smell like rum."

"Good morning to you, too," he sits down. Charlotte hasn't said a word or looked at him.

"Fun night, last night huh? Charlotte says you guys drank a lot." Ryan looks at Christopher sick with jealousy that he's alert, rested, bright-eyed—and not him.

"Yeah...yeah we did. I gotta eat." Ryan's been sitting for less than a minute but he's already chafing under the pressure of pretending everything is normal. "Be right back."

The restaurant features an extensive buffet, with various stations manned by chefs in large white top hats standing over gleaming silver trays, a faux glamour that distracts from the fact that you're paying $50 for soggy eggs. Biding time, he opts for the longest line: Belgian waffles. He aims to distract himself by people watching, by watching the ceiling fans above him whir, by repeating, it's all going to be fine, over and over in his head.

When he gets back to the table, plate piled high with food he now doesn't know if he'll be able to get down, they're discussing plans for the day, which for a split second is a concept beyond his comprehension. The consensus seems to be to just relax at the beach, and once decided everyone settles into silent chewing, an uneasy quiet.

"What's going on?" Mari looks from Ryan to Charlotte, back to Ryan.

"What do you mean?" and "Nothing," they say at the same time.

"We're just really hungover," Charlotte clarifies.

"Well, you can nap at the beach," Christopher says with such good cheer Ryan almost finds it aggressive.

"Should we go get changed, Mari?" They get up from the table, all the while Ryan fights the impulse not to scream, noooo, please stay! "We'll see you down there in like an hour."

"Sounds good," Ryan says, hoping he's hid his dismay that they're leaving and he and Charlotte are going to be alone; an unavoidable contingency that he is nonetheless unprepared for. Mari and Christopher aren't even a table away before Charlotte turns to him.

She has been up since 6 a.m., which is to say, she had a cat nap after she and Ryan came home from the beach around 4:30. She was awakened to a swirl of thoughts that she's been trying unsuccessfully ever since to wrangle into some sort of coherent stance, but it's something like, well we didn't plan that, but it was amazing, and I feel guilty, but maybe that means there's something here, we get each other and, yes, it's going to be messy and complicated, but that's life and we could figure it out and people may get hurt, but don't we owe it to ourselves, and maybe...maybe I love you.

But what she says, hesitantly, quietly, is: "So that happened."

"Yep." He takes a big bite of waffle. If they're just going to rehash the obvious this will be more manageable than he thought.

A pause. "So, what are you thinking?"

"I'm thinking we made a huge fucking mistake. Jesus." He says this more angry than he means to, but he is angry, at himself and a little bit at Charlotte, unfairly, but why did she let this happen? Like the sun rising this morning, slow and steady, a realization sunk into every fiber of Ryan's being: he can't lose Emily.

"Okay then." Charlotte struggles to process this and to absorb his certainty. She didn't know what she expected, but certainly more agonized ambivalence.

"Look, sorry, I'm just not sure what to say...I'm not sure what you want me to say." Ryan looks so pained, she prefers the anger.

"I don't know, but you don't have to be a dick."

"I'm sorry." His voice soft now, he leans over to Charlotte. "I just, I feel really bad, you know? I'm married. To one of your closest friends. What we did was completely fucked up."

"That's how you think of it?"

"Well, duh yeah, don't you?" And then Ryan sees it. She doesn't. She doesn't think this was a mistake, she doesn't regret it, at least not in the same way he does. He stares at her and sees something terrible: hope. This is as striking as it is horrifying, realizing that he could have Charlotte. He never thought this was possible. Sure they'd flirted in law school, but Charlotte has always been for him, unattainable, a tease and an aspiration. A beautiful wild card. God, Ryan loves Charlotte, he always will, but he loves his family more. And now because he's a confused, selfish, self-destructive asshole, he's hurt the two women he loves most in the world. Ryan has come to understand that you're only allowed a certain number of fuck ups in your life; it's like a game of Jenga and each other fuck up is a piece out of the tower, it's only a matter of time before the whole structure suddenly comes tumbling down. He doesn't have any fuck ups left. Charlotte starts to get up. "Yeah, it was a mistake. Let's just pretend that never happened. Obviously. I gotta go." She's all but running out of the restaurant. Ryan calls after her. What he would say if she stopped, he has no idea, but it doesn't matter, because she doesn't.

* * *

She hears the crying before she knocks on Charlotte's door. Mari woke up this morning feeling okay, better, like she could be a normal happy-ish person if for one day. She and Christopher had a really great dinner last night, they'd really talked, and had laughed and had fun, more fun than they'd had in months and Mari realized he was right to insist they come: they needed this. His spirits were lifted and in turn so were hers. And in her happier state, Mari decided she would set aside her anger and her cynical thoughts about Charlotte and have fun on vacation with her friend, which is why she's at Charlotte's door. So they can head down to the beach together, stopping at the lobby store to get good snacks and bad magazines and then pull their chairs close together to read over each other's shoulders.

The crying is unexpected. Mari hesitates and has a horrible thought lurking there in the hall: does she want to deal? She could walk away. But she doesn't, she knocks.

Charlotte opens the door with a red tear-streaked face. She doesn't say a word just turns around and flops down on the bed.

Mari sits next to her. "What's wrong? What's going on?"

Charlotte, staring into space, doesn't answer for a full minute. "I fucked up," she says. But then she thinks, wait, why am I taking all of the credit. "We fucked up," she clarifies.

"Who's we? What are you talking about?"

"Ryan and I." A pause. "We had sex last night."

It is like the air is whooshing out of the room. Mari hears a hollow echo of Charlotte's words bouncing off the walls around her. She had been rubbing Charlotte's back, but she abruptly pulls her hand away as if Charlotte's on fire and stands up.

"What?"

"You heard me, it just happened." Charlotte is already on her way to armoring herself against the regret, the shame and the hurt with a numb practicality that will allow her to move forward. It is what it is.

"What?" This seems to be all that Mari can say. She starts pacing the room and there's a knock at the door.

Ryan. He had come up to apologize to Charlotte and also to hash a game plan (secrecy at all costs), but one look at Mari's face and he sees he's too late. He's furious at Charlotte for betraying him, but then realizes he's standing on shaky ground.

"Mari, I...I can explain."

"No, no actually, you can't." She paces the small room, which feels even smaller by the minute. "I just.... I can't believe you guys did this. To Emily. Your wife. Your friend. Emily, who has been there for all of us. Who's already forgiven you for one big fuck up, Ryan. Who's become one of our closest friends!" Mari is getting hysterical now.

"How could you? It's..." She struggles to find just the word. "It's disgusting."

Charlotte should have known better. She was expecting a little compassion, some sympathy, at least for Mari to hear her out. A steely defensiveness rises up in her.

She's so tired of being the bad guy. "Well, sorry Mari we can't all live up to perfect ideals."

Mari barks out an outraged laugh. "Wait, are you kidding me? Perfect ideals?

Not sleeping with your best friend's husband and..." She turns to Ryan. "...not cheating on your wife is not perfect ideals. It's just common decency."

Ryan collapses on a chair in the corner and buries his face in his hands, wishes futilely for the obvious: that he was anywhere, anywhere but here. They're all quiet for several seconds because no one, least of all not Ryan, knows what the hell to say.

Finally, Mari: "I just don't get it. You have everything, Charlotte, but what? You just had to have Ryan, too?"

"So, I'm the harlot who seduced poor little innocent Ryan. Give me a break."

"Yeah, it wasn't like that, Mari. I'm equally to blame." Ryan can't help but to feel somewhat chivalrous at jumping in to accept the blame here.

"See? And also, I have everything? HA. That just goes to show you, you have no idea what's going on in my life. You're so wrapped up in your own life—and up Julia's ass. " Charlotte is well aware that she's muddying the waters here, but it's something she's been thinking of for a while, Julia is the worst.

"Are you kidding me? Do you even hear yourself? Are we in

middle school? And also, I'm wrapped up in my own life??? My mother is DYING, Charlotte. Do you understand that? And my baby..." Mari can't even bear to get into that. She takes a quick breath, fighting tears, and regroups. "You do have everything, Charlotte—you just don't ever appreciate it. You always want more! It's always poor, poor, Charlotte. And you want us to feel bad for you for the drama YOU create. That's all you do! Create drama. And do whatever you want, no matter who it hurts, like stringing Gabe along!

And sleeping with Ryan! Jesus. Both of you are so selfish and entitled. It's like whatever you want you deserve to have, everyone else be damned. I'm so sick of it."

Ryan sinks deeper into the chair under the weight of Mari's accusations, because she's right. Meanwhile Charlotte, blind with fury, shame, outrage, stands up, walks over to where Mari is standing and stands two inches in front of her friend. "Fuck. You."

Mari stands there for a moment in shocked silence.

"Honestly you two can have each other. I'm leaving."

"Don't go, Mari," Ryan calls out half-heartedly.

By the time Mari has made her way to the elevator bank she's pulled up Delta on her phone and discovered, thank god, that there's a flight that leaves in four hours. She doesn't care how much it costs to change their tickets or buy new ones, this island isn't big enough for her to share it with Ryan and Charlotte and their bullshit. And by the time she gets back to her room, she is in blinding, angry tears. This was supposed to be *a good day!*

Christopher's standing in the middle of the room in bright orange swim trunks applying sunblock. "What's wrong?" he asks when a stricken Mari barrels in and starts slamming clothes in her suitcase.

"I can't talk about it now. I'll tell you on the way to the airport. We just need to leave, okay? Please."

And this is why Mari loves her husband because without another word he starts gathering his stuff in the suitcase. "Okay, let's go home."

* * *

"What now?" Charlotte sits on the bed, staring into space, numb. Ryan sits down next to her, but doesn't say anything.

"Are you going to tell Emily?"

"What, no? No." Ryan is concerned because he thought that this would be obvious. Emily can never know. He'll have to call Mari later, when she calms down, convince her of this, that it was one tragic, awful stupid mistake and will never, ever happen again so what would be the point in telling, in hurting her for no reason.

Charlotte curls up on the bed in fetal position. The full weight of what's happened is slowly sinking in. She'll never be able to face Emily again. Mari will never forgive her. Ryan will always blame her, convincing himself that this was entirely her fault so that he can live with himself. An unbearable sadness settles over her now as she realizes what this, this one night of a stupid, drunken hook up with her best friend, has cost her: everything.

Ryan lays behind Charlotte, spoons her. He braces himself for her to pull away, but instead she starts crying, silent, shaking sobs.

"I want a do over," she says between sobs.

"I know, so do I."

"I mean, everything. Don't you wish you could go back and do everything again, but differently?"

"Every fucking day," he says sadly.

They lie there quietly for a long while, until Ryan suspects that Charlotte, spent, may have fallen asleep. It's going to be a tough twenty-four hours before their respective flights tomorrow, hers at 11 and his at noon. But lying there together, he can see how they will power through, how it will be awkward, but if they try really hard, not unbearable.

"I love you, Charlotte." Ryan's voice is barely a whisper. "I'm sorry." And then after a pause: "It's going to be okay." He gently gets up, tiptoes to the door and leaves without looking back.

Two truths and a lie. This is what a fully awake Charlotte thinks as she turns to lie on her back. The click of the door shutting is the loudest sound she's ever heard in her life. She holds her breath as she listens to Ryan's footfalls echo down the tiled hallway and then they, too, fade away.

Chapter Ten
New York & San Francisco, 2011

It feels like a miracle. Emily's warm breath on the back of his neck. Her arm heavy across his shoulder. Ryan has tossed and turned for the last few hours—nothing new since he hasn't slept well in years. What is new is this: that Emily, in her sleep, just reached for him, pulled herself close to him, so they are spooning, though that's a word that makes Ryan cringe, like moist.

This used to happen fairly regularly; one of them would consciously, or unconsciously, reach for the other across the expanse of their bed in the middle of the night. Right after they moved in together, when waking up with someone else in your bed day after day was still novel for them both, they would actually wake up to find that they were holding hands. But ever since...well, everything, they've pretty much kept to their respective sides of their king size bed. Ryan considers it a win even to be in the same bed still, so he will take what he can get. But this, unexpected, unbidden gesture of intimacy fills him with such a sense of hope that they are finally, finally somewhere better, that he wants to sing, or scream, but he dares not risk moving even a muscle lest sleeping Emily pull away.

Their therapist Sheila's words ring in his head from the end of their session earlier this week: "I'm really proud of you guys. You've worked hard and made so much progress."

Ryan and Emily both sat there smiling like diligent students before a tough, but beloved teacher, filled with pride to have made the grade. And, still feeling flush, they decided, spontaneously, to call the babysitter after their session and ask if she could stay for another two hours, so they could have dinner.

"Strip House?" Ryan had suggested, even though it was overly sentimental, cheesy even, (and maybe a little fraught, too), to return to where they went on their first date and have celebrated at least half of their anniversaries.

"I think that's probably a little too extravagant?" Emily said tentatively. "How about Grace's Diner?"

Not so long ago, this exchange would have been laced with tension. Emily would have felt that Ryan, as usual, wanted to indulge every whim, even though they'd agreed to a budget, an impossibly hard budget designed to get them out of debt. And Ryan would have felt Emily was judging him, controlling him, possibly even punishing him.

There was a likelihood that it would have quickly spiraled, as so many of their arguments did, into such well tread territory, as familiar to them as their children's faces. Out would come the what were you thinkings and the you can't hold this over my head forevers and the you should have thought of that and the if you really loved me you would/wouldn'ts. Which would ultimately build to the worst of all: "Her, Ryan? Of all people. How could you?" Which never failed to wreck him on so many levels.

But now they're learning to give each other the benefit in moments like that—deciding where eat—and that has made all the difference. Sheila has helped them to "reframe their issues," and "take emotion out of the equation," and shown them all sorts of other "tools," disguised as catch phrases that Ryan first thought hokey and a waste of time...until they actually seemed to work.

After disliking Sheila for so long (which he now sees was a classic case of shooting the messenger and deflection) he finally crossed the line to a grudging respect for her and for her patience. After all, he could hardly imagine how it was possible to sit and listen to people's bullshit, their dark, ugly dramas, day in and day out. Ryan would go crazy. A few months ago he told Sheila that and how he was sort of amazed that the tools were working. And she looked at him and Emily, side by side across from her on the grey loveseat, and said, "They work because because you guys love each other and you do the work. You guys are fighters."

This comment made Ryan realize something and hey, isn't that what therapy is all about, life-changing realizations and epiphanies. It was a two-part realization really, a sort of good news bad news scenario. The bad news, and this has slowly unfolded for him over the last year, is that Ryan understands now that he married Emily for all the wrong reasons. It was like a game of musical chairs; he was ready to settle down and she was sitting before him when the music stopped, looking like the poster child for WIFE. He's now had enough of his friends get divorced (or complain incessantly about their wives) that he knows this sentiment is nothing new, so many of his guys friends have explained their marriages in such a way, which is basically: it seemed like a great idea at the time and it was time.

It's not that Ryan hasn't always loved Emily—no question there, he has. But if he's honest with himself, and that's something that's his top priority these days—he loved her for the wrong reasons. Her appeal was entirely based on how she made him feel: adored, admired, and how seamlessly she fit into the glossy vision he had for his life. Of this selfishness, he is ashamed. But here's the good news: His love may have started out superficially, in a way he was too young and immature to understand, but it has grown deeply. Ryan has watched Emily grow up, too, beside him; she's an amazing mother and she kicks ass at work at the gallery and he is awed by her. Her calm, her confidence, her patience. And most of all her strength.

This is why Sheila's comment struck him so much—because he realizes that the thing he loves most about Emily is that she's a fighter. No matter what life (or he) has thrown at her, Emily never wallows or whines, never plays the victim, never gets stuck.

And that's what everyone else seems to do, himself included—rationalize, blame, hide, etc. Because the alternative, namely, dealing with your shit in a healthy, self-aware way, is so fucking hard. It takes work, you have to fight—and Emily does it, and god, he admires her for it. After he had laid everything out for her after Bermuda last year—the hardest conversation of his life—she had left and gone to stay with her parents in Boston—the longest four days of his life. When she got back, they talked, all night. She had made him a promise (even though it was he who should have been making promises): "I'm hurt Ryan. And I don't know how I am going to trust you again. But I'm going to have to try, because I love you and I love our family. I promise I'll try."

It was more than he deserved; they both knew that. But for Ryan the unbelievable takeaway was that Emily knew that he wasn't a dick, he wasn't a fundamentally bad person, he wasn't irredeemable, he just fucked up. And that she understood that he would make it up to her, this he vowed time and time again.

Whereas he once was willing to do anything to get the life he thought he wanted, now he would do everything just to keep the life he already has. And he has made it up to her—in a million ways, large and small—and slowly they are coming out out of their financial and emotional hole, both of which have required more patience and sacrifice and stamina than they knew they were capable of.

There are tough days though; an unforgettable one last Christmas, when Emily came home from her work holiday party after drinking way too much. Ryan found her sobbing in their room. "I want to ask you something," she said when he sat down next to her.

Ryan braced himself.

"Have you talked to her?" she asked in a whisper.

"No, I haven't," Ryan said, rubbing Emily's back. She didn't need to say her name. "I won't." Not that Emily had or would ever ask him not to. She told Mari the same thing too during one of their long heart to hearts; that she didn't expect her not to be friends with Charlotte, that she didn't want her to have to choose sides. Somehow in forgiving Ryan, Emily knew she needed to forgive Charlotte, too. It takes two to tango.

Emily cried quietly for a few minutes and then said something completely unexpected: "It's weird, I miss her. I actually really miss her."

Ryan, of course, knew better than to say, I miss her, too, and actually, he's not sure that he does. Or at least he can't isolate that in the tangle of feelings he has about Charlotte. But he doesn't feel a sense of longing for her or the desire to be in touch with her; he feels like she, necessarily so for a lot of reasons, is a part of his past. He will always love Charlotte.

She allowed him to be the guy he was, however fucked up and flawed. And although it was never really about comparing Charlotte and Emily, he knows that Emily is helping him to be the man he wants to be.

What he does miss, though, is the group, their threesome that grew over the years; the boozy dinners and the late night talks and the constant chatter between them on email and text. He can't lie, there's a void now where that used to be. They do see Mari and Christopher from time to time, but that's gotten harder with work and the kids.

Emily lets out a soft sigh. Ryan still hasn't moved, and her arm is still draped on his shoulder. And for no reason (or every reason), he remembers that it's Mari and Christopher's anniversary this weekend. It seems like just yesterday they were in Florida for their wedding, but then it also seems like a lifetime ago, a surreal mental time warp that confuses Ryan. And if it's Mari's anniversary, it's their weekend, a fact that Ryan is shocked that he is only now thinking about. In another universe, where everything worked out differently, they'd be all together in Thailand, or Buenos Aires, or Austin right now, laughing, dancing, drinking. Ryan is disturbed by how difficult that is to imagine. But it doesn't matter because Ryan doesn't want to be in Thailand or Buenos Aires or Austin. He wants to be right here, in his own bed, with his kids sleeping soundly on the other side of the wall, held by the woman he loves most in the world.

* * *

Fighting the urge to check the time yet again, and having read every Twitter update (she's on a Facebook moratorium), Charlotte flips her phone face down on the bar. She catches her reflection in the beveled mirror, distractedly fixes her hair, and then looks around once again. No one else is sitting at the bar alone. But they did agree to 7 p.m. at ABV in the Mission (she's already read back through their texts and confirmed the time and place—twice). But it's now—fuck it, she turns her phone over and checks it—7:36. It's pretty safe to say her OkCupid date is a no-show.

So much for that distraction, which was her main goal this weekend. So much so that she had agreed to go home last night for dinner with her parents. It was either that or go to a dinner party at her friend Lucy's—full of married people—or hang out alone with her thoughts, so it came down to a lesser of evils thing.

This morning she ran six miles, and then went to both therapy and acupuncture and then got a blow out.

All of this distraction, this staying busy, staying Zen, is all in an effort not to lose her mind like she's lost her friends. This goal has been only marginally successful, especially in the last few weeks. Actually, it was probably July when she began to dread this weekend with as much excitement as she used to look forward to it with. First, she found herself nurturing the tiniest hope that somehow they, Ryan or Mari, would be in touch and they would meet up. Ridiculous, she realizes. A silly pipedream.

Then another idea had flickered: what if I reached out? Her Gmail drafts folder is filled with various missives she's written over the last year; apologies, explanations, pleas for mercy. But they have and will remain unsent because what is there to say, really? And, even if there were magic words, Charlotte isn't brave enough to break the silence. If someone gave her an opening—perhaps she would take it. But she just doesn't have the courage to put herself out there. She's discussed this with her therapist, Wendy, the one she found the very week when she got home from Bermuda last year in her first step to figure out, what the fuck is wrong with me? Turns out, a lot.

When they discuss Charlotte reaching out to Mari or Ryan,

Wendy never fails to ask, "What's the worst that can happen?" Charlotte gets this logic, because basically, it already has. But still, she can't, and anyway this is her least favorite therapy topic, though granted she's always the one to bring it up, so she usually pivots to something about her dad and childhood, because heaven knows there's a lot there. Her therapist is probably secretly writing a case study.

Her second least favorite topic, though one they've been spending a lot of time on is Charlotte's "entitlement issues." Wendy's theory, though she presented it much more diplomatically than this is: Charlotte is basically a poor little rich girl. Which is to say that she grew up in a household that valued getting what you want at all costs and that she was given everything her heart desired or that money could buy and she's internalized this message and value system. Her privilege has made her believe that she deserves things, that she is entitled to things, material and otherwise, and that she can somehow buy or manipulate her way out of her feelings.

So yeah. Wendy tells it like it is, but in a loving way. And her office at least has plenty of Kleenex for when you realize just what an awful human being you are and are filled with a loathing that previously was reserved for evil dictators and pedophiles. But Wendy will never fail to remind her of the pointlessness of beating ourselves up, that we are all a work in progress, etc., etc. To which Charlotte will explain that she just wants to be done, fixed, cured, better. And Wendy will say, "There are no shortcuts." And Charlotte will feel like a jerk, because isn't that part of the problem, she wants what she wants now. And the cycle begins again, a maddening circle.

She just wanted a break from herself and her thoughts, especially this weekend.

Which is why she thought this would be a good idea— meeting a handsome stranger in a dark bar would be the perfect distraction. She could be anyone she wanted to be for the next few hours—even the improved version of herself she was determined to create.

But as they say, everywhere you go, there you are, and here she is alone, in a bar, having been, it's safe to say now, stood up. At least she's sitting at the bar, not facing an empty seat across from her at a table and a waiter who's checking in sheepishly every ten minutes. A small mercy.

She's surprised that she doesn't feel more furious, like how dare him. She's well past angry; she's resigned. People, herself included, are sometimes dicks. That would seem cynical, but to Charlotte it's liberating. When you let go of the idea that everything and everyone should and will bend to your will and will act and behave exactly how you desire, it's liberating. Wendy would be proud of this, Charlotte thinks.

She'll make a point to share at her next session.

The bartender has, all night, reminded her of a certain celebrity that she could not pinpoint until right now: Paul Walker! It's the bright blue eyes. He's been pleasantly distant, so far, but now he comes over to her and places a chilled martini in front of her, one she didn't order.

"It's on the house, beautiful." He smiles in such a way that the complement seems genuine, not sleazy or slick.

"Thank you."

He doesn't ask if she's waiting on anyone, or what brings her in tonight, or how her day was. He just says, "cheers," and leaves her be.

She sips the martini, it's cold, crisp, perfect. The bartender sees her look of appreciation from the other end of the bar and winks at her.

She smiles and raises her glass, decides that maybe it's a good thing her date never showed. You never know.

* * *

Mari has both her hands and feet pressed firmly into her pink mat; is pushing her hips up in the air, in downward dog. This leaves her head only inches away from her round belly.

"Now take a deep breath and push your hips, higher. One

more inch," comes the instructor's soothing but demanding voice. Mari makes an effort to do so and this is when it happens: she farts. Loudly. A hazard of pregnancy that she will never, ever get used to.

Julia, on the mat next to her, immediately collapses in a fit of hysterical giggles.

And because Julia's laughter is contagious—even if it comes at Mari's expense—Mari falls out of the position in a fit of laughter, too. And inexplicably, they just can't pull themselves together, even as the teacher and other students glare at them with utter contempt. Yoga is a serious matter and the 11 a.m. Sunday class at YogaWorks is the hardest class to get into, with a waiting list ten people long every week.

Still laughing, Julia quickly nods towards the exit, grabs her mat and tiptoes out the door, which mercifully they're near, leaving Mari no choice but to grab her mat and follow, silently mouthing her apologies at the un-amused instructor.

Outside she finds Julia still doubled-over. "It never gets old!"

"I can't help it!" Mari whines.

"Well, I can see that. That was the third yoga fart this week. I literally cannot stop laughing...it's too much. It's like every time you bend over you fart." This sends Julia into another fit.

"I'm pregnant! You just wait until you're pregnant."

"Not going to happen. I'm Auntie Julia forever. Especially if it means I keep my dignity."

Mari rolls her eyes and stalks down the narrow hall that leads to the street.

"Come on, let's get out of here. I'm starving."

Mats tucked under their arms, they spill out onto Union Square and blink in the bright sun.

"Holy shit, it's like eighty degrees out here."

"I know. And this fetus is an oven." Mari feels sweat trickling down her back; between the farting and the sweating, not to mention that she feels as big as a house and has months left to go (and grow), Mari can't say that this experience is as glamorous as she had hoped, but still she's grateful. Public humiliation and swollen ankles is the least of the sacrifices she'd be willing to make.

Mari is also actually grateful for the oppressive fall heat wave because she has been trying to forget the time of year; that it's fall, and what she would normally have been doing this weekend. She has no idea if Julia realizes the significance of the weekend, probably not. Christopher does—he tried to get her to go away, first to D.C. (too hot), then to Napa (too far), or a cabin upstate (too quaint). Finally, they agreed they would celebrate their anniversary last night by ordering Thai and binge watching Breaking Bad, and Mari couldn't think of anything more perfect. Besides, technically they had already celebrated their anniversary a little early, with the cruise last month. Mari's parents had always wanted to go on one, and since this summer marked their thirty-fifth wedding anniversary, they all decided to go on an "anniversary" cruise together.

Mari hated the idea given her fear of confined spaces and of the norovirus, especially since she was pregnant. She had just passed the twentieth week mark and was only finally starting to feel calm, feel positive, that she allowed herself to believe that this was really happening and tragedy didn't await again, something she feared she wouldn't have been able to bear. But to be able to see how much her mother enjoyed the cruise, though still weak from her latest bout of chemo, made putting aside her cruise qualms all worthwhile.

There was also the fact that it was bad timing for her to take a full week and a half off work with three months of maternity leave looming. After years of legwork, Mari was bringing Stone and Associates first major high-profile pro bono case to court—a class action suit representing current and past employees of a major media company for racial discrimination. She had been terrified to tell Frieda that she was pregnant, the timing truly couldn't have been worse, as the first trial date is just two weeks before the baby is due. But Frieda took it in stride, shrugging as Mari stammered her news and worries. "Just hire more people to pick up the slack—make sure they're as good as you," Frieda said.

And then, "I'm happy for you, kiddo."

With everything going on, Mari has largely been able to put Charlotte, and Bermuda, and the sticky, murky, complicated morass which is their friendship, or rather, was their friendship, out of her mind. But this weekend, for obvious reasons, it was front and center.

"So, which one?"

Mari, lost in thought, hadn't realized Julia had been talking.

"Sorry, I'm a space cadet."

"Do you want to get burgers or pizza?"

"Burgers! Shake Shack please."

"Done."

"And then fro-yo from Sixteen Handles?"

"You pregnant ladies, you can just do whatever you want and all of us sycophants around you have to bend to your will."

Mari grins. "Yup, that sounds about right."

"Lucky girl."

"I know," Mari said, and she did.

Epilogue
Boston, 2012

The rain pours outside the window in slick sheets—her drenched umbrella lies on the floor, everything feels soggy. Charlotte tries not to see the rain as an ominous omen.

She stares at the muffin she's been picking at, because she's too nauseous to eat. She tries to chalk the nausea up to the fact the she hasn't really eaten or slept in days, since she got the email that Professor Wallace had died and booked the flight that got her to Boston two hours ago. But the truth is, it's the nerves. Any second now, Ryan or Mari will walk into this new sleek coffee shop, a variety of which it seems have completely colonized Boston since she lived here years ago, and Charlotte has no idea what will happen. But she takes it as a good sign that they are even meeting like this; she's still stunned that Mari reached out. Her pipe dream, come true.

Charlotte picks up her phone from the table, reading Mari's email again, for the hundredth time, desperately mining the text and subtext for clues as to how this afternoon might unfold.

Sep 10 (8:01pm)
To: Ryan <lawman02@gmail.com>;
Charlotte <CMayfield@gmail.com>
From: Mari <MaribellaC@hotmail.com>

"Hi-I guess you guys heard about the Prof. I'm so heartbroken. I saw him for lunch last winter and he was in such great health...I know he was getting up there, but he was so strong and energetic. I just...can't believe he's gone. I'm glad I can remember him like that though, as bright-eyed, funny, and of course, fired up about, well, everything, as usual. God, he was an incredible man. Do you remember the time that he roped us into helping him make those blackberry pies from scratch? Because everyone was teasing him about the disastrous concoctions he made for the holiday faculty potluck ever since his wife died.

Why on earth he thought we could make a better pie is beyond me. But, then again, as I recall, it was a pretty damn good pie. Anyway, I'm going to the service on Saturday. I guess I felt like I should let you know. Are you guys going? I figured since it's been a while, it would be good to have a heads up if we were going to see each other (or not). So, let me know if you'll be there.

Either way, hope you're well."

It was Ryan who wrote back first: "We killed it on the pie. Ugh, sorry, bad choice of words, I guess, given the circumstances. I loved the guy. I'll be there on Saturday."

And then Charlotte: "I wouldn't miss it. And I'm looking forward to seeing you guys. I get in on the redeye, and service is at 11 a.m. Maybe a quick coffee before?"

Charlotte remembers her hands trembling as she sent that email. So much for giving up. Instead she'd ask them to get together, almost like nothing was wrong. What was she thinking? She fully expected Mari and Ryan to either ignore her, or make up polite excuses, or even say, are you kidding me? So when Mari wrote back: "Sounds good." And Ryan said, "Cool," it felt like a miracle or, like the most normal thing in the world, which in this case amounts to the same.

So here Charlotte sits, sweating in her black dress, and waiting.

The door opens, ushering a whoosh of chilly air and Charlotte's breath catches, but it's just a mother with a young toddler rushing in out of the rain. She waits for her heart to stop racing, but it doesn't have a chance because seconds later, Mari walks in.

Charlotte has a quick minute to appraise her while Mari shakes out her umbrella and scans the coffee shop. She looks good; her hair is super short now, which is a shock but suits her, and she's put on some weight, but she carries it well. She looks confident, self-possessed, in a way that Charlotte hasn't seen (or noticed) before. Charlotte waves and Mari looks over, smiles. Dare Charlotte even think it, but Mari looks happy to see her, or if not happy, at least not tense.

Charlotte is debating whether she should get up to hug her but shyly stays in her seat as Mari sits down opposite her.

"Hi," Mari says, somewhat formally.

"Hi...Do you...do you want a coffee?" Charlotte stupidly waves at the latte she already has.

"I'm okay for now. Maybe I'll get something later." They are tentative, formal because they don't know how else to be; the memories of their once easy comfort, the specter of their former intimacy hovers in the air like a shadow, a sad vestige.

Charlotte breaks the silence that quickly borders on becoming awkward. "So, um, what's new?" Mari laughs and it feels like a gift. The tension is still there, but it's lifted a little, like the sun burning off morning fog. They can laugh and that's something, everything.

"Well, I guess the biggest, newest thing is, Lena? She's eight months. Did you know?" Mari asks tentatively.

Charlotte didn't know, and that she didn't kills her. Mari had a baby.

"I didn't know! Wow. I'm so happy for you. Pictures stat, please."

Mari pulls out her phone and pulls up her photo roll. "Well, there are about a million here, scroll until you get sick of it."

A chubby baby with a mop of curly hair, huge blue eyes and four bright teeth grins at Charlotte.

"God, she's beautiful, Mari." Charlotte would have said this no matter what, but it happens to be very true.

She passes the phone back to Mari, who lingers on the picture open on her screen—Lena eating pears, her favorite, last week—before putting it back down.

"Thank you. We're taken with her."

"Christopher's good?

"Yeah, he's great. Still at Random House and he's actually writing a book himself.

It takes up all of his free time, which is not much with a baby, and it tortures him, but he loves it."

They both look up then as Ryan walks in. The first thing Charlotte looks for is his wedding ring. She's almost positive she would have heard if he and Emily had split, news of divorce spreads like wildfire on the friends of friend network even off Facebook, but she needed to see for herself and there it is, proof that he and Emily are still together and she feels traces of a lot emotions seeing this, surprise, envy, happiness, but mostly, relief.

"Hi guys?" Ryan approaches them tentatively, unsure, which is so unlike his usual bravado, but endearing nonetheless. He's standing on Mari's side of the table and leans over and kisses and half hugs her quickly. Charlotte, tucked in the booth, wants to say, me too, longs to reach for him to embrace, but she doesn't, obviously.

"I already got coffee," he holds his cup up. "From Union Station. I couldn't wait. The train left at 6 a.m. but I couldn't sleep and this joker kept talking in the quiet car..." Ryan wills himself to stop blabbering on and calm down. This is going to be fine.

The three of them are quiet, no one knows where to begin.

"So...this is weird, no?" Ryan chuckles nervously. "All of us back...here."

"Yeah, and sad," Charlotte says. And then quickly adds: "About Professor Wallace." But she means this, too, this fraught reunion.

"Yeah, he was a great guy. Even though he gave me a B. Still bitter." Ryan laughs.

"So, Mari told me all about little Lena..."

"She's amazing, isn't she?" So Ryan and Mari are in touch. He knows Lena, has probably held her, their kids have probably played together in Central Park. This pierces Charlotte, the cast out, but she plows on.

"How about you...how's...things?" Charlotte can't bear to be more specific than that, to ask about Owen and Caroline who probably have no memory of her, to ask about work or where they moved (she did know that they had lost the apartment), and especially, to ask about Emily. So rolled up in that vague question, she hopes, is everything.

"Good, actually. Really good." And it's true.

He smiles. "We moved to Brooklyn a few months ago, full circle, which is great, the kids love it. I coach Owen's soccer team."

Charlotte waits for the envy, for that cold dark place inside to rise up to her throat, and the cackling witch-like voice to taunt her: See, look at all the happy families and you always all alone. But instead she feels happy, and uncomplicated, unmitigated happiness and this, this more than anything tells her about the progress she's made.

Charlotte turns to Mari. "I'm really sorry about your Mom." Perhaps she shouldn't bring this up because it's too painful, but it needs to be said. She had learned that Mrs. Castillo had died after an abrupt return of her colon cancer from the alumni listserv; one of their other classmates was taking up a collection. Charlotte had sent a check, a woefully inadequate gesture, but something.

"Thank you." Mari says simply. This is something, her mother's death, the fact that she had to face it at the same time as she was dealing with losing her friends, that she can't focus on lest the darkness comes back. So instead she focuses on Lena's chubby legs wobbling as she tries to stand, or the way Christopher looks when he talks about his book, his dream, or the way Julia rubs her own pregnant stomach and tells Lena her best friend will be here soon. In other words, she focuses on the future. It saves her every time.

The trio quickly turns to safer topics, who is speaking at the service, which of their classmates is going to be there, how much Boston has changed. And it feels good, like old times.

"I'm dying to get a steak and cheese from Carmichael's while I'm here, for old times sake's," Ryan says.

"God, that sounds good!" Mari agrees.

"Should we go? Maybe after the service? My flight back isn't until tomorrow morning." Charlotte knows she's being too eager, but she's feels an instant and intense desperation for this to happen. Maybe this is just what they need, to be back in one of their old haunts, to be loosened by a few drinks, to channel their younger selves.

"I can't... I'm taking the 4 p.m. Acela back," says Ryan.

"Oh, I'm on that train, too."

"Okay, yeah, I get it...well, maybe another time." Charlotte knew it was a long shot but still she's disappointed. And if not steak and cheese at Carmichael's, where do they go from here?

"Well, actually, I'm going to be out in Los Angeles for a conference in December.

I think Christopher and Lena will come, too, make it a vacation. Maybe...maybe we can see each other then?" Mari suggests tentatively. It's clear she's just thought of this and that maybe she isn't even one hundred percent convinced of it, but Charlotte couldn't have been happier if Mari had said, I love you and I forgive you and I want us to be close again, because maybe, just maybe this is a way of getting from here to there.

"Yes, of course, I'll come down. I'd love that."

So it appears this is a start. They, all three, sense it. A feeling, equal parts cautious and optimistic, that there might be something to be salvaged, something to be built, from the wreckage of their friendship. It is something that could be everything.

Ryan looks at his watch. "Shit, it's 10:30! We better go if we're going to make it in time. We're never going to get a cab, I guess we walk?"

"We're going to be soaking wet. And late! You know how slow this one walks."

Charlotte nods at Mari.

An old joke since this is something they've teased Mari about for years.

Mari ribs right back and Charlotte reminds them of the time they decided to go pedal-boating in the Charles and got stuck way out there in a sudden thunderstorm.

"Yeah, I believe pedal-boating was her bright idea." Ryan shakes Mari affectionately.

"But then she was almost in tears, convinced that we were going to get struck by lightning."

"Hey! It's more common than you think. Especially in open water!" Mari says.

The teasing and the reminiscing feel good, familiar, promising. They rush to gather their stuff; sodden umbrellas, handbags, cell phones and ready themselves to go out and face the elements, face the future, and face the day, at least, side by side. It's time to say goodbye to an old friend.

About the Authors

SEPTEMBER, SOMEWHERE is a work of fiction, however, the locations, characters, and experiences contained in this story are each influenced by actual events.

Susan Lerner and Nancy Meyer are sisters and best friends. Now in their 70's, they felt that it was time to tell a story that mixes some romance and creativity with their diverse, real life experiences. This story pulls from the authors' combined years of world travel, community service, heartbreak, and happiness.

Throughout the highs and lows of their lives, the authors have always held sacred their families, friends and senses of humor, which has given them the courage to write their first novel at this stage in their lives. They are most thankful for their special bond, which has only deepened while working on this story together. Susan and Nancy reside in southern California.

Made in the USA
Columbia, SC
21 March 2018